a Nerd + a

"Ms. Thompson continues to set the romance world on fire."
—*Writers Unlimited*

"Thompson writes cheeky, sexy romance."
—*Contra Costa Times*

"If you're looking for something fun and sexy, this is the book for you, especially if you have a soft spot for nerds."
—*All About Romance,* on *Nerd in Shining Armor*

Praise for Vicki Lewis Thompson's Novels

NERD IN SHINING ARMOR

"A sharp, sassy, sexy read. Stranded on a desert island? I hope you've got this book in your beach bag."

—Jayne Ann Krentz

"The heart of this story is the endearing development of a relationship between Gen and Jack . . . will likely rescue you from reading doldrums."

—*Romantic Times*

"Thompson's fun, sexy island adventure gets points for casting a nerd in place of a Fabio."

—*Booklist*

"A lighthearted and frisky tale of discovery between two engaging people."

—*The Oakland Press*

"Thompson writes cheeky, sexy romance, and Jack is a delightful hero."

—*Contra Costa Times*

"If you're looking for something fun and sexy, this is the book for you, especially if you have a soft spot for nerds."

—*All About Romance*

"Vicki Lewis Thompson has created a fun-filled Pacific adventure for the absolute delight of her readers."

—*The Best Reviews*

"Shades of Jennifer Crusie! I just loved this book!"

—*A Romance Review*

The Nerd Who Loved Me

Vicki Lewis Thompson

St. Martin's Paperbacks

THE NERD WHO LOVED ME

ISBN: 0-312-99856-2
EAN: 80312-99856-1

Printed in the United States of America

St. Martin's Paperbacks edition / August 2004

St. Martin's Paperbacks are published by St. Martin's Press, 175 Fifth Avenue, New York, NY 10010.

10 9 8 7 6 5 4 3 2 1

To Kelly Ripa and the wonderful staff at *LIVE with Regis and Kelly*. You changed the shape of my career by choosing *Nerd in Shining Armor* for *Reading with Ripa*, and I will be grateful forever.

Acknowledgments

A room full of roses to my editor, Jennifer Enderlin, for her enthusiasm and vision as we continue our pursuit of the wily nerd. And big hugs of appreciation to my fellow writers, who've offered nothing but love and support during this exciting transition. I cherish each and every "Atta girl." Thanks always to my agent, Maureen Walters, and to my family for unwavering support and encouragement.

Chapter One

"At work my mommy wears teeny-tiny, sparkly clothes." Dexter, four going on forty, looked up from the chessboard, his expression innocent. "With red feathers. Did you know that, Mr. Harry?"

"Uh-huh." Harry Ambrewster, M.B.A. with honors, Stanford, class of '92, didn't have a lot of experience with babysitting. Still, he didn't think babysitters normally discussed teeny-tiny, sparkly clothes that a parent was wearing *right this minute*. Thinking of Lainie Terrell in her skimpy outfits made his palms sweat.

He wiped them on his Dockers and adjusted his glasses, determined to keep his mind on chess. After two nights of staying with Dexter while Lainie pranced on the Nirvana Casino stage, Harry had learned that babysitting involved lots of floor time, even when the kid was a bona fide genius.

Consequently Harry sat cross-legged on one side of the coffee table, while Dexter balanced on his knees on the other side, his small body sandwiched between the table and the couch. Actually, Dexter wasn't all that small—more the size of your average six-year-old. That coupled with his intelligence made people assume he was much older. Harry could relate. He'd dealt with that a lot as a kid.

Dexter picked up his knight and moved it within striking range of Harry's queen.

Harry decided to give the kid a break. "Do you really want to move your knight there?"

"Yep." Dexter leaned his chin on both fists. "Have you seen my mommy dance?"

"Sort of." Lainie performed in four out of six numbers staged nightly at the Nirvana Casino. Harry had watched her so many times he had the numbers memorized, although he sat at a back table and hoped she had no idea he was such a regular. She might laugh. Better that she only know him as the boring accountant from payroll, a nerd in glasses who also happened to be a neighbor in her apartment complex.

"I wish I could see her dance."

Harry tried to redirect Dexter's attention. "You do realize I'm going to capture your knight."

"I know." Dexter sighed. "But I really, really want to see the show. Mommy won't let me."

"Mm." Harry picked up Dexter's knight. He hated to beat the kid, but if Dexter didn't learn to pay attention, he'd get his ass whipped whenever he sat down at a chessboard, genius or not. "Well, she shouldn't let you go. The show is for big people." Big people like Harry, who was inconveniently obsessed with a certain sexy showgirl.

He wasn't proud of giving in to his craving as often as he did. He should volunteer to be Dexter's permanent babysitter, because then he'd be forced to spend his evenings playing chess with a four-year-old instead of secretly lusting after the kid's mommy.

Although Harry liked Dexter a lot, he wasn't ready to make that sacrifice and give up his reserved spot at that back table. Not yet. He was only filling in for the regular sitter this week because if he didn't, Lainie would miss too much work and get her long-legged self fired. Then she might leave Vegas, and Harry wouldn't be able to watch her dance anymore.

Logically, that would be a good thing. His fascination with her was doomed on many levels. For one thing, she was far too cool ever to be interested in an accountant. He was all computer spreadsheets and double-entry bookkeeping, while she was all fire and rhythm. His favorite dance number was called "Fever," where she wore fishnet stockings and red satin rose petals over her—

"Check."

Harry blinked. "Son of a b—bucket. How'd you do that?"

"I just—"

"Okay, okay. I see it now." Talk about embarrassing. The kid might have more brain cells than the Sahara had sand, but Harry was no slouch in that department, either, and he had the kid by twenty-nine years. Plus, Harry had only taught Dexter the game two nights ago.

"I didn't checkmate you. You can still get away."

"Right." Harry made the necessary defensive move. Dexter's concentration was way better than his at the moment. Chess was one of the few competitive activities in which Harry was the alpha dog, and he'd obviously underestimated his opponent.

Dexter leaned over the board, and Harry noticed that his curly dark hair needed combing. Dexter had his mother's hair, but hers was long enough to reach her waist when she wore it down. And she had such a tiny waist. And such generous—

"You're not mad, are you, Mr. Harry?" Dexter lifted his head, looking worried.

Harry stared at him, astonished. "Mad? About what?"

"'Cause I almost beat you."

"Good grief, no! Maybe I was mad at myself for not giving my full attention to the game, but I would never be mad at you for doing your best. That's what you're supposed to do."

"So you'll keep playing?" He seemed very anxious.

"Of course." Harry had decided the boy's gray eyes came from his father, because Lainie's were a mesmerizing shade of blue.

Dexter flopped back against the edge of the couch. "Whew. What a relief."

He sounded so adult that Harry couldn't help smiling. A faint memory of his own childhood drifted in. He used to have trouble holding on to playmates for the same reason. "Do people wimp out on you a lot, Dexter?"

The little boy nodded.

"Your mom?"

"Not really, but she doesn't like to sit still for very long."

"Ah." Just as Harry had suspected. High energy all the time. A guy like him, who lived mostly in his head, would bore her silly. And maybe he was afraid she'd bore him, too. Even if they clicked sexually, they might have nothing to talk about afterward.

That happened all the time with him—physical attraction, mental incompatibility. But the scholarly types he'd dated didn't turn him on. He was at an impasse.

"She likes it when we go play in the park, though," Dexter said loyally. "And that's fun."

"I'll bet." Theoretically Harry was all for playing in the park. But as a kid he'd never worked up any enthusiasm for slides and monkey bars, preferring to sit under a tree and work on logic puzzles. Lainie and Dexter had been coming back from the park, their eyes bright and their hair tousled, the day he'd stopped to talk to them on his way to his own apartment. Lainie had confessed her babysitting crisis and he'd leaped into the breach.

"But Mrs. Flippo won't play *anything* with me anymore, not even Chutes and Ladders. I said I'd let her win, but nope, no dice." He tugged at his hair. "And who wants to watch TV all the time?"

"Indeed." Harry felt himself weakening on the babysitting thing. This little guy was starving for mental stimulation. Harry empathized. Maybe that's why his own mother had given up on regular babysitters all those years ago and brought him to work with her.

Unfortunately, work for her had been exactly like work was for Lainie, and Harry had spent his formative years backstage at a casino just like the Nirvana. Doing his homework surrounded by flowery-smelling, nearly naked women had seemed normal at the time.

Looking back on it, he was pretty sure it was suboptimal for a little kid. There'd never been a question of his mom changing careers. She loved dancing—still did, even though she'd retired. In his experience, dancers were passionate about their work.

So he'd made it a practice not to date showgirls. Logic told him they weren't likely to give up their glitzy, exciting careers for nights of reading to the kids and playing chess with Harry. Then Lainie had come to work at the Nirvana and moved into his apartment complex. And just like that—logic had taken a powder. But he would conquer this infatuation that had temporarily caused him to act like an idiot, and once he did, he'd resume looking for Ms. Right.

"Check."

Harry snapped out of his daze and discovered he was in a worse pickle than the last time. Unless he brought all his powers to bear on this chess game, this little sprout might actually beat him.

"While you're thinking, I'll get the cookies, okay?"

Harry nodded, still studying the board. Because he wouldn't take any money for babysitting, Lainie had baked cookies for him. That was a true sacrifice in the middle of summer in Vegas. She must have turned the air conditioner to freeze to compensate for heating up the oven.

First she'd left him peanut butter cookies, then oatmeal, and tonight, the most seductive of all, chocolate chip. She couldn't know his weakness for chocolate chip.

"Here you go, Mr. Harry." Dexter set a plastic plate loaded with cookies next to the chessboard.

Harry couldn't believe how distracting the scent of chocolate and cookie dough was. His mouth watered, and he couldn't keep his mind on the chess game. Lainie had made those cookies, and that was part of the problem. He smelled them and imagined her bustling about the kitchen in her short shorts and tight T-shirt, bending over to slip the pan into the warm oven, pausing to lick the spoon . . .

Dexter picked up a cookie and leaned over the board as he bit into it. A crumb fell on a white marble square. "Whoops." He wet his finger and picked it up. "What are you gonna do?"

Harry surrendered to his urges and picked up a cookie. "Eat one of these." The cookie was incredible. Some people overbaked them and burned the chocolate chips, but this one was totally perfect, the outside a little crunchy and the inside soft and gooey. He moaned with delight.

"My mommy makes good cookies, huh?"

Harry talked with his mouth full, something he never did. "She sure does."

Dexter took another bite of his cookie and studied the chessboard. "I think it's time for you to castle, Mr. Harry."

Harry had come to the same sad conclusion. And he wasn't even sure that move would save him. The kid had him on the ropes. "As soon as I finish the cookie."

"Want milk?"

"Not yet, thanks." Oh, what the hell, he might as well castle and be done with it. Then Dexter would edge in with his king, and in a couple of moves, it would be all over. Harry glanced at the clock, wondering if they had time for a rematch before he tucked Dexter in at eight-thirty.

Just as he'd picked up the rook, someone banged on the door. They hammered on it with a lot of force, like they were ready to break it down. Startled, he dropped the chess piece and scrambled to his feet, adrenaline pumping. This couldn't be good.

He started around the coffee table to get Dexter, and Dexter met him halfway, grabbing him by the legs. Harry lifted the little boy into his arms and held him tight. "It's okay," he said, not believing a word of it.

"Open up!" yelled a guy with a nasal twang to his voice. "I wanna see my son!"

Dexter moaned softly in distress. "It's Daddy," he whispered.

Harry gulped. Lainie had never mentioned a daddy. From the way Dexter was trembling, there was good reason for that.

"I know you're in there! I can see the lights are on!"

Dexter shrank away and buried his head against Harry's neck.

"A man should be able to see his boy!" Dexter's father bellowed. "Dexter! Come on out and let me see how big you are!"

Harry figured the guy had to be drunk, and he'd probably come around now because he knew Lainie would be working. Maybe he thought a babysitter would be intimidated into opening the door to him. Harry decided not to respond. Letting this cretin know that the babysitter was a man might rile him up even more.

"Dammit, I know you're in there. The law's on my side, y'know. A woman can't take a man's son away. Let me in, dammit!" Dexter's father pounded on the door, making it rattle in the frame.

Dexter winced with each blow and tightened his grip around Harry's neck.

Harry leaned down and murmured in Dexter's ear. "Don't be afraid. I won't let him get you."

More pounding. "If you don't open this door, so help me, I'll bust it down!"

Harry wished he had more confidence in the door. He wished they were on the first floor instead of the second. And he wished he'd taken that karate course he'd always thought about. First thing tomorrow he'd check it out. But that didn't help him right now.

Maybe he should dial 911, but Dexter's daddy could be through that door before a squad car pulled up. Besides, even if the police arrived in time, Harry didn't know if Lainie might be a mom on the run. Judging from this performance, she had a reason to run, but the courts could still put her in jail for it. Harry wasn't about to take that chance by alerting the cops.

"Okay, you asked for it." The door reverberated with a heavy thud, as if the guy had just rammed his shoulder into the wood.

Keeping his eye on the door, Harry retreated down the hall toward Lainie's bedroom at the back of the apartment. He'd never been in there, but her floor plan matched his. People usually had heavy dressers in the bedroom, and that could serve as a barricade until Harry decided what to do next.

"I'm scared," Dexter whispered.

"Don't be. I'm right here." Even though Harry's blood was pumping way too fast, he tried to keep his voice calm. Lainie had obviously made a terrible mistake five years ago by letting this Neanderthal close enough to father her child. But Dexter shouldn't have to pay for that by being terrorized.

"He's very big," Dexter said.

Not what Harry wanted to hear. "Well, I'm very smart."

"So what are we gonna do, Mr. Harry?"

"Think." Somehow it didn't seem like enough. The moment called for boldness and daring. Harry wasn't the bold and daring type.

Inside Lainie's darkened bedroom, he glanced around and found a dresser. Unfortunately, the dresser was made of flimsy white wicker. Considering the drawers were probably full of lacy underwear, the dresser lost all potential as a barricade.

Another thud, louder than the first, echoed through the apartment.

"We could go out the window," Dexter said.

"Uh, we're on the second floor." Harry looked at the aluminum-framed sliding window. There was a good-sized tree outside, but the thought of climbing out the window and down the tree while holding Dexter made him queasy. If he dropped the kid . . .

"We could climb down the tree. Like Spider-Man."

The crack of wood splintering narrowed Harry's choices. Lowering Dexter quickly to the floor, he closed and locked the bedroom door. Then he dragged the dresser in front of the door, for whatever time it might give them. After checking to make sure his car keys were in his pocket, he unlocked the window and slid it open. Warm desert air blew in and he realized his shirt was soaked with sweat.

The screen wouldn't come out without lifting the window from the frame, so he punched the screen free and it clattered to the ground below. "Okay." He took off his glasses and tucked them in his shirt pocket before crouching beside Dexter. "We're going to climb out the window and go down the tree, like you suggested."

"Right. Then what?"

"We'll take my car. Don't worry. We'll lose him. Are you with me?"

Dexter nodded so hard his hair wiggled.

"I want you to climb onto my back, wrap your arms around my neck and your legs around my waist. Then I want you to hang on like Velcro. Got that?"

"Yep." Dexter glued himself to Harry's back and got a choke hold on his neck.

Harry adjusted the little boy's grip so the kid wouldn't strangle him during the climb. Then he stuck one leg over the windowsill.

"After we get in your car, where are we going?"

Harry doubled over so he could work both of them through the opening. "To see your mommy."

In the midst of a dressing room filled with laughter, nakedness, and efficient movement, Lainie wiggled into her red rose-petal outfit for the "Fever" number. Halfway through the night's entertainment, the other dancers rode the crest of a performance high. Lainie wanted to throw off her uneasy mood and ride it with them. The crowd was friendly, sweetened up by the comedian the casino had recently hired. Jack Newman had turned out to be a good complement to the musical part of the show.

He'd also indicated an interest in Lainie. Years ago Jack would have been exactly her type, but ever since tangling with Joey Benjamin, she steered clear of party animals. More accurately, she steered clear of all men.

She had a son to raise, and she lived in fear that somebody, someday, would try to take Dexter away from her. If she ever lost Dexter, she'd die, plain and simple.

She was smart enough to know that her profession could count against her if anyone challenged her custody, but she made more money dancing than she would clerking at a department store. Besides, she loved dancing. Still, a judge might not take kindly to a showgirl trying to be a mom. A boyfriend might make the picture even worse.

She'd been thinking of potential custody battles ever since last night, when out of the blue, Joey had called her at work. If only she knew what he was up to. Six months ago he'd seemed more than happy to let her move from Atlantic City to Vegas. When she'd told him she'd waive her rights to child support, he'd seemed even happier. After six months of silence, she'd dared to think she'd cut Joey out of her life, and more important, out of Dexter's life.

And now, this phone call. She wondered if he'd gone through the phone book or if he finally had access to some of his trust fund money and had hired a private detective to find her. Maybe it didn't matter. What mattered was that he'd begged her for another chance. She was through giving him chances, but she didn't want trouble, either.

He hadn't mentioned Dexter, hadn't even asked how he was. That didn't surprise her. When she'd told him she was pregnant, he'd wanted her to get an abortion. Practical as that might have been, she hadn't even considered such a thing. She'd been a little surprised at her strong protective instincts, because she hadn't thought she wanted a baby, but Joey's suggestion had horrified her, and she'd said so.

She could still hear his reply: *Don't make the mistake of thinking I'll marry you, sweetheart.*

With that statement, he'd killed any remaining affection she'd had for him. *Don't make the mistake of thinking I'd have you,* she'd thrown out before turning on her heel. The relationship had gone downhill after that. But for Dexter's sake, she'd tried to keep things halfway civil. She believed kids should know both their parents if at all possible, and she'd hoped Joey would warm to the idea of being a father.

Instead, his drinking had become worse and he'd started to scare Dexter with his loud voice and threatening gestures. She'd had to rethink her strategy.

The dressing room door opened. "On stage for 'Fever,' " called Tim, the stage manager.

Lainie hurried out with the rest of the ensemble.

"Where's your accountant been keeping himself?" asked a blonde named Gina as they filed onto the curtained stage during the intro.

"He's not exactly mine."

"Sure he is. He never takes his eyes off you, and he's been at that back table almost every night, except just recently. I wonder if he's sick or something."

Lainie shrugged. Explaining that Harry was home watching Dexter would start all kinds of rumors, and she didn't need rumors right now, not with Joey popping up again. Besides, Harry might not want anybody to know he was babysitting. Although he seemed to have a crush on her, he'd never asked her out, and he'd had plenty of chances.

Harry might be shy. She certainly hoped that was the problem. Unfortunately, shyness might not be it. He could be like a lot of guys—including Joey—who thought showgirls were exciting but not the sort of woman they'd take home to Momma.

Lainie would hate to find that out about Harry, because he seemed nicer than most, but the evidence was there. She wouldn't go out with him, of course, but he didn't know that. She wouldn't have minded being asked, for the record.

"Curtain," Tim murmured from the wings.

Lainie smiled automatically, gratefully. As always, when the curtain swished open, it swept her worries into the wings where they belonged. For the few minutes of the number, nothing existed but the joy of moving to the music, feeling the energy of the audience, taking the rhythm into every cell of her body.

How she loved this! Dancing before a live audience gave her a thrill greater than sex, which was a good thing, because she wasn't getting a smidgen of sex these days, unless she counted solo sessions with her vibrator. She'd created quite a fantasy life for herself during those sessions. Recently, because there was a rebellious streak in her, she'd thrust Harry, so to speak, into the role of her fantasy lover. Wouldn't he be surprised.

Harry had a much greater appreciation of monkeys as he hugged the tree branch and scrambled for footing on the tree limb. Dexter's breath rasped in his ear and the kid had reclaimed his death grip on Harry's neck, choking off his wind.

Inch by torturous inch, Harry worked his way backward, keeping his balance by using tiny nubs where smaller branches had been pruned. He calculated the limb was about a foot in diameter and angled to the main trunk at approximately forty-five degrees. Somebody used to this kind of thing would have no problem.

Harry wasn't used to it. His palms stung where the rough bark had cut into his hands. His clothes scraped the tree, and he'd already popped a button off his shirt where a stubby twig had caught in the front placket.

Through the open window he could hear Dexter's dad banging around inside the apartment. The noise sounded close, so Harry guessed that the guy was trying to get through the bedroom door.

"Mr. Harry?" Dexter was whispering.

Harry eased down another few inches before whispering back. "What?"

"I have to go potty."

"Hold it."

"Okay, but I have to go really bad."

"Do your best." Harry tried to climb down faster. He could remember being four years old and having to hold it.

His foot connected with the crotch of the tree. Looking down, he judged it was about five feet to the ground. Fortunately grass grew under the tree. "Dexter, I'm throwing my glasses down. Watch where they go, okay?"

"You're throwing your glasses? Why?"

"Because we're going to jump." Harry tried to sound confident.

"Jump? Are you really, really sure about this?"

"Yes." He launched himself from the tree. When he felt the momentum pitching him backward, which would mean landing on top of Dexter, he kicked his feet out behind him so that he belly-flopped into the grass. Dexter bounced down on top, which knocked the air right out of Harry. His lungs burned as he fought to breathe. He couldn't stay here very long.

"Mr. Harry?"

"Nn."

"I can see your glasses."

"G-good."

"But I peed my pants."

Chapter Two

When she was back in the dressing room following the "Fever" number, Lainie's spirits were greatly improved. That particular dance routine never failed to make her feel alive. The only downside to feeling so alive was that she missed sex all the more. She didn't think it was natural for a twenty-seven-year-old woman to go this many years without an actual man in her bed.

Her fantasies about Harry only proved that she was getting hard up for male sex symbols. Still, to be fair, he might have a decent body under those preppie clothes. Plus there was something solid and reassuring about Harry, and feeling safe with a man had become very sexy to her.

Jack Newman was on stage next, so she and the other dancers had fifteen minutes for their costume change. After removing her elaborate headdress, Lainie took time to sip some bottled water before unfastening the front catch of her rose-petal bra.

A sharp rap on the dressing room door prompted her

to fasten it again. Some of the women didn't care who saw them naked, but Lainie was one of the more modest members of the dance troupe. When she was dancing, she threw modesty out the window, but off-stage was a different matter.

Tim stuck his head in the dressing room door. "Lainie? Somebody to see you. Says it's real important."

Instant panic left her shaking. She prayed Joey wasn't standing outside the dressing room door. She had trouble speaking and had to clear her throat. "Did you . . . get his namc?"

"No, but he has a little kid with him who looks like you."

She bolted from the dressing-room stool and nearly knocked Tim over as she barreled through the door. *What if Joey has Dexter?* Then she stared in confusion at the man holding Dexter's hand. "Harry? My goodness, you're a mess! What happened?"

Dexter ran to her, and she dropped to her knees so she could grab him in a hug.

"Daddy was banging on the door," he said. "He went bang, bang, bang, and he wanted to break it down!" He quivered in her arms.

"Oh, my God." Gulping air, she looked over Dexter's head at Harry. He had dirt and grass stains all down the front of his clothes. His shirt was missing a button, he had dried blood on his hands, and his glasses were smudged. More startling than all that, his thick brown hair, always combed and parted perfectly, stood out in all directions. She'd never seen his hair mussed.

"We handled it," Harry said quietly.

Lainie clutched Dexter tighter while she held Harry's

gaze. "Did you fight him? Please tell me you didn't—"

"Mr. Harry was just like Spider-Man, Mommy!" Dexter struggled away from her and started waving his arms as he talked. "Mr. Harry and me, we climbed out the window and down the tree! We got away in Mr. Harry's car, and I helped find his glasses, but I peed my pants, so we had to go to Target and buy me new ones." He took a deep breath and shoved his hands into the pockets of a pair of shorts Lainie had never seen before. "They have Pooh on the pocket."

"Very cool." Her throat closed up. She'd put her son and an unsuspecting guy in danger. She might never forgive herself for that. "I'm so sorry," she said, looking at Harry. "I had no idea that Joey would . . ."

She couldn't finish the sentence, because it wasn't true. She'd had some idea, and that would haunt her forever. When Joey drank, he became unpredictable, which was why she'd decided to leave. The minute he'd called yesterday, she should have quit her job and left Vegas. She'd underestimated him, glossed over the problem, tried to pretend nothing would come of his phone call.

"His name's Joey?" Harry asked.

"Yes. Joey Benjamin. We were never married." She felt compelled to add that last part to somehow distance herself from Joey's behavior.

"Well, he's out of control," Harry said in a low voice.

"I think he's been drinking beers," Dexter said. "Lots and lots of beers."

"Probably true," Harry said. "I haven't called the police, but if you think we should—"

"No. I'd rather we didn't do that. Not yet." She thought of the spin Joey could put on things. She'd told him she was leaving for Vegas, but she hadn't asked him to sign papers giving her that right legally. And she should have, but she'd thought that might put too sharp a point on it. However, without his signature on something, he could accuse her of kidnapping Dexter and taking him out of New Jersey.

She couldn't believe Joey had suddenly become a doting father. That was totally out of character. Something else was going on, and until she knew what it was, she had to be careful. Joey might have the Benjamin money behind him. She didn't want to make a wrong move that would result in losing Dexter.

"Mommy, can I stay and see the show? I could go to bed early tomorrow night."

"I have a better idea." She gave him a quick kiss on the cheek. "What if I take the rest of the night off and we'll do something fun, okay?" Dexter's bedtime was the least of her worries. She had to figure out the best place to hide him until she found out what Joey wanted.

"Like what could we do?"

"We'll talk about it after we get in the car." Obviously she couldn't go home. She calculated how much money she had in her purse and how much room was left on her credit card.

"Can Mr. Harry come?"

"I'm sure Mr. Harry has other things he needs to be doing."

Harry shifted his weight. "The fact is, I—"

"You know, I hate to ask you even one more favor, but would you please stay with Dexter for a minute while I get my things?"

"Sure. But listen, Lainie—"

"I'll be *right* back." She headed off to find Tim and located him in the wings checking out Jack Newman's routine. "Tim, something's come up."

Tim took one look at her face and frowned. "What's the matter, kiddo?"

"I have to leave. Right now. Family emergency. I hate to duck out like this, but—"

"The kid's yours, isn't he?"

"Yes. And I—"

"Don't tell me anything more, okay? I really like you, Lainie, and if you and that kid are on the back of a milk carton, I'm sure there's a good reason for it. That aside, if the police come asking a bunch of questions, I have to tell them whatever I know. So don't give me any more info. Just take off."

"Thanks, Tim." She hugged him and hurried back to the dressing room. Once there she grabbed her clothes off a hook and decided to cover her outfit with her purple raincoat instead of changing. She could mail the costume back to the casino once she was out of here, but right now every second counted. Joey could be on his way over.

When she came back out, she smiled in spite of herself. Harry had crouched down in front of Dexter, and Dexter had crouched down, too, in imitation. So there they were, both hunkered down face-to-face in deep conversation. Her smile faded as guilt set in. Besides Joey, Harry was the first man Dexter had spent any quality time with, and Dexter seemed to be lapping up the attention.

She would be forever grateful to Harry, both for being a friend to Dexter and saving him from Joey at great risk to himself. Unfortunately, she might never see Harry again, which meant she'd have no way of repaying him.

Knowing that, she wondered what on earth she could say to him now. Words seemed so useless. She wanted to do something nice for him, but nothing could be done under the circumstances.

As she approached, she heard them talking about queens and rooks, which meant they were discussing chess. For the past two days Dexter had talked of nothing else. Now that he'd be losing his new chess partner, she'd need to buy him a chess set, learn the game, and force herself to concentrate on it. That was one way she could make up for jerking him away from someone he'd started to care for.

As her heels clicked on the cement floor, both Dexter and Harry glanced up, and as if choreographed, they both stood and faced her.

She held out her hand to Dexter. "We need to go, Dexter, but first we should thank Mr. Harry for all he's done."

"We could make him more cookies," Dexter said. "He's *crazy* about your cookies."

Lainie blushed, and to her amazement, so did Harry. "Cookies don't seem like enough," she said. "But I can send you some, anyway. It's the least I can do. I should—"

"Send them?" Dexter peered up at her. "Why can't he just come up and get them? When we play chess?"

She looked down into Dexter's trusting gray eyes and hated having to quash his dream of endless chess games with his new hero. "You might not be able to play chess with Mr. Harry for a while," she said. "But I'll buy you a chess set and you can teach me how to play. We'll play every day. How's that?"

Dexter looked uncertain. "I don't think chess is your game, Mommy."

"I'll make it my game." Feeling the pressure of time ticking away, she looked at Harry. "I don't know how to thank you. You've gone above and beyond, and I'll never forget that. I'm sorry we have to leave so quickly, but I think we'd better be on our way. I'm sure you understand."

"Lainie, can he recognize your car?"

She blinked. Of course Joey could recognize her car. It was the same one she'd had in Jersey, and she still hadn't painted the replacement fender white to match the rest of the car. Then there was her bumper sticker that said *I HOPE YOU DANCE*. That car would stand out.

"He doesn't know mine," Harry said. "I kept a lookout, and nobody followed us when we left the apartment complex. I guess your chest of drawers is sturdier than I thought."

"What?"

"Never mind. I'll explain later. But we need to use my car to get out of here."

"That's a *good* idea," Dexter said.

"It is," Lainie said reluctantly. Although she didn't want to pile yet another obligation on top of all she owed Harry, she had no other plan. "Thank you. I accept."

"Yay!" Dexter gave a little hop of glee.

"Mr. Harry's only going to drop us off," she said.

"Drop us off where?"

Lainie had no answer for that. She was making this up as she went along.

"At my mother's," Harry said before Lainie could think of an answer to Dexter's question.

Lainie stared at him. "Oh, I don't—"

"You have a *mother*?" Dexter looked entranced by the idea.

"Alive, well, and living about twenty minutes away in Henderson. So let's go."

Lainie's head spun. "You don't have to call her first?"

"I can give her a call on my cell while we're driving. It'll be fine. Joey won't find you there and you'll have time to catch your breath and decide what to do."

"Okay." Lainie vowed she'd stay at Harry's mother's house for an hour, tops. A person could figure out a lot in an hour. Yet she had to admit her problems were bigger than she'd thought. She might be able to hide out in a motel for a while, but no way could she afford another car. Maybe she could pull off a leasing arrangement, though. Holding Dexter's hand, she started toward the stage door leading to the rear parking lot.

"You should go out the front way," Harry said. "I'll bring the car around."

She paused, her brain still buzzing from the shock of what she had to do. "The front?"

"If Joey shows up here, he'd come to the back looking for your car. He'd assume you'd leave that way."

"You're right." She wasn't thinking straight at all, and she had to think straight. Dexter's future might depend on it. Thank goodness Harry was relatively calm. If it took her years, she'd figure out some way to make it up to him for all the trouble she was causing.

"Do you remember what I drive?" Harry asked.

"I do!" Dexter looked happier by the minute. "It's black, and the seats are made out of leather, which is from dead cows, you know. They're old and dead before they take off the skin. Very old and very dead. Leather's okay to sit on if you've peed your pants."

As Harry stepped onto the asphalt heading for his Lexus, he realized he was doing something he never did. He was winging it. That wasn't his normal mode of operation. And here's where winging it had stuck him—taking Lainie, who was still wearing his favorite dance costume under her raincoat, over to Rona's house, where the two women would probably bond.

Anyway, bonding was what he'd come to expect from showgirls. Rona had insisted on buying a condo in Henderson's Emerald Lakes development because all her retired showgirl friends were buying there. They'd formed a five-member pack, calling themselves Temptresses in Temporary Suspension, or TITS for short. Knowing those women, Harry figured the acronym had come first and they'd stayed up nights drinking margaritas until they found words to fit.

So Lainie and Rona would bond, and then Rona would get all mushy over Dexter and start making broad hints about the grandchildren she might never live to see. Oh, yes. Winging was not his style, and this was why. In no time he'd created chaos.

But he couldn't let Lainie try to escape in her black-fendered car with its *I HOPE YOU DANCE* bumper sticker, not after listening to the fury in her ex-boyfriend's voice while he banged on her door. Maybe she'd kidnapped Dexter and brought him to Vegas. Maybe Harry was aiding and abetting a criminal. Well, some things were worth breaking the law over.

A car cruised by him on the way out of the parking

lot. Harry glanced casually at the driver and discovered it was a woman, one of the cleaning crew. He waved and continued toward his car. He was parked six spaces away from Lainie's vehicle. Without looking directly at it, he let his gaze wander around the area. He didn't want to appear as if he might be surveying the lot, in case Joey happened to be there watching for anything suspicious.

A blond guy climbed out of a gold latc-model sedan. Could easily be a rental. Harry's heart hammered as the guy approached, a friendly smile on his face. He was about Harry's height of six-three, but he was built like a linebacker, while Harry was built like . . . an accountant.

"Evening," the guy said, looking at Harry's grimy clothes.

"Evening." Harry's instincts went on alert. If this was Joey, and he'd figured out that Dexter and his babysitter had gone out the window, then Harry's grass-stained clothes could be very incriminating.

"You work here?"

"I do. Groundskeeper."

"Ah. The grounds must have put up a bit of a fight today."

Harry laughed, as if Joey had made a great joke. "I'll tell my wife that. Maybe she'll forgive me for being so dumb as to try trimming the palm trees in the entry with an extension ladder instead of calling in the cherry picker." Harry held out both arms. "As you can see, the ladder fell."

"Don't casino employees wear uniforms when they do that kind of stuff?"

"That's the other reason I'll catch hell from the little woman. I was off duty, doing a little gambling, and one of the supervisors came over and started in about the palm trees. So I told him I'd take care of it. I'd had a couple of beers, so I thought I could take care of it, if you know what I mean."

The blond guy nodded. "Been there, done that."

"I mean it, man. My wife is going to kill me for ruining these clothes. They were a birthday present. Well, better go find my car. I never can remember where I've parked the damned thing." Harry started off across the lot, away from his Lexus.

"Good luck," the blond guy shouted after him. "Say, do you happen to know a dancer named Lainie Terrell?"

Harry nearly passed out. So it *was* Joey. Although he wanted to run, he made himself pause and scratch his head. "Is she a redhead?"

"Nope. At least not last I knew."

"Then I guess I don't know her. I'm a married man, you know. I'm not allowed to check out the dancers."

"Sure you are. What your wife doesn't know won't hurt her."

"Yeah, but she knows *everything*. Well, see ya."

"Right." Joey turned and started toward the back door.

Harry kept walking in the opposite direction, but he located his electronic key in his pocket. Once he heard Joey knock and the door open, he turned and sprinted toward the Lexus. When the lock popped open he threw himself inside only to discover it was hard to start a car when you were shaking. He forced himself to slow down and managed to get the engine going. With a moan of relief, he yanked the car into reverse, backed out with a squeal of rubber, shifted again and floored the gas pedal.

Cars honked as he ploughed his way into heavy traffic.

A quick right, and he pulled under the casino's bright portico where Lainie and Dexter stood waiting. They hopped in the back seat.

"Duck down, both of you."

They obeyed, while Harry maneuvered past a white stretch limo and scanned the portico for Joey.

"Come here, Dexter, and let me buckle you in," Lainie murmured.

"Why are we hiding?" Dexter asked. "Is Daddy trying to find us?"

"I'm sure he is," Lainie said.

As Harry pulled into traffic, still with no sign of Joey, he sighed in relief. No point in telling Lainie that Joey was so close. "Okay, I think it's safe to sit up now."

"Daddy scares me," Dexter said. "He roars like a dragon. Why does he do that?"

Harry waited for Lainie's answer, wondering if she'd smear Joey's name.

"I think it's because nobody taught him that he shouldn't," Lainie said.

"You mean like his mommy? She didn't teach him?"

"His mommy or his daddy. In any case, he missed out on some lessons when he was growing up."

Harry's admiration for Lainie soared. She was putting the best light she could on a bad situation, for Dexter's sake.

"Well, somebody should tell him to stop," Dexter said. "'Cause nobody will play with you if you act like that. Mr. Harry, can we listen to the radio, like we did before?"

"Sure." Harry flicked on the radio, which was on the station Dexter had picked after much changing of channels on the way to the casino. Instead of music, Dexter had settled on an all-talk-show station. Twenty minutes ago the topic had been training your pet. Harry hoped it still was.

"*. . . dealing with erectile dysfunction. Most men respond to direct stimulation of the pe—*" Harry hit the button and got country music. "I think we need some tunes! Right, Lainie?"

"Tunes are a great idea!" She sounded as fake and jolly as he did. "Let's sing along. Come on, Dexter. You know this one. We—"

"What's 'erectile dysfunction,' Mommy?"

Harry choked. The kid had even pronounced it correctly.

In the back seat, Lainie cleared her throat. "Well . . . um, it's not something you have to worry about, Dexter. You know, I really like these new shorts Mr. Harry bought you."

"Me, too. Why don't I have to worry about erectile dysfunction? They said 'most men,' and I'm going to be a man when I grow up, right?"

"Right. But—"

"My mother has a dog," Harry blurted out. It was the first thing he could think of.

"A *dog*?" Dexter's voice rang with excitement. "What kind of dog?"

"A cute little guy named Fred. He loves to lick your face."

Dexter giggled. "I like it when dogs lick my face. It tickles. Mommy, can I play with Fred when we get to Mr. Harry's mommy's house?"

"If you're very gentle," Lainie said. "Fred might not be used to children."

"Fred loves everybody." Harry was very pleased with himself for coming up with a subject to distract Dexter. "He has a little rubber ball, and he'd be so happy if you'd roll it across the floor for him."

"I can do that. I would love to do that. But I still want to know . . . what's erectile dysfunction?"

"Hey, we're here!" Harry pulled up in front of his mother's two-story condo and noticed that Leo's Jaguar sat in the driveway, its pearl finish gleaming in the light from the street lamp. Oops. Apparently this was Leo's night to pay Rona a visit. Harry had meant to call on his cell, but he'd been too busy getting away from Joey and dealing with Dexter's preoccupation with erectile dysfunction.

"The downstairs looks kind of dark," Lainie said. "I hope she isn't in bed already."

Harry figured that was exactly where Rona was, but not alone. "Oh, she likes to save on electricity. But let me give her a quick call, so we don't scare her when we ring the doorbell."

"Harry, I think maybe we'd better—"

"No problem, no problem. I'll just call her," Harry said as he punched in the number.

His mother answered, letting him know she'd checked her caller ID when she called him by name. "Hello, Harry," she said in her "This had better be important" tone.

"Hi, Mom! Hey, listen, I hate to bother you, but—"

"Then maybe you'd like to call back tomorrow? I'm, shall we say, somewhat indisposed at the moment."

"I know."

"You do? How could you know that?"

"I'm in your driveway."

"Oh, for pity's sake, Harry. You're calling from the driveway? Didn't I teach you better manners than that?"

"Yes, you did. But this situation came up all of a sudden, and . . . well, I'm here with Lainie Terrell, one of the dancers at the Nirvana, and—"

"Say no more. We'll be done in two minutes."

"Thanks, Mom, but there's something else you need to know. She—"

"Rona?" Leo said in the background. "Is Harry in some kind of trouble?"

Harry's mother didn't bother to cover the mouthpiece, which meant that she wanted Harry to hear her. "We can only hope so, Leo. He's there with a showgirl, which is a good sign. And if my luck is running, he's knocked her up."

Chapter Three

"Mommy, what does 'knocked up' mean?"

Lainie sighed as she unbuckled Dexter's seat belt. "It's a grown-up expression."

"So I can't use it?"

"No, I'm afraid not." She helped him out of the car.

"Sorry about that," Harry said. "She didn't know Dexter was there."

"I know she didn't," Lainie said. "It's okay. This happens all the time, so don't worry about it." She took Dexter's hand and started toward the front porch where a light glowed.

"So I won't use it, then," Dexter said. "But I still want to know what it means."

Lainie decided this term wasn't quite as tricky as "erectile dysfunction," so she launched into an explanation. "Remember when I told you how a daddy and a mommy get together and make a baby?"

"Yep."

"Well, if they actually make that baby, and the mommy

is pregnant, sometimes a grown-up will say she's knocked up. But little boys can't say that."

"Mr. Harry's mother hopes that you're *pregnant*?"

Harry groaned. "I'm really sorry."

"I think Mr. Harry's mother was making a joke, sweetie."

"You mean like knock-knock jokes? Only this is a knock-up joke?"

"No, I mean—" Lainie was interrupted by high-pitched barking erupting from inside the condo.

Immediately Dexter lost all interest in the conversation. "It's *Fred.*" He began to tremble with excitement. "I'll bet he's glad we're here to see him. I'll bet he's very, very, *very* glad!"

Fred was probably the only one in favor of this invasion, Lainie thought. She couldn't decide which was more embarrassing, interrupting Harry's mother and her lover, or walking into his mother's living room wearing the "Fever" costume and her raincoat. She'd stuffed her clothes in her oversized purse, but asking for a place to change would seem as if she planned an extended stay. This was such a bad idea, but she didn't have a better one.

The door was opened by a tall woman wearing a black silk robe studded with rhinestones, a robe obviously designed for entertaining the man she'd left upstairs. Her short red hair was tousled and she looked a little flushed, but her smile was wide and welcoming as she scooped up a pint-sized dog. "I'm Rona, and I— My God, Harry! You look like you've been shot out of the cannon at Treasure Island!"

"Mr. Harry and me, we climbed out of the window and slid down a tree," Dexter said.

Abruptly Rona's gaze lowered to Dexter. Her eyes widened even more, and then she crouched down, still holding her wiggling dog. "And who have we here?"

"My—" Lainie began, but Dexter stepped forward, earnest and eager.

"I'm Dexter," he said. "And I really, really think Fred wants to play with me."

"Well, I expect he does!" Rona tucked Fred against her side, stood and held out her hand to Dexter. "Come with me, Dexter." She shot Harry an "I'll deal with you later" kind of look. "I have a cup of cocoa with your name on it. And maybe even a cookie."

"We have cookies at home." Dexter slipped his hand in Rona's as if they'd known each other for years. "But we couldn't bring them because we had to leave so fast."

"And it would be so hard carrying them if you're sliding down a tree." She started toward the back of the house. "You can tell me more about that while I'm getting your cocoa ready."

"She likes kids," Harry murmured to Lainie as he guided her inside and closed the door.

Lainie nodded as she fought a sudden lump in her throat. Watching Dexter and Rona reminded her that Dexter had missed out on so many things, including a set of loving grandparents. Joey's family didn't know about Dexter, and as for her folks—her unwed-mother status had been another disappointment to add to their list, which included her ignoring the idea of college and becoming a showgirl right out of high school.

They'd allowed their disapproval of her lifestyle to get in the way of loving Dexter, which was their loss, but also his. After Lainie had paid a few visits to their little house in Brooklyn and received very little welcome, she'd given up trying to get them to act like grandparents. Although Harry's mom had taken to Dexter immediately, she didn't have any history to deal with.

Rona's condo looked like Rona—elegant with a touch of pizazz. Sleek leather furniture and Tiffany-style lamps made it the kind of room Lainie had always longed for and had never been able to afford. Rona was an interesting mom, no question. Dexter wasn't the only one curious about Rona's wish that Harry had knocked up a showgirl. Sounded like Rona wanted a grandchild, and Harry wasn't cooperating.

"Want me to take your coat?" Harry asked as she started to follow Dexter back to the kitchen.

"No!" She clutched the lapels. She'd sweat it out, literally, before she'd sit in Rona's kitchen wearing only her tiny red costume. "I mean, no, thank you. I'm fine. Dexter and I won't be staying long, anyway."

"Where would you go?"

She turned to gaze at him. "I have a few ideas." She had zip.

"Good. Because I didn't want to say so in front of Dexter, but I think you need to keep far away from Joey until he calms down. Do you . . . have legal custody?"

"Yes."

"Whew. I'm glad to hear it, because—"

"To a point. Joey knew I was taking Dexter to Vegas, but I never got him to sign anything official giving me permission. He just said okay, so I left."

"Oh." His expression indicated that he thought she'd made a big mistake handling things that way.

So maybe his life was in perfect order and hers was

unraveling like a cheap sweater. She couldn't help that right now and frustration made her abrupt. "I know it's a mess, and I don't expect you to get involved." She winced at the coldness in her voice. "That sounded wrong. I mean, you've been wonderful, but I can't ask you to do more than this. You've already put yourself out tremendously."

"So you'd rather handle things on your own."

Because he looked so disappointed and rejected, she stepped closer and put her hand on his arm, so he'd know that she appreciated all he'd done for her and Dexter. She didn't remember ever touching Harry before, and she was surprised at how warm and solid he felt.

An old song went through her head—Streisand warbling "he touched me." Apparently it worked even better in reverse, when the woman made the first move. Touching Harry was giving her a real lift.

Too bad she couldn't keep doing it. "I think it's best if I take care of things from here on out," she said, and removed her hand.

An emotion stirred in his eyes, an emotion that whispered of heat and longing. "Okay."

He wants me to touch him again. Cool. She was close enough to catch the scent of his aftershave, and she realized that scent had been part of her recent fantasies about him. The longer she stood next to him, the more those fantasies put on a show in her head. Bad timing, though. Better bring the curtain down on that extravaganza. "We should go see what's happening with Dexter."

"Right."

She liked the sound of his voice. As she turned and started for the kitchen, she realized his voice had also been part of her fantasies. The longer she hung around him, the more she was liable to become susceptible to whatever sexual thing was going on between them. After Dexter had finished his cocoa and cookie, she was calling a cab.

Then she walked into Rona's yellow and white kitchen and saw Dexter on the floor giving Fred a dog biscuit. Boy and dog were having a regular lovefest, and she wondered how she'd ever drag her son away now. Fred chomped the biscuit in no time. Then he climbed onto Dexter's lap and started licking whatever skin he could find—hands, face, ears. Dexter's giggle made Lainie smile, in spite of everything.

Rona closed the door on the microwave and glanced down at them. "If you don't want him to lick, you can tell him no."

"I like licking." Dexter wrapped his arms around the enthusiastic dog. "He can lick me all he wants."

"Well, maybe your mother wouldn't appreciate—"

"It's fine," Lainie said. "I wish Dexter could have a dog, but the apartment doesn't allow pets."

Rona nodded as she punched buttons on the microwave. "Most don't. I remember what that's like, trying to raise a boy in an apartment. It's not easy. Would you two like coffee or cocoa?"

"Oh, nothing for me, thanks." Lainie was torn between wanting to stay for Dexter's sake and needing to leave because she had to separate herself from Harry before she started depending on him.

Dexter already had some major dependency issues going on where Harry was concerned, but Dexter was a kid, and therefore flexible, thank God. Then there was also the fact that by staying, they were imposing on Rona. Lainie had a thing about not imposing on anyone . . . ever.

"I'll take coffee," said a raspy male voice from the kitchen doorway.

"Hey, Leo." Harry turned.

"Hey, yourself, kid." A gray-haired man with a commanding hook to his nose and a Sicilian burnish to his skin grasped Harry's arm with one hand and gave him a playful poke to the jaw with the other.

Lainie imagined she heard "The *Godfather* Theme" playing in the background.

"You look like hell, Harry," Leo said. "What you been up to?"

"Climbed out of a second-story window." Harry seemed proud of the fact.

"No joke? Playing at being a second-story man, huh? I didn't know you had it in you."

"Neither did I," Harry said. "Leo Pirelli, I'd like you to meet Lainie Terrell and her son Dexter."

"Pleased to make your acquaintance." Leo surveyed Lainie, his dark eyes speculative, as he shook her hand. But when he looked at Dexter, his features softened and he walked over and crouched down, exactly as Rona had. "Hi, there, Dex. Looks like you and Fred are buds already."

"Yep." Dexter's face was glowing with joy and shiny with dog spit. He smiled at Leo. "I have a question, though."

Leo looked pleased. "Questions are great. Shoot."

"Mommy and Mr. Harry wouldn't tell me, but I bet you know, 'cause you're a man."

Instantly Lainie knew what was coming. "Dexter, let's not discuss—"

"What's 'erectile dysfunction'?"

Leo blinked and cleared his throat. "An urban legend."

"A legend?" Dexter's forehead crinkled. "You mean like a movie?"

"Never mind, Dexter." Lainie's face grew hot. "That's not a subject to discuss right now." She noticed that Harry had strolled to the end of the kitchen, where a round table sat in a little nook surrounded by windows. She could have sworn she'd heard him choking back laughter.

"But the radio said all men ought to know about it, Mommy! And I'm going to be a man when I grow up, so I need to know! Specially if it's a *legend*."

Rona flipped the switch on the coffeemaker and turned around. "Dexter, I can tell you what erectile dysfunction is, even though I'm not a man."

Leo got to his feet and backed away. "It's got nothing to do with me, I can tell you that much."

"I didn't say it did." Rona smiled at him. "But I believe in answering honest questions."

"Me, too!" Dexter scratched behind Fred's ears.

Rona took the mug of hot water out of the microwave and emptied a package of instant cocoa mix into it. "Well, Dexter, it takes a daddy and a mommy to make a baby. Do you know about that?"

"Yep. I know. Mommy told me. They get together, and then the mommy gets a fat belly, and then the baby comes out."

"Well, if the daddy has erectile dysfunction, that means he can't help make the baby." She took a spoon from a drawer and stirred the cocoa.

"So *that's* all it is." Dexter's shoulders slumped with obvious relief.

"That's all." Rona glanced over at Leo and winked. "No big deal."

"So if the daddy has erectile dysfunction, then the mommy won't ever be . . . that other thing I'm not supposed to say."

Rona turned to look at him. "What other thing?"

"What you said on the phone to Mr. Harry. It means 'pregnant.'"

Leo coughed and looked away, hiding a smile.

Rona's eyes grew wide and then she blushed. "Oh. Um, Dexter, I shouldn't have used that kind of language."

"You're a grown-up, so you can. Mommy said it's a grown-up word."

"Well, this grown-up wishes she'd kept her mouth shut. But thanks for saving my bacon, Lainie." Rona smiled apologetically at her. "I shouldn't have said it. I'm sorry."

"No problem." Lainie wasn't offended in the least, but she was still very curious.

"Dexter!" Rona said brightly. "How would you like to roll the ball for Fred?"

"I would *love* it."

"Ask him to get it for you, and then roll it and he'll chase it. No throwing, though. Just rolling."

"O-*kay*." Dexter leaned close to Fred. "Get your ball, Fred! Go get it."

Fred scampered into the living room and Dexter followed.

"Whew," Rona said. "I'm going to have to watch myself around that little guy."

"Which reminds me," Leo said. "For your information, erectile dysfunction is definitely a big deal." Then as he passed Rona on his way to the double-wide refrigerator, he swatted her on the rump. "To some of us, anyway."

"Dexter caught that on the radio on the way over," Lainie said. "We couldn't shut it off in time and I'm afraid he picks up on everything."

"Nothing to be afraid of," Rona said. "Be glad he's smart." She glanced the length of the kitchen to where Harry was standing. "The only problem comes when they tend to overthink the big questions, like when to marry and who to marry, stuff like that."

Harry gave her a long-suffering look. "I'm going to pretend I don't know what you're talking about."

"Who wants a little Baileys to go in the coffee?" Leo asked, pulling a bottle out of the refrigerator. "I have a feeling this is a good time for Baileys, what with folks climbing out of second-story windows and debating the merits of matrimony. And just let me add, Rona, my love, that you're as skittish about traipsing down the aisle as your son. It's the pot calling the kettle, if you ask me."

"I have my reasons."

"Thanks for the help, Leo," Harry said.

"You're welcome. Will you join me in some Baileys?"

"I think I'd better stick with the coffee for now."

Leo gestured with the bottle. "Lainie?"

"Just coffee for me, too, thanks," she said. She'd decided one cup of coffee would at least show that she appreciated the effort Rona was making, and the scent of freshly ground beans tantalized her. But she didn't dare add anything that might dull her wits.

"Then have a seat, have a seat." Leo waved her toward

the table. The windows looked out on a community pool, glowing blue in the darkness.

Lainie had the urge to go over and close the mini-blinds, but decided she was being paranoid. "I really don't need to be waited on," she said. "Is there anything I can carry over to the table?"

"Those cookies." Rona nodded toward a package of Double Stuf Oreos on the counter.

"Sure thing." Lainie picked up the package and carried it to the table, her four-inch heels clicking on the tile.

"Say, can I take your coat?" Leo asked.

"Thanks, but I think I'll keep it on."

Tapping the spoon on the edge of the mug, Rona glanced over her shoulder. "If you're worried because you have on a dance costume, don't be. We're used to that around here, aren't we, Leo?"

Leo chuckled. "Ain't that the truth. You never know when the TITS are going to start bouncing around."

Lainie stared at him. Surely she'd misunderstood that last part. Surely he wasn't referring to Rona's—

"Oops, sorry." Leo flushed and sent a guilty glance toward the living room, but Dexter was too involved with Fred to hear anything. "I'm so used to talking about them, I sort of forget what I'm saying."

Harry cleared his throat. "Before this gets any worse, I'd better tell Lainie that it's an acronym for Temptresses in Temporary Suspension. Mom and her retired showgirl friends have formed a social club."

"*Oh.* Harry didn't tell me you were a dancer."

Rona straightened her spine a fraction. "For thirty years."

"Wow." Lainie's image of Harry shifted dramatically.

So Rona had been a showgirl. That fit. She moved gracefully and appeared to have a good figure under the black robe. Now Rona's comments added up.

She must have supported herself and her child by dancing just as Lainie was supporting herself and Dexter. It gave Lainie hope to see that life had apparently turned out well for both of them, even if Rona was disappointed that she didn't have any grandchildren yet.

"Everything's ready," Rona said. "Leo, if you'll pour the coffee, I'll get Dexter and help him wash his hands at the sink."

"Oh, I can do that." Lainie automatically assumed her duty as the one in charge of Dexter.

"I know you can." Rona smiled at her, holding her back with a glance. "But let me. You and Harry go sit down. Leo and I are used to working in this kitchen together."

Lainie hesitated and then decided to follow instructions. "All right. And thanks." She took a seat at the table and told herself not to settle in too much. But she'd had so little support in this mothering business and had paid for any and all help she'd had. Here was a woman who relished the job of caring for Dexter, and that felt nice for a change. She listened to Rona and Dexter giggling over the hand-washing and sent the little boy a silent apology for all he'd missed in life.

Leo set down three mugs of coffee. "All her friends have grandchildren," he murmured as he scooted mugs in front of Lainie and Harry.

Harry sighed and pulled his coffee closer. "And you might as well add that I've selfishly deprived her of that."

"Well, it's time," Leo said.

"But I haven't—" Harry broke off when Rona and Dexter arrived. Rona carried her coffee and a cup of cocoa mounded with whipped cream. Dexter clutched a stack of napkins, which he carefully parceled out to everyone.

Rona set down both drinks. "I'll go get the special chair."

Dexter looked up. "Special chair?"

"For special people."

"Like me?" Dexter grinned. He was obviously reveling in the attention.

"Exactly like you." Rona tweaked his nose before walking back to the kitchen. She returned with a combination stepladder and chair that put Dexter at the perfect height to reach the table.

Dexter climbed into it and beamed at the group. "Great. Now let's clink."

Leo stared at him. "Clink?"

"He means toast," Lainie said. "Whenever we have a special occasion, we clink our glasses together." She'd had to create special occasions out of ordinary things like finding a penny on the sidewalk, because they'd had so few real occasions to toast.

"Then we should definitely clink." Rona picked up her mug of coffee. "Here's to making new friends."

Everyone followed her lead, tapping mugs together and reaching way across the table to make sure they clicked mugs with Dexter. Lainie had thought she didn't miss this kind of social interaction, but being here tonight showed how tiny her circle had become. That wasn't healthy for her or Dexter, and she needed to fix it, right after she decided what to do about Joey.

After taking a sip of her coffee, Rona reached for an Oreo. "How long have you been at the Nirvana, Lainie?"

"Just six months. It's a great job." She wanted desperately to keep it, but if Joey started threatening to take Dexter, she'd have to leave. "Where did you work?"

"The Sands, which is gone now, and Caesars Palace. I miss it. That's why the girls and I put on shows in the rec hall, just to prove we can still shake our booty."

Dexter looked up, his mouth rimmed with a whipped-cream mustache. "Can I see your show? Mommy won't let me see hers."

"I'd love you to see it, snookums."

"Good." Dexter drained his mug of cocoa. "Can I be 'scused to go play ball with Fred, now?"

"Yes, you may," Lainie said. She needed him to leave so that she could give Rona and Leo an explanation for ruining their evening. "And be very careful. Roll the ball, don't throw it."

"I promise, Mommy." Then he was off.

Lainie watched him go. "It's way past his bedtime."

"I have a spare room, if you want to set him up in there," Rona said eagerly. "He does look a little tired."

Lainie turned back to her. "Thank you, but we really need to go. I'll call us a cab, right after I fill you in on what brought us to your doorstep in the middle of the night. You deserve that much, for being so kind."

"A cab?" Rona seemed scandalized. "Why would you do that?"

"I'd better explain about Dexter's father." So she did. As Lainie talked, Rona looked increasingly worried and Leo's face grew dark and menacing. Lainie decided she'd never want to make an enemy of Leo Pirelli.

"So that's the story," she said at last. "I should have asked Joey to sign papers before I left New Jersey, but I was afraid putting something official like that in front of him would make him change his mind about letting us go. I was hoping he'd just forget about us."

Rona's jaw tightened. "I can't imagine a man forgetting about a son like Dexter. Anyone can see he's a very special little boy."

"He can beat me at chess," Harry said.

"Really?" Rona blinked in surprise. "I didn't think anybody could beat you at chess."

"Well, I was a little distracted."

"Nevertheless, apparently Dexter ranks several notches above the average four-year-old." Rona glanced over at Lainie. "Have you had him tested?"

Lainie shook her head. The pediatrician, the eye doctor, and the dentist had been all she'd been able to manage. Testing Dexter's brain power hadn't seemed necessary. She knew he was very smart. She assumed his smart genes had been passed down from Joey's father, the business tycoon. Lainie had never met him, but from Joey's description, the man was a genius.

Leo cleared his throat. "Let's get back to the matter at hand. From what you're saying, Lainie, I gather you don't think Joey can be trusted around little Dex."

"That's right. When he drinks too much, he loses control. He wasn't this bad when I first met him, but over the years he's gotten worse."

"You should have heard him tonight." Harry pushed his empty mug away. "Yelling like a crazy man."

"So why didn't you call the police?" Rona asked.

"Well . . ." Harry glanced over at Lainie.

Her heart swelled. "Because he thought I might be a mom on the run, and he didn't want to get me in trouble. Thank you for giving me the benefit of the doubt, Harry."

He shrugged, and a faint flush tinged his cheeks. "It wasn't hard. Here was this maniac Dexter was scared to death of, versus a woman who really cared about her kid."

"So you went out a second-story window," Leo said with a grin. "That's my boy. So, what can we do about this situation? How can Rona and I help out?"

Their kindness made her want to cry, but she wasn't about to let herself do something so embarrassing. "That's an extremely generous offer, but I wouldn't dream of getting you two involved. This is my problem, and I'll handle it." She wished that she'd followed through on getting a new cell phone. She'd canceled the old one, not wanting to give Joey a link to her. She'd meant to get a different one but hadn't taken the time. It would have come in handy now. "If I can borrow a phone, I'll call a cab."

"That's not necessary," Harry said. "I'll take you wherever you want to go."

Rona leaned both arms on the table and gazed at Lainie, her eyes filled with concern. "And where would that be, honey? You definitely don't want to go back to your apartment tonight."

"I'll . . . I'll stay with a friend." She hadn't made any friends who were close enough that she'd feel comfortable plopping herself on their sofa for the night, especially with Dexter in tow. Come to think of it, Harry was her closest friend. She needed to take a cab to disguise the fact that she'd have to stay in a motel and maybe even hop a bus out of town in the morning.

Leo shook his head. "Lainie, give it up. You have nowhere to go, and we all know it. Here's the deal—Rona and I aren't about to let you take a cab to a motel, leaving yourself and your kid open to whatever this looney tunes father might do if he manages to track you down."

"But—"

"We don't know what kind of resources he has," Leo continued, cutting her off. "You say his dad's extremely wealthy. That means there could be private detectives on this. Now, I can tell you're an independent woman—" He paused to give Rona a telling glance. "I happen to be well acquainted with the type. If we were only talking about you, that would be one thing. But we need to keep Dexter out of this guy's clutches."

"Exactly," Rona said. "And because we can't get the police involved, I think our best bet is to confuse the heck out of this moron and anyone who might be working with him. Fortunately, I have the perfect plan."

Harry groaned. "God save us."

Leo laughed. "Like I didn't see that coming." He glanced at Lainie. "Prepare yourself. Rona's a champion planner. True, her plans usually sound a little wacko at first, but trust me, they work."

"At least hear me out," Rona said. "If you hate the plan, then we can discuss alternatives, but I'm guessing you are flying by the seat of that fancy dance costume you're wearing."

Lainie realized she'd been made. Rona and Leo were too streetwise to be taken in by her vague references to nonexistent safety nets. And they were absolutely right about keeping Dexter safe. She wasn't sure what to make of Harry's groan when Rona announced that she had a plan. However, because Lainie had no plan, she'd be a fool not to listen to Rona's ideas.

"Okay, Rona," she said. "I'd like to hear what you have to say."

Chapter Four

Harry wanted Lainie and Dexter to be safe. He wanted that more than anything. But he couldn't be blamed for being suspicious of whatever plan his mother had cooked up, given her single-mindedness about grandchildren. She currently had possession of a potential grandchild, and Harry didn't think he'd be able to get Dexter out of here with a crowbar.

In addition to that concern, Harry had caught a whiff of matchmaking in the air whenever his mother glanced at Lainie. Of course Lainie would appeal to her—she saw herself thirty years ago and longed for a daughter-in-law she could relate to. She might let her emotional reaction to Lainie's situation overrule logic, but Harry wasn't about to do that. He planned to help as much as he could and keep his emotions strictly out of it.

Rona leaned forward and lowered her voice. "My first concern is for that little boy in there."

Leo nodded. "It's safe to say that's everybody's chief concern. So what have you got, Boom-Boom?"

Harry was used to Leo's pet name for his mother, at least as much as he could ever be, but he wondered what Lainie would think. From her quick little smile he gathered that she thought the nickname was cute.

However, right now Rona was all business. "Lainie, I think it would be good if you got out of town for a while."

"I agree," Lainie said.

"But I don't like the idea of dragging Dexter all over the place, especially if he figures out that you're running from his dad. And he would figure it out. Besides, with the two of you together, you'd make life easier for any private detective Joey might have hired, because you'd leave visual clues all over the place. We can disguise you, but people will remember Dexter. He's that kind of kid."

Harry couldn't fault his mother's reasoning. He also knew where she was going with it.

"Therefore, I suggest leaving Dexter here with me."

"Now there's a shocker," Harry said.

His mother ignored him. "I'm retired, so I can devote all my time to Dexter. He loves Fred and I think he already likes me a little bit. And he'd be safe. We have great security in this complex."

"Damn straight you do," Leo muttered.

"That much I can vouch for," Harry said. "The word's out. Try anything funny around the Emerald Lakes area and you're liable to be wearing cement overshoes."

Lainie's eyes widened.

"Metaphorically speaking," Harry added.

"Right." Leo smiled. "Cement overshoes went out in the forties."

Lainie glanced from Harry to Leo, obviously trying to decide if they were pulling her leg.

"Take my word for it," Harry said. "If you leave Dexter with my mom, it's like locking the kid away in Fort Knox. All you'd have to worry about are the sugar highs from unlimited cookies and whether the TITS would spoil him so completely you'd never get him straightened out." Harry didn't know why he was supporting his mom's plan, except that for the first time since he'd arrived at the Nirvana with Dexter, Lainie seemed to be perking up.

Even so, she shook her head. "I couldn't possibly impose on you like that, Rona."

"Impose?" Rona looked at Lainie in disbelief. "Honey, haven't you been paying attention? I'm desperate for the grandmother experience. If you left Dexter here with me for a few days, you'd be doing *me* a favor."

Lainie glanced toward the living room. The joyous sounds of boy and dog drifted down the hall as if to put an exclamation point on Rona's statement.

"Obviously Fred would love it, too," Rona said. "As you can see, he's crazy about kids. The TITS bring their grandchildren over here specifically to give Fred a thrill."

And Harry was beginning to feel very, very guilty. He'd known his mother wanted a grandchild to spoil, but he hadn't realized to what extent. Shit, he was even depriving *Fred*. His mom was treating this visit from Dexter as if she and Fred had hit the Quartermania jackpot.

It wasn't like Harry didn't want to marry and have kids. He'd been a little slow about it, but he definitely saw that in his future. Apparently he needed to make it a bigger priority, though, considering he wanted a family and his mom *really* wanted him to have one.

"You're making a convincing case," Lainie said to Rona. "I've been worried that Dexter is missing out on having grandparents fuss over him."

"Your parents don't visit?" Rona asked gently.

"Uh, no."

She looked so sad at that moment that Harry clutched his coffee mug to keep from reaching for her hand.

"That's too bad," Leo said, his voice gruff. "A damned shame."

"Then I think it's settled." Looking for all the world like Judge Judy at the conclusion of a case, Rona folded her manicured hands on the table. "Dexter will stay here for a few days, and you can take a little trip with Harry."

Harry almost fell off his chair. "Wait a minute, I—"

"A trip with Harry?" Lainie made it sound like the last thing in the world she wanted to do.

Well, that got his hackles up. "For your information, I'm a fairly decent traveling companion." Yep, his mom was doing the matchmaking thing, and he should watch his step. But Lainie didn't have to sound so horrified at the thought of being stuck with him.

She blushed bright red. "Oh, I'm sure you are a *wonderful* traveling companion! I didn't mean it like that. I was caught by surprise, and I was sure you wouldn't want to do it, anyway, so I was only—"

"All right, you two," Rona said. "Settle down and listen to what I have to say before you jump to conclusions."

Harry knew there was only one conclusion that made sense, and he'd already jumped to it, walked around on it, and recognized it as his mother's handiwork. If he was wrong he'd eat Fred's dog food, but he didn't think he was wrong. Rona had dreamed up a way to have

Dexter to herself and throw her unmarried son in the path of matrimony in one brilliant maneuver.

"Anybody change their mind about that Baileys?" Leo asked.

"I'm thinking three fingers of bourbon, personally," Harry said. "But I have a feeling I'll be driving somewhere soon, so I'd better pass."

"Everybody wait here a minute." Rona pushed back her chair. "I need to get something. Anybody need more coffee while I'm up?"

Leo stood and picked up his mug. "Let me get whatever it is, Boom-Boom. I'm going for the Baileys, anyway."

Rona sank back to her chair and smiled at Leo. "Thank you. If you could please bring me that invitation from the time-share people in Sedona, I'd appreciate it."

Leo chuckled. "You mean the one addressed to Mr. and Mrs. Fred Ambrewster?"

"That's the one."

Lainie burst out laughing. "They sent a time-share invitation to a dog?"

"It happens all the time." Harry really liked hearing her laugh. "You can't blame them. Mom's listed in the phone book as 'Fred and Rona Ambrewster.' "

Rona sniffed. "Go ahead and make fun of me, but I think it's smart to give the impression there's a married couple living here."

"Yeah," Leo called from the kitchen, "and guess how many of your neighbors call me Fred?"

"I think it's a great idea," Lainie said. "My number's unlisted, of course, but if I should ever list it, I'll remember that strategy. I suppose you wouldn't even have to have a pet. You could just stick a guy's name in there. Who would know?"

"Of course, Rona could solve the whole problem." Leo came back with his mug full, the coffee carafe in his free hand and the envelope stuck under his arm. "She could marry me and then there would be an actual married couple living here. No subterfuge necessary. But I can't seem to convince her of that, and I've been trying for twenty years."

Rona glanced at him. "Our arrangement suits me just fine. And it suits you just fine, too, so be quiet. If I ever said I'd marry you, you'd run for your life."

Leo winked at Harry. "Smart woman, your mother." Then he handed her the envelope and started pouring coffee all around.

"And don't you forget it." Rona took a letter out of the envelope. "Anyway, Leo and I are curious about this time-share."

"Rona is curious," Leo said. "Me, I'm not so sure about the time-share concept."

"Well, I think it looks beautiful. So Harry, you and Lainie could drive down there tonight, listen to the pitch tomorrow, and let us know if it's worth our making the trip. They include two nights' lodging, so the only expense would be the meals."

"But the letter's addressed to you and Fred," Harry said. That was the least of the problems, but the only one he could say in front of everyone.

The big problem, the huge, gigantic, super-humongous problem, was how he'd react to all that time alone with Lainie, in a resort setting, probably bedding down in the same complimentary suite. Sure, it could get her out of town for a few days and perhaps throw Joey off the trail, but Harry would be smack-dab in the middle of the biggest temptation he'd had to face in years.

"So be Fred for a few days," Rona said. "I was planning to have Leo be Fred, so why not you? My friend Suz said they don't check ID on these deals as long as you look like you're a decent prospect. Besides, your last name matches."

"I'll bet I'd have to register a credit card at the front desk for incidentals."

Rona waved away the objection. "They won't ask. When was the last time you registered a credit card at a hotel and had anybody look twice at it? If they do, tell them Fred's your nickname and Harold is your real name. If the credit card signature matches, they'll be fine with it."

"But my name doesn't match anything," Lainie said.

"I know, sweetie," Rona said. "But you won't be asked to prove who you are. I was planning to give you some of my clothes to take along, and among the various TITS members we should be able to come up with some wigs and spare pairs of glasses. You don't want to be recognized as yourself."

Harry had to admit it was a neat little plan. He had plenty of vacation days coming because he never went anywhere, and he was caught up at work. Hell, he was always caught up at work. Dependable Harry. Boring, but dependable.

At any rate, if Joey turned out to be your average disruptive bully, he'd probably give up after a few days of searching fruitlessly for his son and ex-girlfriend. This could be a simple, if temporary, fix for the problem, giving Lainie time to figure out how to solve her dilemma once and for all.

Of course, Lainie might refuse to go along with the plan.

"Okay," Lainie said. "I'll do it."

Joey couldn't believe Lainie had given him the slip. Her car was still in the parking lot, though. And it would stay in the parking lot. He'd disconnected the battery and parked his car right next to hers, so when she came back, even if he'd fallen asleep in the car, he'd wake up when she got somebody to come out and help her.

But after fifteen minutes of trying to catch some Zs, he realized he was both hungry and thirsty. Well, hell's-a-poppin', if he wasn't parked right behind a casino, which served food and drinks twenty-four/seven. He could easily order some food, have one drink while he was waiting for it, and get another one to bring out here with the sandwich. Even if Lainie showed up, she wouldn't be able to have the car fixed and drive away in the time it would take him to get some eats.

He walked around the building and in through the front. The place smelled and sounded like money—even with the new machines that paid in paper vouchers instead of coins, money lust was in the air. He'd always loved that about casinos. You could walk in a poor slob and walk out a rich dude in a couple of hours. All you needed was a stake and luck.

His luck was due to turn. It had to turn, or he was in way too much trouble. But all he had to do was link up with little Dexter, and he was golden. The kid was his. He had a legal right to him.

Locating the nearest bar, he took a seat.

"What'll it be?" asked the bartender, a young punk who didn't look old enough to drink.

Joey ordered a beer and a turkey sandwich. The beer came immediately, and he chugged half of it. Then while he waited for the sandwich, he dug in his pocket for quarters and stuck three in the poker slot machine built into the bartop. The first game paid off with twenty quarters, which he took as a good sign. He must have whooped a little, because the bartender came over to take a look.

"Nice going," the guy said.

"Chump change." Joey fed three more quarters into the machine. "One of these days, I'm going to be rolling in it." Then, because he knew the bartender probably heard that all the time, he felt compelled to look this yahoo in the eye and add, "Seriously."

"Wouldn't that be nice?" Obviously the guy didn't believe a word of it.

"I'm not kidding around." Joey finished off the beer. "I'm going to inherit a freaking fortune." He motioned to the empty glass. "Hit me again."

"Sure thing." Pretty soon the guy brought another beer plus the turkey sandwich.

Joey decided to ignore the sandwich for now and concentrate on the beer. It felt real good going down, and he'd had a tough night. "See, I wasn't supposed to inherit everything at first."

"Is that right?" The guy edged away, like he didn't want to get drawn into the conversation.

But Joey knew how to grab listeners, by God. If there was one thing Joey Benjamin knew how to do, it was keep people entertained. "See, it's all about sexual preferences."

Immediately the guy was back. "Like, what do you mean?"

"My older brother Emil popped right out of the closet two weeks ago, and my billionaire, Bible-thumpin' daddy's not leaving him one thin dime, now. I'm next in line for the dough, but my daddy wants a guarantee that I can pass on the family fortune to my own flesh and blood when the time comes."

"So you're looking to get someone pregnant?" The guy was totally involved in the story. "Because I'll bet you'd have women lining up, if they knew about this deal."

"I can't take that chance. See, I had mumps as a teenager, and the docs said I'd be shooting blanks from that point on."

"Wow, that sucks!"

"Except five years ago, to my surprise, I got my girlfriend pregnant, so I do have a kid. Might be the only one I'll ever have, but I have one."

"So you're all set, then!"

"Yeah." Joey gulped some more beer. "Except I never told Daddy about that kid. You know how it is. He doesn't think people should have sex outside of marriage." Joey snorted. "Probably not inside of marriage, either. And if he knew the kid's mother was a showgirl, well, we won't even go there. Anyway, I figured what he didn't know wouldn't hurt him."

"But now you want him to know about the kid, at least."

"Right." Joey picked up his sandwich. "My little

brother Ronnie is so sure he has this sewn up. He even had his sperm tested, the little prick, and I mean that literally. But yours truly has already sired the next Benjamin heir, so I'm light-years ahead of Ronnie and his freaking sperm count. With luck I can gloss over the showgirl part. The thing is, now I have to find that little dude, or my ass is grass."

"I don't get it. Your kid is missing?"

Joey spoke through a mouthful of turkey sandwich. "It's sort of complicated. I'll find him, though."

"Man, in your shoes, I'd be scouring the countryside for that ticket to my inheritance."

"That's exactly what I plan to do." Joey polished off his second beer and waved to the empty glass. "I just need to wet my whistle real good first."

Lainie's reasons for accepting Rona's suggestion revolved around Dexter and what would be the best thing for him. So even though she'd said yes, she needed to check with her son and make sure he was okay with the plan.

"Or rather, I'll do it if Dexter says okay," she added. "If you don't mind, I'd like to go in the living room and ask him privately."

"Sure." Rona smiled. "No problem."

Excusing herself from the table, Lainie tightened the belt of her raincoat before walking into the living room. She was sweating under that vinyl coat. Borrowing some clothes from Rona would obligate her even more, but by now her own clothes were probably a wrinkled mess, not fit for a trip to a resort. And she'd love to get into something more comfortable. Her sequined thong wasn't designed for sitting around a kitchen table drinking coffee and chatting.

When she reached the living room, she found Dexter sprawled on the floor cuddling Fred. Dexter hadn't heard her come in because he seemed to be engrossed in telling Fred a story.

"But those aliens trying to take over the world hadn't figured on Dexter and his Superdog Fred," Dexter said. "Those two zapped the aliens like crazy, and they started running to their spaceship. Then they took off and went back where they came from, a nebula far, far away. So Dexter and Fred, they were heroes, and they had a big parade and got to ride in a convertible with the top down, and they got to eat all the cookies they wanted, and that night, they all went to see a dance show. The end."

"Great story," Lainie said.

Dexter looked up, his expression worried. "Hi, Mommy. Do we have to go, now?"

"That's what I want to talk to you about." She crouched down next to him.

"Can we come back again, though? Me and Fred, we like each other a lot."

From his prone position, Fred wiggled and thumped his tail on the rug.

"I can see that." Right then and there, Lainie made a promise to herself. She would figure out a way for Dexter to have a dog. She'd been too quick to take the apartment they lived in, or maybe *used* to live in was more like it. The future was uncertain. But once this business was settled about Joey, she'd keep looking until she found a place that allowed pets.

"As it turns out, Miss Rona has asked if you'd like to stay here for a while."

Dexter's eyes grew round with excitement. "*Stay* here? You mean sleep here? With Fred?"

Lainie nodded. "Miss Rona said you could stay here while I take a little trip with Mr. Harry."

"Where're you going?"

"To check out a vacation place and see if Miss Rona wants to go there someday."

"So why don't we *all* go? You, me, Mr. Harry, Miss Rona, Mr. Leo, and Fred. All of us. We could get a van."

Lainie smiled at the picture of such a trip. "Miss Rona doesn't want to go right now, and she would love to have you stay here with her to keep her and Fred company."

"I could do that," he said eagerly. "How long do I get to stay here?"

She noticed he'd phrased it as if he didn't want to leave, ever. Poor kid, he really needed grandparents, not to mention a dog. "Oh, about three days." She reached out and stroked his hair. "But remember, we've never been away from each other for three days." She was grateful that he was smart enough to understand how long that was. She didn't have to worry that he'd agree to something and not know what she was talking about.

He looked at her with great seriousness. "Will you miss me a whole lot?"

"I'm sure I will." She got a lump in her throat just thinking about it.

"It's only three days." He sounded so much like her that she nearly laughed. "You'll be fine, Mommy. Before you know it, you'll be coming back."

"I guess you're right." She admitted to being a little

bit jealous of Rona and Fred, who had captured Dexter's devotion in no time at all. But because they had, she could more easily deal with this problem. Maybe during the trip, Harry could help her decide what to do about Joey.

She would love to know how Harry looked at this plan. She hoped he wasn't too irritated that his mother had swooped in and complicated his life with this trip. He acted hesitant, and she could certainly understand that. Harry didn't seem to know what to do regarding her. He seemed attracted, and yet maybe he didn't want to be attracted.

Well, three days of forced confinement should give her the answer to the puzzle of Harry Ambrewster. But she wasn't sure how she'd manage to leave her kid for that long. "So you're sure you're okay with this idea?" she asked.

"Mommy, I'm *great* with this idea. But are you going to be lonesome without me?"

"Probably." She leaned down and kissed his soft little boy's cheek. He smelled of doggy drool. "But like you said, before I know it, I'll be back."

Chapter Five

The minute Lainie was out of the room, Harry skewered his mother with a look. "Just so you're aware, I know exactly what you're doing."

Rona laughed. "I know you do. I haven't been able to get anything past you since you were two."

"Now don't go getting upset with your mother, kid," Leo said. "I agree with her that this is the best way to handle things for right now. And I'm not interested in marrying you off. It's only that I hate bullies, and I'd like to see if my guys can smoke this one out."

Harry lowered his voice. "I can give you a description."

Leo became more alert. "You saw him?"

"Yeah. Blond, about my height, hefty. Not fat, just solid. Looks like a jock. I'm guessing he played football in high school."

"That helps, knowing what to look for," Leo said. "Anyway, somebody needs to get Lainie out of the way while I put my boys on it, and she seems to be short on friends to help her out."

"Of course she is," Rona said. "The poor thing's been looking over her shoulder ever since she got here." She studied Harry for a moment. "So you've been babysitting?"

Harry shifted in his seat. Pretty soon his mother would discover that he had more than a neighborly interest in Lainie, even though he'd been trying to disguise it. Rona was no dummy, either. "I happened to find out that her regular sitter wasn't available this week, so I said I'd fill in."

"That was nice of you." Rona tapped her manicured finger against her mouth. "I'm trying to remember the last time you offered to babysit for someone's child. Let me think. That would be . . . never."

"Don't go making a big deal out of it. I'm sure the offer had something to do with remembering how you had to struggle to find sitters."

"Which doesn't take away from the fact that you did a nice thing. And on top of that, you didn't call the cops when Dexter's father showed up." Rona smiled at him. "I think you like her."

"Which is what you're banking on," Harry said, feeling testy. "But don't get too fond of Dexter, okay? Because Lainie's not my type."

His mother rolled her eyes. "She's exactly your type. You'll never convince me that those mousy girls you've been going out with lately are the kind who will make you happy."

"I just haven't found the right woman, Mom. Simple as that."

"Well, I would think a showgirl would be perfect for you. They're the sort of women you know best. Which reminds me, I need to round up the TITS, but before I do that I want to make Dexter's bed. I'll bet he's pooped. So if you two will excuse me, I have things to do."

"Need me to help with anything?" Leo asked.

"Thanks, but I can handle it." Rona smiled at him. "You're a nice guy, you know that?"

"I keep telling you."

She laughed and headed upstairs.

Leo sipped his coffee while he watched her go. When she was out of earshot, he put his mug down. "I know what your problem is, kid."

"What problem?"

"With women."

"I don't have a problem with women."

"Sure you do. Otherwise you'd be settled down by now. Lord knows you have the disposable income to do that. Which reminds me, why haven't you moved out of that tiny apartment and bought yourself a decent house?"

"Because I—"

"You like your new neighbor?" Leo winked.

"No, that's not the reason." But it was part of the reason, one he hated to admit to himself because it wasn't logical. "I can't see buying a place until I find the right woman."

"You of all people should be after the investment and the tax write-off."

"I have this place as an investment and tax write-off." He'd told his mother that she was doing him a favor by living in the place and paying him a nominal rent. It saved her pride, and he was glad for that.

"Okay, okay. But you're not making progress on the marriage front, and I say it's because the ones who float your boat haven't been smart enough for you, at least so far. Am I right?"

"I suppose there's some truth to that. But I'm sure that eventually—" Harry closed his mouth when he heard Lainie's high heels clicking in the hallway leading from the living room.

"Take it from me, kid," Leo said in a low voice. "You wanna go for the gusto first, and then check out the brains of the operation. I don't care how smart a woman is, if she doesn't flip your pancakes, then forget it."

"Hey, that's my mother you're talking about. Watch it."

"I'm just sayin'."

"I know what you're saying," Harry muttered. "And I wish you'd quit saying it." Then he glanced up as Lainie walked into the kitchen. "So what does Dexter think about staying here?"

"He's crazy about the idea," she said with a trace of sadness in her voice. "I'm the one with separation anxiety. I'm sure Dexter will be fine. He's practically asleep right now, lying on the living room rug with Fred."

And just like that, Harry was sucked in again, wanting to comfort her, wanting to take her in his arms and tell her she was making the right decision, tough as it was for her.

Because he wasn't about to do anything like that, he searched for a role he could fill. "I think my mom is getting his bed ready upstairs. Why don't I carry him up there and we'll tuck him in?" He didn't have to look at Leo to know the guy was grinning like the cat who ate the canary. Leo was enjoying the hell out of watching Harry maneuver through this situation. Harry figured Leo had the right to enjoy it—the guy had pulled Harry's sorry butt out of several dicey situations when Harry had been a clueless teenager.

"That's a good idea." Lainie looked about ready to cry.

Harry realized that once they were on their way to Sedona, he could have a blubbering woman on his hands. He'd better throw a box of Kleenex in the car before they left. Under no circumstances should he pull over and let her cry on his shoulder. Comforting a woman built like Lainie could be a slippery slope.

He pushed back his chair. "I'll go get him, then."

"I'll see if Boom-Boom's ready for you," Leo said.

"I don't have his PJs." Lainie sounded upset. "He's not used to sleeping in his clothes."

Harry started down the hall toward the living room. "If I know my mother, it'll just be for tonight. She'll take him shopping tomorrow."

"Shopping? But what if Joey or some private eye he's hired is lurking around and sees them?"

"Yeah, you're right." Harry turned, almost colliding with Lainie. "Okay, so maybe she'll send a member of the TITS out shopping for her. We can even suggest that, if you're worried about it."

"Then I'll pay her back for whatever they buy."

"Don't even suggest it." There in the darkened hall, he had the insane urge to kiss her. They were standing close enough that it would be an easy move. "Mom would be insulted."

"But she shouldn't be spending money."

She smelled so damned good. He loved listening to her breathe, loved watching her lips move when she talked. "Don't worry about the money, either. She wouldn't spend it if she didn't feel she could. She went too many years pinching pennies to be wild with money." And Harry would deposit a hefty sum in her account when he got back and tell her it was an unexpected stock dividend.

"So what about you? How can you just leave work?"

"I can. I'll call the office from Sedona in the morning. It'll be fine."

Lainie sighed. "And Tim won't expect me to be coming back, so I guess I should just relax and let things happen."

"Probably." But he didn't dare do that, or they'd be in a lip-lock in no time flat. He needed to move on down the hall, and do it now, before he acted on a stupid impulse and planted one right on that full mouth of hers. "Let's go get Dexter." He started toward the living room again.

"Harry . . ."

He glanced back, and she looked so vulnerable he had to clench his body against the urge to wrap his arms around her.

"Thank you," she said. "For everything."

"You're welcome."

"I'm sure you're a terrific traveling companion."

He smiled at that. "I guess you'll find out." Then he concentrated on walking straight to the living room without passing Go or collecting two hundred dollars.

When he crouched down to pick up Dexter, the strangest thing happened. Fred growled at him. Fred had never growled at him. Fred wasn't a growler. He was a cute little lapdog who licked whatever bare skin he could reach and wiggled with ecstasy when he got a good tummy rub.

"Omigosh," Lainie said. "He's *guarding* Dexter. That is so cute."

"That is so weird. He's not a guard dog." He lowered his voice. "It's okay, Fred." He still couldn't get over this little fluff ball acting like a Doberman. He wanted to laugh, but that might wake Dexter, who was sound asleep, his arm around Fred. "I'm not going to hurt your new friend. We need to take him upstairs to bed. You can come, too. I'm sure he'd like that."

Fred whined and thumped the floor with his tail. Harry took that as a sign that Fred wouldn't bite him if he scooped Dexter up off the floor. Fortunately, as he lifted Dexter, he didn't feel the prick of Fred's teeth.

Dexter was a good-sized four-year-old, and Harry grunted a little as he stood up with Dexter in his arms.

"Let me help." Lainie moved in close. "He's too heavy."

"Nah, I have him." Harry wasn't about to let on that he had the least bit of trouble hefting a four-year-old and carrying him up the stairs. But this was the second time tonight he wished that he'd paid more attention to his physical conditioning recently. As a college kid, he'd worked out in an attempt to change his nerd image. Unfortunately, nobody had noticed, so he'd given up his gym membership.

Maybe he'd rejoin after he came back from Sedona, although that wouldn't help him now, when he was faced with jock-type ex-boyfriends and a sleeping kid who needed to be hauled up to bed. This turn of events had caught him off guard.

As he started toward the stairs, the jingle of dog tags told him Fred was right on his heels. "Make sure he doesn't get in front of me and make me trip," he said to Lainie.

"I'll just pick him up and carry him." Then she started laughing. "Oh, man, does he love to lick. I'm getting a real face washing. Hey, that tickles, Fred. Come on, stay away from my ears."

Dogs had all the luck. Harry tried not to listen as Lainie giggled her way up the stairs behind him, but her reaction to Fred's tongue was turning him on. Harry wanted to be that dog, held against Lainie's breasts while he licked every bit of exposed skin.

At the top of the stairs he turned right and headed into his mother's guest room. She and Leo were still in there. Rona cradled her cordless phone against her shoulder while she helped Leo adjust a comforter over the twin daybed. She waved Harry over as she turned back the sheets.

"Not your purple wig," she said into the phone. "We don't want her to attract attention. That short blond one would be great, though. Cherie's bringing over her long red one. Yeah, the one she thinks makes her look like Nicole Kidman."

Harry carefully laid Dexter on the bed and started taking off his shoes.

"This dog's going nuts," Lainie murmured.

"Here." Leo walked over toward her. "Let me take him until we get that little shaver under the covers." He scooped the dog from Lainie's arms. "Hey, you, settle down," he said in his gravelly voice. "Or you'll make me mad. You wouldn't like me when I get mad."

Harry glanced over his shoulder at Leo and the dog. Leo would never raise a hand to Fred, but the dog minded

Leo better than anyone else. Come to think of it, most everyone minded Leo. You didn't mess with a guy who had Leo's connections. It wasn't healthy.

Even Fred seemed to understand that. Rona was the only person not intimidated by Leo, but then, she didn't scare easily. Harry had been about eight when three burly high school kids had followed him home, threatening to "depants that little nerd." Rona had boiled out of the house in her short-shorts, cropped top, and thigh-high boots and sent those three scurrying for cover. She would have made a good Amazon warrior.

"No, no clothes," Rona said to whichever member of the TITS she'd called. "She's close enough to my size that I can dress her. Well, okay, if you must, you must. You do have some stunning nightwear, Suz. I'm sure she'd appreciate that, come to think of it."

Harry gulped. *Stunning nightwear?* Apparently the TITS had decided Harry had procrastinated on this marriage deal long enough, and they were going to reel him in, using Lainie as bait. They might want to check with Lainie on that score. Just because he had a weakness for her didn't mean she had a weakness for him, especially a guy who didn't have washboard abs. More like motherboard abs.

Once relieved of Fred, Lainie moved over beside Harry to help undress Dexter. They worked together and managed to slide off the Pooh shorts Harry had bought him.

"That's good enough," Lainie murmured. "He can sleep in his shirt and underwear." As she pulled the covers over him, she sniffled softly.

Harry turned his head in time to see her brush her

cheek with the back of her hand. His arm was around her shoulders before he could stop himself. "He'll be fine. They'll have a great time together," he said softly, giving her a reassuring squeeze.

"I know." She sniffed again. "B-but I've never left him for this long. Only the few hours when I was working. I–I don't know if I can do it."

"You can do it. Think of it this way—you're helping make it very difficult for Joey to find him."

Leo eased Fred down on the bed. "And remember, he has a new friend to keep him company. Easy does it, Fred. That's a good dog."

They all watched as Fred stepped carefully over Dexter until he was in position to curl against Dexter's side. Then, with a little doggy sigh, Fred plopped down and put his head on his paws.

Lainie reached out and scratched behind the dog's ears. "Take good care of him, Fred."

Fred's tail thumped twice.

From the doorway, Rona flipped off the light switch, leaving the room dark except for a little night-light near the baseboard. Leo headed out the door.

Finally Harry realized he was standing there holding on to Lainie in a tantalizingly dark room. He released her and stepped back. "Let's go downstairs."

"Okay." She sounded hoarse. With one last glance at Dexter, she walked through the door.

Lainie couldn't imagine what she'd do without Harry. Right now he was her security blanket, whether he wanted to be or not. His mother was into matchmaking—any idiot could see that—and most guys didn't appreciate having a mother interfere in such things. Rona didn't have hidden agendas. She had agendas that were right out on the table for everyone to see.

Stunning nightwear, indeed. The doorbell rang as Lainie started down the stairs. Amazingly, Fred didn't come barreling past her to check out whoever was at the door. That comforted Lainie, knowing that the little dog had appointed himself Dexter's protector. Fred wasn't big enough to be a real threat to anyone, but he'd sure as heck let someone know if Dexter was in danger.

By the time Lainie reached the first floor, the TITS were marching down the hallway toward her. In the flurry of introductions, she had trouble keeping names and faces straight. There were four of them, all tall, as she would have expected from former members of Vegas chorus lines. They greeted Leo and Harry with enthusiastic hugs and noisy kisses on the cheek. Lainie felt like she was backstage at the Nirvana.

Eventually she figured out Suz, a brunette, was the other member of the group besides Rona who'd kept her figure, and Suz was also the woman who'd brought the nightwear. No sooner had they gathered in the kitchen than Suz pulled a red, floor-length nightgown from the shopping bag she'd brought in with her.

"Here's my contribution to the cause." She held it up against her still-impressive bust line. "Is this gorgeous, or what?"

While all the women exclaimed over the beauty of the nightgown, Lainie stared at its plunging neckline. The nightgown was gorgeous, prettier than anything she'd ever owned. But by wearing it, she'd be hanging a sign around her neck that said "Take me, Harry."

No doubt about it, that outfit pretty much committed her to having sex on this trip. Harry might be able to resist his mother's manipulations, but he wouldn't be able to resist Lainie in that nightgown. She peeked in his direction to see how he was reacting.

He'd turned his broad back to the group and was rapidly clinking ice into glasses as he helped Leo bartend. But the tips of his ears were pink. And he was throwing ice around so wildly that a couple of cubes skidded across the counter and onto the floor.

Lainie thought his discomfort was very cute. His tush wasn't so bad, either. And come to find out, he had satisfyingly broad shoulders, plus his thick brown hair looked extremely touchable. In spite of knowing it was probably a bad idea, she began imagining what it would be like to seduce Harry. Obviously she had his mother's blessing to do exactly that.

Something else was slowly sinking in—as much as she didn't want to leave Dexter, as tough as it would be to think of spending three days without seeing his adorable little face—Dexter was the reason she hadn't had sex with a man in the past four years. She'd thought, all things considered, that Dexter would be better off if she didn't date. So for a long time, sex had been a solo affair for her.

Now she'd be going away for three days with a living, breathing man, a man she'd had secret fantasies about, a man taller than she was. Nice. They'd be sharing a room at a resort. Suz was loaning her a nightgown that would bring Harry to his knees. If Lainie wanted to end her long period of celibacy, now was her chance.

"So how are they supposed to get reservations for this time-share thing?" asked a woman in snug pants that didn't disguise a single one of her bulges. "Don't you have to call in advance?"

"Nah, you don't," said a blonde wearing long rhinestone earrings that flashed as she shook her head. "If they think they have a hot prospect, they'll find a place for you. Harry has a way with people. He can call them when the office opens up and say they happen to be in the area and want to take the tour. I'll guarantee he gets a room."

"I'm sure that's true." Suz tucked the red nightgown back in the bag. "Harry always was a smart cookie. Remember, Harry, how you used to help us do the crossword puzzles between numbers backstage when you were a little kid?"

"Sure do." Harry didn't turn around, just kept working on the ice situation.

"You were our mascot, Harry," said the blonde with the rhinestone earrings.

"That he was." Suz accepted the gin and tonic Leo handed her. "Thanks, Leo. You're a peach."

Leo distributed mixed drinks ranging from margaritas to White Russians. Lainie could tell that this kind of gathering happened all the time, and that Leo had memorized the favorite drinks of each club member. He was a peach, just as Suz had said. Rona was a lucky woman, Lainie thought a little wistfully. And Harry was lucky, too, having all these adopted aunties.

"Lainie, sure you don't want something to drink?" Leo asked. "It's not like you'll be driving, and you've had a rough night."

"No, thanks, Leo." She smiled at him, and he smiled back. Depending on how things worked out, she'd like to stay friends with Rona and Leo, both for Dexter's sake and for hers. A relationship with Harry wasn't required for that.

"I brought the red wig," said a woman with fingernails painted maroon with silver lightning bolts on each nail. She pulled it out of her shopping bag and laid it on the table in the alcove.

Lainie remembered that the red-wig person was Cherie.

"Here's my blond one," said Suz.

Bags began to crinkle as all the women pulled wigs out and laid them on the table.

Then Cherie started laughing. "It looks like a fancy hamster convention on that table. Rona, go get your camera."

"We should take a picture of all of them lying on the table, and then another one of all of us wearing them," said Suz.

"And then switch!" said the snug-pants woman, the one Lainie had pegged as Babs. That meant the blonde with the rhinestone earrings was Trixie.

Rona clapped her hands together. "Girls, girls. We're not here to party. We need to get these two on their way. Cherie, if you'll make a fresh pot of coffee, I'll take Lainie upstairs and get her outfitted and packed."

"What's Harry doing for clothes?" Leo asked.

"Oh, I don't really need clothes," Harry said. When that was met with shrieks of laughter, he turned the color of a stoplight. "What I mean is—"

"I keep a small stash of things upstairs," Leo said quietly. "Take them. You should at least have clean undies and a couple of shirts."

"I'll pack you a bag, Harry," Rona said. "Come on, Lainie. Let's get you upstairs and out of that raincoat."

"I was meaning to ask about the raincoat," said Cherie. "Lainie, are you wearing your costume under there?"

"Um, yes."

"Oh, well, we *have* to see it! Professional curiosity, right, girls?"

Lainie had no choice but to open her coat.

"Ooh-la-la," Trixie said. "Take the coat off so we can see the whole thing. Damn, there's nothing like red, you know?"

Feeling more like a stripper than a dancer, Lainie took off the coat.

"Turn," Cherie said, making a circle with her lightning-tipped finger.

Lainie turned.

The women all sighed, almost in unison.

"Boy, if that doesn't take me back," said Babs. "What I wouldn't give to be back out there."

"It's a young woman's game," said Cherie. "We had our run. Oh, to be that tight again."

"The only way I can be tight is to have three White Russians in a row," said Trixie. Her earrings flashed in the light. "By the way, what tune did you use that costume for, Lainie?"

Lainie was about to answer when Harry blurted out, " 'Fever.' "

All heads swiveled in his direction.

"Um, it's a catchy tune," Harry said, his color high.

"Oh, you bet it is." Suz walked around Lainie and surveyed her costume. "Gorgeous, Lainie. I can just see it for 'Fever.' Cherie, weren't you at the Sands with me when we did that number?" She put down her gin and tonic and started to hum and move her hips.

"That's right, I was!" Cherie got up from the table and came over to join Suz. "I think we started out like this." She threw one arm up in the air, tossed back her head, and thrust one leg out straight in front of her.

"And then we did this." Suz executed a high kick that any dancer on the Strip would envy.

"Show me the routine. I wanna try it." Babs got up to join them, tight pants and all.

"And then Lainie can show us hers," said Trixie.

"No she can't," Rona said. "Lainie and I are going upstairs to pack, and I hope by the time we get back, somebody's made that coffee. Come on, Lainie. Once they get started on a dance routine, there's no stopping them."

As Lainie followed Rona up the stairs, she heard Leo call out, "Who needs a refill?" He got several takers.

"I've known those girls for thirty years," Rona said. "They helped me raise Harry."

"They seem really terrific."

"They are." Rona led the way into her bedroom. "I just hope they didn't overwhelm you."

"Are you kidding? I wish I could stay and hang out with them."

"I wish you could, too. Oh, excuse the mess. Leo and I . . . got a little carried away."

That was putting it mildly, Lainie thought. The floor was strewn with clothes obviously taken off in the midst of passion. A black bra dangled from a lampshade. A lacy pair of black panties drooped from the bedpost. Pillows were scattered over the bed, and the comforter and sheets hung off the mattress and dribbled to the floor.

"I want to assure you that nothing like that will go on while Dexter's here," Rona said. "In fact, I'll probably send Leo home. I never used to let him stay over when Harry was a boy."

"You didn't?"

"No. Harry had a father, and I wanted him to remember who that was and not get his father all mixed up with Leo in his mind." She opened a door into a walk-in closet. "Let's see what I can find for you."

Rona had the kind of organized closet system Lainie had always dreamed of. It would be good to be Rona, she thought. "I haven't even dated since Dexter was born," she said. Why she'd felt the need to mention that, she wasn't sure.

"Oh, you poor dear."

Maybe that was why. She wanted some sympathy.

"I know how that is," Rona said. "I didn't date until I met Leo, and by that time, Harry was thirteen and old enough to understand a few things. But I still didn't let Leo stay over." She started pulling outfits from their hangers. "This would look good with your coloring. Not this. Ah, this one." She thrust the clothes into Lainie's arms.

"Were you, ah, married to Harry's father?" Lainie hoped she wasn't prying.

"No." Rona said it with great fondness. "We might have married, if he'd lived."

"Oh, dear! He died? Was it Vietnam?"

Rona turned to her with a tiny smile. "He died from having too much sex with me."

Lainie gulped.

"I'd better explain, before you think I'm some sort of

wild woman. Well, I am, but not that wild." She opened a drawer and pulled out some silky underwear. "Paul was sixty-five when we met and I was twenty-two. He was a chemistry genius at UNLV and a confirmed bachelor. Then he saw me dance and became infatuated. He begged me to go to bed with him, and I took pity on him and agreed."

"And you got pregnant?"

Rona laughed. "Wouldn't have been possible that first time. Poor Paul was so out of practice he couldn't get it up. Talk about your erectile dysfunction. He was the poster boy for it, and he was positively humiliated. His solution was to create a drug in his lab that would solve the problem. It was probably similar to Viagra, but much more crude, and certainly untested."

"My goodness."

"So he took the drug, and we had quite a night, Paul and I. He gave me incredible pleasure, more than I've ever had before or since. He was very well endowed, you see. I fell a little bit in love with him that night, so when the condoms ran out, I didn't care. I was sure he'd ask me to marry him. We had at least two rounds of unprotected sex, and then he had a heart attack and died."

Lainie gasped. "You mean . . . while you were . . ."

"Fortunately not in the middle of sex. He got up to go to the bathroom and keeled over."

"Oh, dear. That's so sad. And incredible. Sad and incredible."

Rona gazed at Lainie. "Harry's a lot like Paul. He looks very much like him, and he's obviously inherited Paul's mind. Very smart people sometimes have trouble figuring out what they want."

"Even not-so-smart people," Lainie said.

"True, but Harry has a tendency to overthink things. And I would hate for him to be sixty-five years old before he finds the love of his life."

"Rona—"

"I'm not putting that responsibility on you, so don't worry. You have your own problems. I'm just . . . glad the two of you can spend some time together. You never know. You just never know."

Chapter Six

That "Fever" costume was going to be the death of him yet. Harry pretended to watch the TITS as they put together an impromptu performance in the kitchen, but all he could think about was the moment when Lainie had taken off her coat and turned so the women could see her costume from all sides. Of course he could see her costume from all sides, too, what there was of it.

From the back, she was nearly naked, with a thong-type deal revealing her perfectly rounded ass, and an almost backless effect above that. The front wasn't much more concealing, with the rose petal thingies somewhat covering her gorgeous breasts but leaving plenty of cleavage to fuel his fantasies. Add to that the red high heels strapped to her slender ankles, and the black fishnet stockings . . . it was a wonder he'd been able to keep from getting a woody right there in front of everyone, including his mother.

At the moment Lainie was probably changing out of the costume, peeling the tight-fitting cups from her breasts, sliding the thong from between her legs. Oh, damn, he was so dead. If she wore the red nightgown that Suz brought, the inevitable would happen in Sedona.

With all the racket going on in the kitchen as the TITS proceeded to enjoy themselves as usual, Harry didn't hear Rona and Lainie come back until they were both standing in the arched doorway of the kitchen.

Leo noticed them first. "Well, don't you look nice, Lainie."

Harry turned to find the showgirl transformed into his all-American traveling companion, Mrs. Fred Ambrewster. She wore a pair of his mother's khaki Capris, a white knit top that clung to her breasts in a most inviting way, and a pair of upscale flip-flops with thick cork soles. She'd pulled her hair into a ponytail and taken off her stage makeup. She almost looked wholesome. Almost. A small rolling suitcase sat by her feet.

Rona pulled a second one into the hallway and left it there. "All set."

"What about the wigs?" Cherie asked, gesturing toward the assortment still sitting on the table.

"Just put them in the shopping bag with the nightgown," Suz said. "You wouldn't want to pack them in a suitcase, anyway."

"Shouldn't she wear one? I thought that's why we brought them, so she'd be disguised," asked Cherie. "I vote for mine."

"You're right, she should wear one." Rona walked to the table and picked up Cherie's long red wig. "Come on in the powder room with me, Lainie, and I'll fix you up."

"It's my wig," Cherie said. "I want to help."

"We'll all help," Suz said. Whereupon all the women crowded around the tiny powder room off the kitchen.

Harry couldn't see a thing.

"These showgirls, they're really something else, huh?" Leo said, still sipping his coffee and Baileys as he watched the free-for-all surrounding the powder room.

"You don't have to tell me. I've known this bunch all my life."

Leo grinned at him. "Yeah—Harry the mascot. Is that why you grew up such a quiet kid? Was that your way of dealing with all that high energy?"

"No. If I hadn't been exposed to that atmosphere, I might have ended up an even quieter kid. I was born quiet."

"See, you're making my point for me. You need that kind of stimulation. And I'm betting that underneath, you like living on the edge."

Harry snorted. "Thank you, Doctor Freud. I'm telling you, I want a plain vanilla life."

"So you say."

"I do. The point is, I—" And then he forgot what his point was, as the mass of femininity parted and Lainie came out of the powder room looking for all the world like Nicole Kidman. "Damn," he muttered. "She's even hotter than I thought."

"Now see, that's the kind of exciting surprise that keeps a man on his toes."

"Or knocks him from here to next week."

"Have fun, kid."

As Lainie/Nicole came walking toward him, a smile on her face, Harry realized he was in so far over his head that nothing could save him.

"Cheaters!" Suz said. "I almost forgot. Who brought some?"

Instantly the TITS made for their purses and pulled out a selection of reading glasses. Typically, they were outrageous—cat's eyes, rhinestone encrusted, psychedelic.

Rona threw up her hands. "All too flashy. Doesn't anybody have a pair of plain-looking glasses?"

Silently Leo reached in his breast pocket, pulled out a pair of black-framed glasses, and handed them to Rona.

"Perfect!" She took them with a smile. Then she paused. "Aren't these expensive? Like designer? I know the girls all buy theirs at Walgreens, but I seem to remember that you—"

"Forget it." Leo waved her off. "I have another pair at home. Besides, they're just magnifiers—weak ones at that. And I'm sure Lainie will bring them back to me."

"I don't even need to take them," she said. "I'm sure the wig will do the trick."

"Let's see how they look." Rona opened the earpieces and slid the glasses on Lainie as if she were a practicing optometrist. "Oh, that's better. It makes you look really different. I think you should take them."

All the TITS murmured in agreement.

As for Harry, he'd been hoping the glasses would make Lainie less sexy, but no such luck. From the neck up she looked something like the nerdy girls he'd gone out with. From the neck down, she was one-hundred-percent showgirl. For a guy like Harry, it was an irresistible combo.

• • •

Each member of the TITS gave Harry a hug and goodbye kiss, and then they did the same with Lainie. She had the weird sensation that she was leaving the wedding reception with her new husband, instead of escaping from her ex-boyfriend. Maybe it was the way Rona and Leo acted like doting parents fussing over details like a thermos of hot coffee and sandwiches in a thermal lunch sack. Or maybe it was the way the TITS treated Harry like a favorite nephew.

Or maybe it was the way everyone crowded to the front window to wave as Harry backed the Lexus out of the driveway. Lainie waved back and fought tears. She'd forced herself not to peek in on Dexter again, knowing that seeing him sleeping so peacefully with Fred would tear her up.

"So we're off," Harry said, taking the road to the interstate.

"Mm." Lainie was afraid to talk, for fear she'd start crying. Then she'd have to take off Leo's glasses, and she liked wearing them. They made her feel safe, somehow.

"I know it's tough to leave Dexter, but—"

"Don't talk about it."

"Okay." He reached one long arm behind the seat.

At first she thought he was going to give her a hug, which would make things worse. Instead he set a box of Kleenex in her lap. She stared at that box of Kleenex and thought about him deliberately putting it in the car, for her, because he knew she'd probably cry when she left Dexter.

The box of Kleenex might be the sweetest thing any

man had ever done for her. And it was all that was required to open the floodgates. With a wail, she whipped off Leo's glasses and grabbed a fistful of tissues.

She cried for at least five minutes. She couldn't be sure how long she sobbed, but she was amazed at the unending cascade of tears that poured out of her. When she was done, about half the box of tissues was gone and the floor mat looked like somebody was stockpiling for a snowball fight.

At last she tapered off to a trickle. Through bleary eyes, she glanced sideways at Harry. He stared stoically ahead, his jaw clenched. She could imagine how he must have hated driving down the road with a blubbering woman.

"I'm sorry," she said. "That was really embarrassing." She blew her nose and put Leo's glasses back on. There. That was better.

"Sounded like you needed to do that." His voice was gruff, but friendly.

"Apparently, but I hate that you had to listen."

"I hate that you're so upset. I wish I knew some way to make things better."

"You did." She gave him a watery smile. "You brought the Kleenex. That's what set me off, you being thoughtful enough to do that."

"So I *made* you cry? Oh, man, that sucks."

"No, no, it was a good thing. Good from my standpoint, anyway. But I've never cried like that in front of a guy. I know you all can't stand to see a woman lose it."

Harry cleared his throat. "That's because it makes us want to do something to fix the problem."

"So you can stop the leak." Her laughter was unsteady,

but thankfully she was laughing instead of crying. "Emotional plumber to the rescue."

"Well, yeah. I mean, if you're crying that hard, it's because things are really screwed up and you don't know how to fix them, right?"

"Sometimes." She thought about her experience with tears. She'd cried when Dexter was born, because he was so sweet. "Not always."

"Okay, I know about happy tears, but those were not happy tears. I know unhappy tears when I hear them."

"I was definitely upset, but not because I couldn't fix something that's wrong. Oh, I won't deny that I have a bad situation with Joey and I'm worried about Dexter, but that isn't why I was crying."

"You were crying because you didn't want to leave him, though."

"There's a lot more to it than that." Lainie felt herself begin to relax. The car had a smooth ride as it wound through the hills toward Hoover Dam, and Harry at the wheel was extremely reassuring.

"So tell me what made you cry," he said. "We have a little time."

"We do, at that. You want some coffee, or part of a sandwich?"

He shook his head. "Not yet. It's nice to just . . . talk."

She had to agree. She hadn't spent much time talking to adults recently, specifically, male adults. She couldn't remember the last time she'd ridden alone in a car with a man. Yes, she had many problems, but riding down the road with Harry, she felt a lightness that she hadn't felt in years, like something wonderful was about to happen.

"So you were explaining the crying thing."

"I'm going to try to explain it without crying."

"Then you don't have to explain anything," he said quickly.

That made her laugh again. "If I start getting choked up, I promise to change the subject immediately."

"Good. Because that last bout nearly killed me. You sounded like your world had collapsed. I can't take it."

"My world is collapsing, and not because of Joey." She took a deep breath. "For the first time tonight I found out what it felt like for Dexter not to need me."

"He still needs you. That's not—"

"Of course he does, but he's branching out, and that's what he should be doing. It's just that I've never had to share his affections before. And eventually he'll grow up and start living his own life. We won't be a team forever." She got that much out, but noticed that her voice quivered on the last part.

It wasn't leaving Dexter that was so hard, although that wasn't easy. But mostly it was leaving him and knowing it was the first of a whole string of goodbyes. She'd never faced that before, hadn't had to. Tonight both she and Dexter had passed a milestone.

"Makes sense," Harry said. "But you have a lot of years before Dexter moves on to a life of his own."

"They'll go fast." Lainie swallowed a lump in her throat as they rounded a turn and caught their first glimpse of Hoover Dam, awash with lights. Once they crossed the dam, she'd be in Arizona, a totally different state from Dexter. But she wouldn't think about that. "The dam is beautiful, isn't it? A real marvel."

"Uh-huh." Harry glanced over at her. "A real marvel."

She didn't think he was talking about Hoover Dam. It wasn't every day—or night, to be more accurate—that she was called a marvel. She decided to enjoy the warm glow of his praise. They'd only come a short way from Vegas, but so far, this had been a most excellent trip.

Joey was thinking he needed to get back to his surveillance of Lainie's car, when a hot-looking blonde slipped into the seat next to him. Joey took in the long legs and the great boobs and immediately pegged her as a dancer. He had a real fondness for dancers, with the exception of Lainie, who was giving him major grief at the moment.

"Hey, Stuart, give me a JD on the rocks," the blonde said. "I've had one helluva night."

"Comin' right up, Gina." The bartender who had served Joey scooped ice into a squat glass and splashed a generous amount of Jack Daniel's over the cubes.

Joey tweaked to a couple of things. If the bartender knew this Gina, then maybe she was a dancer here at the Nirvana. If she was a dancer at the Nirvana, she might know Lainie.

He turned to her. "Nobody who looks like you should ever have a bad night. Let me buy you that drink."

She glanced at him. "No, thanks."

He held up both hands. "No strings attached. This is not a pickup, I promise."

"I get a discount anyway. It's no big deal." She pulled some money out of her purse as the bartender set her drink down on a cocktail napkin.

"Okay." Joey smiled. He had a terrific smile, thanks to good orthodontia, and he'd used that smile to get himself many things in life. Unfortunately his creditors had offered to rearrange his smile. "Just trying to convince you the world's not such a bad place."

"It's not." Gina sipped her drink. "But our last number got fouled up, so we got yelled at, and it wasn't our fault. One of the dancers took off right before we were due to go on, and she's an important part of the number."

Pay dirt. Joey had predicted his luck was about to change, and bingo. "Sounds damned inconsiderate, to me."

"Yeah, well, I shouldn't complain. From the looks of things, she's got big problems. Something to do with her kid. She left so quick, I have to wonder if she has some legal problems with custody."

"Wow." Joey signaled for another beer. "Must be, if she didn't even stay to finish the night's work. She had to know she was making it tough on the rest of you."

"Yeah." Gina took another swallow of her drink. "Oh, well."

"You have a good attitude about it, at least." Joey sat there drinking his beer. If Lainie had taken off with Dexter, then whoever had taken the kid out that back window had also driven him to the casino and likely driven both of them away from here, since Lainie hadn't used her own car. Joey needed to find out who that was.

But maybe he shouldn't head right for the subject. "So how long have you been a dancer?"

"Six years. Well, six years getting paid for it. I've been dancing ever since I could walk."

"I'm sorry I missed the show. I'm here on business and it's kept me going until a little while ago. This is my first chance to relax."

As she neared the bottom of her drink, she became more friendly. "What kind of business?"

"I work for my dad. You know those plastic toys in airports, the ones parents buy to take home to their kid? He contracts overseas for the manufacture of that kind of stuff. Plush toys, too."

"Really?"

"Yeah. It's kind of a goofy way to earn a living, but he's made it extremely profitable. Want another drink?"

"Sure, why not?"

Joey motioned to the bartender. "Yeah, my dad works with manufacturing plants all over the world, but none in Nevada yet. I'm supposed to check that out for him. So why don't you tell me about your family?" Actually, Joey had talked long and hard to get the old man to fund his trip out here.

His dad would have a fit if he knew Joey was paying a private detective out of his trust fund account. And even his trust fund wouldn't be enough to bail him out of the fix he was in. Man, did he owe a lot of money. But at least now he had the company credit card in his wallet.

He was going to use it tonight for these drinks, in fact. He'd used it earlier tonight, too, but he wished now he hadn't stopped off at the little bar before heading over to Lainie's apartment. He'd been pooped after the flight and had decided to relax a little before doing the hard work of picking up the kid. But as he'd sat there drinkin' and thinkin', he'd gotten riled up about the whole situation. He'd come on a little strong.

Even so, he might have been okay if the usual babysitter had been there. He'd been told she was an older woman named Mrs. Flippo, and he'd figured handling her would be a piece of cake. But he'd bet the keys to his Vette that Mrs. Flippo hadn't been the one who'd carted Dexter out a second-story window.

Unfortunately, after four beers, Joey had needed to pee and hadn't been in shape to run around the building and catch them before they left. He suspected the person was a guy, because it would have taken upper-body strength to get the kid out the window and down the tree. Either a guy or a very athletic woman.

"So my sister was, like, 'I'm going to be a dancer, too,' but she has no sense of rhythm," Gina said. "She might have the body for it, but not the moves."

Joey clicked back into the conversation and realized Gina had been telling him about her family, exactly as he'd requested. He hadn't heard a word of it, but that was okay. He'd always been able to fake being a good listener.

"I really would like to see you dance," he said. "And I'll bet by tomorrow night you'll have that last number all fixed."

"I'm sure. Tim's interviewing dancers in the morning."

"So you think your friend is really gone for good?"

"Tim seemed to think so, but I'm not so sure. Something's going on with that accountant. I just don't know what."

"Accountant?"

"Oh, this guy who's an accountant in payroll, Harry Ambrewster. I'm sure he has a major crush on Lainie, and considering that he looks like he has bucks, I think she should go for it. But she keeps saying there's nothing between them. Then, tonight, there he was, with her kid. And he looked like he'd been wrestling with the kid in the grass or something. The whole thing's weird."

"Sounds weird." *Harry Ambrewster*. This investment in a couple of drinks had paid off in spades. And Joey had a strong hunch he'd met this jerk in the parking lot. Tree trimming, indeed.

Joey finished off his beer and handed his credit card to the bartender. "Well, Gina, it's been a pleasure, but I have several appointments tomorrow, so I have to call it a night."

She looked at him in surprise. "So you really aren't going to hit on me?"

"Nope. Just wanted to share some friendly conversation."

"You don't even want my phone number?" She acted disappointed.

"That's okay." He quickly signed the credit card slip. "Maybe I'll make it to the show tomorrow night. If I do, I'll send a note backstage."

"You do that. Except . . . I don't even know your name."

"Steve. Steve Horton." Then he flashed her his killer smile and left. Belatedly he realized that maybe he shouldn't have used a fake name at the same time he was paying with a credit card, but he was so used to giving fake names to women in bars that it had become a habit. Ah, the bartender probably hadn't heard him, anyway.

As he headed for the exit, he reached for the cell phone in a holster on his belt. His phone call would get the private detective out of bed, but Joey didn't give a damn. He needed info on Harry Ambrewster, and he needed it like yesterday.

He was standing outside, finishing up his call to the

detective, when security approached him. He flashed them the famous Joey Benjamin smile. "How's it going?"

"We need you to come with us," said the larger of the two. "It's been brought to our attention that you introduced yourself to a young lady using one name, and signed a credit card with a different name."

Joey chuckled. "I gave her my drinking name, gentlemen. You know how that is, right? You never give a woman your real name unless you plan to see her again."

Neither of the guys smiled. "If you'll just come with us, sir, we can get this all straightened out."

Shit. Maybe his luck hadn't completely turned around, after all. "Certainly, gentlemen. Whatever you say."

Chapter Seven

About midway between Kingman and Flagstaff, Lainie fell asleep. Harry had encouraged her to roll up her raincoat and use it for a pillow, and finally, after several big yawns, she'd taken his suggestion. In no time she was in dreamland.

Harry checked the gas gauge and decided he wouldn't fill the tank in Flagstaff, after all, because the stop might wake her. He was sure she could use the rest. By all rights he should be exhausted, too, but adrenaline pumped through his system, more powerful than caffeine. For the next three days, and more significantly, two nights, he'd be spending all his time with a woman he found way too appealing. More so every hour they were together, in fact.

He glanced over at her. Leo's glasses had slipped down her nose, making her look like a bookworm who had dozed off in the middle of a chapter. He wondered if she read books. He'd been so preoccupied with her dancing—face it, with her *body*—that he hadn't considered her mind. Wasn't that chauvinistic of him? Instinctively he knew she was smart, though. With a son like Dexter, she would have to be or he'd drive her crazy.

From Dexter Harry had learned that Lainie didn't like to sit still long enough to play board games, but that didn't mean anything. Some people didn't like board games. He tried to remember if he'd noticed books lying around in the apartment. All he remembered were kids' books, which Dexter was already reading by himself, of course.

Thinking of the boy reminded him of what Lainie had said about Dexter, that she was beginning the process of letting him go. She'd organized her whole life around that kid, and she was right that someday he wouldn't need her to do that. In Rona's case, Leo had come along at the perfect time. Harry remembered being thirteen and wondering if his mom would be lonesome when he went off to college.

Sure, she had her girlfriends, but even at thirteen Harry sensed they might not be enough company for her. Then along came Leo, who soon became like a member of the family. He must have felt very much like a family member the night he'd managed to get an underage Harry out of a sleazy strip joint minutes before a police raid.

Then there was the night a couple of years after that when Leo convinced an irate hotel manager not to press charges after Harry had organized a chess marathon in one of the suites. He'd felt so worldly, booking a suite for this event, but the jocks had crashed it and in no time the party had raged out of control. All Harry's attempts to be cool had turned out like that. Finally he'd given up and accepted his boring nerd status.

At least being a nerd paid well, so he could buy toys

like a Global Positioning System for his Lexus. The GPS indicated he had a choice of routes to Sedona, and he decided on I-19 out of Flagstaff instead of the winding road down through Oak Creek. The hairpin turns on US 89 would have jostled Lainie awake, and she looked so peaceful.

But when he turned at the exit for Sedona, the sun peeked over the horizon, a fiery ball of gold, and he decided he couldn't let her sleep through the next few minutes. He'd been here for an accounting seminar a few years ago and he knew that sunrise on the red rocks of Sedona should not be missed.

"Lainie." He reached over and touched her arm.

"What?" She came awake in an instant. "What's wrong?" She glanced around, disoriented, then squinted at Harry. "Oh." She collapsed against the seat. "Whenever somebody wakes me up like that, I think something's the matter with Dexter."

"I'm sorry. Didn't mean to scare you." He wasn't a parent, had no idea what the instincts of a parent could do to a person. Watching Lainie was making him a little nervous about the day when he would become a daddy. Apparently he'd turn into one big throbbing nerve.

He grimaced. One look at Lainie, all rumpled and pink from sleep, and he *was* one big throbbing nerve, although this nerve was located in a very specific spot. "I didn't want you to miss the drive into Sedona. I didn't think you'd ever been here before, and with the sun coming up, it's . . ." When he heard a soft snuffle, he glanced over and discovered she'd drifted back to sleep.

He didn't want to shake her again and bring on her emergency response, but the sun made the red rock formations glow like huge embers rising into the blue Arizona sky. She would be sorry if she didn't see it. So he began singing the title song from *Annie.* He didn't have the greatest voice, but he knew the words. A guy raised by a showgirl knew his show tunes.

She opened one eye. "Do you do this kind of thing a lot? Not ever dealing with you first thing in the morning, I wouldn't know, but I should warn you I'm not a morning person, and someone who sings about the sun coming up is not getting a special award of merit from me. And FYI, you're flat."

"Lainie, you have to sit up and look at this. Here you are, driving into Sedona for the first time, and the sun's coming up. This is a peak experience. You don't want to sleep through this. People pay thousands of dollars and travel hundreds of miles to see this, and sometimes it's cloudy, and they don't see anything."

With a martyred sigh, she struggled to a sitting position, complaining all the way. "I hope this is worth it, because I was having such nice dreams, and I— *Oh . . . my . . . God.*"

"Told you."

She whipped off Leo's black glasses. "Harry, this is like out of a movie. Am I awake?"

"Finally, thanks to me."

"Look at that rock! It's gorgeous! It's incredible. It's . . . exactly the color of my favorite lipstick!"

Harry laughed, happier than he remembered being in ages. "You'll have to show your lipstick to me sometime."

"It's at home. Or what used to be home."

"Don't think about that now. Just enjoy the view."

"I'm enjoying. I had no idea. When your mother said

'You can go to Sedona,' I thought it might be some tourist trap. But these red rocks are awesome. I wouldn't have missed this for the world."

"So you're not mad at me for waking you up?"

"Good grief, no! I've seen pictures, but I never thought . . . You figure the pictures are touched up, you know? What's in that rock, that makes it so reddish? When I tell Dexter about this, he'll definitely want to know."

"Oxidized iron." He was pleased that he could tell her. "It's sandstone with oxidized iron in it."

"Harry, I love this place. I totally love it."

"Good. Then I'm glad we came."

"Me, too! Okay, I see signs of civilization ahead, so I'd like to request a bathroom and a cup of coffee, in that order. And if we can have a cup of coffee with a view, that would be awesome."

"I can arrange that." He glanced at his watch. "After breakfast we'll call the time-share people."

"What if they won't give us a room?"

"We'll find somewhere else to stay in Sedona. But we're not leaving, if that was your question."

"That was my question."

"Well, that's my answer. I want you to get your fill of red rocks." And he couldn't help wondering if, in the process, she'd get her fill of Harry Ambrewster. According to the saying, familiarity was supposed to breed contempt. That didn't seem to be working for him. Familiarity was breeding lust. But he couldn't speak for her.

"In case I forget to say it later, thank you for bringing me here," she said. "I know it's just a dodge to confuse

Joey, but it's a pretty darned wonderful dodge. I feel as if I've landed in paradise."

"Yeah, me, too." Now if the snakes would stay out of the garden, they'd be all set.

Rona couldn't throw Leo out at two in the morning after he'd spent the past few hours making drinks for the TITS and periodically climbing the stairs to check on Dexter. So she'd told him no funny business, and he'd promised her he was too tired for funny business. They were both dead asleep when the phone rang at three.

Rona switched on the light and answered it, her heart pounding. She hated middle-of-the-night calls. Fortunately, it was for Leo, one of his boys checking in with some information. She passed the phone over.

Leo's "boys" weren't really his sons, but sometimes he treated them that way. Rona didn't ask too many questions about Leo's business. From comments he'd dropped, she thought he might be mixed up in the underworld somehow. She'd seen all the *Godfather* movies, and Leo fit the profile.

Another clue was that he didn't talk about work. Men in the underworld didn't discuss their jobs with their women, for obvious reasons. Rona had once asked Leo if he'd ever killed anybody, and he'd said no. However, that didn't mean anything. If he was the boss, he'd have someone else do the dirty work. Rona had decided it was safer not to pry. With her, Leo was a pussycat, and that's all she cared about.

He said goodbye to whichever of his boys had called and handed the phone back to Rona. "Well, that was easy."

"What?"

"The boys have already located Joey Benjamin."

"No kidding?" Rona rolled to face him. She was wide awake. She'd only had Dexter in her care for a matter of hours, and already her mother tiger instincts were functioning. "Where is the slimeball?"

"Security at the Nirvana questioned him because he used a credit card registered to Joey Benjamin to pay for a bar tab, but then the bartender overheard him giving one of the dancers a different name."

"But it is really Joey?"

"Oh, it's really him, all right, and he happened to pull a dumb stunt, which confirms what I thought when I heard about the breaking and entering. He's not the sharpest tool in the shed. Of course, dummies can be dangerous, too."

"Where is he, now?"

"In his hotel room." Leo folded his pillow and propped it behind his head. "Security let him go eventually, but not until they got a boatload of info on him. Lainie wasn't kidding about the guy's rich father back in New Jersey. We could connect him with breaking and entering over at Lainie's place and probably get him in jail, but daddy's lawyers would probably have him out in no time."

"Plus we don't want the cops involved and get into the whole custody issue." Rona propped her chin on her fist. "I think he has a legitimate claim to Dexter, and if he has money behind him, he might be able to take that kid away. The court could say a father with beaucoup bucks would be better than a Vegas dancer barely making ends meet."

"Well, thanks to the bartender who served him the drinks, we also know why he wants custody. Apparently he needs to produce the kid he's sired in order to inherit the family fortune. Plus, he ran up some impressive gambling debts in Atlantic City, and if he doesn't get into daddy's good graces soon, some very scary guys will come looking for their money."

"Dammit!" Rona flopped back on her pillow with a groan. "That means he won't give up."

"No, he won't, not with those stakes. But we've bought a little time to strategize. What I can't figure out is why he didn't notify the authorities about Lainie and Dexter going missing. I'm wondering if maybe he's never told his parents about the kid. If his old man is upset about a gay son, he might not be happy about an illegitimate grandson, either."

"So now he needs to rewrite history before he shows up with this heir."

Leo glanced at her. "That's what I think. Well, my guys are watching him, so he won't get away with anything while he's working on his revisionist history. But what I don't know yet is whether he's operating alone or if he's hired somebody to help him. I have this place covered, but I'm thinking somebody should mosey down to Sedona to make sure Lainie's okay."

Rona shivered. "Because if Lainie's out of the picture, Joey's free to make up any story he wants."

"Exactly. And if he's worried about getting roughed up or worse by his creditors, he could be desperate."

"Well, at least for now, she has Harry."

Leo smiled. "I love the guy, you know I do. But I don't think he's up to this. A few years ago, maybe. During that short time he worked out at the gym, he was lean and mean."

"Harry was never mean!"

"It's an expression. Anyway, lately he's been getting soft. I don't know if his instincts are sharp enough."

"He climbed out of that second-floor window with Dexter," Rona reminded him.

"Yeah, he did. I'm proud of him for doing that. But I'm still not so sure that—"

"I know, I know. I agree that someone should drive to Sedona and look out for both of them," Rona said. "But it needs to be you, because anyone else might interfere with the romance that seems to be blossoming. I'd love to get a wedding and a ready-made grandchild out of this deal."

Leo sighed. "I already planned on being the one to go."

"Thank you, Leo. Promise me you'll be discreet."

"Don't worry, Boom-Boom. They won't even know I'm there."

Lainie almost forgot to drink her coffee, she was so busy looking at the red rock formations stretched out as far as she could see. She and Harry had finally settled on a little corner coffee shop with a terrace facing a good part of the view, but they couldn't have gone wrong almost anywhere in town. Sedona was one big postcard.

"I can't imagine how anyone gets anything done around here," she said. "I would be forever staring at this place." She had to prop her glasses halfway down her nose so she could peer over them, but she didn't mind. Sitting here, she couldn't bring herself to mind anything at all.

"I suppose you'd get used to it after a while."

"Hard to believe."

"Yeah, I know." His voice sounded sweet and gentle, not exactly the kind of tone you'd use to discuss the scenery.

Lainie glanced across the table and realized he wasn't looking at the view at all. He was looking at her. And he had a goofy smile on his face.

She imagined her expression was about the same, but she got it from looking at the red rocks. She found it hard to believe that Harry felt about her the way she felt about this view. But if he did, that could complicate matters quite a bit.

She thought about his determination to wake her up on the drive in so she wouldn't miss anything. He must like her at least a little to have cared about that. "Not many guys know the title song from *Annie,*" she said.

"I know plenty of songs, believe me." He hesitated. "And dance routines."

"Because you were the mascot?"

"That's right. I wasn't wild about learning all that stuff, but I was outnumbered."

"Oh, Harry." She couldn't help smiling at the thought of him reluctantly performing for his mom's friends. "Did you just hate it?"

"Not really. I tolerated it." A glimmer of amusement lit his brown eyes. "It's not all bad, being the center of attention."

"Nobody else had kids?"

"Not in the beginning. It plays hell with a dancer's career if she gets pregnant, especially if she doesn't have any savings." He continued to gaze at her. "I guess you know all about that."

"I certainly do. I took off as little time as possible with Dexter. And I counted on my girlfriends, just like Rona did." But she'd had to leave that support system in order to get away from Joey, and she missed it desperately. She'd just started making friends at the Nirvana, and now she might have to leave again.

But feeling sorry for herself wouldn't help. She finished off her cinnamon bagel slathered with blueberry cream cheese. "I guess we need to call work and the time-share."

"You're right." He let out a little sigh and started to get up. "I left the phone in the car."

"Sit, sit. I didn't mean to rush you. It's very nice right here, and I'm sure you'd like to finish your coffee. And you haven't even touched your bagel."

He sank back to the chair. "Okay. I'll go in a minute." But he didn't pick up his bagel, just continued to stare dreamily in her direction.

"You're dead on your feet, aren't you?"

"I'm okay."

"No you're not. You're punchy. Maybe we should look for a park or something so you can grab a nap in the back seat."

"Nope. I'll be fine." He seemed to gather himself together with great effort before he picked up his coffee cup and drained it. "Okay. You stay here and hold down our spot. I'll go get the phone."

"I could get the phone."

"I'll get it. Enjoy your view."

"All right." She decided arguing with him would only make him more tired, so she stayed. But instead of taking in the red rocks, she watched him walk to the car, which was parked about half a block away. Before the trip, at Rona's insistence, he'd changed into a pair of Leo's imported slacks and one of his Italian silk shirts. Both were black, and casually elegant. Mafia clothes.

The clothes plus the shadow of a beard darkening Harry's jaw made him look a little intimidating, maybe even a little dangerous, especially when he wasn't giving her that goofy grin. Then she remembered what Rona had said about Harry's father being well endowed. And that Harry looked a lot like his father.

For all she knew, Harry had an outstanding package under those borrowed Italian slacks. She'd always thought of him as dependable and trustworthy, two qualities she currently craved in a man, but she hadn't ever thought of him as mysterious, sexy, and well hung. As he walked to the Lexus, also black, she noticed a couple of women besides her ogling him.

He moved well, striding down the sidewalk with a smooth, easy rhythm. That might be left over from the days he'd been forced to learn dance routines, or maybe he'd inherited his physical coordination from Rona. One thing was clear—Harry had hottie potential.

She felt like going after him and slipping her arm through his, to let those women know they'd better back off. If anybody was going to find out what was under those black slacks, it would be her. Then she had to laugh at herself. She had no claim on Harry.

However, until this moment, she hadn't considered that anybody else would want to stake a claim, either.

Judging by the two women surveying Harry's progress to the car, he had the ability to turn heads. Who knew?

When he locked the car and started back carrying the phone and the time-share envelope, she turned toward the red-rock view, not wanting to be caught staring. He would die if he knew that his mother had revealed the details of the night he'd been conceived. And if he thought she was checking him out to see if he'd inherited the family jewels, he'd turn the color of those rock formations.

But she'd managed one quick look at his crotch, and what she'd seen looked promising, very promising. Funny how the rock formations she'd been so enthralled with a moment ago took on a whole new meaning as she gazed at them now. Good thing no one lounging on the terrace could read her mind as she surveyed the various projections thrusting proudly into the air. Well, let some of those folks go without real sex for five years and see how preoccupied they'd get when faced with a bunch of phallic symbols.

Harry lowered himself into his seat opposite her. "Want more coffee?"

Damn, but he looked good to her right now. Maybe any guy with a pulse and a package would look good to her right now, but Harry had the advantage of being on the premises. "No, thanks. But I'd be glad to get you another cup while you make those calls."

"You know what? Maybe that's a good idea. I am feeling a little groggy, and I'd hate to accidentally buy one of these time-shares." He reached for his wallet. "Let me give you—"

"I've got it." Grabbing her purse, she left the table

before he could hand her any money. He hadn't let her buy coffee and bagels originally, although she'd tried. She was used to paying her own way, and accepting so much generosity bothered her.

By the time she came back with his coffee—one cream, no sugar—he was finishing a call.

"Great," he said. "We'll be there within the next thirty minutes."

"They took us?" She sat down and put his coffee in front of him.

"They not only took us, they seemed ecstatic about it. I wonder if business is slow. She said they'd make us an offer we couldn't refuse."

Lainie grinned. "A promise that certainly goes along with your outfit."

He glanced down at the black-on-black ensemble and laughed. "Yeah, no kidding. Do I look like I should have an Italian accent and a shoulder holster, or what?"

She thought he looked wonderful, but decided against saying so. "I've been meaning to ask you about Leo. Does he really have Mafia connections?"

"I don't know." Harry took a swallow of his coffee and raised the cup in her direction. "Thanks for this." Then he started in on his bagel.

"You're welcome. So you really don't know about Leo, or you're not supposed to tell anyone?"

He put down his bagel. "I really don't know. When I was about eighteen I asked him flat out. He gave me this look and said, 'That's not a good question, kid. I'd appreciate it if you wouldn't ask me that again.'"

Lainie was surprised at how well Harry mimicked Leo. "You sound just like him."

"I've practiced. When I was a teenager, I thought it would be so cool to talk like that."

That made her smile.

"Anyway, I respect the hell out of the guy, and if he doesn't want to tell me, that's okay. I know Mom thinks he's connected to the underworld somehow."

"Really?"

"Yeah, but she doesn't ask questions, either. The TITS all worship the ground he walks on. They don't care what connections he has. All they know is the Emerald Lakes Condominiums are the most crime-free in the town of Henderson."

Lainie thought of Dexter, who would be awake and playing with Fred by now. "You don't know how happy that makes me."

"I probably have some idea. At least as happy as I am knowing my mom is safe. I owe Leo on several counts but that's the most important one." He took another bite of his bagel.

"They have an interesting relationship."

He chewed and swallowed. "Tell me about it. I used to wish they'd get married, but I'm beginning to wonder if that would work for them."

"Their current arrangement certainly works. When I walked into the bedroom it looked like a tornado had—" She stopped abruptly when she realized he probably didn't want to hear what his mother's bedroom had looked like. "Well, they seem to get along, is all I meant."

"Uh-huh." Harry drank the rest of his coffee quickly. "Ready to go?"

"Did you call work?"

"Yep. I'm officially on vacation, but I'm afraid Tim's looking for your replacement."

"I'd expect him to." She pushed back her chair and tried not to think about the great job she'd just tossed aside.

"Now, remember that I'm Fred and you're Rona." Harry stood and dumped their trash in a nearby can.

"What do we do for a living?" she asked as they walked toward the car.

"We can still have our same jobs at the Nirvana."

"Should we have kids?"

He glanced at her with a startled expression. "Kids?" He looked as if he'd taken the question literally.

"I mean, if the time-share people ask about kids. What do we say?"

"Oh." He cleared his throat. "Let's say we have Dexter."

"Okay." She continued toward the car, still mulling over the idea of having kids with Harry. It was an appealing idea. "I just thought of something. We're supposed to be married, but we don't have rings."

He stopped in the middle of the sidewalk. "You're right." He glanced around. "You know what? This place is crawling with Indian jewelry stores. Let's go get a couple of rings."

"Real rings? Surely we don't have to spend the money on real rings."

"We don't, but I will." He took her arm and guided her toward a shop where the windows glittered with silver and turquoise. "We should be able to find matching silver bands, maybe with some inlaid turquoise."

"No, Harry." She resisted. "This store is too nice.

How about one of the more touristy ones? We can find something cheaper."

He turned to face her, his expression stubborn. "But what if I don't want to buy you something cheap?"

"But what if I don't want you to buy me something expensive? I already feel uncomfortable about all you and your mother and Leo are doing for me. Now you're talking about buying me jewelry." But the real reason went deeper. She had never gone ring shopping with a man, and Harry was the sort of guy she wouldn't mind going ring shopping with. The nicer the jewelry store, the more she was liable to get into the fantasy. That could be a huge mistake.

He looked into her eyes. "Think of it as a souvenir of the trip."

"Then I should pay for my own."

He blew out a breath. "You are a very exasperating woman. I just want to get you this one simple thing."

It's not simple. "I know we could find them cheaper down the street."

"But you deserve . . ." He paused. "Look, the people around here know cheap silver jewelry when they see it. We need to have something decent if we're going to pull this off."

"If we stayed in a motel instead of this resort, we wouldn't have to do any of this."

"Dammit, Lainie, I want to give you a nice experience here! Why do you have that bumper sticker if you don't intend to live by it?"

She flushed. People were staring, and she certainly didn't want to become conspicuous, in case Joey had somehow figured out where she was. But Harry had struck a nerve with that last comment. *I HOPE YOU DANCE.* Her bumper sticker was old, and she hadn't thought about it much in the past five years. Maybe she had played the martyr for too long.

He sighed. "Listen, I'm sorry." He grasped her gently by the shoulders. "Don't look like that. I shouldn't have said what I did. I know you've been struggling to make a good life for Dexter, and it hasn't been easy. I have no right to—"

"But you've hit the nail on the head." She looked up at him. "I've been so busy sacrificing myself to care for Dexter that I've forgotten how to take a little pleasure for myself."

Pleasure. The word hung in the air between them, gaining significance the longer they stood staring at each other.

He released her and swallowed. "Um, I take it that means you'll let me buy the rings."

"Yes." She was egging him on, and she didn't care. She'd been handed a golden opportunity to have some fun for a change. "In fact, I'll let you do anything that makes us both feel good."

Chapter Eight

I'll let you do anything that makes us both feel good. Lainie's words echoed through Harry's fevered brain as he guided her into the nearest shop displaying silver and turquoise jewelry. Unless he missed his guess, she'd just invited him to have sex with her. And oh, God, how he wanted to.

But he had to keep his wits about him. She was probably extending that invitation out of gratitude. In fact, logically her response had to be all about gratitude. It didn't compute that a woman like her would be lusting after a guy like him.

If she was offering out of a sense of obligation because she thought she owed him, then that should cool his jets. He wasn't having sex with a woman because she thought it settled a debt. And sure enough, he was soon in control of himself again. He approached the counter where an older woman dripping in turquoise smiled hopefully and asked if she could help.

"We're looking for matching bands," he said.

The clerk's eyes brightened. "Let me offer my congratulations!"

Harry didn't know what to say. He wasn't used to lying. "Uh, thanks."

"Yes, thank you," Lainie said softly, edging up to the counter.

Immediately the clerk's jovial manner disappeared, as if she sensed this wasn't your average loving couple. "What price range were you thinking of? We have some reasonable silver bands in this case." She moved to her left and unlocked the back of the glass display counter.

Harry swore under his breath. Their lack of excitement about buying the rings could have the clerk imagining all sorts of stuff, like Lainie being pregnant and him being forced to marry her. He shouldn't care what the clerk thought, and if he'd been the only one involved, he wouldn't have. But he didn't like the idea of someone casting Lainie as a woman shoved into a loveless marriage. Such a move would be a crime for a woman like Lainie.

So he wrapped his arm around her and pulled her close to his side. "We want something really nice," he said. "Really, really nice."

Lainie glanced up at him, obviously startled by his move. "Now, Harry, let's not go overboard. I don't want you spending a lot of—"

"I know you don't, sweetheart." Damn, that word sounded good applied to Lainie. He smiled at her. "You're always saying that, but let me treat you, okay?"

The surprise faded from her expression and a soft gleam came into her eyes. "Okay." She paused a nanosecond. "*Sweetheart.*"

He gulped. Her saying the word was about fifty times more powerful than him saying it. And the weird thing was how she was looking at him, as if she liked calling him that. The idea that she might genuinely be attracted took some getting used to.

The clerk reverted to her original level of enthusiasm. "All righty, then! I have some beautiful Zuni pieces with inlaid turquoise, opal, and onyx. In fact, I have a few in gold, if you want to go that route."

"That's a possibility," Harry said, feeling giddy. She might really be attracted to him. How cool was that? Yet it couldn't amount to anything, but still . . . she wasn't repulsed by him.

"Not gold, Harry." She slid her arm around his waist and squeezed gently.

"Why not?" He was ready to buy the priciest ring in the store, just because he felt so psyched.

"Well, we decided to go with the nontraditional bands, so ending up with gold, even if it is Southwestern, seems like a cop-out. We should stick with silver, don't you think?"

When she had one arm wrapped around him and he could feel the heat of her body through the silk of Leo's imported shirt, he couldn't think at all. He gazed down at her, his brain a pile of mush. "Whatever you say, honey."

Lainie winked at the clerk. "Did you hear that? I should get that statement in writing."

"Absolutely." The clerk gave her a woman-to-woman grin. "You don't want amnesia setting in once the honeymoon's over. Now take a look at these, and tell me if any of them suit your fancy."

"You decide, Lainie." Harry had never worn a ring in

his life. He glanced down at Lainie's tapered fingers and noticed with surprise that she wasn't wearing any, either. He'd never noticed that before, but it made sense. All her spare cash was tied up in raising Dexter, not buying jewelry.

Instead of picking out one of the inlaid turquoise pieces, Lainie pointed to a silver band engraved with a geometric design. "That's very pretty."

Harry wasn't fooled. He didn't know much about jewelry, but even he could tell that she'd picked the cheapest ring in the display. "I like this one better." He picked up an intricate design of inlaid turquoise, a pearl-colored stone that was probably opal, and a black stone that must be the onyx the clerk had talked about. "Try this."

Lainie shook her head. "I like this one." She put the engraved silver band on her left-hand ring finger. "See? It even fits."

"It's too big. See how it wiggles when you move your hand?" And it looked way too much like a cereal-box prize to suit Harry. "Come on," he said. "Humor me and try this one."

She got a stubborn look in her eye. "Now, Harry."

He stared right back at her. "Now, Lainie."

"It's a very lovely piece," said the clerk.

Lainie glanced down at the ring in Harry's hand, then back up at him. "You know how I feel about this. And you said I could decide."

"You can. Just try this one on. For me."

She blew out a breath.

Newfound confidence made him bold. He took off the engraved silver ring she was trying to get him to buy and replaced it with the more expensive one. The gesture of sliding it on her finger sucker-punched him in the gut. *With this ring, I thee wed.* He hadn't meant to imitate that part of the wedding ceremony, but in essence, he had.

She caught her breath, and one glance at her pink cheeks told him that she'd thought exactly the same thing. The trouble was, he was getting all warm and fuzzy about this moment, when he needed to remember that in his case, good chemistry seemed to lead to disastrous relationships. Of course, to mess with his head even more, the ring fit as if made for her.

"We'll take it," he said, deciding they needed to buy the rings and get the hell out of there before he started imagining a walk down the aisle with this woman.

"I hope I have a matching band for you," the clerk said. "There isn't one here, but maybe in the back. Give me a moment to look."

The minute she was gone, Lainie started to pull the ring off. Harry grasped both of her hands to stop her.

"It's too expensive," she said.

"It's not, Lainie." He let go of her hands before he brought them up to his mouth and started kissing her fingers. "And we need to buy the rings and get going."

"That's twice you've called me by my real name, and I think I've slipped up with your name, too. Aren't we supposed to be Fred and Rona?"

"Yeah, but it shouldn't matter until we get to the time-share place."

Lainie groaned. "I'll never remember to call you Fred. Not in a million years. You don't look anything like a Fred."

"Is that good or bad?"

"It's not good or bad. You're just not a Fred. Freds are

crotchety middle-aged guys with a little pot belly and a bald spot."

"That pretty much describes Fred, the dog, except for the bald spot." He was afraid to ask for her image of a guy named Harry.

"Anyway, I can't accept a ring this expensive. It makes me feel like a gold-digger."

He smiled at her. "Silver-digger."

"Whatever. The engraved silver is more than I anticipated, and the inlaid rings are out of sight. I'm not here to take advantage of your generosity, and I—"

"But it looks good on you." He held up her hand so they could both admire the ring. "Think of it as a souvenir of your first trip to Sedona."

"Souvenirs are supposed to be cheap trinkets." But her eyes said she was weakening. "Besides, if she can't find a matching one, this whole argument is wasted. I'm sure she can match the engraved silver ring, though. There are a bunch of those in the case."

"I found one!" The clerk hurried out of the back room. "Definitely a man's size, so now we have to pray it fits. You have pretty big hands."

Harry had a totally illogical feeling that the ring would fit. He wasn't prone to flashes of intuition and didn't much believe in them, but when he held out his left hand and the ring slid right on, he wasn't surprised.

"Perfect!" The clerk beamed at them. "I'll get two ring boxes so you can keep them safe until the big day. When is the wedding?"

Harry blurted out "tomorrow" at the same time Lainie said "next week." The clerk blinked.

"I'm, uh, trying to talk her into making it sooner," Harry said.

The clerk opened her mouth to say something.

"Oh, you know what, Harry?" Lainie glanced at her watch. "We have to get a move on if we're going to make that meeting."

"You are so right." He fished his credit card out and handed it to the clerk. "We're running late."

"I understand." The clerk didn't look as if she understood anything, but she processed the credit card quickly and tucked the rings into small velvet-covered boxes. "I wish you both the best," she said as she plopped the boxes and the completed sales slip in a bag and handed it to Harry.

"Thanks." He fished in his pocket for the car keys as he followed Lainie out the door of the shop.

"We need to get our story straight," she said as he helped her into the car.

"Doesn't matter anymore. From now on, we're Mr. and Mrs. Fred Ambrewster." He closed the door and walked around to his side of the car. This whole marriage charade was weirding him out. Damned if he didn't feel as if he were whisking Lainie off to a honeymoon hotel.

On the drive toward the time-share, Lainie didn't say anything except to point out the signs for Crimson Canyons so he wouldn't take a wrong turn. She sat with the bag in her lap and stared out the window, as if lost in thought.

"Are you okay?" he asked finally.

"Uh-huh." More silence.

"You're awfully quiet." And he wasn't used to that with her. She was such a bundle of energy that her silence worried him.

"Sorry." She straightened and smiled at him. "I didn't mean to be quiet."

"It's fine if you want to be. You don't have to apologize. I just wondered if something was wrong."

"No." She opened the bag and took out the ring boxes. "I was just thinking how my life is totally different from the way I expected it to turn out when I was a little girl." She opened both boxes and took out the smaller ring. "I should probably put this on now."

"How did you expect things to turn out when you were a little girl?" He probably shouldn't be asking, but then, he probably shouldn't be doing any of this.

"Oh, you know. I thought I'd meet a nice guy, get married, and have kids, in that order." She slid the ring on her finger.

Seeing her with that ring on made him wish for something that wasn't remotely logical. "So you didn't plan to be a dancer, originally?" He sounded way too hopeful, as if he wanted her to say dancing was a passing phase, something to pay the bills.

"I always wanted to be a dancer."

His hopes evaporated. That's what his mother had said, too.

"When you're a little kid, you think you can have it all," she continued. "I was going to be a famous dancer with a husband who managed my career. And we'd both take plenty of time off to play with our babies. You know, the Hollywood version of fame and fortune."

He envied her, having dreams that big. He was too

damned smart to allow himself those castles in the air. He'd studied statistics and kept himself grounded in reality. And right now that seemed incredibly boring compared with her fantasies.

"There it is." She pointed toward a billboard next to the road. "Crimson Canyons Resort. They don't even call it a time-share."

"They didn't call it that in the brochure, either. They say we're invited to purchase 'vacation ownership.' I'm sure that's because the word 'time-share' got some negative press years ago." Harry turned down the winding road, avoiding potholes that would play hell with the suspension on his Lexus. "Somebody needs to get out here with a few buckets of asphalt, though."

"Maybe the weather's hard on the roads here."

Harry thought the weather in Sedona wasn't a whole lot different from the weather in Vegas, which meant Crimson Canyons had no excuse for the lousy road, but he kept his mouth shut. He didn't want to rain on Lainie's expectations for the place. The road ended at a nearly deserted parking lot that wasn't in any better condition. At the edge of the parking lot stood a rambling stuccoed building in need of a fresh coat of white paint.

"I guess they're going for the rustic look," Lainie said.

"If so, they've taken it too far." Just beyond the building stretched a golf-course fairway, but what should have been an expanse of emerald green was mostly dusty brown, with dots of green here and there. Harry wasn't much of a golfer, but even he knew this course was suboptimal.

"The setting's gorgeous." Lainie peered at the red rocks rising on all sides of the resort property. "It might be nice to have a time-share here. I'll bet the units look better than this clubhouse."

"Without good amenities, it wouldn't have a whole lot of resale value." He sounded like such an accountant. Well, he was an accountant, and he shouldn't try to act otherwise.

"Oh, I wouldn't ever sell it. I'd come for my week every year. I'd learn how to play golf and tennis. I'll bet they're having trouble with a fungus on the golf course, and that's why it looks like that. They'll fix that problem. You have to look past some things, and consider the overall value."

"Maybe." Harry pulled into a parking spot and turned off the motor. From here he could see a group of two-story buildings with a Spanish-villa feel tucked alongside the browned-out fairway. Red-tiled roofs blended with the rock formations rising to the west and south of the property. From here, the units looked halfway decent. Maybe Lainie would turn out to be right, and the actual accommodations would be fine.

"It's so peaceful here," Lainie said as she climbed out of the car. "So relaxing."

Harry thought it might be quiet because not a single other soul was crazy enough to visit this rundown place. Even so, listening to the eagerness in Lainie's voice, he wanted to pull out his checkbook on the spot. But he wasn't here to buy a time-share for Lainie. He was here to throw her ex off the track and give her time to figure out what to do. Grabbing the other small velvet box, he took out the ring and put it on.

As he started to leave the car, his cell rang. He pulled

it from its holder on the dash and punched the talk button. "This is Harry."

"Harry, it's Leo. I have news about Joey."

Instantly Harry was out of the car and headed for Lainie, as if Joey might be hiding behind one of the low-growing junipers lining the parking area. "What about him?"

"He wants the kid in order to prove he can give his old man an heir. If he produces Dexter, his old man will make him next in line to inherit the family business, which is a considerable amount of moola. Not only that, but he's racked up a huge gambling debt, more than he can pay. I'm sure he wants daddy's protection from his creditors, and he won't get it unless he shows up with the old man's grandkid in tow."

"What about Lainie?"

At the sound of her name, Lainie turned. Her smile disappeared when she saw Harry's expression.

"I think mostly she's in his way," Leo said.

Despite the heat rising from the asphalt, Harry felt cold. "What does that mean, exactly?" He could guess, but he didn't like guessing about something this important.

"I'm not sure yet, kid. We're watching Joey and trying to find out if he has other people working for him. There's billions at stake with the inheritance, and the guys he owes money to aren't the kind you want to mess with. I'm worried the pressure might make Joey do things he might not consider under different circumstances. Are you in the time-share yet?"

"Not yet."

"Get going, then. You need some protective coloring. Once they assign you a place to stay, keep low."

"Right. Listen, Leo, I—"

"Gotta go. Talk to you soon." The line went dead.

"That was Leo," Harry said, answering Lainie's unspoken question. "Let's go in. I'll tell you what he said on the way."

She grew pale. "Dexter. You have to tell me if Dexter's—"

"Dexter's fine." Harry had to assume that much, or Leo would have said something about the little boy.

Color flooded back into her face. "Thank God. Nothing else really matters."

Harry didn't contradict her as he opened a creaky wooden door and ushered her through it, but he knew plenty of other things mattered. If she was an obstacle to Joey's inheriting a fortune, no telling what he had in mind for her. Harry was no bodyguard, and Leo damn well knew that. One of Leo's men should be posing as Fred Ambrewster, not Harry, the accountant. But that meant one of Leo's men would spend the night with Lainie, and Harry didn't like that idea, either.

Well, he might not be brawny, but he was smart. He'd stick like glue to Lainie, and anyone who wanted to hurt her would have to go through him to do it. He hoped that would be enough protection, at least for the next few hours.

Leo replaced the phone in the holder on the dash of his silver Jag as he pulled off the interstate and started toward Sedona. Cell phones sure helped guys in his line of work. He could call from anywhere and not give away his position. Harry had assumed he was still in Vegas, which was as Rona had wanted it.

And he would try to play it the way she'd asked, at least in the beginning. He understood why she wanted him to stay in the background and give Harry a chance to fall for the lovely Lainie. Shoot, Lainie even came prepackaged with a little kid, and Dexter was a charmer. Poor Rona was such a frustrated grandma. He wouldn't mind playing the grandpa role, come to think of it.

So he couldn't let Harry know he was here. An on-site bodyguard could put a real damper on their romance. But if Leo sensed that anyone was lurking around town hoping for a chance to nab Lainie, then Leo would move in, even if it meant spoiling the moment for those two. Fortunately, he had thirty years of experience and instincts that he trusted completely.

And he'd left Eric and Brett, two of his best, guarding Rona's town house. They were also unobtrusive, but no one would get to either Rona or the kid. Joey Benjamin might have a little money behind him, but after all his years of working in Vegas, Leo wasn't intimidated by a little money.

Chapter Nine

A musty smell and the sound of flutes, drums, and chanting greeted Lainie as she walked into the Crimson Canyons lobby. She was pretty sure this used to be the living room of what had apparently been converted from a house to a sales office. Posters featuring Sedona's red rocks were tacked on the wall with pushpins, and over the empty fireplace hung an Indian rug that had been visited regularly by moths.

Other than a desk in one corner, the only furniture was a ripped Naugahyde sofa and two mangy armchairs. No one was in the room. A small tape recorder on the desk clicked off, having come to the end of the cassette providing the flute-and-drum background music. With surroundings like this, she was in no danger of being swept away by the ambiance.

Then again, there was Harry, a huge part of the ambiance, a guy whose solid presence was really growing on her. She could tell she was getting to him, too.

She had no doubt she could seduce him the minute they were truly alone.

But she had a sneaking suspicion he didn't want to get permanently mixed up with a dancer. So if she had sex with him, she had to be clear in her mind why she was doing it. Curiosity, partly. Sexual deprivation, mostly. Vibrators were a poor substitute for the real deal.

She'd also have to forget the thrill of pleasure he'd given her when he'd slipped the ring on her finger. It could have been a special moment if he'd wanted to make it into one. Quite definitely he hadn't wanted to. 'Nuff said on that score.

Harry leaned toward her. "We don't have to stay. Maybe we should go somewhere else."

"No, it'll be fine." Lainie wasn't about to have Harry spend money on a hotel room when this one came free. Besides, they'd promised Rona they'd check the place out. Maybe it was a diamond in the rough.

"Seriously, this is shaping up to be a disaster. I think we could find a better—"

"Is there something I can do for you?" A middle-aged woman in a long skirt and oversized sweater came into the room. Her name tag read "Thalia Jenson."

"We're Rona and Fred Ambrewster," Lainie said before Harry could open his mouth. "We called earlier about an appointment to discuss a time-share."

"Resort and vacation ownership," Thalia corrected gently. "Certainly. If you'll come this way, we'll get you registered for the room and I'll notify Dudley that you've arrived." She went over to the desk in the corner, sat down and picked up the phone.

As she punched in a number, presumably to contact their salesman Dudley, Harry turned to Lainie. "You know, I really do think—"

"Come on, Fred." Lainie took him by the arm. "We agreed to take the tour, so let's get on with it."

Harry lowered his voice and leaned closer to her. "But what if the units look like this?"

"We'll cross that bridge when we come to it," she said under her breath. "And I'm sure they're an improvement."

Harry rolled his eyes. "Anything would be an improvement," he muttered, but he walked with her over to the desk.

Thalia hung up the phone and smiled at them. "Dudley's on his way." Then she powered up her ancient desktop computer. "Your stay will be complimentary for two nights, and I just need a credit card for any extra charges you might make."

Lainie wondered if there would be any question about names as Harry handed over his card. But as Rona had predicted, Thalia keyed in the number without giving it a second glance.

After thanking Harry and returning his card, she gave him two metal door keys and a crudely drawn map of the premises. A big red *X* was on one of the numbered units. Then she laid out name tags, Sharpie pens, and a tour registration form. "If you'll fill these out, I'm sure Dudley will be here any minute."

"Okay." Harry started printing *H-A-R* with the Sharpie.

Lainie noticed and clapped a hand over the name tag, getting a palm full of ink for her troubles. Maybe seeing those keys to the room they'd be sharing had messed with his concentration. "Let me do yours," she said, balling up his attempt and shoving it in her purse. Then she wiped her hand on a tissue. "Nobody can read your handwriting."

"They can so." Harry looked peeved. "If I print, and I was pr—"

"May we have another name tag, please?" Lainie asked sweetly.

"Sure." Thalia placed another peel-and-stick name tag on the desk. "We have plenty."

Lainie carefully printed *F-R-E-D* on the tag, peeled off the backing, and slapped the sticky side onto Harry's silk-covered chest. Mm, that felt good, pressing her hand right over his heart. "There you go, Freddy," she said.

Harry looked down at his chest and apparently the light dawned, because he glanced at her with understanding in his big brown eyes. "Oh."

"Exactly." Lainie printed *R-O-N-A* on her tag, peeled off the back and smoothed it over the shirt the real Rona had loaned her. Funny that Rona had hair about the color of the wig Lainie was wearing. Her scalp was starting to itch a little, and she'd be glad to get into their room and take the wig off. *And what else will you be taking off, Lainie girl?* She shivered, still not sure whether sex with Harry was a great idea or the worst one she'd had in five years.

Harry had started filling out the form, and thanks to her intervention on the name tag thing he seemed to be with the program. He used his mother's condo address and telephone number. Then she watched him hesitate over her age and was gratified when he listed her as twenty-five instead of her true age of twenty-seven.

Then he put down his age, and Lainie found out he was thirty-three. No wonder his mother was impatient about grandkids. Harry needed to settle down. What he didn't need was the kind of mess she'd made of her life, which was another reason to avoid sex, or at least make it clear the fun would be temporary.

"Fred and Rona, you're a sight for sore eyes!"

Lainie jumped, nearly colliding with Harry as they both turned to face their salesman and his Texas twang. Small and wiry, Dudley looked as if he'd been dried in the sun like a piece of beef jerky. He wore a long-sleeved cowboy shirt, boot-cut jeans, and a battered cowboy hat, all of which looked authentic. Except for the lack of a horse and six-guns, he could have stepped right out of the eighteen-hundreds.

"Dudley Shearson," he said, sticking out a weathered hand first to Lainie and then to Harry. "We're gonna have more fun than a hog in mud today. I hope you brought your checkbook, 'cause you're gonna need it!" Dudley was a hand-pumper.

"Good to meet you, Dudley." Harry extracted his hand from Dudley's enthusiastic grip. "And we probably should get started with—"

"Oh, we'll get started, all right. We'll get started with a bang. You're gonna love what I'm about to show you, Rona and Fred. Follow me, folks." Dudley picked up the registration form from the counter and took off at a good clip toward the rear doors of the building. "Henderson, huh? I have me a cousin who lives in Henderson. Ray Atkins. He's a good ol' boy, deals in those portable toilets they use for construction and special events, ya know? Like rock concerts and such. Handles the overflow. Get it? Overflow!" Dudley cackled happily at his own joke.

Lainie glanced at Harry and raised her eyebrows. Harry shrugged as if to say it didn't matter how weird their salesman was. And it didn't. They weren't in the market for a time-share.

"Ray, he never goes out on the Strip, though." Dudley opened the door and gestured for Lainie and Harry to go out ahead of him. "Says he wouldn't be caught dead there. Just a tourist trap, a place to fleece you out of all your hard-earned cash."

Lainie kept her mouth shut. It didn't matter if Dudley insulted his prospects or not, since the prospects were bogus.

Once they were on a walkway outside, Dudley glanced at their registration form and did a double-take. "Oh, say, you two work for the Nirvana! Now there's a classy place. Yessir, I've been to the Nirvana, and I give it the Dudley Shearson seal of approval. I don't give many outfits that honor, let me tell you. Now if you'll step over this way, we'll take a golf cart to the units."

Although the golf cart looked as if it had seen better days, Lainie was relieved they wouldn't have to walk. Sleeping in the car had helped some, but she was still feeling tired, and she could imagine how exhausted Harry was. Even so, he helped her into the back of the cart before climbing in beside her. What a guy.

Dudley slid behind the wheel, talking the whole time. "Ah, yes, the Nirvana. Great place. I wouldn't give you a plugged nickel for any of the other casinos up there, but the Nirvana's my kind of establishment. My accountant told me to stay away from all forms of gambling, but you know how accountants are. Never want anybody to have any fun."

"I wouldn't go that far," Harry said.

Dudley glanced at their registration again. "Oh, I see you *are* an accountant, Fred. Well, there you go. You're out of the mold, because here you are looking at resort ownership. You obviously know how to have fun." Then he cranked the key on the golf cart. When it wouldn't start right away, he jiggled the key and gave the dash several hard thumps. Finally the motor caught.

"Is this thing gas-powered?" Harry asked.

"Yup. When it decides to go, anyways." Smoke belched from the rear of the cart.

"I thought everyone had gone to electric."

"Not everybody!" Dudley sang out as he put the pedal to the metal and they took off so quickly that Lainie's and Harry's heads snapped back.

Backfiring all the way, they careened down the golf path as fast as the little cart would go. Harry anchored one arm around the canopy brace and the other around Lainie, to hold her steady. She appreciated the gesture on many levels. Being held by Harry was turning out to be one of life's pleasures, but in this case it also was one of life's necessities. They had to hang on to each other to keep from being tossed out of the cart.

Seemingly oblivious to the wild ride he was giving them, Dudley kept up his monologue. "I had some folks several days ago from the state of Washington, and he works for a paper company, so I asked him if his company made toilet paper, and he said sure, so I told him I'd hook him up with my cousin Ray."

Harry leaned down and put his mouth close to Lainie's ear. "Can you believe this guy sells anything?"

"Nope." But Lainie could believe that having Harry murmur in her ear was worth enduring whatever Dudley dished out. It didn't matter what Harry said. Just his warm breath and his rumbly voice got her all hot and bothered.

"Hey, Fred," Dudley called over his shoulder. "Maybe you'd like this fella's name, the one with the warehouse full of TP? I'm sure he could cut you a deal for the Nirvana. Since you're an accountant, I'm sure you're always looking for ways to trim that old budget, right? Whoopsie." He hit the brakes and laid a strip of rubber on the golf path. "I was so busy talking I almost drove right past the first model."

Lainie had the giggles. She pressed her lips together to control herself, although she probably didn't have to worry about offending Dudley. He continued his monologue about budgets and toilet paper as he climbed out of the cart and beckoned them toward a wrought-iron patio gate. Dead weeds choked the area on either side of the gate.

Harry stepped down and held out a hand to help Lainie as Dudley proceeded through the gate, still talking.

"Now watch your step and keep an eye out for rattlers," Dudley said. "Don't want either of you getting bit."

"Rattlers?" Lainie scrambled back into the cart. "What do you mean, rattlers?"

"Yeah, exactly what *do* you mean?" Harry glanced

nervously around him. "Some of us aren't wearing boots, you know."

"Aw, they won't bother you, so long as you make a lot of noise to warn 'em off. They just hate being startled."

"If noise is all we need, then we should be golden." Harry looked over at Lainie and rolled his eyes.

"That's what I'm telling ya. Just follow ol' Dudley's instructions, and you'll be fine. Come on in, folks, and prepare to be charmed by Crimson Canyons." Dudley opened the sliding glass door into the time-share unit.

Once again, Harry held out his hand to Lainie. "We'll stomp our feet the whole way."

She put her hand in his. What a terrific sensation, holding hands with Harry. "Like you said, if it's noise we need, we're all set." She lowered her voice. "I've never heard such a motormouth."

"I'm guessing he's fueled up on about ten cups of coffee." He guided her down. "I'm ready to buy something just to shut him up."

"Well, control that urge, Fred."

His eyes got all warm and melty. "Easier said than done."

She didn't remember hearing that husky tone in his voice before, and it hit her right where she lived. She wondered how long Dudley would torture them with his sales pitch, such as it was. Once they ditched Dudley, they could lay claim to their room, and she could hardly wait to see what happened after that.

"Right in here, Fred and Rona. This is our one-bedroom model, perfect for a couple with no kids, or if you have kids, a place to get away from the little cowpokes. Never could stand rug rats, myself, but some people swear by them."

This time Lainie didn't try to hold back her laughter. "I have a rug rat at home, Dudley, and I'm nuts about him."

Dudley might have blushed. In a guy as brown and weathered as Dudley it was hard to tell. He pulled their registration form from his coat pocket and looked at it. "Why, so you do. And knowing you folks, I'm sure he's a crackerjack."

"Oh, he's that, all right," Harry said.

"Spoken like a proud papa." Dudley waved them inside. "Now come and take a look at this place. You're gonna love it."

As Lainie walked through the gate ahead of Harry, all the while making sure to create as much noise as possible scuffing the soles of her shoes against the paving stones, she thought about Harry as a father. If only she'd taken a shine to someone like Harry five years ago, then Dexter would have a great role model instead of the sorry excuse for a man that Joey Benjamin had turned into.

Of course, she hadn't thought there was any chance Joey would get her pregnant. His story about the mumps making him sterile had been real. Joey wasn't smart enough to make up something like that.

Then she realized she'd never asked Harry what Leo had called about. But now was not the time, with Dudley able to listen in. She stepped through the patio door into a living room that seemed in slightly better shape than the lobby. A colorful blanket had been thrown over the sofa, and a braided rug was positioned on the carpet in front of the fireplace. It wasn't directly in front of the fireplace, but that was probably the maid not being precise.

Dudley was talking again, this time about the smallness of the kitchen and the largeness of the bedroom, which he said was the right proportion for a getaway. Then he winked at Harry, man-to-man. On Dudley's lined face, a wink looked very strange.

Harry glanced around the living room. "How old are these units, Dudley?"

"Now there's a very good question, Fred. I promise to get an answer for you when we get back to the clubhouse. Now, Rona, take a gander at this bedroom and tell me it's not perfect for a couple of lovebirds."

Lainie could tell from Harry's expression that he was thinking of abandoning the idea of staying here. No doubt he had higher standards than she did. She would be fine here, though, unless the bedroom was horrible. Following Dudley's suggestion, she walked over to the doorway and peeked inside.

Okay, so it wasn't the same as a room at the Bellagio, but the bed was a king, and right now it looked extremely inviting. She'd never owned anything bigger than a double bed. Sure, the headboard and dresser were a little cheesy, but that bed was all she needed. And try as she might to keep the image from taking over, she pictured Harry in it with her.

She turned and discovered Harry standing in the doorway. He too was staring at the bed. He swallowed. Then he looked at her. Lust shone in his eyes.

Her heart beat so loud it echoed in her ears. She forgot to breathe as she fought the urge to grab Harry and pull him down on that mattress with her. He wanted that, too. She could see it on his face.

He took a step into the room . . . and stopped. Closing his eyes, he shook his head. When he opened his eyes again, the lust was gone.

He's decided not to have sex with me. She was sure of it, and that made up her mind once and for all. Harry wasn't the kind of guy who had temporary sex with a woman. Come to think of it, she wasn't that kind of woman, either.

In the living room, Dudley continued his monologue, babbling about the number of cable channels available in the area. Then he appeared in the doorway. "Well, folks, can you two see yourself having a high old time in this kind of setup?" He leaned against the doorframe, his hat tipped back from his forehead, a grin on his face.

"Uh, we need to continue with the tour," Harry said, still looking at Lainie, regret plainly reflected in his gaze.

"Why even bother with the two-bedroom model?" Dudley said. "The trouble with a two-bedroom, if you don't mind my saying so, is that you have yourself two bedrooms, and people tend to fill up that space, which means your privacy is shot to hell. Now some people might not want privacy, but I can tell you two are very interested in your privacy. I can see that you—"

"We'd better look at the two-bedroom," Lainie said, forcing herself to break eye contact with Harry. Then she glanced back at him. "Right, Fred?"

He blinked as if coming out of a trance. "Right. A two-bedroom."

"Okay, but I can't see you in a two-bedroom. You're a one-bedroom couple if ever I saw one. However, if you insist on seeing a two-bedroom, then I'm obliged to show you a two-bedroom, isn't that right? Back to the golf cart we go." He turned and walked outside.

Lainie swallowed her disappointment that she wouldn't be having sex with Harry, but that was the breaks. They had to make sure they were on the same page, so they could proceed. "Okay, here's the plan. We'll look at the two-bedroom. Then we can pretend we can't make up our mind between the two, which gives us an out."

"I think we should look at the two-bedroom and leave. There's no reason to stay here. We can find a better place."

She didn't want a better place. If she wasn't going to have sex with Harry, it didn't matter where they were. "It would be stupid to spend the money when we don't have to. Besides, Leo expects us to be here. We've successfully passed ourselves off as Rona and Fred. And nobody's around. That makes it the perfect hideaway. If we go somewhere nicer, we're bound to be more visible."

Harry sighed and rubbed the back of his neck. "I guess you're right. Let's go look at the two-bedroom."

"And remember, you want the one-bedroom and I want the two-bedroom, and we can't agree."

"Right." He glanced at her. "So if we are going to stay in one of these units, I'll take the couch."

She nodded. "Of course. Any other arrangement would be crazy."

"Yeah."

Harry followed Lainie out onto the patio. Whew, close call. And Lainie knew it, too. He had to make sure they were never again in a position where they stood within jumping distance of a mattress big enough to do all the things he envisioned doing with her.

He was so busy thinking about those things that he lagged behind and barely made it onto the cart before Dudley took off at top speed again. As they jounced down the path toward the two-bedroom model, every bump threw Lainie up against him. He was forced to put his arm around her again, and that ate away at his decision not to have sex with her.

He'd thought about it and thought about it, and finally decided, during that moment when he'd wanted her so much he couldn't see straight, that it wouldn't be fair to either of them. Nothing could come of it, and he cared too much about Lainie to have casual sex with her. But his decision was being put to the test by the unrelenting temptation of breathing in her scent, listening to her voice, feeling her touch, watching her every move.

Even Dudley had picked up on the sexual heat between them and hoped to use it as a sales tool. Throughout the tour of the two-bedroom, Dudley kept mentioning the intimacy of the one-bedroom and how necessary that kind of privacy was for a married couple if they hoped to keep the marriage hot. Dudley, of course, was not married. Harry wasn't surprised.

Lainie did exactly as she'd suggested earlier and promoted the idea of the two-bedroom, saying it was more flexible and made more sense for a family. Harry argued for the one-bedroom, and watched the color rise in her cheeks, because his preference labeled him as wanting the uninterrupted sexual opportunities Dudley kept hinting they'd have.

Oh, God, did he want uninterrupted sexual opportunities. But he wasn't going to allow himself to have them. He was going to sleep on the couch and be strong enough to deal with the frustration. Somehow, he'd make it through the next two nights without giving in.

Chapter Ten

Sitting at a plastic table next to the resort's murky pool, Lainie wondered if they'd sold any time-shares at Crimson Canyons. The concept was great and the view spectacular, but the resort left about fifty things to be desired. She decided to concentrate on the red rocks beyond the bedraggled golf course. Thunderclouds billowed up behind the formations, and Lainie wished she had some kind of camera for souvenir pictures. No telling when she'd be able to get back to Sedona.

As Dudley droned on about payment plans and credit reports, she glanced at Harry to make sure he hadn't spaced out again. Good thing she'd checked, because Harry wasn't paying a bit of attention to Dudley. Instead he was staring off into space, his eyes glazed over.

"So if you'll just sign here." Dudley shoved a paper in front of Harry. "Then I'll send you on your way to your complimentary suite."

Barely looking at the document in front of him, Harry took the pen Dudley handed him and prepared to sign.

Obviously all he'd heard was "complimentary suite" and he was ready to put his name on anything. Besides not wanting him to sign anything, Lainie was worried about what name he'd use.

She couldn't wait to find out. Reaching across the table, she grabbed his arm. "Fred! We have to talk about this! Don't you dare sign that before we've hashed out our differences."

He looked startled. "Uh, isn't this just a release verifying that we've taken the tour, so we can legitimately occupy our room?"

"Why, no," Dudley said. "That there's the contract for a one-bedroom resort ownership. The way you were nodding at what I said, I thought you understood that's what I was talking about. You want the one-bedroom, you understand the terms I just explained, so the only thing left is signing the contract."

Harry scanned the paper in front of him and a red flush spread up from the collar of his shirt. "Uh, no, we haven't decided on a one-bedroom, yet."

"Or a two-bedroom," Lainie added.

"We each want something different," Harry said. "So that's the crux of the problem."

Wasn't that the truth, Lainie thought. But right now, the issue was a time-share they were most definitely not buying, because they weren't Fred and Rona Ambrewster.

"Tell you what," Dudley said. "If you buy that one-bedroom today, you can upgrade to the two-bedroom later. How's that for solving your situation?"

"I don't think that would be the answer for us," Harry said.

"Definitely not." Lainie decided more ammunition

was needed to blast them out of Dudley's orbit. "You don't know Harry. Stubborn as a mule."

"Wait a minute," Harry said. "I can be as flexible as the next—"

"Harry?" Dudley shoved back his hat. "I thought this here was Fred."

Lainie could have kicked herself. She would have to add that comment and then slip up on the name thing. And Harry was so blitzed from lack of sleep he hadn't noticed. "It's my pet name for him," she said. "It's spelled *H-A-I-R-Y,* because Fred is . . . well . . ." She glanced at Harry, who was studying the underside of the umbrella with great concentration. The corner of his mouth twitched.

Dudley grinned. "Okay, I get it. See, that's what I'm talking about. Couples who have pet names for each other aren't going to let a little space problem stop them from buying a love nest in Crimson Canyons."

Lainie groaned. She'd lost ground instead of gaining it. "I'm telling you, if we get the one-bedroom, I'll never talk Fred into the two-bedroom, and it will be a source of constant friction in our marriage."

Dudley leaned toward her. "Rona Ambrewster, have you seen the spark in your husband's eyes when he looks at you? That's what can happen to folks when they fall under the spell of this place. You want to fan that spark, Rona. One bedroom, two bedrooms, makes no never mind, but it's my considered opinion you'd do best in the one-bedroom."

Lainie shook her head. "I want that extra bedroom or nothing at all."

"And if that's not being stubborn, I don't know what

is." Harry crossed his arms and gazed across the table at her.

"I'm practical. You're stubborn."

He threw up his hands. "Then I guess it's nothing. You see, Dudley? I'm afraid we won't be buying a unit in Crimson Canyons."

"Of course you will! Now I'm not supposed to do this under normal circumstances, but you two need that one-bedroom. I'll throw in a free golf cart if you sign the contract right now."

Just what they needed, Lainie thought, a free golf cart just like the backfiring bucket of bolts they'd been riding in.

"Sorry." Harry pushed back his chair. "We won't be buying."

Dudley put a hand on his arm. "Buy her the two-bedroom, son. Sure, sometimes you'll have to drag the in-laws along, but once in a while you'll have her all to yourself, and with two bedrooms, you'll have more space to play, if you know what I mean." He waggled his bushy eyebrows.

"Nope." Harry stood. "I'm not buying her a two-bedroom."

"And I'm not agreeing to a one-bedroom." Lainie stood, too. "So that's that."

"No it's not," Dudley said. "Normally I'm not supposed to do this, but I'm leaving the offer open for the next twenty-four hours. I'll check with you folks periodically during your stay, because I'll bet my hat that you'll change your mind before you leave here. And I love this old hat."

Lainie exchanged a horrified glance with Harry. The

thought of Dudley checking on them periodically was most unpleasant.

"I guarantee we won't change our minds." Harry stuck out his hand in farewell. "So we wouldn't want to waste your valuable time. Spend it on people who are better prospects. We appreciate your time, Dudley."

"Absolutely," Lainie said. "And Fred's right. We're terrible prospects. A complete dead end."

Dudley laughed. "I don't believe that for a minute. I've been watching you two lovebirds, and you might be having a little spat about how big the unit should be, but that'll all get worked out in due course. I'll just keep this offer open, and we'll write it up before you leave, mark my words."

"No, no we won't." Harry looked a little desperate. "Don't leave the offer open, Dudley. Close the offer. Lock it up and throw away the key."

"You let me be the judge of that." Dudley reached in a folder and pulled out a map. "Did they give you one of these?"

"Yes," Lainie said. "We're all set."

"Your suite isn't far from the models I took you to see. I can give you a lift over there, as a matter of fact."

"No!" Lainie and Harry blurted out together.

"No, thank you," Lainie said, not wanting to be rude. After all, Dudley, or the company he worked for, were giving them a free room for two nights. And she and Harry had never been legitimate customers. "We appreciate the offer, but we can find our way."

Dudley nodded. "Then get along with you. Take care of the fightin' and the makin' up, and I'll be checking with you later."

"I hate to have you doing that, Dudley." Harry pushed back his chair.

No kidding. Lainie would second that one. She'd thought Dudley was a temporary inconvenience, but apparently he was about to become their new best friend.

"No problemo. You two go have fun, now. Whoopsie, there's my beeper. I'll see you folks later." Dudley hurried back across the pool area toward the lobby.

"Where was that beeper when we needed it?" Harry gazed after him. "I've never worked so hard in my life for a free room."

"Are we ever going to get rid of him?"

"Yeah, we are. Starting now by getting out to the car and down to our suite before he shows up again. After that, we're not answering the door or the phone."

"Sounds like a plan." A very intimate plan, one that would keep them closed in that room together for quite a while. But they weren't having sex. Harry didn't want to, and she didn't want to. Case closed.

Harry pulled the resort map from his shirt pocket and consulted it. "If I have this place figured out right, we can take that path over there and get to the parking lot without going back through the lobby and risking a run-in with Dudley."

"Then let's do it." She kept pace with his brisk strides as he started down a gravel path to their right.

"And for your information, I'm neither."

"Neither what?"

"Hairy or stubborn."

Whoa, mama. She sure wished he hadn't brought that up and refocused her thoughts on a naked Harry. "I was just covering the name slip-up."

"I figured that, but I wanted to set the record straight."

"Consider the record straight as a ruler." Now that he'd broached the subject of body hair, she thought about his mother's description of his father's sexual equipment and wondered if he'd also be willing to set the record straight about whether he'd inherited said equipment. Probably not. Damn, she could be giving up a most excellent experience. But it was for the best. Neither of them wanted to indulge in cheap, meaningless sex. Neither of them—

"Stop!" Harry put out his arm, keeping her from continuing down the path beside him as he came to an abrupt halt. "Get behind me," he murmured. *"Now."*

"What is it?" Squiggles of fear danced in her tummy, but she wasn't about to use him as a human shield. "Joey?"

"Nope. Snake. Under that bluish-green bush on the right next to the path. Are you going to get behind me or not?"

"No, I am not." She saw the snake now, coiled and staring straight at them, its tongue darting in and out. It looked big.

"Lainie, just do it."

"So it can bite you instead? I don't think so."

"I'm bigger than you are, so I could take the bite easier. Plus I don't make my living as a dancer or have a little guy to take care of, so if I happened to be laid up—"

"Stop talking like that. You're no less valuable to society than I am." She didn't want Harry in danger. She hated the idea, in fact.

He blew out a breath. "You are one uncooperative woman, you know that?"

"For all we know you'd have a worse reaction to the bite than I would."

"Okay, I can see we're getting nowhere, so how about if we both back up, very slowly."

"That's more like it." She kept her gaze riveted on the snake. "How far can they reach when they, uh, strike?"

"Let's not use that word."

"Well, it would be good to know when we're out of range."

"I don't know the answer to that. Let's hope we don't find out the hard way."

"Right." Heart pounding, she took a step backward. The snake didn't move, but neither did Harry. She poked him. "Hey, buster, you're not backing up."

"I want to stay here until you're a ways back. Then I'll move."

"That's what you think." She poked him again. "I'm not taking another step until you do."

"I do believe we're finding out who the stubborn one is around here."

"Yeah, you arc. Start backing."

He sighed. "Okay." He took a step and the snake remained where it was.

"I'll bet it doesn't really want to bite us," Lainie said. "We're too big to be lunch."

"I'm not giving that snake the benefit of rational thought. Keep backing."

"I'm backing at the same speed you're backing."

"Hey, folks!"

Lainie jumped at least a foot in the air and Harry said a few words she'd never heard him use before.

Dudley clapped them both on the back.

"Say, did you happen to notice you're walking backward?"

Harry's breath hissed out from between clenched teeth. "Damn it, there's a snake up ahead, Dudley. Right next to the path." He kept his attention on the coiled snake. "We're trying not to get bit, if it's all the same to you."

Dudley started laughing. "Oh, that's only Gertie. She's a gopher snake, and we like having her around to control the rodents and such on the premises." He stepped around Lainie and Harry and walked toward the snake. "Go on, now, Gertie. You're scaring the customers."

As he scuffed his boot in the gravel, the snake uncoiled and slithered off through the bushes.

"It sure as hell looked like a rattlesnake," Harry said.

And he'd been willing to sacrifice himself to protect her. "It looked exactly like a rattlesnake," she said. "I don't know how anyone can be expected to tell the difference."

Dudley turned and walked toward them. "If you're going to be a resort owner, then you need to be able to tell your average rattler from your average gopher snake."

"We're not going to be resort owners," Harry said.

Dudley waved a hand as if to dismiss that piece of information. "Your rattlesnake has a triangular-shaped head." Dudley created the shape with his thumbs and forefingers. "That's so there's a place to store the venom, in the back of the jaws. Your gopher snake has a more oval kind of head. Study the head and you'll know what you've got. And there should be rattles on the tail, but sometimes you can't see those. I remember a time when I was showing the resort to some people from Arkansas, and we—"

"Thanks, Dudley." Harry put a hand on his shoulder. "We need to be on our way, now."

"I understand, I understand. I'll be checking with you folks shortly to see how you're getting along, see if you've come to your senses on this purchase."

"Goodbye, Dudley." Harry grabbed Lainie's hand and tugged her down the path.

"Thanks for the snake lecture," Lainie said over her shoulder.

"No problemo, little lady."

Lainie hurried to keep up with Harry. "Did he just call me 'little lady'?"

"Yeah, and maybe he fancies himself as a miniature version of John Wayne. I couldn't care less. Let's get out of here."

"Right." She liked racing down the path, hand-in-hand, but once they reached the parking lot, he let go of her. And that would be the end of touching for the rest of the trip. It had to be, because touching Harry made her want to forget her principles. Touching Harry made her want to have cheap, meaningless sex. A whole lot of it.

With great relief Harry helped Lainie into his black Lexus, a haven from all things reptilian. Then he climbed behind the wheel and closed his door with a satisfying thud. He hit the button for the locks as an extra precaution, although he didn't think snakes could get into cars when the doors and windows were closed.

Finally he started the engine and turned on the air. Now this was how life was supposed to be. He leaned back against the headrest with a sigh. Safety.

"This has been rough on you," Lainie said.

He closed his eyes. "I was doing fine until we tangled with that snake. I'm not a fan of snakes." He was petrified of snakes, but he didn't want to admit the depth of his fear to her. Men were supposed to protect women from creatures like snakes.

"I suppose they have a right to live like everything else."

"I suppose." He opened his eyes, sat up, and put the car in reverse. "I'd just like it if they'd live somewhere other than in my vicinity."

"I can't imagine they have a real problem with snakes around here."

He smiled at her. Smiling was easier in a snake-free world. "What, are you working for Dudley now?"

"Yeah, I am." She smiled back. "Normally he's not supposed to do this, but he's giving me a cut of his commission plus a Ferrari if I convince you to forget about the snakes."

"Don't put it past him." Harry followed signs directing them toward the units they'd recently visited. "The guy is obviously having a tough time selling time-shares. Between the product and his technique, it's a wonder he makes a living at this."

"Maybe this is the only job he can get."

Harry sighed. "Now I'm starting to feel sorry for the guy. He looks like an honest-to-goodness cowboy, and I wonder how many of them can find work these days. But I sure hate to think of him popping up every few hours while we're here."

"We just won't answer the door or the phone, like you said." She covered a yawn with one hand.

That triggered an answering yawn in him, and he

realized he was bone tired. That was a good thing, actually, because being tired could take care of his urges where Lainie was concerned.

"What did Leo have to say on the phone this morning?" Lainie asked.

Oh, yeah. Leo. And Joey. Harry had been so exhausted and preoccupied with sex that he'd nearly forgotten their original reason for being here. "Well, I don't want you to get too worried about this, because Leo and his guys are on top of it."

"Harry, I'm too tired to get worried about much of anything."

He nodded, understanding completely. "It seems Joey's run up a bunch of gambling debts."

"That's no big surprise. He was always looking for the big score. But what does that have to do with Dexter?"

"Joey would get back in good with his dad, not to mention be in line to inherit a fortune, if he can prove that he has a kid. His money problems would be over."

"Inherit? His older brother Emil is supposed to inherit. Joey was very bitter about that."

"Turns out Emil's gay."

Lainie started to giggle, and after a while Harry was worried that she wouldn't stop.

He pulled up in front of the unit they'd been assigned, turned off the motor, and glanced at her. "Are you okay?"

"Uh-huh." Hiccuping, she wiped her eyes and looked at him. "It's just too funny, that's all. Ending up with a gay son must be the worst thing Doyle Benjamin could imagine. But I don't see how Joey's going to present him with a kid born out of wedlock to a showgirl. That won't fly with old Doyle, either."

"My guess is he won't present Dexter in that light." He decided not to outline all the possible ways Joey could change the story about Dexter. "Let's go in." He reached for his door handle.

"Wait a sec, Harry."

He turned to find her watching him, all traces of her giggling fit gone.

"I'm beginning to get the picture," she said. "Joey would be better off if I didn't exist, right?"

"I don't think you have to worry about—"

"Not that I think he's capable of something so drastic," she added quickly, as if to reassure herself, "but the fact remains that without me, he could make up any story about Dexter he wanted."

Harry felt the grip of a fear that made snakes seem like child's play. "That scenario's not possible, Lainie."

"It's possible, but not probable. Joey's a blowhard and he can get riled up at times, but I can't picture him doing anything that violent." Despite her confident words, she'd begun to shiver.

"It doesn't matter what he's capable of or not capable of," Harry said quietly. "Because he'll never get close enough to you to test the theory."

"Because of Leo?"

"No, because of me."

Chapter Eleven

Lainie had never had a protector before, and she loved the feeling. "Thank you, Harry. That means a lot."

"You're welcome." He opened his car door and grabbed his cell phone from the dash. "And the first order of business is to get us both safely inside that timeshare unit. I can call Leo once we do, and find out if he's learned anything more."

Lainie wanted to check on Dexter, too. "I'd like to call your mother, if that's okay."

"Definitely okay. Here, you take my phone. Let's make this transfer quick, in case anybody's watching us."

"Do you really think they are?"

"Probably not, but I'd like to get you inside before we worry about the suitcases. Do you have the key?"

She held up one of the metal keys. "Right here."

"Good. Let's go."

Lainie didn't really believe that Joey would be lurking around, waiting for a chance to pounce on her, but adrenaline pumped through her anyway as she hurried to the entrance and shoved the key in the lock. It wouldn't open the door.

"Dammit! Let me try."

She stood aside so Harry could fool with the key. She tried not to be spooked by the fact they were standing out here exposed, but she couldn't help glancing around.

"There. Finally!" Harry opened the door. "Quick, get in there."

She scooted in and Harry followed, closing the door after them.

He flipped the security lock into place. "At least there's a security lock in this fleabag. Stay here and I'll check around."

Her heart thudded faster. "Oh, I'm sure nobody's hiding in here."

"Probably not. But that's how they do it on TV. The bodyguard checks everything in advance."

"Is that what you are, then?" She thought it was the cutest idea.

He adjusted his glasses. "Well, uh, Leo told me to keep an eye on you, so I guess that's my job description. I realize I'm not exactly trained for this, but I'm the only—"

"I'm honored to have you as my bodyguard."

He looked pleased. "I think I will check the place over. Better make sure Dudley's not hiding in the closet, ready to leap out and make us an offer we can't refuse."

"No kidding." She smiled, to let him know she appreciated his attempt to lighten the mood. She was a little unnerved by the situation with Joey, but she hated to admit being afraid of him. That seemed to give him more power, and she didn't want that. "While you're checking around, I'll call your mother."

"You know what, that's a new phone and I don't have the number on speed dial yet. Let me write it down for you." He moved toward a notepad on the end table nearest the door.

"That's okay. I know it."

He glanced at her in surprise. "You do?"

"I saw it when you wrote it on the registration form."

"Yeah, but that was hours ago."

"And your point is?"

He shrugged. "I'm only thinking that most people wouldn't see a phone number once and remember it. You must have a really good memory."

"I guess. I don't work at it, though. I just see something and it sticks."

He studied her for a moment. "Have you ever heard of a photographic memory?"

"I think that's what I have. Dexter does, too, but then, he's way smarter than I am. Don't get the idea I'm a brain or anything. I'm a one-trick pony when it comes to intelligence."

"Maybe, maybe not." He gazed at her a little longer, as if absorbing this new piece of information. "Well, I'd better make my tour. Here's the car keys." He tossed them in her direction. "If you hear me yell, take off."

She caught the keys in midair. "As if I would do that! First I'd call 911, and then I'd grab a lamp and come help you."

"Because you think I couldn't handle it?"

"No, because I couldn't leave you in the lurch."

He sighed. "Lainie, you're the one in potential danger, so I'm supposed to hold them off so you can get away. I don't know much about how this is supposed to work, but I do know that."

She thought of Harry, who probably didn't have a violent bone in his body, fighting bravely with some intruder while she ran away. She'd never be able to leave him when he was in trouble, but he seemed to need her to say she would. "Okay." She mentally crossed her fingers behind her back. "If something happens, I'll go for help. How's that?"

"Better. I'll go check around." He turned and headed into the bedroom.

If she thought for a minute there was anyone waiting for him, she wouldn't let him go alone, but nothing about this unit felt ominous. After years of being on her own, she trusted that the fine hairs on the back of her neck would warn her if danger lurked nearby.

Maybe that's why she hadn't sensed any threat when they'd nearly stepped on that snake. Harry had freaked, and his panic had transferred to her. But if she'd listened to her gut, she would have known the snake was harmless.

Right now, her gut told her Joey wasn't out to bump her off. But he was after Dexter, and that was scary enough. She turned on Harry's cell phone and dialed Rona's number. While she was waiting for it to ring, she glanced around the living room. It was a little more rundown than the model, but a similar colorful blanket was draped over the sofa. This time the rag rug was positioned on a different section of the carpet, near a worn easy chair.

Rona answered on the second ring. "Harry?"

"No, not Harry. Lainie." She heard Harry opening

closet doors and swishing aside the shower curtain. His earnest inspection of the premises made her smile. "Harry loaned me his cell phone so I could call and find out how Dexter's doing."

"Great! He's right here. Would you like to talk to him?"

"Thanks, I sure would." Lainie felt a lump grow in her throat. She was so far away from her little boy, several hours by car. But he was better off in Rona's condo, guarded by Leo's associates, than he would be with her.

"Hi, Mommy!" Dexter sounded very happy.

That made the lump in Lainie's throat get bigger. He really was fine without her. "Hi, sweetie. Are you having fun?" Silly question. He was obviously having a ball.

"Yep! Did you know Fred slept in my bed all night?"

"That's wonderful."

"He follows me *everywhere*, even when I go potty! He waits outside the door. He loves me soooo much."

"I'm sure he does. You're a lovable guy."

"That's what all the ladies say. We're playing this game called Texas Hold 'Em. Usually they play with money, but today they're playing with M&M's because I'm just a little kid." He paused and pride crept into his voice. "But I have the biggest pile."

"I'm sure you do." So the TITS were teaching Dexter to play poker. Not only that, they were smart enough to play with M&M's, maybe because they'd learned that Dexter could clean out their savings accounts in no time.

Dexter lowered his voice. "Do you think I should let them win a few hands, Mommy? I don't want them to quit."

Lainie didn't know what to tell him. She knew how

Dexter ached for companions, and so few people could keep up with him. Yet she hated to encourage him to lose on purpose, to do less than his best. She'd have to trust the TITS not to abandon this lonely little boy. "I think they're smart enough to know when you're not playing your hardest, and they might be insulted. I say go for it, Dexter. My guess is that they'll hang in there with you."

"I sure hope so. Because this is very, very fun. Here's Miss Rona. Bye, Mommy. I miss you." He smacked a kiss into the phone.

"Miss you, too." Lainie was telling the truth, but she wasn't sure about Dexter. Between his extreme intelligence and her single-mom status, he'd stayed way too isolated, and she could see that now. She'd find a way to fix it once this mess was over.

"I promise I'm not filling him full of sugar," Rona said. "He can't eat the M&M's, at least not now, when they're the only way he can keep score."

Lainie hesitated. "Rona, is it a problem, that he's winning?"

Rona laughed. "A problem? You should see what a kick we're getting out of watching that little rascal clean up. And it's for M&M's, after all. I think these women are mature enough to lose a few M&M's without getting bent out of shape."

"I'm glad, because he loves playing games, but he has trouble finding people to play with him because he always seems to win."

"But he's so cute about it. I can see you've taught him not to gloat."

The praise felt good. She hadn't had much validation

of her parenting skills. But she didn't think she could take credit for Dexter's attitude. "He figured that one out himself. It's bad enough that he beats everybody, but if he rubbed it in, he'd be even more unpopular."

"He's a great kid, Lainie. Thank you for letting me borrow him for a couple of days."

"But I'm the one who should be thanking—"

"Nope. I'm in my element. All the TITS are loving this. So how are things there?"

Now there was a loaded question. Harry had come out of the bedroom and was checking the lock on the back slider that went into the patio. "Why don't I turn you over to Harry and he can fill you in?" Lainie said.

She walked over and handed the phone to her newly minted bodyguard.

He seemed to mentally brace himself before he put the phone to his ear. "Mom? Yeah, it's been quiet. I talked to Leo."

Lainie walked into the bedroom, not wanting to eavesdrop on his conversation. She wished Rona hadn't been so obvious about her matchmaking attempt. That was another good reason not to have sex with Harry. He should be saving himself for a woman who could actually end up being his wife.

The unit was stiflingly hot, so she located the air-conditioning control on the wall in the bedroom and flipped the switch on high. The blast of air coming through the bedroom vents wasn't very cool yet, but it would probably take a while. She glanced at the bed and noticed that the quilted spread was torn in several places and the stuffing was coming out.

So this unit wasn't kept up as well as the models. Oh,

well. She still longed to stretch out on the bed, torn spread or not. With the air conditioner on, she could make out the low murmur of Harry's voice but not what he was saying. Unfortunately, that low murmur turned her on.

She had no trouble coming up with ways to seduce him. She could strip down and get in the shower, leaving the door open. She could take off her clothes and climb into bed with the sheet draped strategically to showcase her assets. Or she could leave her underwear on and walk into the living room like that.

But she wouldn't engage in any of that behavior. She wondered how much longer Harry would be on the phone, and what the two of them should do once he hung up. Peeking out of the bedroom doorway, she discovered all six feet, three inches of him sprawled on the sofa, his head propped against the back while he talked on the phone. He'd laid his glasses on the coffee table and his eyes were closed.

"Yeah, Leo, I'll be careful," he said. "We'll play it safe, I promise."

She remembered that he'd wanted to check with Leo, so he must have called him after ending the call with his mother. Harry looked like he'd been run over with Dudley's golf cart. He was in no condition to be seduced, even if she hadn't decided to be noble and not do it.

Instead she felt the urge to stroke his forehead and brush back the lock of hair that had fallen out of place. He looked so vulnerable, this straitlaced man who had appointed himself her bodyguard.

"I'll keep you posted, Leo. Bye." Eyes still closed, Harry slowly lowered the phone and stayed where he was, his long legs stretched out, his arms resting slackly at his sides.

He'd probably been awake for more than thirty hours. Squeezing his eyes shut, he started to get up. Then he groaned and flopped back against the sofa.

Lainie stayed very still and watched the rhythm of his breathing change as he drifted toward sleep. Once he tried to rouse himself again, but it was no use. He'd reached his limit.

When she was absolutely sure he was asleep, she went back to grab a pillow from the bed before taking off her shoes and walking over to the sofa. Placing the pillow against the armrest, she got to her knees and started gently taking off Harry's shoes. Although he snuffled softly in his sleep, he didn't wake up as she worked him out of his loafers.

Taking off his shoes was the most intimate thing she'd done with Harry, and she was enjoying it way too much. She'd never pegged herself as having a foot fetish, but once she'd successfully pulled off his shoes, she decided to take his socks off, too. She hadn't seen naked male toes in a long time. Funny what a girl could miss.

Harry, it turned out, had elegant toes. His second toe was longer than his big toe, which she'd heard somewhere indicated a link to the aristocracy. She would believe that of Harry. He had a little bit of dark hair on his toes, just enough to make them look very masculine. His toenails were clipped neatly, which she would have expected.

She wondered if he'd ever had a woman suck on his toes. Some guys loved it and some were too ticklish to enjoy the sensation. She'd learned that stroking a guy's feet could be very stimulating for him, but she might be out of practice with that. She might be out of practice for the whole sexual routine. What a depressing thought, especially now that she was going to forgo the pleasures of the flesh with Harry.

Some said sex was like riding a bicycle and everything would come back once you got started. She was also worried that using the vibrator had conditioned her to the point that she could only have orgasms that way. Some women had that problem, she'd heard. Well, she wouldn't be finding out this trip, sad to say.

As she contemplated Harry, she decided he'd rest better if she could get him horizontal, so she stood and grasped his shoulders. Then she tried to push him toward the pillow. No dice. He felt nice and solid, though. Touching him, feeling the warmth of his skin through the black silk shirt, was making her mouth water.

She pushed a little harder. "C'mon, Harry," she murmured. "Lie down."

He moaned softly in protest and struggled in her grasp.

She stepped back, not wanting to wake him up. She sure would love to unbutton that shirt, but she could find no justification for undressing him some more. He could sleep with his shirt buttoned, no problem.

"Gotta stay . . . awake." His speech was slurred.

As she peered closer, she could see his eyes moving behind his closed lids and knew he must be dreaming about their predicament and talking in his sleep. Poor guy. Even asleep he was worried about protecting her.

But if he stayed like that, he'd end up with a vicious crick in his neck. She decided to try working with the other end of his body. If she lifted his feet and swung them around, maybe he'd be off balance and slide right down to that pillow. Hefting his feet up off the floor took some effort, but when she finally maneuvered them onto the sofa, sure enough, he toppled over onto the pillow.

"Mm." He smiled and snuggled his cheek into the plump surface.

"That's it," she murmured, perching on the edge of the coffee table to gaze down at him. "Get some rest."

He sighed in his sleep.

What a sweet guy, to interrupt his life like this. She reached out to comb his hair back from his forehead. His hair was silky and she allowed herself to keep stroking it, petting him like a puppy. It wasn't only sex she'd missed all these years, but the tiny pleasures like running her fingers through a man's hair and grabbing onto shoulders with some bulk to them. She liked the crisp scent of a man's shaving cream and the deep sound of male laughter. But dating seemed so risky with a little guy as impressionable as Dexter.

Before she started dating again she needed to know that Dexter understood the concept of testing out potential stepdads. He had to realize that her true love might not show up right off the bat. Dexter was smart about a lot of things, but he might have trouble with that program until he was much older.

She finally made herself get up and move away from Harry. He was fine here on the sofa, and she might as well rest, too. They were as safe as she could imagine them to be for now. Maybe she could get a little sleep.

Walking into the bedroom, she pulled off the red wig, took out the hairpins, and massaged her scalp. Much better. Then she shucked her pants and shirt and climbed under the covers. She expected to fall asleep immediately, but instead she started worrying about Joey. He would want to have Dexter in his life for sure, now.

Of course she didn't want Joey to have anything to do with Dexter, but Joey was his father and had legal rights. He might also have access to some money by now—not the billions he was hoping to inherit, but an allowance from the trust fund each of the boys had been promised when they reached thirty. Even with gambling debts, he might have the resources to fight her for custody.

Not only that, she had to consider whether she could rightfully deprive Dexter of being the heir to the Benjamin fortune. But there was Joey, who obviously hadn't changed his drinking habits. Every instinct told her to keep Dexter away from Joey, no matter what the cost. Still, she hadn't planned on the cost being billions of dollars.

Dexter was extremely smart and probably needed private school and special attention to make the most of his brains. With the right education he might invent something important or find a cure for some dreadful disease. She had an obligation to nurture his abilities, but she was financially limited.

The problem seemed to have no solution, and various plans made her thoughts spin like a roulette wheel. Eventually she wore herself out enough to drift toward sleep.

The cutesy tune on Joey's cell phone woke him a little after noon. Swearing, he vowed to change the damned tune ASAP. He didn't like waking up under the best of circumstances, and he couldn't classify his current circumstances as anything but crappy. He should have had his kid and been on his way back to New York by now.

The phone call turned out to be from the PI he'd hired, who had traced Lainie and the kid to a condo in Henderson which belonged to Harry Ambrewster's mother. The PI was pretty sure Lainie had left the kid there with the mother when she'd driven off with Ambrewster, although no one had seen the kid, so the PI wasn't absolutely sure of that.

As Joey heard this news, his mood improved. He couldn't figure why Lainie would take off and leave the kid, but that made life nearly perfect for him. All he had to do was talk some middle-aged broad into letting him take his own son out for an ice-cream cone, and he was in the money.

He'd made a mistake the night before by having a few drinks and letting himself get all riled up about the situation, but he wouldn't make that mistake again. Today he'd stay off the booze, take some Excedrin instead, and concentrate on what he had to do. A lot was at stake, here. His freaking life, in fact, if he didn't get the money to pay his debts. He could have a drink later, after he'd accomplished his mission.

"Want me to keep the condo under surveillance?" the PI asked.

Joey thought of all he was paying this dude and decided on a better plan. "Give me the address and I'll watch the place," he said. "You find out exactly where Lainie is. I need to keep track of her." Then he hung up.

It had occurred to him that life would be much simpler if Lainie didn't exist. Then he'd automatically get the kid and he could make up any story he wanted about

Dexter's mother. Maybe he'd get lucky and she'd meet up with an accident.

Well, why not? After all, Emil's coming-out party had been a huge stroke of luck. All the events since then had been sort of shitty, but he had a feeling that streak was about to end. Today he'd pick up Dexter or know the reason why.

Chapter Twelve

The sound of knocking woke Harry from a very erotic dream that featured Lainie most prominently. He couldn't help noticing as he struggled up from the sofa that something else was prominent as a result of that dream. Damn, he hadn't meant to go to sleep. Geez, it was hot in here. And where was Lainie?

The knocking persisted as he stumbled to his feet—his bare feet, he noticed. Someone had made off with his shoes and socks. He located his glasses on the coffee table and shoved them on before proceeding. Then he set off, erection, sweaty clothes, bare feet and all, hoping no one had kidnapped Lainie while he slept.

Fortunately he spied her right away. Standing in the bedroom doorway, he was relieved to see her sound asleep in bed, cuddling one of the extra pillows to her chest. Much more of that knocking and she was liable to wake up, though. He had a good idea who the knocker was, and if he was right, Dudley was getting a piece of his mind.

Fortunately his erection had gone down a fair amount by the time he checked the peephole in the door. Sure enough, Dudley stood outside, and he was raising his fist to knock some more.

Harry unlocked the door in a flash and swung it open while Dudley was in mid-swing.

Dudley nearly toppled over with the force he'd brought to bear on his knocking effort. But he straightened immediately and grinned at Harry. "Ready to buy that one-bedroom unit yet?"

"You don't want to hear what I'm ready to do with that one-bedroom unit." Harry wasn't usually the type to get upset, but he was ready to take Dudley apart for disturbing their rest, especially Lainie's. "Harassing people is no way to get their business, Dudley."

Dudley stroked his chin, seemingly unfazed. "You might think that's true, but in fact, folks often need constant prodding to do what they know in their hearts is the right thing."

"Let me put it this way." Harry's right temple began to throb. "Leave us alone or I'll be forced to report you to the resort."

Dudley nodded. "I can see you feel right adamant about this."

"You have no idea."

"Tell you what." Dudley leaned forward and tucked a card in Harry's shirt pocket. "Call me later today, when you've made up your mind."

"I have made up my—"

"That's what you think. Go spend some more time with that little lady of yours. And you should turn on the air-conditioning unit, son. It's too hot in there to fan the flames of love." Then Dudley winked and headed down the path.

Harry closed and locked the door. Then he padded back to check on Lainie. She was still asleep, thank God. Walking over to the temperature control on the wall, he discovered the air-conditioning *was* on. Obviously it didn't work. Figured. He glanced at the bedside clock and found out he'd been asleep a couple of hours.

Apparently that was enough for now, because he was wide awake. Gazing at Lainie in that big bed would be enough to keep any guy bright-eyed and bushy-tailed.

From the doorway of the bedroom he glanced back toward the sofa and noticed the pillow she must have put there. The last thing he remembered was disconnecting his cell phone after talking to Leo and then battling to stay awake. Apparently he'd lost the fight.

He pictured Lainie kneeling down to take off his shoes and socks, and he started getting hard again. She'd been undressing him, and he hadn't even known it. Such a thing didn't seem remotely possible.

She'd not only removed his shoes and socks, she'd managed to get him prone on the sofa with a pillow under his head. He sure would have liked to be awake during all of that. Her tenderness toward him inspired more than simple lust. He was slowly coming to realize what a terrific person she was, the kind of woman a man could easily fall for.

He glanced into the bedroom again. She'd folded her clothes and laid them neatly on one of the upholstered chairs next to the window. The wig was history, too. She wore only her underwear. From here he could see one thin bra strap resting against her bare shoulder. The pillow she clutched covered her breasts. Her spectacular breasts. He licked dry lips.

Then he closed his eyes and silently recited the reasons they shouldn't have sex. It couldn't go anywhere. They might find themselves getting emotionally involved, and she had way too much going on in her life to deal with an emotional involvement. Sex between them would only complicate matters in the long run. Oh, but in the short run . . .

No. He wasn't going to weaken. With a shake of his head he pushed himself away from the doorjamb. Now would be an excellent time to bring in their suitcases.

After that he should probably figure out what to do about food. He considered whether they should chance room service, or if the food would be as bad as he thought it might be. Then again, maybe there was no room service, which presented a problem. Leo had recommended staying low until Joey made his next move, so how would they feed themselves?

Harry sat on the sofa to put on his shoes and socks, all the while imagining Lainie taking them off for him. He wondered what she'd been thinking about. Then his mind wandered to topics he had no business contemplating, like wondering what she did about sexual urges. She had to have them. Maybe she resorted to solo sex.

And that was definitely something he had no business contemplating if he intended to keep his hands off her during this trip. And that was the best plan, the logical plan. He wouldn't do either of them any favors by acting on his impulses.

Checking to make sure his car keys were in the pocket of his slacks, he picked up a key from the scarred coffee table. Then he slipped out the door as quietly as possible and blinked in the bright sunlight. The air smelled of cedar and flowers. The rusty-hinge cry of a raven drew his attention to a big black bird soaring overhead. Other than that, everything was quiet. Storm clouds still hung on the horizon, but above him the sky was bright blue.

Fortunately, there was no Dudley. If the guy so much as showed his face again, Harry was going to file a complaint with the resort. He hadn't wanted to get the guy fired, but maybe Dudley deserved to be fired.

On the other hand, filing a complaint might not be such a good move. The more attention Harry brought upon himself, the more likely someone would discover that he was not Fred and Lainie was not Rona. So he couldn't risk reporting Dudley, after all. His threats had been empty ones, but maybe Dudley didn't realize that.

Harry walked toward the car and pushed the button on his key ring that popped the trunk. As he lifted out both overnight bags, he tried to decide what to do if Dudley persisted. A few minutes ago he'd been ready to punch the guy, which wasn't his usual response at all. Physical violence never solved anything. Every person with half a brain knew that.

He put down the suitcases, closed the trunk, and glanced around with the uneasy feeling that someone was watching him. Probably paranoia brought on by talking to Leo. Still, his heart pounded as he picked up the suitcases and walked quickly back to the front door.

The feeling of being watched continued. He surveyed the area one more time and caught himself literally sniffing the air, as if he needed all his senses to protect himself and Lainie. That was ridiculous. What he probably needed was a gun or a can of Mace—something that would disable an attacker. But he'd never used anything like that, so he'd be a danger to himself and Lainie with such equipment.

Finally he put the key in the lock, opened the door, and shoved both suitcases inside. He was inside with the door locked and the security latch on in no time. Embarrassingly, he was breathing hard, and there was probably no reason in the world for that.

He forced himself to close his mouth and breathe through his nose. He ought to settle down and get back in control. But by breathing deeply through his nose, he picked up the scent of Lainie's perfume. It rose over the musty smell of the carpet and the stale odors in the kitchen to sing him a siren's song. He fought the urge to walk straight into the bedroom and strip off his clothes.

Ironically, having fast and furious sex seemed like the logical thing to do, because they were in a crisis, and people always had sex when they were trying to release the tension from a crisis. He'd seen it a million times on TV, but he'd never experienced the feeling firsthand. Suddenly he was convinced that he should live for the moment, because he might not have many moments left.

He shook his head and laughed. Talk about melodramatic. Leo would get a real kick out of knowing he'd scared the shit out of his favorite accountant. Leo loved to shake up Harry's careful existence.

Come to think of it, maybe Leo had overemphasized the danger, just to put Harry on the hot seat. Or maybe not. A guy with Joey's temperament who was in trouble with bad guys and had his sights set on inheriting a billion-dollar business was capable of anything. No matter how often Harry told himself nothing was going to happen, the size of Joey's debt and the scope of that inheritance changed the game.

So he and Lainie would be careful. Right now he was sweaty and grungy. He could do with a cool shower and a shave. He'd feel much more like facing whatever was coming their way after getting cleaned up. With luck his mom had tucked some shaving supplies in the suitcase she'd packed for him. One way to find out. He swung it up on the sofa and reached for the zipper.

The overnight case belonged to Leo—he could tell by the smooth black leather. No cheap fabric for Leo, who liked to travel first class. Inside the suitcase was another change of clothes and a small black leather case.

Harry zipped it open, knowing he wouldn't be so fortunate as to find an electric razor like the one he normally used. Sure enough, the case contained an old-fashioned shaving mug, a brush, and a metal razor that took disposable blades. Who used stuff like this anymore? A guy like Leo, obviously.

Rona had thrown in a travel size of shaving lotion and some stick deodorant. She wouldn't want him to be either prickly or smelly during this trip, which she hoped would net her a daughter-in-law. Harry's conscience pricked him. Of course his mom wanted more family around her, and Harry was her only hope of getting that. He'd let her down on that score.

Picking up the small leather case, he walked through the bedroom into the bathroom. On the way he couldn't help glancing in Lainie's direction. He shouldn't have.

She'd abandoned the pillow she'd been clutching to her chest, turned over on her back and tossed the sheet aside, no doubt because of the heat. Harry gulped. The fit of that white lacy bra wasn't any more revealing than one of her costumes, but knowing it was underwear seemed to make a huge difference to his fevered brain.

He stood as if nailed to the carpet, his attention riveted on the generous swell of her breasts barely contained by the scalloped edge of the bra. She was a woman with cleavage to burn, even lying on her back. Oh, to bury his face between those soft breasts and . . .

She moaned in her sleep and turned on her side. That moan went right through him, bringing his penis to life as he imagined hearing her moan for a different reason, because he was caressing her and bringing her to a climax. He clenched his jaw. Then, calling on his famous control, he walked into the bathroom and quietly shut the door. He'd have to handle temptation one moment at a time and hope he'd be strong enough.

Inside the bathroom he set the black case on the counter and turned on the water. The pipes creaked and groaned. He winced, afraid the noise would wake Lainie, after all, but it was too late. The groaning stopped, and he got out Leo's shaving supplies. Funny how using a mug and brush made Harry feel more manly. He'd always gone for the efficiency of a portable electric razor, figuring this lather-and-blade method was too much trouble.

He took out the razor, a heavy thing with a pearlized handle. His fingers dislodged something, something that felt remarkably like . . . uh-oh. Peering into the case, he realized that what he'd thought was some sort of plastic liner to protect the leather was actually a layer of black condom packets.

Water splashed into the sink unnoticed as he stared at

the stash of little raincoats. In all his X-rated thoughts about Lainie, it had never once occurred to him that they'd be hampered by a lack of this exact item. That was a testament to his level of distraction and fatigue, because he *always* remembered condoms. He was diligent about safe sex.

A lack of condoms would have been one more thing to keep him in check, because he couldn't imagine going out to actually buy the things during this trip. Had he even made the mistake of starting something with Lainie, at some point in his lust he would have remembered that they had no protection. Then all activity would have come to a screeching halt. Or maybe not. There were alternates to penetration.

Ah, geez. Were there ever alternates. And now he was focusing on those, too. He was in hell, is where he was—trapped for two days with the sexiest woman alive coupled with his own puritanical conscience. And . . . he pawed through the bag and counted . . . eight condoms. Yep. Hell.

The sound of a shower running filtered gradually through Lainie's sleepy haze. It had been five long years since she'd listened to someone else take a shower. She was the only shower-taker in her apartment. Dexter still liked baths.

So Harry was in the shower. And she was hot and sticky, because the air-conditioning was not working. She would love to be in the shower, too. With Harry. But she'd told herself that was a bad idea. However, Harry was naked in the shower. How strong could anyone expect a woman to be, when she'd gone without sex for five long years?

Okay, what if she announced to him that she only wanted one meaningless sexual experience? She could assure him that she had no permanent designs on him, but that she needed one male-induced orgasm or she'd go crazy. It seemed like a reasonable request.

Now was the time to ask, when he was already naked. Then there would be no awkward undressing scene, no chance for second thoughts. One quick orgasm, that's all she needed. Then she'd leave him alone for the rest of the trip.

True, she had no condoms, but surely he could figure out how to give her an orgasm without condoms. And she'd do the same for him. That was only fair.

So it was decided. One little orgasm wouldn't matter so much, would it? After that she'd be a good girl. Leaving the damp bed, she unhooked her bra and tossed it on her pile of clothes. Then she stepped out of her panties and walked toward the closed bathroom door. As she opened it, the sound of a washcloth slapping against bare skin stopped.

The shower curtain tucked inside the rim of the bathtub was opaque, darn it. She would have loved a sneak preview through a clear one. Even so, her imagination painted a vivid picture of Harry standing on the other side of that curtain, water dripping off his . . . everything.

"Who's there?" His voice rose in alarm.

She wanted to seduce him, not scare him to death. "Just me," she said.

"Oh." Long pause. "I, uh, thought I'd take a shower." He sounded very, very nervous.

"I think that's a great idea. It's hot, and some cool water would feel wonderful." She stepped over to the tub.

"I'm almost done. In fact, I've been in here long enough. If you want to have the bathroom next, I'll be out in no time. No time at all. And we need to find out what's wrong with the air conditioner." He was definitely in panic mode.

Five years was too long to go without sex. Oral sex wasn't the whole program, but she could make do with that for the time being. She reached for the shower curtain.

"Lainie? Are you still out there? Listen, I was thinking we need to figure out what to do about eating."

"Let me give you a suggestion." She pulled aside the curtain. Oh, yeah. This would be excellent.

She'd never seen him without his glasses, and he seemed a lot more rugged without them. He looked pretty good without clothes, too, as he stood there with water sluicing off every naked inch of him. All that wonderful equipment was just waiting for her to enjoy.

Harry didn't have the muscle definition of a jock, but he had great shoulders and a nice chest covered with just the right amount of dark hair to make him look very male and very yummy. As the spray from the shower pattered all around her, dampening her skin and making her nipples tighten even more, she pondered her next move.

As for Harry, he wasn't moving at all. He clutched a washcloth in one hand and a bar of soap in the other while he stared at her with a shell-shocked expression. If she hadn't been so sexually excited, she might have laughed. His frozen stance looked like a risqué addition to Madame Tussaud's Wax Museum. He could be titled *Man in Shower*.

Then a part of him moved, the part that interested her the most right now. If she got the attention of that certain part, they were in business. Sure enough, in no time that area of his anatomy was fully deployed and ready for action. Now he could be titled *Aroused Man in Shower.*

He must have been squeezing the bar of soap really hard, though, because suddenly it squirted out of his hand and smacked against the wall of the tub enclosure. They both jumped at the loud noise.

Then they spoke at once.

"Lainie, I—"

"Harry, I want—"

He gulped and spoke again. "I'm not sure this is a good idea."

She glanced down at his rigid penis. "Then you'd better have a talk with your buddy."

"Any man who opened a shower curtain and found you naked on the other side would have this reaction." His chest rose and fell with his rapid breathing.

She gazed into his eyes. "I have two things to say to you. First of all, I don't want a relationship, so don't worry about repercussions. I want one meaningless orgasm. Just one. Then we'll go back to our regularly scheduled program. Second of all, it's been five years since any man has seen me naked and vice-versa. I'm a sex-starved woman."

His gaze locked with hers and his throat moved in a slow swallow. "I . . . I see."

"I hope so. You'll love this, Harry. And so will I." She reached out and wrapped her fingers around his thick penis, using it as a grab-bar. "I'm coming in, ready or not. But I think you're more than ready."

She had that right. He'd been hovering on the edge of readiness for weeks and had stepped over the line into complete readiness several times in the past few hours. When she grabbed hold of him and lifted one long leg over the edge of the tub, he surrendered with a groan.

The washcloth dropped with a splat into the water swirling over the bottom of the tub as he reached for her. He needed both hands free, one to cup her head and one to explore all the magical territory he'd dreamed of every time he'd watched her dance. Her breasts alone were enough to keep him occupied for a very long time. Fingers splayed, he reverently curved his hand over one generous breast as the blood surged through his body in a tsunami wave of lust.

She still had a firm hold of his penis as he backed her against the wet marble and gazed down at her flushed face. He could barely believe that he was about to satisfy every craving he'd had, starting with kissing those full lips. But she'd have to let go of him or he wouldn't make it through even a kiss without coming.

"Turn me loose," he murmured, his voice thick and a little shaky with anticipation. "I promise I'm not going anywhere."

"But I love the feel of you." She rubbed her thumb along the underside of his shaft. "It's been so long."

"Then maybe you've forgotten what's liable to happen if you keep that up."

"No." Her smile was one-hundred-proof seduction. "I haven't forgotten." She began to stroke him more firmly.

He closed his eyes as an orgasm rushed closer. "Lainie, stop." Reaching down, he held her wrist. "Or I'll come."

"Maybe I want that. Maybe I want to make you lose control."

He tightened his grip on her wrist. "No, not yet. You're the one who's gone five years without sex. And besides, the man's supposed to satisfy the woman first, so you need to let me—"

"No, you let me." She tugged his head down and brushed her mouth against his, teasingly. "Here's the deal. I know for a fact that if you let go now, you'll be able to spend more time on me. I'm being selfish, actually."

Before his brain completely left the building, he checked out her premise and found it worthy.

"Kiss me, Harry. Kiss me while I make you come."

So that's how their first kiss turned out. He let go of her wrist, let go of his expectations of himself and let go of his control. Bracing both hands on the marble behind her head, he lowered his mouth to hers.

She kissed him hard, and he kissed her back just as hard, thrusting his tongue inside as she gave him the most amazing hand job of his life. This wouldn't be an episode where he polished his reputation as a guy who could outlast anyone. But, ah, hell, who cared? What she was doing to him was beyond fantastic.

Maybe later on he'd be embarrassed by how easily she'd worked him up, but for the moment he was having a terrific time kissing her and abandoning himself to this headlong rush to an orgasm. Then he was there, and he had to stop kissing her so he could gasp for breath between groans of ecstasy.

He came so hard his ears buzzed, but that didn't block out her soft laugh of delight.

"Wonderful," she said. "Just wonderful. Oh, Harry, I'm having so much fun."

He couldn't speak for her, but he was already having more fun than should be legal. She'd asked for one meaningless orgasm, but he doubted he could stop with just one. Not when he had a shaving kit full of eight condoms.

Chapter Thirteen

Lainie hadn't planned her seduction quite that way, but once she'd laid her hands on Harry's stiff penis, she'd felt compelled to see what she could do with it. Maybe she'd been challenged to break through Harry's straight-arrow persona and find the wild man she sensed lurking under all that buttoned-down behavior.

Mission accomplished, at least for this little space of time in the cool water streaming out of the shower. He remained with his hands braced on the marble behind her head and his eyes squeezed shut as he fought for breath. She wondered if he knew how vulnerable he looked. In the aftermath of an orgasm that had left him trembling, he probably didn't even care.

But it was a defining moment for her, because she was seeing a side of him that she guessed not many people did. It was a side that she could get quite fond of, and that could be dangerous. She couldn't get too fond of Harry.

He opened his eyes, blinked and shook his head. "Wow."

"You liked that?"

"Oh, yeah." His gaze traveled down her body. "But it looks like I baptized you in the process." He seemed almost proud of the fact.

She smiled, thinking how cute he was after a climax. "Fortunately we're standing in the shower."

"So we are." Pushing away from the wall, he turned, stepped into the spray, and snagged the washcloth where it lay on the floor of the tub.

When he returned to her, his hair was plastered to his head and water dripped from his eyelashes. "We should call the Guinness Book of World Records. This could end up being the longest shower in history."

And she didn't want him feeling guilty about that later. She wasn't sure where he stood on the ecology issue of it all. "Want to shut off the water?"

"No." He stroked the wet washcloth over her breasts. "Some things are more important than water conservation."

She had to agree. No man had ever sponged her down before, and she wanted him to have all the water he needed for the job. The cotton terry moving over her nipples had never had that effect when she was using a washcloth. Then again, she'd never lingered over the process. And Harry was a man with a surprising talent for lingering, given how efficient he was normally.

"Your skin turns rosy pink when I do this." He re-wet the washcloth in the cool spray and rubbed lazy circles over her breasts and tummy, paying special attention to her nipples.

She sighed at the unaccustomed pleasure of being caressed. "I have . . . sensitive skin." How she'd lived for five years without a man's touch, she'd never know. This was pure heaven.

"Am I being too rough?"

"No . . . oh, no." She closed her eyes and leaned her head back against the marble. "I—I love it," she admitted.

"I thought so. Every once in a while you make this little hum deep in your throat."

She hadn't even been aware of doing it. Eyes still closed, she focused on the texture of the washcloth moving over her skin. Then an even better tactile sensation joined the caress of the cotton terry. He began following the path of the washcloth with his tongue. When he reached her nipple, he paused to suck on it for a while.

Yes. In the years since she'd experienced this, she'd forgotten the incredible sensation that suction could produce, how it could zing straight down between her legs and nudge her closer to a climax. As if reading her mind, he moved the washcloth between her thighs.

The first stroke of the wet cloth made her gasp and open her eyes. She'd nearly come with that single touch. She was on fire. With a soft groan he dropped the washcloth and sank to his knees in front of her. With the last bit of her restraint she managed not to beg him to hurry.

Water pelted his head and shoulders as he hunched down and leaned in. Then he settled his mouth right where she wanted it, and in seconds she arched against him, crying out in ecstasy as wave upon wave tore through her grateful body. At last. At long last a man's tongue had replaced a vibrator as her source of pleasure.

Even more wonderful, the man in question knew instinctively what to do with his tongue. As she started sinking back to earth, Harry zeroed in and took her up again. She clutched his head and called out his name, delighted more than he could know that her bodyguard seemed to have a gift for oral sex.

After presenting her with a second glorious climax, he rose from his knees and kissed her full on the mouth. She wrapped her arms around his slick shoulders and clung to him, dizzy with appreciation. That's when she became aware that he was sporting another powerful erection. Apparently the orgasmic urge was catching.

He lifted his mouth from hers and gasped for air. "Time to move to dry land."

She'd meant to end with one climax apiece, but he'd actually given her two, so how could she leave him in this condition? Her body vibrated with aftershocks, and she felt a real obligation to return the favor. She watched him turn around and shut off the water, and this time she had the presence of mind to admire his butt. Great butt.

Apparently he had to come back for some more mouth-to-mouth before he could go on with whatever plan he had. Once again he pressed her up against the marble wall and kissed her like there was no tomorrow.

"I thought . . . you wanted to get out," she managed to say when they came up for air.

"I do." He cupped her breasts in both hands and squeezed as he nipped at her earlobe. "But I can't seem to stop touching you. One look at you and I have to have more. And more, and more. Mm." He leaned down and sucked on her breast.

She was in pleasure overload, but surely his package needed relief. She began to fondle him, thinking that this time she'd treat him to a blow job. "I want to give you—"

"I have a plan," he murmured against her breast. With a groan he released her. "I have to stop kissing you or I'll never . . . okay . . . stay there . . ." He stepped out of the tub and skidded on the wet floor as he hurried toward the sink.

"Harry! Be careful!" Deciding the tub situation was becoming way too dangerous, she climbed out and grabbed a towel. It was skimpy, but it would have to do. She threw it on the wet floor so neither one of them would fall. Besides, the towel would cushion her knees while she took care of that big ol' erection of his. She sank down on her heels, preparing to coax him to come over and let her make him happy.

But as she glanced up, she noticed that he'd grabbed the small black case that had been sitting on the bathroom floor. He dumped the contents, which bounced off the counter. And just like that, black condom packets littered the white tile floor.

He didn't give her time to think about that strange turn of events, because he was already ripping a packet open and rolling a condom over his penis, which redirected her thoughts to the obvious conclusion that she was about to have a complete sexual experience. They could make each other happy simultaneously, and that was worth waiting for.

She started to get up from the floor. "The bed?"

"Right here." His voice rasped with need.

Then right here it would be. She wasn't particular. So what if her head was on the hard tile and the towel was already soggy from all the water they'd sprayed on the floor? She had Harry fully aroused and fully protected, and life didn't get much better than that.

Once she was horizontal he got to his knees and moved in, parting her thighs and bracing his hands on either side of her, gazing down with enough heat to melt the polar ice cap. He was breathing hard. "I've never done it on a bathroom floor." Then, with one push he was inside her.

She'd never done it on a bathroom floor, either, and it might not have been her first choice. But she would have risked a bed of nails to experience this—the slide of a warm, thick penis deep into her vagina. Oh, yes. And when it came to using his equipment, Harry had instincts that she'd bet he wasn't even aware of.

There was nothing calculated, nothing mechanical about his strokes. For all his desperation to get inside, once he was there he tuned in and created a rhythm that was all about her needs. This kind of empathy couldn't be taught.

She blossomed beneath him, gripping him so she could feel the muscles moving in his butt. Each thrust was a miracle of sensual delight as he took his cue from her eyes, her breathing, her little cries of delight.

She loved the wild abandon of dancing, but this . . . this had dancing beat by a country mile. And here came another orgasm, riding in on the shaft of his penis. Delirious with joy, she made the tiny space ring with her cries.

Only then did Harry's rhythm change. As he increased the pace, she knew he'd returned the focus to himself, but for all that time until she came, he'd concentrated on her. What a guy. And he deserved a rousing finale to such a great performance.

Lifting her hips, she met each stroke with an answering swivel. He groaned and pumped faster. She kept the action going, calling on her dance training to give him the ride of his life.

He began to pant, and his eyes glazed over. They moved faster, and faster yet. When he came, his roar of satisfaction told her all she needed to know. She'd pleased him a great deal. And pleasing Harry was a worthy goal.

Joey parked his rental car in front of the condo address the PI had given him. Nice place, but nothing spectacular. He'd done the right thing getting the medium-priced bouquet of mixed blooms at the grocery store instead of paying florist prices. If he'd been trying to butter up his own mother instead of Harry Ambrewster's, he'd be looking at first-cut roses in a gold box, with a price tag to match.

Too bad his mother didn't run the Benjamin, Inc., operation instead of his father. Joey could always get around her, but Doyle Benjamin was another story. Still, if Joey showed up with a four-year-old son and could put the right spin on how he happened to have said son, Doyle might be so excited about a male heir that all Joey's previous transgressions would be forgotten.

Once that happened, Joey would go through his mother to get the necessary cash to pay off his debts. He had one more week to deliver the money. If he didn't come up with it by then . . . He didn't want to think about what they'd do to him.

Popping a breath mint into his mouth, Joey picked up the bouquet and climbed out of the car. He missed his Vette and had thought about renting something more exciting than an Escort, but he'd finally decided against spending the money. Someday he'd be able to stop nickel-and-diming every situation, but first he had to get Dexter on board.

He crunched down on the breath mint so he'd be finished with it by the time he got to the front door. He wanted his speech to be clear and his manner pleasant. Her name was Rona. He needed to remember that and call her by her first name. And smile. Hell, he could do this.

Even so, his palms were sweaty by the time he rang the doorbell. So much was riding on him getting his kid back, and he wasn't even positive Dexter was inside this condo. But if he was, then Joey was taking him out, today. Enough of this Vegas trip.

The woman who came to the door looked damned good for someone in her fifties. If Joey had met her in a bar, he might have considered hitting on her. His mother didn't look that perky, but then, she had to live with Doyle.

"Rona Ambrewster?" Joey said, giving her his charm-the-birds-from-the-trees grin. "I understand you're baby-sitting my son, and I brought these as a gesture of my appreciation." He held out the flowers and waited for her to smile back. Women usually smiled back at him.

This one didn't. "I don't know what you're talking about," she said.

Noises came from inside the house. First he heard women laughing and the clink of ice in glasses, which reminded him he could sure use a drink. Then . . . bingo. He identified the high-pitched voice of a little kid. Could easily be Dexter, although after six months, Joey wasn't confident he could recognize Dexter's voice. Little kids all sounded the same, anyway.

He had to believe Dexter was in there. He cleared his

throat and reapplied his smile. "Look, Rona, you've probably been told that I'm a terrible guy. I have to admit that I was out of line last night."

Her eyes were cold and unwelcoming, not a good sign. "I'm afraid you have the wrong house," she said.

"Rona, I love that little guy. I've been going crazy wondering where Lainie had taken him. I finally found out, and now I want to see my son. Surely you understand that, a father's love for his only son."

"There's no child here," she said, cool as a cucumber, even as childish giggles coming from the back of the house made a liar out of her.

"I know he's here, Rona." Joey's smile became harder to maintain. "I want to see my son. A son needs a father's influence."

Rona's gaze flicked over Joey's shoulder, and at last she smiled. "Hey, there. I wondered when you two might decide to pay me a visit."

Joey turned to find out who she was talking to and nearly bumped into a couple of guys wearing casual clothes and mirrored shades. They had the build of men who worked out . . . a lot. Fear knotted in his gut. He had another week, damn it. They couldn't come and get him when he had another week.

He glanced around, hoping to spot a workman's truck of some sort, which would mean Rona was having some work done today. Instead a black sedan was parked behind his rental car.

This didn't look good.

"Hey, Rona," the blond guy on the left said. "We just waited to see if maybe you were getting a flower delivery from Leo."

"Yeah," said the guy on the right, whose look included a shaved head and an earring. "But on closer inspection we can see this isn't the type of flower arrangement Leo orders. He favors the pricier stuff."

"Exactly," Rona said. "This gentleman has the impression that I'm babysitting for a little boy. I've informed him that I'm not."

Under different circumstances Joey would have flat-out accused her of lying, but the way these two goons were scowling at him, he might not want to do that. He just prayed they weren't connected with the Atlantic City crowd. "Maybe I was mistaken about the kid," he said.

"Obviously," said the guy with the shaved head. "And we have rules against soliciting in this neighborhood, so we'd like to ask you to move along."

Some neighborhood association this is. But he couldn't exactly rush into the house and drag Dexter out, not with these two incredible hulks blocking access to his car. The more they talked, though, the more he became convinced they weren't with the Atlantic City crowd, which was a relief. "Okay, I'll leave," he said. Damn it to hell, now what?

The two guys left a space between them so he could squeeze past, but just barely.

"I'd advise you not to frequent the area," said the blonde.

"Right, right. I get the message." Joey was becoming royally pissed. Dexter was in there. He'd bet the keys to his Vette on it. And for some reason, the place was guarded like the Pentagon.

Normal people didn't have bouncers lurking around, so what was up with Rona Ambrewster that she did? Just his luck, too. Any ordinary middle-aged broad would have taken his flowers and invited him in.

He got into his car and threw the flowers on the passenger seat. As he started the motor, he glanced out the window to see if the musclemen were still watching. They were, both of them standing there with their arms folded and their legs spread like they were in a James Bond movie. Rona's door was closed.

Grinding his teeth, Joey drove away, resisting the urge to gun the motor. With his cheap bouquet and cheap rental car he probably looked like a loser to those guys. But they didn't know who they were dealing with.

He'd work this out, and he'd have the last laugh or know the reason why. There had to be a way to get to the kid. Too much depended on the outcome. He couldn't give up.

So that's what it was like to have sex with a dancer. As Harry's brain gradually began to function again with the return of normal blood flow, that was his first thought. He'd imagined sex with Lainie would be spectacular, but he hadn't figured on dance moves as part of the experience. He should have, but he hadn't.

Now as they lay sprawled on a surface that wasn't designed for comfort, he wondered how amazing Lainie would be in an actual bed. All this time he'd thought sex with her would be great, but something he could forgo, considering the big picture. He'd been operating from limited information and had come to an entirely faulty conclusion. Sex with Lainie had suddenly become the big picture, the little picture, the only picture. Giving it up would take all the will power he had.

She stroked his back and sighed. "Thank you, Harry. A million thanks. I'd forgotten how wonderful that felt."

His cheek rested against her shoulder, and he knew he needed to get up from this definitely uncomfortable position, but for a minute longer he'd ignore the ache in his knees. "You're welcome," he said. "You were . . . terrific."

He couldn't say he'd forgotten how wonderful sex felt. He'd forgotten nothing, but he had a whole new point of reference. There was sex, and there was sex with Lainie. Totally different categories.

"I meant what I said, about not wanting anything more than this," she said.

"You mean we're done, now?" Suddenly that sounded like the worst news he'd ever heard.

"Well, I got the impression you thought it was a mistake to get involved with me, so if we don't do this anymore, we won't be involved. Not really."

"Lainie, I don't think I can stay with you in this timeshare and not do this some more."

"Oh. I'm sorry."

"Don't be sorry. I'm not." Maybe later on, when his brain wasn't saturated with hormones, he'd remember to be sorry. But not now.

"So you think we could have more sex, with the understanding that what happens here stays here?"

"I think we can do that. I can't imagine you want a relationship right now."

"Of course not," she said quickly. "I'm just thrilled to take a break from celibacy, even for a couple of days."

"Then it's settled."

"Right. All settled. And thank you, Harry."

"No problem." Man, was he ever a generous guy, sacrificing himself for the cause.

"Exactly, because I promise I won't be a problem, at least not any more than I've already been."

He lifted his head to gaze into her eyes. "You're not a problem. You just gave me the most memorable sex of my life." He hadn't meant to say that, but he couldn't have her thinking she was a burden to him. Far from it.

"Yeah?" She smiled. "That's good to hear."

That smile burrowed right past his defenses and grabbed hold of his heart. As if he didn't have enough to deal with, knowing how good the sex was, now he also was starting to like her. Really, really like her. And the trip was only a few hours old.

Chapter Fourteen

Having sex in the bathroom had certainly broken the ice, Lainie discovered. With luck it hadn't also broken her tailbone. But as Harry helped her to her feet, all her parts seemed to be intact, and one particular part was totally rejuvenated thanks to Harry.

Harry. He looked so mussed and adorable, with his hair standing out in all directions and a pleased little grin on his face every time he glanced her way. Even more darling, he'd reached for the glasses that he'd left on the bathroom counter. Once he put them on he looked like a naked mad scientist. Too cute.

"I don't know about you, but I'm starving," he said.

"Me, too. Now I remember that I'm always famished after sex. Food seems to taste twice as good."

"We should probably find out if this place has room service." He headed out of the bathroom and into the living room.

Uh-oh. In most cases, room service equaled big bucks,

and she didn't have a lot of money to burn. "Um, that's probably too elaborate. Too much food."

He turned back to her. "I thought you were famished?"

"Maybe not so much. Look, you could leave me here and find a fast-food place. A hamburger would suit me fine, so—"

"Is this about the money?"

She gazed at him, unable to lie. "Yes, it's about the money."

"That's all I needed to know." He started back into the living room. "If there's a menu around here someplace, we'll order something. I'm not leaving you alone to go off and buy food."

"Then we can both go. I'll put on my wig."

He shook his head. "Leo told us to lie low for a while, which I interpret as staying right here. You have to stop worrying about the money, Lainie. The room's free, and I can afford room service. The only question is whether they even have it."

"I know you can afford it, but I hate sponging off anyone."

He glanced over at her and grinned. "Now there's an interesting choice of words. Reminds me of certain activities in the shower."

A flush warmed her skin. "That's exactly the point. You've generously agreed to have sex with me while we're here, so for me to cost you money, besides, is . . . what's so funny?"

"You." He crossed back to her and drew her into his arms. " 'Generously agreed to have sex,' indeed. As if this were a sacrifice on my part."

She began to feel better. As if she could feel bad, cuddling skin-to-skin with Harry. If she could just get past her pride, lying low and ordering room service also meant they wouldn't ever be far from a bed.

Harry might be thinking that same thing. She could feel his penis stirring, and it was nice to know that a simple cuddle could have that effect.

"Seriously, Lainie. Any guy would give his eyeteeth to be in my shoes right now."

She smiled up at him. "You're not wearing shoes."

"So I noticed." He cupped her bottom in both hands and squeezed gently. "And neither are you, Lady Godiva. We'll have to put on some clothes, which is the downside of this room service plan. I love having you naked, plus that air conditioner is definitely not working right."

"Without clothes, it's not so bad."

"Without clothes, I could forget all about the air-conditioner problem."

"But we need food." She had to think about Harry's welfare. He was a big guy. They'd finished off the sandwiches and coffee on the way to Sedona, and since then he'd had nothing but coffee and a bagel. She wouldn't want him to get weak. Reluctantly, she stepped out of his arms. "I'll go put on my clothes and my wig. They're in the bedroom."

"And I'll stay right out here, instead of following you into the bedroom."

"Okay." As she backed away from him, she couldn't help laughing from pure happiness. How cool to be wallowing in mutual lust.

"Oh, I almost forgot," he said. "I brought your suitcase in, if you want anything out of it."

She glanced toward the door and saw the suitcase Rona had packed sitting there. "Oh, right. The one that contains the red nightgown." She walked over to the rolling bag and grabbed the handle.

"Don't put on that nightgown."

She winked at him as she pulled the suitcase toward the bedroom. "Later."

"Overkill."

Flashing him another smile, she rolled the suitcase through the bedroom doorway. What a marvelous invention sex was. She felt like a million bucks.

Ten minutes later she came out of the bedroom wearing a pair of shorts and halter top and met Harry walking out of the bathroom where he'd obviously been combing his hair.

He'd put on dark slacks and a black T-shirt. He gave her a quick once-over. "Marginally better."

"Same goes for you. You should wear black T-shirts more often. It makes you look really hot."

"I am really hot. It's got to be ninety-five in here."

"No, I meant hot as in 'studly.' "

He blushed. "I'm not the kind of guy who's designed to look that kind of hot."

"Who says?"

"I do. Black T-shirts belong on mysterious types like Leo, or tortured musicians or buff guys who lift weights three times a week. I'm an accountant."

"And I say you look great in a black T-shirt. Why can't an accountant be a hottie?"

"Maybe some accountants can, but I'm just an ordinary—"

"Not even." She walked over and gave him a quick

kiss. "Let's order lunch, and we'll ask them about the air conditioner. Did you find a menu?"

"Yeah. It's on the desk, and we might be better off with fast food. The trouble is, I don't think we should leave right now."

"Oh, how bad can it be?" She walked over and picked up a laminated sheet of paper with a couple of cigarette burns on it. Then she started to laugh. "I think they go out and buy fast food to fill these orders. The menu sounds like what Dexter and I see every time we go get a burger."

Harry sighed. "You're probably right. And I guess we're stuck with it."

"Fine by me. Maybe we can even order a toy for Dexter. He'd love that. Right now he's collecting— Hey, our message light's blinking." Her initial stab of alarm disappeared almost immediately. "But it can't be too important. Anyone we know would have called your cell phone."

"Which means it's Dudley."

"Probably. I didn't hear it ring, though." She thought about what they'd been doing that had made it impossible to hear the phone.

"Me, either. But I'll bet it's Dudley. While you were asleep he came by."

"Now there's a surprise. What did you say?"

"I wasn't very nice, but that doesn't mean I got rid of him for good." Harry crossed to the phone and punched the message-retrieval number. Then he listened to the message and grimaced. "It's Dudley." He paused. "Dudley wants to know if the magic of the place has worked for us, yet."

She felt the space between them vibrate and wondered if they'd take time for lunch, after all. "It's worked for me," she said.

"Me, too." He continued to stare at her.

"Food, Harry. We need to concentrate on food. We don't want to end up getting sick because we didn't eat." Four years of being a mother had made her more sensible in some ways.

"You're right. Pick something for both of us. I don't care." Glancing back at the phone, he punched the button to erase the message. "Got a selection?"

"Two cheeseburgers with fries sound okay?"

"Why not? What do you want to drink?"

"There's a coffeepot and coffee in the kitchen. We can brew that. It might taste better than what we order from this so-called room service."

"Good thinking." He punched another number and gave their order. "And this may sound strange," he added, "but does a kid's toy come with that? It does? Then we'd like one to take back to . . . our son."

Lainie thought he was the sweetest man, to remember to ask about the toy. In the process he'd confirmed they were getting fast-food burgers, which was what she was used to, anyway.

"Oh, and the air-conditioning unit doesn't seem to be working," Harry said. "I wonder if you could send somebody to check on it." He paused. "Who? Oh, that's okay. Actually, it's starting to get cool. Never mind. We're fine. Just the food is all we need. Thanks. Bye."

Lainie looked at him in confusion. "You think it's getting cooler in here?"

"No, but the person who took our order sounded a lot like Thalia, who checked us in, and she was about to send Dudley to repair the air-conditioning."

"Good grief!" She stared at Harry. "You don't suppose that there are only two people running this operation, Thalia and Dudley?"

"I sure as hell hope not, because that means there's a fifty-fifty chance that Dudley will be bringing our burgers."

Lainie started to laugh. "I don't think you'll be recommending this time-share to your mother."

"No kidding. Can't you see Leo here? He's used to five-star treatment."

"There's some consolation. At least we saved them a trip. Guess I'll go brew us some coffee."

"Okay. While you're doing that, I'll—answer my cell phone," he said as it rang, interrupting him.

Lainie went to make coffee, because the sound of the cell phone sent a wave of anxiety rolling through her and she didn't want Harry to know how worried she was. What if Joey had found a way around Leo's security and snatched her son? She'd make Harry break all the speed limits getting back to Vegas.

Moments later, Harry came to join her in the minuscule kitchen area. "Dexter's fine," he said.

She pushed the switch to start the coffee brewing and turned to him. "I'm sure he is."

"No you're not. You were standing at the counter with your shoulders hunched like you expected bad news. So that's why I told you about Dexter first. He's fine, still with my mom, still being corrupted by the TITS. Last Leo heard they were teaching him dance routines."

"Oh." She pictured that and smiled. "Just like they did with you."

"I could have predicted it. Anyway, he's fine."

"And they're welcome to teach him all the dance routines they want." Her heart felt a hundred pounds lighter. "Thank you, Harry. You're right. Every time the phone rings, I think terrible thoughts." She had the urge to go over and kiss him, but that could lead to things they'd decided to postpone, so she managed to contain herself.

"Apparently Joey's hired a PI, though, because Joey showed up at Mom's house early this afternoon, and he would have needed a detective to figure out where—"

"Omigod." She clutched her stomach. "He went there? We have to move Dexter. We need to tell Leo that—"

"Joey got nowhere." Harry crossed to her and put his hands on her shoulders. "It's okay. Leo's guys were watching the whole time, and when they thought it was necessary, they moved in and warned Joey to leave and not come back."

"But he will come back, won't he?" Panic clawed at her. "He'll try something else, maybe break in during the night. We need to call Leo. We need to go back to Vegas, if Joey's found out where Dexter is. I have to keep Joey from getting to him."

"Lainie, it's okay." His grip tightened. "I know you haven't known Leo very long, but I have. For years the guy has made sure that Rona is never in any danger from break-ins, and now that she's keeping Dexter, the surveillance is heavier than ever. She's got a top-of-the-line alarm system, but even that's not as effective as Leo's guys keeping a twenty-four-hour watch, which they're doing."

She looked into his eyes and willed herself to calm down and think rationally. "Except for a babysitter I've hired for the evenings, I've never trusted Dexter's welfare to anyone. It's really tough to stay here when Joey's after him. I feel like I need to be there to protect him."

"I know." He massaged her shoulders. "I'm sure that's a natural reaction, but I'd stake my life on Leo and his guys. They're not going to let anybody into that town house who doesn't belong there."

She had to believe that or go crazy, but she still didn't like the idea of being separated from Dexter now that Joey had found out his whereabouts. "But I wonder if I should have stayed there, too."

"No offense, but you're wound pretty tight right now, and I think Dexter would pick up on it."

She nodded, knowing it was true. "You're right, and I don't want to scare him, but—"

"Then stay down here until you have a plan. Or do you have a plan?"

"Uh, well, sort of . . . no."

"Then we can talk about it. Maybe if we toss some ideas around, we'll come up with some kind of direction."

Instead of agreeing, she glanced away. For all these years of raising Dexter, she'd been the only one making decisions. Sure, she hadn't always made the right ones, but she'd become used to the role. After all, he was her kid. But on the other hand, she had no clue what to do about this situation.

Meeting his gaze again, she vowed to be more flexible. Harry was smart, and he might be a big help in coming up with a strategy. She'd be a fool to look a gift advisor in the mouth. "All right," she said. "I'd appreciate that."

"Good. We can talk while we eat."

Harry could feel Lainie's resistance when he suggested helping her formulate a plan. He tried not to get his feelings hurt over it. She'd been on her own for so long that getting advice from others probably seemed like a mistake. But if Joey had hired a PI, then he was committed to getting Dexter back, which wasn't surprising, considering the stakes.

Leo had also warned Harry that the PI might be looking for Lainie, too. Or there might be a second guy on the case, depending on how much money Joey had at his disposal. In any case, Harry and Lainie had limited time before somebody figured out where they were. Leo wasn't sure what Joey would do with the information, but he wanted Harry to be aware of the possibility they'd be tracked to Sedona.

That news could come out later, Harry decided after seeing the way Lainie had reacted to the first bit of data. In the meantime, they could have lunch and maybe talk about a long-range plan for dealing with Joey. A knock on the door told him that lunch had probably arrived.

"There's our lunch." Lainie started toward the door.

"Wait."

She glanced over her shoulder in surprise. "But I heard a voice call out 'Room service.' "

"That doesn't mean it *is* room service. Don't you ever watch TV?"

"Actually, no, I don't. During the day I'm with Dexter and at night I'm dancing. Although I get your point. But if Joey was just at your mother's house, he couldn't be on the other side of the door."

"No, but . . . he's hired at least one person to help him, and we don't know exactly what instructions he's given out."

"You think Joey might have hired a hit man?" She laughed and continued toward the door. "No way. He's an ugly drunk, but he wouldn't dream up some assassination attempt. That's not Joey."

Harry curbed his impulse to throw himself in front of the door. She was probably right and there were no hit men prowling around Sedona ready to pick her off. "Check the peephole, anyway. Please."

"If it makes you happy."

"It does. And let's pray it's not Dudley, either."

She peered out. "Not Dudley. Thalia. She's holding a tray with a sack of food from the Golden Arches. Shall we assume it's our lunch, or a hired gun in disguise?"

"Now you're being ridiculous."

"Just making sure I'm not taking a wild chance by opening this door."

"All right, already! Open the door!"

She did, and Thalia walked in.

"My goodness, but it *is* warm in here," she said. "Maybe I should send Dudley over, after all."

"No, we're fine," Harry said. "Perfectly fine."

"Absolutely fine," Lainie said.

Thalia looked doubtful. "Well, if you're sure."

"Very sure." Harry handed her a tip. "Thanks for the lunch."

"You're welcome. Enjoy. I have to tell you, though,

it's cooler outside than it is in here. The clouds are coming in and there's a breeze."

The minute she was gone, Lainie headed for the sliding doors onto the patio. "Let's eat outside."

"I wonder if it's a good idea." Harry reviewed Leo's instructions and tried to decide whether eating lunch on the patio outside their room fell within the guidelines of lying low.

"It looks safe enough." Lainie gestured through the sliding door. "There's a covered porch and walls on either side, so someone would have to see us from the golf course. That's assuming anyone's trailed us to this point, which I seriously doubt."

Once again, Harry had to admit she was probably right, and it would be nice to sit out there, catch a breeze, and watch the storm clouds rolling in over the red rock formations. "Okay," he said. "Go put on your glasses, so you're wearing the full disguise. I'll take the tray out there and set us up."

"Be back in a flash." She headed into the bedroom.

Harry unlocked the slider and opened it. Eating out here was probably okay. They could go a little stir-crazy if they confined themselves to the room for two days. Or maybe not. Maybe they'd just spend the entire time in bed, having amazing sex.

The prospect of doing that was incredibly exciting. He seemed to have no limits when it came to Lainie, and if he didn't tone down his response to her, she might think he was fixated on that particular activity. Which he was. He didn't know how a guy could help it with a woman like Lainie.

The patio furniture consisted of a round plastic table and two plastic chairs. Harry used one of the napkins in the bag to scrub off the table a little. Then he laid out the burgers, fries, and packets of ketchup and mustard.

Finally he poured two mugs of coffee, but he wondered if they'd really drink it. Hot coffee didn't sound very good. He took it out anyway, because Lainie had made it. The menial little chores took his mind off Lainie's body for a little while.

By the time he was ready to sit down, Lainie came out wearing Leo's glasses. The transformation to a studious vamp made him want her all over again.

The glasses also made him remember that photographic memory of hers, and he wondered if she was smarter than she realized. If all she'd cared about was dancing, then school might not have interested her much. She could be a classic underachiever.

"This is great." She sat down across from him and opened the lid on her burger container. "Oh, where's the toy?"

"I guess still in the bag." He rummaged around and came up with a little plastic action figure. He had no idea what it was supposed to represent.

"Perfect! Dexter's been wanting this one!" Lainie took the toy and set it carefully beside her place. "He'll be so thrilled."

"Good." Harry discovered he no longer cared about the food. As hungry as he'd been a minute ago, he was ready to forget about eating and haul her back inside. They had seven condoms, which wasn't many for two days, but he was ready to rip open another packet and take his chances on running out.

She opened the ketchup and mustard and doctored her hamburger, totally intent on her task. What a treat to be with someone who was completely happy with a fast-food burger and a toy for her son.

After picking up her hamburger, she glanced at him. "Is something wrong? Did I use too much of the ketchup and mustard?"

"Nope. I just like watching you."

Her cheeks grew pink. "Oh. Well, you need to eat and stop staring at me. You're making me self-conscious." She took a bite of her burger.

"Sorry." He opened his burger container. "It's just that you're so . . ." He thought of a million adjectives, but none of them quite captured the essence of Lainie. She was indescribable. "Oh, never mind."

"Eat, Harry."

"Right." He applied himself to the job. They ate with only the distant rumble of thunder breaking the silence. Yet Harry didn't feel uncomfortable, as if they should be talking. He and Lainie had fallen into an easy companionship that he hadn't experienced often. Maybe that was because of their unusual circumstances.

He'd told her they'd toss around solutions to her problem with Joey, but he hated to bring Joey into this peaceful setting. Sitting here eating a hamburger with Lainie would most likely turn into one of his favorite memories.

She'd finished off most of her hamburger when she spoke again. "I've been wondering something. Would you ever have asked me out? If this hadn't happened?"

He paused, a French fry halfway to his mouth. "I don't want you to take this wrong, but probably not."

"Because I'm a showgirl?"

"Well, yes and no. It seems like whenever I'm physically attracted to a woman, the relationship never works out."

She looked puzzled. "Why not?"

He didn't have the faintest idea how to explain it without insulting her by implying she wasn't his intellectual match. And he was beginning to suspect that might not be true, anyway. She was plenty smart. But she'd asked if he would have asked her out, and he'd given her a truthful answer.

"It's okay, Harry," she said softly. "I'll bet you want a wife who's home at night with the kids. I understand that."

"That's not really it. Besides, you've done a hell of a job with Dexter."

"I'm not so sure. He's lonely. But I'm not trained to do anything else, and I couldn't make good money at another job. Plus, for a single mom, it's actually easier to be home during the day and get a sitter at night. I see more of Dexter than I would if I worked days."

He nodded. "That's true."

"Never mind, Harry." She reached across the table and stroked his arm. "I get it. The main problem is that we like each other so much, but I would be horrible for you, especially now that I'm in this mess with Joey."

"Not horrible." Not even close, he thought.

"But not what you want."

Right now she was everything he wanted. But still, he was nervous. His erotic impulses had always landed him in trouble.

She smiled. "I just have to say, though, that you have

one heck of a package, and you're not afraid to use it."

He choked on his French fry.

"Well, it's true."

He coughed into his napkin. "Nobody's ever said that to me before."

"Are you offended?"

"No, I'm flattered." He looked across the table at her. "Not to mention turned on. Do you think we've given enough attention to this meal?"

"Could be." Behind the dark-rimmed specs her eyes sparkled. Then she leaned down and glanced under the table as if checking the condition of his lap. "Are things happening I should know about? Maybe we—" She paused, and her eyes widened.

"What?" He looked down at his lap. Sure, he was tenting the material of his slacks a little bit, but not enough to send her into shock. "Is something wrong?"

"Harry, don't move. There's a snake right behind you."

Chapter Fifteen

Harry felt the rush of pure terror. A snake in front of him was bad enough, but a snake *behind* him? Holy shit. But he was sitting with a woman he hoped would think well of him, a woman he hoped to have great sex with in a little while, unless snake fangs sank into his leg and he had to be airlifted to the hospital and shot full of anti-venom.

In any case, he didn't want Lainie to think he was afraid. He *wasn't* afraid. He was petrified, literally unable to move. Clearing his throat, he managed to say the only words his brain would spit out. "How big?"

"Pretty big. Listen, it might be Gertie again, the gopher snake we saw before."

He latched on to that suggestion like a drowning man. "Yeah. Heh, heh. I'll bet it's old Gertie, come to pay us a visit." But logic quickly doused that hope. Considering the distance old Gertie would have to cover, the chance was slim that this snake was the same one they'd seen before.

"Harry, you're white as a sheet."

He gulped. So much for making her think he was the soul of courage. "I'm not . . . real good with snakes."

"Most people aren't."

But it seemed to him she was a lot calmer than he was. "And I seriously doubt this is Gertie."

"I told you that to calm you down. But the fact is, I don't think it is, either."

"Why not?" His voice squeaked.

"I can see something that looks like rattles on its tail. And besides that, I just have a gut feeling that this one's the real deal."

"Go inside." He was shaking like a leaf and he might end up getting bit, but he'd be damned if she would. Not on his watch.

"Harry, we've had this argument before. I'm not going inside and leaving you out here with a six-foot rattler."

"*How* long?" He hoped he wouldn't pass out, although then if the snake bit him he wouldn't know about it. There were some compensations to being unconscious.

"About six feet, give or take a few inches. At least that's my best guess."

He felt dizzy. But before he slid right out of his chair in a dead faint, he needed to get her out of harm's way. "Damn it all, Lainie, get inside. Let me deal with this . . . this . . ." This monster from the bowels of the earth. Yeah, like he was going to deal with it. But at least she'd be out of harm's way and wouldn't continue to watch him cower.

"I'll do no such thing. I can see what the snake's doing, and you can't. So how about if you start slowly getting out of your chair while I watch the snake?"

"I . . . um . . . don't know if I can." He was shaking so bad he wasn't sure he could stand up. Hell of a thing to have to admit to the woman you had the hots for.

"Sure you can, Harry." She looked into his eyes. "Think about how nice it will be when we're both inside, all safe, and we can take a little siesta in that king-sized bed. Wouldn't you like that?"

He nodded. But first there was a damned snake to deal with.

"Then slowly get out of your chair and walk toward the sliding door."

His heart was beating so loud that he could barely hear her, but he could read her lips. He concentrated on those lips, thinking of all the wonderful things she could do with that mouth of hers, once the snake was on the other side of a solid glass door.

"The snake's lying there quietly, Harry. I don't think he cares about you. He probably ate something a while ago, and he needs to sleep it off."

"Uh-huh. Well, I can promise you one thing."

"What?"

"Dudley just lost himself a sale."

She laughed. "See? You're making jokes. You'll be fine. Now get out of the chair."

Harry thought about Lainie, naked. Unless he got out of his chair, he might never see her that way again. He and this snake would have a Mexican standoff that could go on for hours. Then eventually the snake would get bored and bite him, and that would be the end of fun and games with Lainie.

Bracing his hands on the top of the table, he eased out of the chair. "What's the snake doing?"

"Lying there."

"Do they have to be coiled up to bite?"

"I don't think so."

"There goes another tiny hope blown to smithereens." He straightened and accidentally bumped the chair. It scraped on the concrete and the noise seemed to echo. His hair stood on end as he waited for razor-sharp fangs to sink into his calf. When they didn't, he swallowed and checked in with Lainie. "Still the same?"

"So far."

Harry took a stiff-legged step toward the door. He felt like Frankenstein's monster, lurching along. "How's Mr. Snake?"

"Motionless."

He took another awkward step. "You need to stand up, too."

"Right." She carefully rose from her chair while she kept her attention on the ground behind him. "Keep going."

"Come with me."

"I will." She backed up a step. "I . . . cripes! It's moving!"

Harry grabbed her and threw open the sliding door. They leaped in together, falling to their knees. Harry reached back and slammed the door closed so hard the glass shook.

"We made it!" Braced on her hands and knees, Lainie gasped for air.

So maybe she hadn't been as calm and collected as she'd looked. He took comfort from that. Still on all fours himself, he drew in several long, shaky breaths.

Now that they'd made it inside and the snake hadn't,

Harry was filled with a morbid curiosity. He had to see exactly what had spooked him so bad. If it was only Gertie, he was going to be pissed.

"Let's see what it's doing now," he said.

"Okay."

They both rotated on their hands and knees until they were facing the door. With a loud yell, they scuttled backward, far away from the door.

The snake was poised, head lifted, staring right at them. Its forked tongue darted in and out.

"It's a rattlesnake," Lainie whispered.

"Damn straight it is." Harry swallowed hard. "It's Jaws of the Desert, that's what that is, come to terrorize us." He shivered, even though he knew the snake couldn't get through the door.

"What should we do?" Lainie murmured as if afraid the snake might be able to hear her.

"Call housekeeping?"

She started to giggle.

"What's so funny?"

"First of all, I doubt there is a housekeeping department. Thalia's probably all the housekeeping department they have. And what would you say, anyway? 'Hello, housekeeping? Could you send a maid over right away? There's a gigantic rattlesnake cluttering up our patio'?"

"So who would you call?" he asked, miffed that she was making fun of his suggestion.

"Oh, I dunno. Maybe a SWAT team. That's one heck of a snake."

"I don't like the way it's looking at us, either."

Lainie sat back on her haunches. "It is pretty creepy,

being eye to eye with a rattlesnake. And you're right—we should call somebody. They need to know this snake is around."

"They need to remove this snake to a snake preserve, or whatever it is they do with them." Harry got up slowly, as if sudden movement might cause the snake to do . . . something. He didn't know what, but he wasn't taking any chances. Walking over to the sliding door took great effort, but he did it, staring down at the snake as he approached. It didn't seem fazed by him at all.

He reached over and locked the door. "That's probably totally unnecessary, but I feel better now."

"I'm glad you did it. Even though I know he can't get it, I can still imagine that somehow he'd use his head to nudge it open."

"I was thinking the same thing." He picked up the desk phone. "Let's see what Crimson Canyons wants to do about this reptile." When Thalia answered the phone, Harry described the problem. He was proud of the matter-of-fact way he discussed the size of the snake. There was almost no quiver in his voice.

"We'll send Dudley right over," Thalia said.

Harry groaned. "Don't you have anybody else who can do it?"

"Dudley's our resident snake catcher. I'll have him over there in five minutes, if you'll please keep an eye on the snake."

Harry resigned himself to having Dudley show up. He was better than nobody. "Actually, the snake's keeping an eye on us."

"Well, don't be a hero and try to catch it yourself. They can be very dangerous."

"Oh, okay. I was thinking of it, but if you don't recommend—"

"Definitely not! Stay inside and let Dudley handle this."

"If you insist." Feeling better after playing macho man for Thalia, Harry hung up and turned to Lainie. "Dudley's coming over to take care of the snake."

"We should have known."

"We should have. Thalia said he's the resident snake expert."

Lainie stared at him. "You don't suppose that Dudley arranged for this snake?"

"No, although at first it crossed my mind, too. But even Dudley wouldn't sic a snake on us to give him an excuse to come by. That plan could backfire, big time."

"You're right, of course." She paused. "And I'll bet that's why they keep him on as a salesman, because he'll take care of any snakes that show up."

"They keep him on as a salesman because a real salesman wouldn't be caught within fifty miles of this place. I hope he knows his way around snakes, is all I'm saying. I thought I never wanted to see Dudley again, and now I can hardly wait to lay eyes on the guy."

"But we have to remember to be Fred and Rona, and I don't know where Leo's glasses are. I guess they fell off when we leaped inside." She started searching around on the floor. "God, I hope I didn't—"

"I see them." Harry walked over and picked up the glasses. One earpiece had snapped off. "One of us must have landed on them."

"Well, shoot." She stood and came over to look at the glasses. "I'll have to get Leo new ones, but right now we need a temporary fix. I'm not supposed to be able to see without them."

"We don't have time." Harry glanced out the door and noticed Dudley coming across the dried-up fairway grass holding a stick with a loop on the end and a large plastic cooler. "He's here."

"Then let me balance them on my nose as best I can. Is my wig on straight?"

"Let's see." Harry took a quick look. "A little bit of your real hair is sticking out." He tucked it out of sight. "That's better."

"How about the glasses?" She perched the glasses on her nose and glanced up at him. The glasses wobbled a little, and she laughed.

Later, Harry admitted to himself that was the exact second he fell in love with Lainie Terrell. At the time, he blamed indigestion for making his chest feel tight. Indigestion was a logical explanation for that funny feeling beneath his breastbone. It couldn't be good for his system to eat a burger and fries and then be scared out of his wits by a six-foot rattlesnake. Yeah, that was it. Indigestion.

"Are you okay, Harry?" She peered up at him. "You look sort of . . . confused."

He took a deep breath. "I'm fine. And if you don't move your head too much, the glasses should stay on. Maybe Dudley won't notice."

"Maybe he'll take the snake and leave."

"Don't bet on it."

Dudley walked to the edge of the patio, set down the cooler and waved to them.

Harry waved back. After all, the guy was there to remove the snake. "He's smiling at us."

"Dudley or the snake?"

"Dudley. I don't know what a smile on a snake looks like. Anyway, I think Dudley plans to turn this into a follow-up sales call. He won't be able to resist the opportunity."

"Then I guess we'll deal with him after the snake's captured. But Harry, do you think that cooler is big enough?"

"I told Thalia that it was six feet, and she said Dudley knew his stuff." Harry's pulse picked up as Dudley approached the snake, which was still stretched out in front of the sliding door with its head raised, staring at them through the glass.

"Maybe we're supposed to keep the snake distracted so he can sneak up on it," Lainie said.

"So how would you do that?"

"I haven't a clue. But it sounded like a good idea at the time."

"Anyway, too late." Harry gulped as the snake's head swiveled in Dudley's direction. Then the snake's tail lifted, too, and a dry rattling sound penetrated through the glass door.

"Omigod." Lainie whimpered. "This is too scary."

"No kidding. I hope to hell he knows what he's doing. A snake that size could definitely put a guy in the hospital."

"He's talking to it," Lainie said.

"You think?"

"Look. His lips are moving."

Harry concentrated on Dudley's mouth, and sure enough, he seemed to be murmuring something to the snake. "What would you say to a snake?"

"After this is over, you could ask him."

"After this is over, I'm going to completely erase it from my memory bank. At least I'm going to try." If he didn't succeed, he could be looking at a few major nightmares.

"Good luck on that," she said. "I know I'll never forget this."

Harry didn't suppose he would, either. He hoped his nightmares would also include some good parts involving sex with Lainie. "Dudley just keeps on coming," he said. "Like he's not afraid at all." Harry was getting seriously jealous of Dudley's manly display of courage in the face of snakes.

"You wouldn't be afraid, either, if you knew more about them and did this kind of thing all the time."

"Thanks for the vote of confidence, but I'd rather walk over hot coals on an hourly basis than do this all the time." Harry held his breath as Dudley came ever closer, holding the looped stick in front of him like a pole vaulter about to spring.

The capture happened so fast that Harry wanted an instant replay to see exactly how Dudley managed it. One minute Dudley and the snake were eyeing each other, and the next Dudley had a noose around the snake's neck and was dangling it in the air.

"Wow," Lainie said.

Harry's jealousy grew. He wanted to hear that tone of reverence when she was referring to something he'd done. "Impressive," he said, because he had to be truthful.

"I think the snake actually started to strike, and he got that noose around its neck right before it could bite him."

"Could be. Man, that's a long snake."

"But he's getting the whole thing in the cooler. Look at that. Just feeding it down in, bit by bit."

"He has to take the noose off before he can close it up, though." Harry realized he was sweating. "That could be dicey."

"Except that his reflexes are amazing."

Harry wondered what his reflexes would be like if they were really called to the test. Fast reflexes didn't usually come into play when you were dealing with computerized spreadsheets. Then again, he could add a column of numbers on a calculator faster than anybody he'd ever met. Oh, yeah, Lainie would probably swoon if she knew that.

"There he goes," Lainie said. "Almost in . . . almost . . . done! Slick as a whistle."

Harry had to give the devil his due. The snake was inside the cooler with the lid locked down, something Harry couldn't have accomplished in a month of Sundays. And Dudley had kept him, and more important, Lainie, from getting snake-bit.

He let out his breath. "Let's go thank him. He certainly deserves that much."

Lainie grinned. "Just don't buy a time-share out of gratitude, okay?"

"I won't if you won't." He started toward the sliding door.

"You know, if this place was a little nicer, and I had the money, I'd do it in a minute."

"You would?" He glanced back at her in surprise. "Even with rattlesnakes lurking around?"

"Sure, you have to be careful, but Harry, look around

at the scenery! Don't you think the red rock formations are incredible? Have you ever seen anything so beautiful in your life?"

He gazed at her, taking in her flushed cheeks, her crazy red wig, and the precarious glasses. "No," he said softly. "No, I haven't."

Chapter Sixteen

Lainie could tell from the way Harry approached the cooler full of snake that he was worried that even with the locked lid, the snake might find a way to make a break for it. Harry obviously had a serious snake phobia, and yet earlier he'd been ready to face this rattler alone while she scampered inside. She didn't meet guys like that every day.

She wondered if his jitters would make him forget who he was supposed to be. Maybe she ought to help him out. "Well, Fred, that's that," she said. "No more snake, thanks to Dudley, here."

"Yeah, Dudley. Thanks, man." Harry held out his hand.

"Aw, no problem." Dudley shook both their hands and looked pleased with himself. "That there was a big one. At first I thought maybe you'd mistaken Gertie for a rattler, but looks like you found yourselves the genuine article."

"What will you do with it?" Harry kept glancing nervously at the cooler.

"Oh, I'll let it go."

"What?" they yelled in unison as they nearly tripped over each other putting some distance between themselves and the cooler.

Dudley grinned. "Don't worry—not around these parts. I'll take it for a ride out into the desert, find a deserted spot far from civilization. You might see another snake while you're here, but you won't see this one again, I promise. It's *vaya con dios* to this rattler."

"We might see another one?" Harry's attention shifted to the browned-out edge of the fairway. "How many snakes are running around out here?"

Dudley adjusted his cowboy hat. "Hard to say, but less than there used to be, that's for sure. You have to remember they were here first. Then Crimson Canyons came in and took away their home. From the snakes' point of view, we're the ones trespassing, not them."

Lainie gazed at the cooler. "Now I'm starting to feel sorry for it. Aren't you, Fred?"

Harry eyed the plastic cooler with suspicion. "I wouldn't go that far."

"I'm dying of curiosity, Dudley." Lainie's glasses started to slide down the bridge of her nose and she pushed them back in place. "Were you talking to the snake?" In spite of herself, she was starting to admire Dudley's empathy for wild creatures.

Dudley nodded. "I figure it never hurts to apologize for booting him out of his home. He would have taken a big bite, if I'd given him the chance, though. And I don't blame him. I wouldn't like being lassoed and thrown in a cooler, myself. Still, it beats getting killed."

"Right," Harry said. "It's a good thing you're doing."

"I'm just hoping this snake business hasn't riled you up too much. I'll bet until the snake came along, you two were enjoying your lunch and toasting your decision to buy a one-bedroom. Am I right?"

"No you're not," Harry said. "I'm afraid we're still unable to agree on which size to buy. And then the snake came along, and to be honest, that affects our decision. I mean, we have a four-year-old."

Lainie had to hand it to him for coming up with that. He was very convincing, too, playing the concerned father. He'd be a good daddy someday.

Dudley nodded. "And you're right to consider your boy's safety, but you're living up in Vegas, am I right?"

"Yes, we are," Harry said. "And where we live, there aren't any—"

"But you're not about to convince me there aren't any rattlers in the state of Nevada, because I know better." He chuckled. "Some two-legged ones, also, but we won't go into that. That little boy of yours will get older, maybe go into the Boy Scouts, or take a school trip somewhere, and eventually he'll be wandering around in snake country. Boys do that."

"I didn't," Harry said. Then he glanced over at Lainie as if sorry he'd admitted it. "I mean, not much, anyway."

Dudley stroked his chin. "I believe it's better to expose kids to the great outdoors and teach them to be careful than to keep them locked up and ignorant." He turned to Lainie. "Don't you, Rona?"

She caught her glasses before they tumbled to the ground. Then she repositioned them. "In theory, yes, but in reality—"

"Of course, of course. Moms tend to get nervous

about dangerous situations, and that's when the dad has to encourage some exploration, right, Fred?"

Harry cleared his throat. "Dudley, we're not buying a time-share."

"We like to refer to it as resort ownership, and yes, you are buying a unit. You just don't know it yet. But I know it, and that's all that counts."

Lainie decided to provide some backup. "Fred and I really aren't buying. You need to move on to other prospects." She had a sneaking suspicion there were no other prospects. "But thank you for taking care of the snake. Now we need to let you get back to—"

"You seem to have a problem with your glasses, Rona. Here, let me take a look."

Before she could stop him, he'd swiped the glasses right off her face. "It was a freak accident," she said. "I'll have them fixed when we get home."

Dudley examined the glasses and whistled. "Pricey spectacles you have here, Rona. If you'll give me the broken piece, I might be able to do something with them. Otherwise I'll wager you're looking at a couple hundred bucks."

She groaned, although it wasn't surprising to find out that Leo had expensive taste in glasses as well as clothes.

"Don't worry about the glasses, sweetheart," Harry said. "It's no big deal."

Easy for him to say. He wasn't the one who had to pay to replace them. But she had to pretend to be grateful for his understanding, so she smiled at him. "Thanks, sweetheart. I'm glad you're not upset."

"Let me work on them," Dudley said. "Is the earpiece inside? Let's go get it." He started toward the sliding door.

Harry caught him by the shoulder. "That's not necessary, really."

"But you can't expect your wife to spend the rest of your vacation holding her glasses up to her face. Give me a couple of hours and I'll have them good as new. Then when I bring them back, we can write up the contract."

A muscle twitched in Harry's jaw. "No contract, Dudley. And as for the glasses—"

"The glasses are no big deal," Lainie said, jumping in to help.

"Of course they are," Dudley said. "So let me—"

Harry tightened his grip. "Can I talk to you privately, man-to-man? Excuse us for a minute, sweetheart."

Dudley looked surprised, but he nodded, and the two men walked several yards away.

Lainie was dying to know what wild story Harry was feeding Dudley as the guys put their heads together, but they had to be talking about her, because Dudley kept glancing her way.

Finally they walked back, and Dudley stuck out his hand again. "I wouldn't want to get in the way of creating new life," he said, "so I'll mosey on down the path."

Harry cleared his throat in such a dramatic way that Lainie had sense enough not to question Dudley's very strange statement about creating new life. She shook Dudley's hand. "Thanks again for capturing the snake."

"Just part of the job. If you need to reach me, this here's my cell phone number." Dudley pulled a battered business card out of his pocket and handed it to Lainie. "I can be reached most any time. You two take care, now."

Harry clapped him on the shoulder. "Thanks for understanding."

"Like I said, I've never had rug rats, never wanted 'em, but for those who do, I say, go for it." He picked up the cooler and the pole he'd used to catch the rattler. "So long, and happy populating." He headed off across the golf course.

"Happy populating?" Lainie turned to Harry. "What on earth did you tell him?"

"I said this was your fertile time."

"My *what*?" Her jaw dropped.

He shrugged and looked sheepish. "He picked up on all the chemistry between us, so I decided to play on that to get rid of him. I said we wanted to give little Dexter a sister or brother, and your broken glasses were really no problem because I planned to keep you in bed with me the rest of our stay here, so whether you could see well didn't much matter."

"Oh." She wondered if he had any idea how a statement like that turned her on. Come to think of it, this was her fertile time, which might explain why she could think of little else but doing the wild thing with Harry. Was it possible she might be ready to jump almost any available guy?

No. She had a fertile time every month, and she'd never had this kind of a reaction. Sex with Harry was more than just sex. She'd felt something significant going on once they finally got naked.

She wanted to feel that significant stuff again. Now. Thunder rolled in the distance as clouds blocked the sun. She smelled rain in the air and could think of nothing she'd rather do than romp in that king-sized bed with Harry while the rain came down.

"I guess we should go inside," she said. "I wouldn't want to make a liar out of you."

Thunder rolled as Leo tucked his high-powered binoculars in their case and started back down a rocky trail. Two seconds later a fat drop of water hit his cheek. Great. Just great.

He'd have to make like a mountain goat in order to get back to his car before the rain hit. His black Italian loafers were covered with red dust, and if he didn't hurry they'd be covered with red mud, too, damn it.

The things he did for Rona. Slipping and sliding his way down the loose shale, he almost fell twice. His silk shirt was spotted with rain and his shoes were a disaster by the time he reached the parking lot of Crimson Canyons and ducked inside his Jag.

First thing he did was reach for his cell phone and punch the speed-dial button for Rona.

She answered immediately. "What's up?"

Hearing her voice made him long to wrap his arms around her and nuzzle that long, elegant neck of hers. "I just ruined a pair of five-hundred-dollar shoes, I'll have you know."

"Never mind your shoes. What's happening down there?"

Leo relaxed against the soft leather seat and realized his back ached. First the long drive and then a hike, for chrissake. He was old and tired of playing these games, but this was too sensitive a matter to turn over to his boys. "You'll be happy to know that I see encouraging signs."

"Such as?"

Leo had decided not to tell her about the six-foot rattlesnake. Some things a mother didn't need to hear, especially when she knew Harry was terrified of snakes. "After lunch, they went back inside with their arms around each other. And they were moving out pretty good, too. I sensed eagerness there. Definitely eagerness."

"I love it! This is wonderful, just wonderful."

"Tell that to my shoes."

"It's your own fault. Everyone else I know has at least one pair of jogging shoes, but not you. You insist on these imported leather jobs that cost a fortune and are no good for anything."

"I don't jog." He felt crabby and he missed Rona. "I don't even want someone to think I might jog. I'm not interested in the whole jogging mentality."

"Then stop complaining because you ruined your shoes."

"I didn't know I'd have to climb up some godforsaken trail to get a good view of the proceedings." And he was lucky he hadn't run into any snakes, himself. The one Crocodile Dundee had taken out of Harry and Lainie's patio was enough to make him decide to do future surveillance from the parking lot or the golf course . . . in a cart, thank you very much.

"What's that noise I hear in the background?"

"It's raining on my car." Leo nudged off his muddy shoes and winced at the mess they'd made on his carpet. "I'm gonna have to have the Jag completely detailed after this."

"You have the Jag completely detailed every week.

Listen, any sign of other people creeping around the area?"

"Not so far. I just hope your son follows my instructions and keeps her inside during their stay." Leo flexed his toes and thought about how nice a hot tub would be about now, especially if he could be in it with Rona.

"I don't know if I ever mentioned that those are excellent instructions, for a number of reasons," she said.

"Yeah, and I know your reasons, you matchmaker, you. So far, so good. He ordered room service, which was the right move. I wish they hadn't decided to eat outside, but then, he's not trained in this kind of thing, so we have to make excuses for him."

Rona laughed. "And if they hadn't eaten outside, you wouldn't have anything to report."

"I know, but I'd like it better if they stayed tucked in there until we find out what else this joker has in mind." Leo listened to the rain beat down on the roof of the car and wished he'd brought an umbrella.

"I'd like it if they stayed tucked in there, too, especially if they're getting chummy."

"Rona, you can't pick out your son's wife. He has to do that."

"That's all well and good, but he's dragging his heels." She lowered her voice. "You should see the TITS making over this kid, Leo. And he's so smart. I'd like to see one of their grandkids beat the pants off everybody at Texas Hold 'Em."

Leo groaned. "Don't let yourself get attached," he said. But he knew it was already too late. Rona had lost her heart and there was no getting it back.

"I won't, but think of it. I was feeling sort of behind

everybody else, but this little boy would catch me up right away!"

Leo shut his eyes. He wanted Rona to be happy. He'd dedicated a good part of his life to that endeavor. But he felt helpless to satisfy her passion to have a grandchild. "Tell you what," he said. "When this is all over, we'll take a trip to Tahiti. How about that?"

"Only if we can take a certain four-year-old."

Leo groaned again. "Rona—"

"Just kidding. So what do you think of Crimson Canyons? Should we buy a time-share down there?"

Shit, he should have warned her not to identify the place. "Rona, you can't count on cell phones to be secure."

"Whoops. Sorry. I should have thought of that. Well, I doubt anybody's listening, anyway. That ex of hers isn't very smart. Anyway, I've gotta go. Suzanne just brought over her video of *SpongeBob SquarePants,* so we're going to take a break and watch it. Bye, Leo. And thanks."

"You're welcome." Leo disconnected the phone. He hadn't bothered to ask who *SpongeBob SquarePants* was. There were some things he really didn't want to understand.

But he had to agree with Rona on Joey's lack of intelligence. In fact, he was counting on it. Unfortunately, Joey might have hired somebody smarter than he was. Leo stared at the cell phone. He should have warned Rona, but he'd forgotten. He really was getting too old for this.

Harry wasn't sure what had inspired him to make up a story about wanting to get Lainie pregnant, but now that he had, he couldn't get the idea out of his head. And the instrument which could actually accomplish that feat was primed and ready for the task. Too bad he'd manufactured the whole concept.

Even so, they would have sex, and soon. They lost no time getting through the sliding glass door, although this time they didn't end up falling to their knees. Once they'd closed and locked the door, they both started for the bedroom, flinging off clothes as they went.

As thunder rumbled outside and rain pattered against the windows, Harry made a dash for the bathroom to snag the black case with the condoms in it. In spite of his ridiculous urge to make the story he'd told Dudley one hundred percent true, he wouldn't follow through on that urge. He didn't even want to marry Lainie, let alone get her pregnant with his kid.

So why was he thinking how much fun that would be as they ripped back the covers and tumbled onto the mattress? Vaguely he realized it was a lumpy mattress, but he didn't care. He was too busy thinking how wonderful it would be if he could make a baby with Lainie. Yet making babies had been something he'd studiously avoided ever since he'd lost his virginity.

"Hurry," she said, rolling to her back. "I feel like I'm ready to come just thinking about having sex with you."

He grabbed a condom and ripped open the package. "I know what you mean." And putting this latex barrier on seemed like one step too many. He'd never had that thought before he was about to have sex. Not ever.

"That is one impressive piece of equipment you have there." She stared at his penis, her chest heaving. "If I had to go five years without sex, at least I'm getting my just reward."

"I'm feeling pretty rewarded myself. Now come here, you." He leaned down and kissed her as he shoved deep, blotting out all thoughts of the last time she'd had sex, because it had been with that creep Joey. And Joey hadn't used a condom.

"How's that?" he murmured against her mouth.

"Outstanding," she whispered, lifting her hips and wiggling against him. "I hope we're going to do this all day, because I feel like I could."

"Me, too." He locked himself in a little tighter and concentrated on not coming. But the rain slapping against the window pulled at him, coaxing him to pour himself into her.

He held still and gazed down at her. "Don't move for a minute, okay? I'm going to hang out right here and try to exercise a little control. I want this to last a while."

"Good idea." Her breath came in tiny gasps. "Let's do . . . a little savoring. I could . . . I could go for that."

"Close?"

"Very."

"And I can guarantee if you come, we both come." Talking helped put his mind back in charge. "I can't hold up under those spasms, not to mention the power of suggestion, knowing you're having a climax."

"You can feel it when I come?" Her breathing was steadier, as if she'd pulled herself back a little, too.

"Oh, yeah."

"I always wondered about that."

"But were afraid to ask?" He loved the view from here. He could watch her eyes dilate if he moved even a fraction of an inch. She looked good in the red wig, which had managed to stay put through all their gyrations. He had the novelty of getting it on with a redhead this afternoon, when this morning she'd been a brunette.

But there was no mistaking the perfect fit he remembered as he slid inside her. Then there was the sense of completion he'd had the first time and felt all over again now, as if they'd been carved from the same block of wood a long time ago and were now finally reunited.

"Can you feel this?" she asked.

He moaned as she contracted her pelvic muscles, massaging his already aching penis. "Uh-huh. You could finish me off with a couple more of those."

"It's Kegels."

"Say what?"

"Kegel exercises. To keep me tight and fit."

"You get any more fit and I'll have the staying power of a rabbit."

She smiled. "What do you know about rabbit orgasms?"

"Nothing, but they do everything else quick, so it's logical." And after this conversational break, he thought he might be able to thrust without losing it, so he tried that.

"Mm." Her arms tightened around him.

"That was a happy sound."

Her breathing quickened again. "That's because . . . you're delivering a whole bunch . . . of happy."

"That's my intention." And he must have gotten a second wind, stamina-wise, because suddenly he felt like he could keep up this rhythm forever. "Now do the swivel," he murmured.

She gulped for air. "You liked that?"

"I loved that."

"Think you can take it?"

"Bring it on."

"Ooo . . . *kay*."

Did she ever. He'd thought he had his buddy under control, but once she lifted her hips and began that bump-and-grind routine, he had zero control. Soon he was bellowing and plunging into her with the same frenzy as he had this morning. They made the mattress bounce and squeak like a trampoline.

He felt the tug of her orgasm right before he shot into the stratosphere. Kapowee. Shazam. Bliss. Ah, Lainie. Lainie, Lainie, Lainie.

Chapter Seventeen

Joey drove back to his hotel, dumped the flowers in the nearest trash bin, and headed for the bar. So much for staying sober and buying flowers. The bitch hadn't even let him in the door. Sliding onto a stool at the bar, he ordered a gin and tonic.

What he needed was a plan, and he could think better with a drink in his hand. Unfortunately, he wasn't any closer to a solution as he neared the end of his second G and T. Getting to the kid, which he'd thought would be easy, had turned into a major deal. He'd blown it the first night and now the kid seemed to be guarded better than his dad's compound in Upstate New York.

His cell phone rang as he was in the midst of ordering his third drink. He fumbled a little pulling it out of the holster attached to his belt and nearly dropped it. Stupid things were too small. He'd always thought so, but if they were any bigger they'd be a pain to haul around. Finally he got it up to his ear.

"I just picked up a cell phone communication between

Rona Ambrewster and a guy named Leo. I'm virtually positive that Lainie Terrell and Harry Ambrewster are at a time-share resort called Crimson Canyons. I looked it up on the Internet and it's in Sedona. Want me to check it out?"

Joey thought of the money that little jaunt would cost and heard the *ka-ching* of a cash register in his head. Besides, it wouldn't do any good for the PI to go there. Joey was the one who had to talk to Lainie.

"How far is it to Sedona, anyway?" he asked the PI.

"About five hours or less. I have the make of the car she left in, and the plate number. Wouldn't take long to give you a definite on their location."

"Why don't you give me the description and plate number, instead?"

"I could, but look, Joey, you're not trained for this. And I'm not sure who this Leo character is, but he's got guys out there, too."

"Tell me about it," Joey muttered.

"I'm only saying you could run into some problems. You'd be better off letting me—"

"I'm smarter than I look," Joey said, taking a swig of his third drink. "Give me the info."

"Okay. Your call." The PI rattled off the information.

"Hold on, hold on. I wasn't ready. Let me get something to write with." He grabbed a waitress as she went sailing by. "Let me have your pen."

She handed him the ballpoint pen clipped to her order pad and stood tapping her fingernail against her tray while he slid his napkin out from under his glass.

"Okay, give it to me again," Joey said. The napkin tore twice as he tried to write on it, but eventually, after the PI had repeated the license number three times, he had it. Once the napkin dried he could tuck it into his pocket and he'd be all set.

"I really think you need to let me handle this," the PI said again.

"I have it under control. Thanks." Joey disconnected the phone and started to tuck the pen in his shirt pocket.

"I need my pen back," said the waitress.

Joey glanced up at her. Not bad. A good figure, and a blonde, to boot. Ever since having to deal with Lainie, he'd sworn off brunettes. He gave her his killer smile as he handed back the pen. "Sorry about that. How rude of me."

"It's okay." She gave him the once-over.

That was all the encouragement he needed. He had a good package and it had fallen into disuse recently. He didn't like to go more than a couple of weeks without some horizontal aerobics. "I'd like to make it up to you," he said softly. "For being so rude."

"It wasn't *that* rude. It's only a pen."

"Yes, but it was *your* pen. Let me do something nice for you."

"Like what?"

He figured if she was still standing here talking to him, he was in like Flynn, but he decided to sweeten the deal. "The thing is, I'm about to come into some money, a *lot* of money, and I don't have anyone to celebrate with. When do you get off work?"

She glanced at her watch. "In about thirty minutes. Was that what your call was about?"

"Yeah. Later on I have to go to Sedona to make some arrangements, but I'd love to have a little going-away party before I leave."

"Are you staying here?"

"Uh-huh. Right upstairs. How does a bottle of Dom Pérignon and a bowl of chocolate-covered strawberries sound?"

She gave him a sly smile. "Like a going-away party?"

"That's right. Just you and me. Let me have your pen again." He took it from her outstretched hand, turned her palm up, and started to write his room number on it. Women loved that.

Except he had to take a minute to remember what his room number was. Then he discovered her hand was damp and the pen wouldn't write on such a wet surface. He hoped she wasn't the type to have sweaty palms during sex. He hated that.

"Just tell me," she said after he'd made several tries and only managed to smear ink on her.

So he just said the number, straight out, which wasn't nearly as smooth as his special routine of writing it on her palm. He'd never dealt with sweaty palms before. But she had good boobs and a nice tush, so maybe sweaty palms wouldn't matter.

After she left, he downed his third G and T and left the bar feeling a whole lot better. He'd work off some of his frustration by having some hot sex with the waitress, and then he'd head down to Sedona. If that loser of a PI could make it in five hours, Joey could do it in three and a half, easy.

Lainie had drifted off to sleep, lulled by an excellent orgasm and the steady drumming of rain on the window. When she opened her eyes, the rain had stopped and the light in the room had dimmed to a soft gray. She lifted her head so she could see the red numbers on the digital clock beside the bed. Nearly six. They'd slept the afternoon away.

Harry snored softly beside her. She took a moment to gaze at him. Of course he wasn't wearing his glasses, and his hair was tossed every which way by the sleep and the activities that had preceded sleep. Oh, such activities. Looking at Harry, she could feel herself getting excited again. He was the source of so much pleasure.

Maybe her memory wasn't very good, but she didn't remember feeling nearly this satisfied when she'd had sex with other men. And there hadn't been all that many, despite what her parents thought. With a sigh she lay back on the pillow and wished, for the millionth time, that she'd been able to please her parents.

But it seemed that from the time she'd first tried out for the pom squad and made it, they'd been unhappy. The outfits were too skimpy, they said, and the routines too suggestive. For her part, she'd loved every minute. Of course being on the pom squad meant lots of dates, and her parents hadn't liked that, either.

They seemed to assume she was turning into a wild girl, and she hadn't been, but they'd made her mad enough to act like it. Going from the pom squad in high school to a casino stage in Atlantic City had seemed like a natural step to her, but they'd been horrified. They'd never come to see her dance.

Maybe her sadness about her parents had been part of her attraction to Joey, who had some complaints about his parents, too. He'd acted like such a fun guy at first, and she'd been intrigued with how he'd initiated their first night of sex. He'd invited her to the bar for a drink after the show, and then he'd written his room number on the palm of her hand, which she'd thought was cute.

Then he'd left, giving her time to decide whether to take him up on his offer or not. She'd felt like a very daring woman when she'd knocked on his hotel room door later that night. He'd ordered up champagne and chocolate-covered strawberries, which had made her feel special.

She remembered the strawberries, but not much about the sex. During the months following that, she could count on one hand the number of climaxes she'd had. Her sexual experiences with Joey had been nothing compared to the chemistry she'd found with Harry. She would remember being in Sedona with Harry for a very long time.

The rain must have made the temperature drop considerably outside, because the room had cooled off quite a bit. She would have loved to open the window and smell the rain, but an open window might not be a great idea, considering that she didn't know Joey's whereabouts. So she'd stay right here in bed, lumpy though it was, and enjoy the fact that she was lying next to Harry. Waking up next to Harry on a regular basis would be sweet, but it wasn't something she should wish for. Her life wasn't destined to turn out like that.

"What time is it?" Harry's voice, sleepy and relaxed, flowed over her, making her smile.

She turned to find him gazing at her in a dreamy, unfocused way. He looked so lovable and cuddly. "Nearly six."

"You know, this could be the worst bed I've ever slept in. It creaks and groans and I'll bet there's stuffing coming out of the mattress. But I don't even care."

"Neither do I," she said. "But it is pretty bad. Lumps everywhere."

"And swaybacked. There's a big dip in the middle."

"I noticed. Oh, look what it made me do." She rolled toward him and kissed him on the mouth.

"I take it back. This is a terrific bed." He returned the kiss in spades, wrapping his arms around her and flopping onto his back so she was sprawled on top of him. Sprawled on top of Harry was a terrific position to be in, and she planned to make the most of it.

She got situated so her bottom touched his ever-ready penis. She thought of the drug his father had taken, the one that had caused Harry to be conceived, and wondered if a tiny bit of the drug had been passed on somehow. If she'd paid more attention in biology class, she might know if that could be possible.

In any case, Harry sure made a girl feel wanted when his pride and joy stood proud and joyous at a moment's notice. She rubbed her breasts lazily over his chest as he kissed her and stroked her back. Apparently they were both ready for round three.

She lifted her mouth from his. "Did you count the condoms?"

"Six left."

She ran her tongue around his mouth. "We're about to use another one."

"Yeah, we are." Gazing up into her eyes, he reached out with one long arm, patting the surface of the night table as he searched for the black case holding their stash.

"Wait, you're going to knock it on the floor." Bracing one hand beside his head, she stretched her other arm toward the case and laughed as her nipple hit his nose.

"Easy there." He caught her swaying breasts in both hands. "You could put out an eye."

"Which would give you an incredible story to tell, now wouldn't it?" She fished in the case and pulled out a black foil packet.

"No kidding." His voice grew husky. "Stay like that a sec, if you can. I want to—"

Yes, he certainly did. She would hold still for this kind of treatment any day. Gripping the side of the night table, she balanced above him while he sucked on her nipples until a glorious pressure built low in her belly.

Maybe it was his enthusiasm. Maybe it was his technique. Maybe it was simply the kind of magic that happened whenever he touched her. Whatever the reason, within moments she trembled on the edge of a climax.

"You have to stop." She eased away from him.

"Why?"

"Because I was about to come, and then I would have lost my balance and fallen on you. I pictured teeth being knocked out and black eyes. It wouldn't have been pretty."

He grinned at her. "Really? You were that close?"

"I was. Embarrassing, huh?"

His dark eyes shone in the faint light from the window. "No, wonderful."

"I'll tell you what's wonderful." She got on her hands and knees so that she could edge backward until she'd cleared his elegant package. Then she sat on his thighs and waved a hand toward his penis. "This. This is wonderful."

"That old thing? I've had it for years."

"I must say you've maintained it beautifully. It looks practically brand-new." She ripped open the condom packet. "And now I'm going to dress it up so it can go visiting."

She'd never put a condom on a man, but now she had a burning urge to try it with Harry. She had a burning urge to try all sorts of things with Harry. No telling when she'd get to have sex again.

"Don't do it yet."

"No?"

He groped on the night table once again and found his glasses. "I want to watch you put it on." Sliding his glasses onto the bridge of his nose, he propped his hands behind his head. "Okay, go."

"You don't think I know how, do you?"

"I have no idea if you do or not, but I've always wanted to watch a woman do this, and nobody's ever offered before."

"Well, guess what? I've never offered before, either."

"You haven't?"

"Never felt like it." She took the flattened roll of latex out and tossed the foil package on the floor. "Ready?"

"Yeah . . . and I'm glad you feel like it this time."

She glanced at him, and even in the dim light she could see the tender look in his eyes. "You're not falling for me, are you?"

"Why?" he said softly, too softly.

"You are, aren't you? Harry, don't fall for me. I'm the wrong girl for you, and you know it."

He didn't say anything to that, just continued to look at her with that warm, melting expression on his adorable face.

"I mean it." She pointed a finger at him. "When this is over you're going to have to forget about me."

"That'll be tough." His voice held twenty kinds of caring in it. "I've never had a woman sitting astride me with her red wig half off and a condom in her hand. How am I supposed to forget that?"

She put the condom between her teeth and adjusted the wig.

"Or that." His smile flashed in the pale light.

She took the condom back out. "I'm glad I'm entertaining you." Secretly she was glad. She knew he wouldn't be able to forget her any more than she'd be able to forget him, but she wanted him to remember the fun times, not the woman who'd filled the floor of his car with used tissues while she sobbed.

"I've never been more entertained in my life."

"Good. And now, for my next trick, I'll roll on this condom. No, wait. I think it's better if I suck on it first."

His tone changed from soft to eager. "Suck on what?"

"The condom, so it goes on easier . . ." She smiled when she saw his obvious disappointment. "You thought I meant something else, didn't you?"

"Uh, well, I—"

"I should have thought of that, instead. I'll bet the condom would go on slick as a whistle afterward, too."

He trembled and swallowed hard. "M-maybe."

"How about if I just tuck this condom behind my ear for now, so I won't lose it?"

He gave a little gasp of laughter. "You're too much."

"Let's see if I am or not." She wrapped her fingers around his penis and lowered her mouth.

Harry tasted as good as he looked. In the past she'd

performed this task to please the guy, because they all seemed to love it to death, but she hadn't exactly relished the experience. Either five years had changed all that, or Harry made the difference. Whatever the reason, she was having a great time.

From what she could tell from Harry's reaction, he was having a pretty good time, himself. He moaned a lot and blew air out between his clenched teeth. After a few minutes he begged her to stop before he came.

She lifted her head, more than ready to climb aboard, but she also wanted to give him whatever he wanted. Making him happy was becoming a favorite thing of hers. "You're sure? Because if you're liking this, I can go the distance."

"I know. Take that thing out from behind your ear." His voice was tight with strain. "And be careful how you put it on."

"You've got it." She put the condom in her mouth for good measure, getting it good and moist before settling it in place. "Are you watching?"

"You bet."

She rolled the condom down, taking it slow so that she'd do it right and be careful, like he'd said. "Just like a stocking," she murmured. "There you go." She gave him a little pat. "Was that fun?"

He dragged in a breath. "Yeah. Almost came twice. Yeah. Fun. Now do me."

She was on a short fuse, herself, and quite ready to make use of his magic wand to whisk them both to paradise. As she lowered herself, taking him in, she sighed with pleasure. This was so good. So very good.

"Nice." Breathing hard, Harry bracketed her hips with his large hands. "Go for it."

"Hang on." She braced her palms on his chest.

His grip tightened. "I've got you."

Taking a deep breath, she moved up and down slowly at first. Slow didn't last long, though. Soon she felt the need for speed, and the room filled with their moans. She loved being in charge, loved hearing him urge her on.

"Yes!" he called out, panting. "Like that . . . there . . . I'm coming!"

And so was she, blasting through the barriers between them. For a precious few seconds she knew the miracle of merging with another human being. For a precious few seconds, she allowed herself to be in love.

Lainie was right, Harry thought as they lay side-by-side in the aftermath of another fantastic round of sex. He was falling for her. And that wasn't good.

Shrouded in darkness, perfectly suited to each other sexually, they could push aside all the issues and enjoy themselves in this bed until morning. But this bed wasn't reality. It was a magic-carpet ride, but eventually they had to come back to earth.

He should probably break this idyllic mood before he completely lost focus. "I know this is a touchy subject," he said. "But I think, given the stakes, we can assume Joey won't just go away."

She greeted his comment with silence.

"Would you rather not talk about it?" he asked, starting to cave already. Okay, so maybe they could stay on this magic carpet a while longer.

She cleared her throat. "I need to talk about it."

Rolling to his side, he propped his head on his hand. Security lights outside the window provided just enough light for him to see her profile. She seemed so vulnerable, and he wanted desperately to help.

"So I was thinking," he began, "that if you called his hand and took him to court, you might be able to demonstrate that he's been an indifferent father and bring up his drinking problem. That could give you some leverage."

"I, um . . . maybe."

"If it's the money that's stopping you, let me—"

"No, Harry." She swallowed. "I couldn't accept that kind of financial help. I'm already feeling guilty about what you've done so far."

"Don't." He reached over and stroked her cheek. "In case you can't tell, I'm having the time of my life."

She took a long, shaky breath. "Me, too, except when I start thinking about Joey."

"I know, and I wouldn't have brought him up except that you have to leave here with a plan."

"Uh-huh." She stayed quiet for a little while. "But even if I took him to court, I might be going up against the Benjamin empire. All Joey has to do is convince his father to try and get Dexter away from me, and I'm toast."

"Maybe not." But Harry could see her point. Usually the person with the most money had the best legal team.

"I've thought about taking Dexter and disappearing, and I might have done that before I found out why Joey wants him. Now I have to consider what's fair to Dexter. He has a chance to inherit a billion-dollar business."

"But if that means somehow being separated from you, the money isn't worth it."

She turned over and pulled his head down for a gentle kiss. "Thank you for saying that," she murmured.

"It's true." He cupped her cheek in his hand. "He needs your influence."

"I think so, too, but if he's the rightful heir to that fortune, I can't stand in his way." She sighed. "I don't want to have to work out a deal with Joey, because I really don't like him or trust him with Dexter, but I may have no choice."

Resistance to that idea made Harry's stomach knot, but he had no right to reject anything she came up with. Dexter was her kid. "Do you think Joey would be willing to compromise, so everybody wins?" So far, Harry didn't see Joey as the compromising sort.

"Honestly? I don't have a lot of hope that he would, especially if he's drinking. But I don't know how else this can be solved." She paused. "And all this discussion is giving me an appetite. Are you getting hungry?"

"Yeah." He was surprised to discover that he was once again starving, but when he concentrated on her, he was able to block out all thought of food. "Yeah, I'm getting hungry. I guess we should order from room service again."

"Harry, let's not. Let's take a drive into town and eat there. I think we need to get some fresh air and clear our minds."

"You mean clear our minds of all this sex?"

She laughed. "All the fresh air in the world won't do that, but I like being outside. I'm not good at being cooped up too long."

He remembered Dexter had told him that, which had led him to believe she'd be bored with a stick-in-the-mud accountant who liked to sit quietly and play chess. So far she hadn't acted bored, but now she wanted some different scenery. If only he could agree, without worrying about consequences.

"I know what you mean," he said, although he could have stayed in with room service, no problem. "But I don't know if it's safe. Leo said—"

"I know what Leo said, but Harry, Leo might be a mobster. You told me it was possible."

"It's possiblc." Even probable, he thought.

"So naturally, Leo is going to expect the worst from Joey and imagine all kinds of bad things, like Joey will want to bump me off, or have me bumped off, just because that would give him clear access to Dexter."

Harry had to admit that's exactly what Leo was worried about. Consequently he'd made Harry worry about it, too.

"Joey is not going to try to kill me, or even have me killed," she said. "That's the kind of thing you see in the movies, but I know this guy. You have to have more grit than Joey has to pull off something like that. Even if Joey showed up, so what? I need to talk to him."

"What if he shows up drunk and starts acting unreasonable?" Harry remembered all too well the bellowing idiot who'd appeared outside her apartment door. Joey under the influence seemed capable of almost anything, despite what Lainie said.

"If that should happen, we'll get the restaurant to call the police. An arrest for disorderly conduct can only help my cause, right?"

She was making lots of sense, and he was beginning to feel like a little old lady, afraid of his own shadow. "You're right," he said. "We'll take a drive into town. What could happen?"

Chapter Eighteen

Although Rona loved showing off Dexter to the TITS, when dinnertime arrived she decided he'd had enough stimulation for one day. Dexter might think differently, but she had to be the grown-up and choose for him. Smart as he was, he was still only four years old.

She stood up from the poker table during a break in the action and stretched. "I don't know about everyone else, but I'm exhausted."

"Not me!" said Dexter, who was almost hidden by a mountain of M&M's.

Rona had expected him to say that, but she'd seen him rubbing his eyes two minutes ago. She glanced at Suz, who could be counted on to back her up most times. "How about you, Suz? You about ready to pack it in?"

"I am. Tomorrow's another day, right, Dexter?"

"We're gonna *quit*?" He looked crestfallen.

"Even Fred's worn out." Rona pointed to the little dog,

who was conked out in his bed in the corner of the kitchen.

"But I'm not," Dexter insisted. "I could play for eons, which is a really long time."

"So I've heard." Babs winked at Rona. "You know what? I'm not only tired, I'm hungry." She patted the spot where her tight pants stretched over her tummy.

"Have some M&M's." Dexter scooted a handful toward her. "I have about five hundred here."

Babs glanced down at the handful she had left in front of her. "I noticed. And thank you for offering, but I was thinking pizza. Do you like pizza?"

"Yes, if it's cheese. I don't like it with stuff on it."

"Oh, me, neither." Trixie's long earrings flapped against her neck as she shook her head. "I hate pizza with stuff on it."

"I like stuff," Babs said. "Lots of stuff. We need to split this order."

"And after pizza, we call it a night," Rona said. "Okay?"

"Then I say we wait on the pizza," Dexter said. "If anybody's *really* hungry, they can have as many M&M's as they want. My treat."

"I know what we can do." Cherie tapped her maroon nails on the table. "We can order the pizza, one cheese and one with stuff. Then we'll bet on exactly what time the pizza guy gets here. It'll be like the grand finale."

"Yeah!" Dexter brightened.

"And we can bet on how many mushrooms they put on," Suz said.

"And olives, and green peppers, and tomatoes," Babs said.

"Not the tomatoes," Suz said. "You'll get little mooshed-up pieces and you won't know how to count them if they're, like, torn but almost attached."

Dexter nodded. "I think we need some rules."

And the debate was on. Rona could see it taking way too much time. "You can all hammer out the rules. I'm ordering. One plain cheese and one with everything."

"Except anchovies!" Babs said. "Ick."

"Babs, you always do that," Suz said. "And I love anchovies."

"Well, I put up with pepperoni because of you."

"Three pizzas, then." Rona was by God going to get this show on the road. "One plain cheese, one everything but anchovies, one everything but pepperoni."

"That's silly," Suz said. "Get one with pepperoni and anchovies. I'll pick off the pepperoni and Babs can pick off the anchovies."

"Ask me if I'll even *touch* an anchovy. Gross!" Babs said.

Suz turned to her. "Then I'll pick them off for you. What a baby. Here, have an M&M and be quiet." She picked up one from Dexter's pile and popped it in Babs's mouth. "Now let's get the rules for this pizza bet settled."

As they began to haggle over whether to bet on clumps of sausage, Rona phoned in the order. Once they'd finished the pizza, she would definitely shoo them out. Dexter needed some quiet time. Amazing how protective she'd become in less than twenty-four hours.

When she returned to the table, Suz glanced up. "How long did they say?"

"Thirty minutes."

Suz nodded. "Okay, I take six forty-two."

"Six thirty-eight," said Trixie.

Dexter stared at the clock. "Six thirty-six," he said.

No one commented on the fact that Dexter could tell time. Anyone who had massacred the group so completely at Texas Hold 'Em was guaranteed to be able to tell time. Rona had to keep reminding herself that he was only four, and he'd been going nonstop ever since he and Fred woke up at seven.

So had she, come to think of it. Maybe she was imagining how tired Dexter was because she was exhausted keeping up with him. She was used to the pace of a retired woman—leisurely breakfast at eight, plenty of time to read the paper, taking Fred for a little walk, lunch with the girls.

Dexter had been so disappointed when they'd had to let Eric walk Fred this morning and Brett this afternoon. If it weren't for that damned Joey, Rona could have taken Dexter and Fred to the park down the street and run them both around so that Dexter would have been ready for a nap. Then again, if it weren't for Joey, she wouldn't have Dexter here in the first place, so in a strange way, she owed Joey Benjamin for being such a jerk.

"We never decided about sausage," Trixie said after everyone had bet on the pizza arrival time.

"I say sausage clumps are too nebulous," Suz said.

"Nebulous?" Dexter said. "Is that anything like nebula?"

"I don't know, Dex," Suz said. "I never thought about it."

"I certainly never thought about it," Babs said, "because I don't have the foggiest idea what 'nebulous' means."

"It means you don't get to bet on sausage, is what it means," said Trixie.

"And I notice nobody's answered Dexter's question," Suz said. "Rona, you must have a dictionary around this place, for your crosswords. Maybe we can all learn something."

Rona went into the living room and pulled out the dictionary she kept with her stack of crossword puzzle magazines. For all she knew, Dexter would be able to work those puzzles better than she could. Harry had been able to at Dexter's age.

Then she remembered the box stored in the back of her closet. She'd thought she had nothing but the TITS and Fred to amuse Dexter, but that wasn't true. She had a box of Harry's toys, and she'd forgotten all about that. Now she really wanted the TITS to vamoose, so that she could haul out that box for Dexter. But pizza was coming and bets had been made. She'd have to be patient.

Back at the table, she looked up "nebulous" and read off the meaning.

"Lacking definite form," Suz said. "That's sausage, for sure. You've got your big globs, your little globs, and your tiny bits of broken globs. You can't count sausage like you can pepperoni."

"Okay, you convinced me," Cherie said. "But what about this nebula connection? Isn't that like a star or something?"

"A diffuse mass of interstellar dust or gas," Rona said, reading from the dictionary, just as she used to do when Harry was a little boy. "So the words are related, like Dexter thought."

"Way to go, kid." Cherie reached across the table and

tapped him on the nose. "You smart little dickens."

Rona beamed. Dexter was a smart little dickens, and all the TITS knew it. The bragging rights stopped here. Finally.

The rules for what was now being called the Great Pizza Bet had barely been established when the sounds of yelling came from out front. Fred leaped from his bed and ran to the door, barking frantically.

Rona's heart started racing. Not Joey again. Please not Joey. "Dexter, stay put. You girls, stay here with Dexter." Then she ran to the door, scooped up a wiggling Fred, and brought him back, shoving him into Trixie's arms. "Keep him here, too."

"Call us if you need backup," Suz said.

"I will." Trying not to hyperventilate, Rona headed for the front door again. Even though she knew Eric and Brett were keeping watch, she still worried that Joey would somehow slip through. And she didn't know if Joey's buddies would show up with him.

Some kind of scuffle was going on out there, though, so maybe they'd caught Joey trying something. She held her breath, crossed her fingers, and looked through the security peephole in her door. The peephole gave her a worm's-eye view of chaos.

Eric and Brett had the pizza guy flat on the sidewalk. Eric was holding the guy's wrists and Brett's knee was firmly planted in the guy's back. She could only imagine what had happened to the pizza, but the deliveryman wasn't looking so good. From what she could tell, he was kind of a scrawny type, no match for the likes of Eric and Brett.

She unlocked the door and flung it open. "Hey, he

was bringing us our dinner! Let him up!" With the door open she could see that one pizza box had popped open and the pizza, the plain cheese Dexter and Trixie had ordered, hung halfway out of it. The other box, pretty much flattened, lay near the bushes. So much for betting on the mushrooms and pepperoni.

The pink glow of sunset reflected off Eric's shaved head as he glanced up. "You ordered pizza?"

"Yes! So let him up." Visions of a lawsuit danced in her head.

"I was only trying to deliver a pizza! Who are you guys?" wailed the delivery boy.

"He wouldn't show us any ID," said Brett, whose blond hair was barely out of place as he continued to keep his knee in position. "Then when we tried to grab him, 'cause we thought he might be after Dexter, he pulled some kind of spastic kung fu number on us."

"It's hapkido!" the guy said. "I've been taking lessons!"

Eric clucked his tongue. "I'd get a refund for those lessons if I were you. That was pitiful."

"Plus, you shouldn't have tried to assault us," Brett added.

"*I* shouldn't have assaulted *you*? Hello! I'm the one with the face planted on the pavement, here! I'm just trying to do my job, and I get attacked by two rejects from the WWF! That's exactly why I took that course in self-defense, to make me feel safer when I deliver pizza."

"And how's that self-defense course working out for you?" Brett asked.

"Don't tease him," Eric said. "And Rona, you should

have paged us. We would have picked up your pizza. I mean, this guy, he could've been anybody."

They were right. She'd been so intent on getting the TITS fed and out of her hair that she'd forgotten about security. It was so hard to remember these things if you weren't used to them. Earlier today she'd said something she shouldn't have on the cell phone with Leo. If anything she did should put Dexter in danger, she'd never forgive herself.

"I'm sorry," she said. "And I'm sure he really is the pizza man."

"I really am the pizza man. The pissed pizza man, I might add."

"Then I guess we can let you up." Brett took his knee out of the guy's back and Eric released his wrists.

The pizza man got up, dusted himself off, and glared at Rona. "I hope you have good insurance, because you're going to need it."

Exactly what she'd been afraid of. "Look, I'm really sorry. I didn't realize—"

"Hey, buddy." Brett put an arm around his shoulder. "What's your name?"

He shrugged off Brett's arm. "Neville, Neville Ordway. And I'm not your buddy. Remember my name, though. You can expect to hear it a lot as we work this out through the court system."

Rona groaned. "Surely that won't be necessary."

"Of course it won't," Eric said. "Here, Neville. Maybe this will ease your pain." He held out several bills, fanned to show the denomination clearly.

Rona gasped at the amount of the bribe, but she hoped it worked. No telling how much Neville could get if he decided to press charges. She hated to think that she'd cost Leo more money, so if Neville took the bribe, she'd just tell Leo to forget the Tahiti trip. Instead she'd dress up in a grass skirt and give him an extra-special blow job. He only went on those trips because of the vacation sex, anyway.

Neville shook his head. "You can't buy me off that easy. Just pay for the pizza. We'll settle the rest before a judge."

"Land sakes, what have we here?" Suz pranced through the open door and sidled over to Neville. "Well, aren't you a cutie?"

Rona stared at her friend, who'd suddenly developed a thick Southern accent. In the forgiving light of sunset, Suz could have been thirty-five, and she was acting twenty-five. She'd fluffed her short brown hair and unbuttoned her blouse to show off what was still impressive cleavage. Then she'd tied the tails of the blouse under her breasts to emphasize her flat tummy. In her low-rider shorts and her sequined mules, she was what used to be called a dish.

Neville looked like he completely agreed. His eyes did a cartoony thing where they seemed to bulge out of his head, and his Adam's apple bobbed. "Uh, hi."

"Hi, yourself, sugar." Suz meandered toward him, hips swaying. "If I'd known somebody as gorgeous as you delivered the pizza, I'd have been ordering every night. I like my pizzas hot and my deliverymen even hotter."

Neville gulped. "We deliver seven days a week."

"Honey pie, I'm sure you deliver *all* the time." Suz batted her eyelashes and took a deep breath, which expanded her chest another couple of inches.

"Uh . . . well . . . I do my best. Would you, um, do you . . . want to see a menu? I can get you a menu from the car. Then if you ever want to order something—"

"I can think of several things I'd like to order, and I'm sure you'd bring them all right to momma." Suz linked her arm through his. "Let's you and me go get that little ol' menu and take a look." The two of them walked over to a beat-up sedan sporting a lighted PIZZA sign attached to the passenger window.

Rona could have kissed Suz for such a successful distraction. Maybe they'd get out of this okay, after all. She turned to Eric and Brett. "I'm so sorry, guys. I never dreamed ordering pizza could cause this much trouble."

Eric watched Suz and Neville over by the car. "If we're real lucky, Suz and her vamp routine might handle it for us. I have to say I was worried when he wouldn't take the cash. That was a good payoff."

"I hope Suz handles it," Brett said. "Because if we all get hauled into court, Leo will shit a brick."

"Ain't that the truth," Eric said. "We never would've tackled him if he'd just shown us some ID and convinced us he wasn't working for Joey Benjamin, but he freaked and went into this weird kind of martial arts stance, so we reacted."

"I understand," Rona said. "When it comes to protecting Dexter, we don't want to take chances. I could kick myself for ordering the— Omigod, will you look at that."

"I'll be damned," Eric said. "Neville's leaving. I wonder if she paid him for the pizza?"

Suz came back up the walk, grinning. "By God, I've still got it! And we're in the clear."

"I'm not sure I want to know how you did that," Rona said.

"Oh, I suggested that the two of us might get together sometime, and I might even do it, although I'd have to keep my condo really dark. He's probably all of nineteen. Anyway, the pizza, such as it is, is free."

Rona was afraid to celebrate yet. After the impact of Suz's charms wore off, Neville could still decide to make a stink. "So you're absolutely sure he's not going to press charges?"

"Not after I told him why he shouldn't."

"Which was?" Brett asked.

"I said he needed to think about why this house was guarded by a couple of thugs."

"Hey!" Eric and Brett said together.

"Look, would you rather have Leo climbing your backs because the guy charged you with assault? I used the word 'thugs' on purpose. I said Rona was protected because she was the girlfriend of someone he wouldn't want to mess with, a guy of Sicilian descent. He got my message and left."

Eric and Brett exchanged a glance and then they both shrugged.

"Okay," Eric said. "That works, I guess."

"You could say 'Thank you,' " Suz said.

Brett bowed. "Thank you. And let me add that you do look hot in that outfit, considering your age, and all."

Suz glanced at Rona. "Okay if I deck this punk?"

"Sure."

"We were just leaving," Eric said as he grabbed Brett's arm. "Let's resume our post, Brett. And keep your mouth shut, okay? Sheesh. If that was a compliment, you need some serious tutoring in how to get women."

"Considering my age, indeed," Suz said as she leaned down to pick up the flattened box of pizza.

"Suz, you're amazing." Rona slid the cheese pizza back into the box. If they brushed off the bits of gravel, they could eat most of it. "Thank you."

"Ah, it was fun. I haven't tried that Southern routine on a guy in ages."

Rona picked up the pizza box and started toward the door. "You should try it more often."

"No, thanks. One round with Neville will satisfy my quota for the year, if I even decide to take him on. Mostly, men are too much work."

"I don't know. Leo is a real comfort sometimes."

"I'm sure he is. Leo is one in a million. I'd have to kiss a creek full of frogs before finding the likes of Leo. Listen, is he really connected to the Mafia?"

As always, Rona felt a surge of excitement as she contemplated Leo's mysterious world, a world he referred to in vague terms. "I don't know for sure. He doesn't talk about it."

"Well, there you go. That clinches it for me. So, are you ready to face the wild bunch?"

"They're not going to like what happened to the pizza."

"That is for damned sure." Suz pried the lid off the smashed box. "Oh, dear. I don't think we'll be able to bet on this one."

Rona laughed. "No, we'll have to switch to your date with Neville. I'll bet he calls you tomorrow."

"Yeah, and if he calls, and if I agree to see him, we can bet on how many times he gets it up."

"But we can't make that bet in front of Dexter."

Suz looked horrified. "You think I'd bet on something like that in front of Dexter? I have grandchildren, too, you know!"

"I know. Sorry to have suggested you would."

"It's okay." Suz patted her arm. "When you first start out, you're bound to be really protective."

"Right." As Rona followed Suz inside, she realized that Suz had just made two assumptions: (a) Rona was now officially classified as a grandmother, and (b) she would continue to have that status. Damned if that didn't feel wonderful.

Chapter Nineteen

Lainie made Harry wait in the living room while she primped for her date. She'd explained to him that after five years, she deserved a little primping time before she left for dinner with an honest-to-goodness man. She hoped that suggesting dinner hadn't been too greedy on her part.

But Harry had made it plain that he had the money to spend and enjoyed spending it on her. That felt really nice. Since she'd been concentrating on Dexter for the past few years, she'd forgotten many things about the dating process, and this was one of them—the satisfaction of making herself pretty for the man who'd offered to buy her dinner.

Fortunately she always carried makeup in her purse, so that part she hadn't needed Rona to provide. Rona had loaned her a killer black skirt, though, and a black silk tank. The short skirt paired with her spike-heeled sandals from her dance costume looked damned hot, if she said so herself. Because she hadn't been dating, she hadn't bought anything like this for herself in ages. She missed the fun of clothes shopping, but she wouldn't trade Dexter for a million shopping sprees.

Still, dressing up tonight felt terrific. She was beginning to like the red wig, maybe because she'd had sex with Harry twice while wearing it. So far this trip had shot way past her expectations. And she hadn't even worn the red nightgown yet.

She planned to give it a trial run tonight after dinner. It was hanging on the back of the bathroom door, ready for deployment, phase two of her evening seduction routine. Applying one last coat of lip gloss, she screwed the brush back into the tube, set it on the counter, and stepped back to evaluate her work.

Not bad. She ran her hands down her hips, smoothing the snug little skirt. Going out to dinner with a guy she really liked had a special, Christmas-morning feel to it. And after all this great sex, her body felt sleek and honed in a way that dancing couldn't duplicate.

The only part of this caper that didn't feel so good was knowing everything would soon end. So she worked hard to keep her mind focused on the here and now. She knew the time was drawing closer when she'd have to contact Joey. He'd given her his cell phone number when he'd called to say he wanted to get back together, and her brain had recorded it even though she hadn't really wanted to remember.

That meant she could call Joey anytime she wanted to. She hadn't told Harry that, because she was postponing the call. But she'd have to make it. The only answer to her problem was working out a compromise with Joey. Dexter deserved to have a shot at that inheritance.

She'd never thought of him as being a grandson of Doyle Benjamin, but he was, after all.

For tonight, though, she'd treat herself, because it had been so long since she'd enjoyed male company. For a little while, she wouldn't think about Doyle or how she'd work things out with Joey. Harry was taking her to dinner, and after dinner would come all the possibilities suggested by the red nightgown. If she concentrated on dinner, the red nightgown, and Harry, she wouldn't have a chance to think about the other stuff.

With that resolution fresh in her mind, she made her entrance into the living room. Harry sat—like men traditionally sat while they waited for the women in their lives—sprawled on the sofa looking bored while he leafed through a couple of old magazines that had been left on the coffee table. At the click of her heels on the tile floor, he glanced up.

His expression as he looked her over was worth every second she'd spent getting ready. He reminded her of the way Dexter surveyed a hot fudge sundae, although there was a definite difference. In addition to eager anticipation, Harry's eyes gleamed with a healthy dose of lust.

She did her share of ogling, too. Harry had cleaned up pretty good, himself, which made his male appreciation that much sweeter. Leo's imported clothes—gray silk shirt and black slacks—had turned Harry into a European playboy type. An intellectual European playboy.

He cleared his throat. "I think we've come to the part where I try to convince you to reconsider the room service option. Or better yet, postpone dinner for about two hours until we satisfy . . . other cravings."

She smiled. "So I look good to you?"

"In case you haven't noticed, I'm wiping the drool off my chin. Are you absolutely sure we have to leave?" He gave her a wolfish grin. "I could make it worth your while to stay, little girl. I'll give you treats."

"I'm sure you would." Mental images of sex on the coffee table, her legs wrapped around his neck and her red sandals still on her feet, tempted her more than a little. But she really wanted a dinner date, too. Still, it was his call, because he was paying. "We can stay in if you want."

"But you want me to take you out," he said gently. "And I would love to do that. Let's go." He stood, pulled car keys out of the pocket of his slacks, and picked up his cell phone. "We should probably keep this around, though."

"Probably. And in case I haven't said it enough, I really appreciate going out tonight. This dinner date means more than you know."

"I should never have questioned the idea of going." He unlocked the front door and opened it for her. "I think it's a crime that you've had to live like a nun all these years and give up any kind of social life. I understand it, but still, what a sacrifice."

"Your mom did the same for you." She stepped into the warm night.

"Yeah, she did, and after seeing it from your perspective, I'm starting to feel guilty as hell about that." He pressed a button on his key ring and the car's parking lights flashed as the locks clicked open.

"I'm sure she wouldn't want you to. I'd never want Dexter to feel guilty. By the way, shouldn't we be watching for snakes?"

"Ah, geez. I forgot about the damned snakes. Let's

get in the car. We can discuss guilt and motherhood in the nice, safe restaurant." He hustled her around to the passenger side and in through the car door. Then he sprinted to his side and hopped in, slamming his door shut. "That's better." He slipped the cell phone in its holder on the dash.

"You could have let me get my own self in, if you were so spooked," she said, laughing.

"I could not." He looked offended. "This is your first date in a trillion years, and we're going to do it right. Snakes or no snakes."

"Harry, you're a peach." She didn't remember where that expression had come from until after the words popped out of her mouth. One of the TITS had called Leo that.

"Thanks." He gave her a smile and started the engine. "You're more than a peach. You're an entire fruit salad."

"Why, thank you, Harry. Are compliments part of this dating experience, too?"

"Nope." He drove slowly through the parking lot of the resort. "Compliments are what you should be getting on a regular basis, regardless of the circumstances. And I think— Hey, look, there's a silver Jag like Leo's. I guess that's a common color."

"You don't think it *is* Leo, do you?"

"Nah. He wouldn't come down here, even if he thought we needed looking after. He'd send one of his boys. But that reminds me, maybe I should call him and tell him what we're doing. He'll complain, but that's just Leo and his mobster orientation, as you said."

Lainie turned around to get a better look at the silver Jag. She thought she saw someone sitting in it, a guy, maybe, but in the darkness she couldn't tell for sure. She faced forward with a shrug. If Harry didn't think Leo would drive all the way down here, then Harry would know. He'd been around Leo more than she had. But she had a funny feeling that the car did belong to Leo, and that Leo had been sitting in the car. It wasn't a logical explanation, just a feeling.

She was probably wrong. Harry was talking to Leo right this minute on the cell phone, and if they'd just passed him in the parking lot, surely Leo would have said so and told Harry to wait up. She didn't really want Leo to be down here. On the serious side, that would mean he was really worried about her safety, and on the not-so-serious side, Leo hanging around could put a real crimp in her plans to screw Harry's brains out tonight after dinner.

But Leo must not be here, because Harry wasn't indicating anything like that during his conversation. From Harry's comments, she could tell that Leo wasn't happy that they were leaving the resort to go to dinner. She had to make allowances for Leo's attitude, though, because he didn't know Joey.

"We'll be in a restaurant, Leo," Harry said, sounding reasonable and patient. "We won't have anything to worry about." He paused. "I promise to be very careful. But just so you know, Lainie thinks we're overreacting about Joey." He paused again. "Yeah, I see your point. I'll keep that in mind. Bye, Leo."

Lainie waited, expecting Harry to explain that last part to her. When he drove along in silence, she decided to ask. "What point was Leo making? What are you supposed to keep in mind?"

He hesitated. "Well, like you said, Leo's in the kind of business that breeds paranoia."

Apparently Harry wasn't eager to share Leo's insights with her, which meant he didn't think she'd like hearing them. Too bad. "And?"

"Oh, he's got some psychological theory going, that because Joey is Dexter's father, you'd be slow to accept that he might be capable of really bad things."

"And you thought that might be true?"

He glanced at her. "I don't know, Lainie. I've never had a kid, but I suppose, if I did have one, I might want to ignore warning signs about the mother." He returned his attention to the road. "It's logical that you wouldn't want to believe bad things about the other parent, because that puts everybody in an awkward situation, including the kid."

She decided there was no point in contradicting that argument. "All right, let's say I can't let myself believe that Joey wants to have me killed so he could get his inheritance." Yet every time she tried to take the concept seriously, she had to laugh. It sounded so melodramatic and unlike Joey.

"The thing is, people can get crazy when billions of dollars are on the line," Harry said.

"Billions of dollars have always been on the line, Harry. If the thought of inheriting it could drive Joey nuts, why hasn't he already bumped off his two brothers? Oh, and he might as well waste Doyle while he's at it, to make sure there's no doubt who gets to take over."

"See, that would take a really violent person." Harry stopped at a red light. "I'm not saying he's that bad.

He might have resigned himself to not getting the business, but then here comes a real shot."

"But it's not a real shot. There's no chance in hell that Doyle will turn over his empire to Joey. Joey's not supersmart to begin with, plus he has a drinking problem. Even if he paraded a hundred male heirs in front of Doyle, I don't think Doyle would be stupid enough to turn things over to him. Emil is the smart one. I'm not sure about Joey's younger brother, but Emil would have been the perfect choice."

"But does Joey understand he doesn't have a shot, even with Dexter?"

She thought about Joey's delusions of grandeur. In his mind, he was always on the brink of fame and fortune. "No, I suppose not. He might be kidding himself that Dexter's the answer to everything."

"So in his mind, you could be the only obstacle to that dream," Harry said. "And don't forget that he owes some underworld characters a whole lot of money. I hate to say this, but I think Leo may have reason to be paranoid."

Lainie sighed in resignation. "If everyone's so convinced, then maybe we should turn around and head back to the resort."

"I didn't say that."

"But I want to be a grown-up about this. I may be sick of having Joey Benjamin rule what I do, but that's the consequence of getting involved with him in the first place."

"You were young." Harry gave no indication he was ready to turn back.

"And I thought I knew everything. Seriously, let's go back to the resort and order hamburgers again. Or chicken nuggets. Maybe Joey's hanging around Sedona waiting for a chance to wrap piano wire around my throat." She doubted it, but everyone else seemed to think it was a distinct possibility.

"We'll go to the restaurant."

"Are you sure?"

"I'm sure. This place will be fine."

She glanced at him. "You say that like you picked one out."

"Of course I picked one out." He smiled at her. "That's what you do on a real date. While you were getting ready I called Thalia and she suggested a place. I tried to make reservations, but they didn't take them. They said we should have no problem getting a table, though."

"All righty, then." She relaxed against the seat, ridiculously happy to be following through on the date. "What's the name of this restaurant?"

"The Cowboy Club. It's an institution in Sedona, but even more important, it's in the heart of the business district. Thalia suggested lots of great-sounding restaurants, but quite a few of them were in outlying areas. I wanted to make sure we'd have plenty of people around."

"That's smart. The more people, the better, if we're going for security."

"I was, plus . . ."

She waited, but he didn't finish the sentence. "Plus what?"

"Never mind."

"Harry, you can't start to say something and then just quit. That's not fair."

"Yeah, I know, and I'm too damned honest for my own good. But I felt guilty having you think I picked a restaurant in the middle of Uptown Sedona strictly for security reasons."

She tried to guess what he was talking about. "I know. You don't want me to know you have a problem with directions and so you picked a place on the main drag because you'd have no trouble finding it."

"No, I'm terrific with directions. I also have an onboard GPS."

"Then you'd better tell me your other reason. Because if you don't tell me now, I'll pester you all through dinner."

"You'll laugh."

"Try me."

He cleared his throat. "I, um, like the idea of people seeing you with me. There. Now you know my darkest secret."

"You want to show me off?" The idea thrilled her.

"Pretty unevolved, huh? Not to mention dumb. I'm never going to see these people again, so why do I care whether they think I'm man enough to be dating a woman who looks like you?"

"Oh, Harry." She reached over and touched his arm. "You're more than man enough."

"You don't have to say that."

"I know. And I wouldn't, if I didn't think so. I'm . . . well, I'm honored to be going to dinner with you tonight."

He slowed down to turn left toward the main section of town. "It's not like you have a lot of guys to choose from."

Her heart squeezed as she realized how truly vulnerable he was. Maybe he'd inherited his father's shy nature along with the intelligence and sexual equipment. "If I could be going to dinner with any man in the world tonight, I'd still choose you," she said.

The dim light from the dash was just enough to reveal his little-boy smile of delight. "Thanks," he said.

As Joey drove his rental car through the darkness toward Sedona, he thought about what Mandy, the waitress, had said to him a couple of hours ago. They'd been relaxing on the bed drinking champagne after he'd come the first time, which had been lickety-split. Faster than a speeding bullet.

He wasn't going to blame himself for that, either. He'd been too long without, and once she'd stripped off that waitress uniform, seeing her 40-Ds bobbing in front of him had almost been enough to do the trick. Then she'd decided to work on him a little first, and her sweaty palms had turned out to be an asset when it came to hand jobs. Next thing he knew, Old Faithful had erupted.

Because the first session had been so short, he'd decided to treat them both to a second round, but that meant a recovery period. He'd ordered up another bottle of champagne and they'd propped themselves against the headboard while they drank it. Mandy had turned out to be his kind of girl—happy to drink champagne out of the bathroom glasses because they held more than the flimsy champagne flutes room service had brought.

In the process of drinking and talking, Joey had ended up telling her the whole story about how Lainie had selfishly taken his only kid away and how important the little guy was to him, in many ways. By the time they'd gone through most of the second bottle, Mandy was getting mad on his account. She was also getting drunk, but Joey didn't care about that. He liked that she took his side against Lainie, though. That felt really good.

"You jus' need to get rid of her," Mandy had said, waving her drink and nearly spilling it on the sheet.

"How?" Joey had asked, watching Mandy's tits jiggle.

"Who cares? She did you wrong. Get rid of her."

"Maybe I will." Announcing that had made him feel more manly and in charge of his destiny. He'd made her put her drink down and they'd gone at it again. He enjoyed having sex with a woman who was smashed, because then she was more likely to let him put it wherever he felt like putting it.

Mandy had given him plenty of leeway in that department. Because he had more staying power this time, he'd been able to try out everything she had to offer. Right before he'd come again, she'd looked over her shoulder and asked if he'd be sure and remember her when he was a billionaire.

"Yeah," he'd said. "Definitely." Then he'd shot his wad.

He'd left her there to sleep it off, but not before getting her phone number. It was always nice to have a few good phone numbers in case he was ever in Vegas again.

He liked Mandy. Besides giving him a good time, she'd given him something to think about. Lainie *had* done him wrong. He wouldn't mind finding a way to get her out of the way. Maybe during the drive he'd think of how he could do that.

Chapter Twenty

Harry had to settle for a parking spot a block north of the restaurant, but when he saw the number of people milling around he wasn't particularly worried that the walk to the restaurant would be risky. Matter of fact, it would be gratifying. It wasn't every day he escorted the likes of Lainie Terrell to dinner. Maybe he could be forgiven for feeling smug as he helped her out of the car and took her hand as they started down the sidewalk.

Technically he hadn't orchestrated this moment. Even more technically, he'd had pretty much zero input. It was more like he'd been shoved into the right place at the right time. Therefore he had no right to this feeling of manly pride as he watched other guys looking at him with naked envy in their eyes.

He was feeling it, anyway. Pity the poor slobs who could only look, while he had the privilege of touching. Soon he'd have to return Leo's imported clothes and resume his stodgy life that revolved around unyielding numbers on a spreadsheet. In the meantime, he was strutting along beside the hottest babe in town, and the words "spread" and "sheet" took on whole other meanings.

Because guess what? Lainie would be spending the night in his bed and wrapping those long dancer's legs around his waist. In fact, she'd let him know in many subtle ways how much she looked forward to doing that. Now *there* was an astounding factoid. Lainie wanted *him*. If he'd been afraid she'd try him out and find him lacking, that fear had been put to rest.

Lainic squeezed his hand and leaned her head close to his. "Harry?"

"What, Lainie?" He squeezed back, thinking that she smelled delicious. Maybe she wanted to whisper something outrageous in his ear, just to tease him about the activities they'd enjoy later. Taking her out in public after the kind of sexually stimulating day they'd had was a definite turn-on. He wondered if everyone could tell they were lovers and sort of hoped they could.

"I think someone's watching us."

Harry laughed. Damned if he didn't feel at least ten feet tall right now. "They sure are. And it's not us but *you* they're watching. Every guy within gawking distance would sell his soul if he could be me tonight. And I don't blame him a bit."

"No, that's not what I mean." She tugged him to a stop and murmured urgently in his ear. "I keep catching a movement out of the corner of my eye, and when I look around, I see someone disappear into a doorway. Then, after I quit watching, there's that sense of someone following us again."

The glow faded from Harry's evening. Hell. He'd let his ego get in the way of his assignment, which was to protect Lainie. Leo had made him promise to be careful, and instead he'd been parading down the street like a dork, soaking up the moment. Lainie had been the one keeping an eye out, not her appointed bodyguard, aka Harry the Clueless. That's what happened when you sent an accountant as a stand-in for James Bond.

Wondering if it was too little, too late, he turned around and scanned the area. On this warm August evening, with the pavement still damp from the rain and the breeze cool and fragrant, people were everywhere. He saw kids with ice-cream cones and grandmothers nibbling squares of fudge. Shops were still open and tourists strolled along with plastic bags full of souvenirs. Some teenagers were horsing around near the crosswalk, and a young couple with a baby in a stroller sat on a bench.

On the surface, the scene looked perfectly safe. He didn't see anyone who posed a threat, but then, he was obviously no good at this. He looked closer, needing to find a bad guy, any bad guy. Surely somebody in the area was acting suspicious.

Okay, what about that fellow window-shopping on the other side of the street? He didn't seem to have much of a purpose to his behavior, so he could be a pretend tourist up to no good. His build was similar to Joey's, and his hair was about the color Harry remembered from that quick encounter in the back parking lot of the Nirvana.

"You mean that guy?" he asked, pointing to the window-shopper.

"No. The person I catch glimpses of is dressed in

dark clothes. That guy has on light-colored shorts and a white T-shirt. And he's on the wrong side of the street."

"So you're sure that's not Joey looking in the store window?"

"I'm absolutely sure. Joey's heavier than that, and besides, his hair's a darker shade of blond."

Harry had found a potential villain, and he wasn't giving up that easy. "He could have changed since you last saw him."

"It's not Joey. I can tell by the way he stands. Joey sort of slouches, but that guy's posture is much straighter. And if you need more proof, here comes the woman who's probably his wife."

"She could be part of his disguise."

"Harry, trust me, that's not Joey. And it's not the man who's been following us, either. Sometimes a tourist is just a tourist."

Harry's eyes narrowed as a dark-haired woman came up to the man he'd picked out as villain material. The woman dangled a wind chime she'd obviously just bought, and the man shrugged. It was the shrug that convinced Harry this was just a husband waiting for his souvenir-buying wife. Joey wouldn't have the acting ability required to manufacture that shrug.

"Okay, so that's not Joey," he said. "But look around and see if you notice anybody who could possibly be him, or someone who looks vaguely like him. You're disguising yourself. Maybe he is, too."

"Joey? Not likely. I keep telling you, he's not the devious type. If he had been, he never would have stood outside my apartment yelling the way he did. Think about it . . . he would have waited until I came home and tried to sneak up behind me."

"All right, but he could have hired someone to do his dirty work." Harry continued to scrutinize each of the people in the immediate vicinity.

"You and Leo have spooked me enough that I'm starting to believe that one, especially after I thought I caught someone following us."

Now Harry was seeing boogeymen everywhere. Maybe even the little kid with the ice cream was actually a dwarf who'd been hired as a hit man. "But you don't see that person now."

"No, but I never got a good look at him, anyway. Whoever it is probably ducked into one of the shops and won't come out again as long as we're standing here staring in that direction. We'll have to move quickly to catch him following us."

"Then here's what we'll do. Let's keep on walking toward the restaurant, and when I say 'now,' we'll both spin around and see if anyone's there."

"Harry, that's going to look very strange."

"Ask me if I care." Ten minutes ago he'd been focused on appearances while he forgot about guarding Lainie. Now he'd gladly look like a fool if it meant he'd catch whoever was lurking behind them.

What he'd do with that person once he caught them was unclear at the moment. He hoped they weren't armed, but that was probably a vain hope. If they were lurking, they were packing. He'd seen his share of stalker movies.

He turned back to face in the direction of the restaurant

and took Lainie's hand. "We'll take five steps and then spin around. Ready?"

She gave him a nudge in the ribs. "Then how about five steps forward, five steps back, spin around, spin around, kick to the left, kick to the right—"

"Cut it out. This will work."

"You're probably right. I'm just nervous, and I get silly when I get nervous." She fidgeted with one of the curls of her red wig. "I don't know if I'm ready to catch this person or not. If we actually find out someone scary is following us, then what?"

"I'll dctain him."

She looked doubtful. "With what?"

Harry had been wondering the same thing. He'd seen some six-shooter replicas in the window of a shop. Maybe if he had one of those, he could convince someone he was armed and dangerous. Yeah, right.

"You don't have the slightest idea what you'll do if you catch him, do you?" she asked.

"Well, not exactly, but I'm sure I'll think of something when the time comes."

She blew out a breath. "You could end up getting beat into a bloody pulp. Or worse. I don't want you to try taking this guy on, whoever he is. Did you bring the cell phone?"

"No, but I doubt you could knock anybody unconscious with it, if that's what you were thinking."

"I was thinking you could call Leo and ask his advice."

Harry didn't want to call Leo. Leo had advised against this dinner outing, and now they might be in some sort of sticky situation as a result. Leo was an "I told you so" kind of guy, which made Harry loath to give him the chance.

"Tell you what," he said. "Let's go eat, just as we planned to do. Then I'll leave you in the restaurant with plenty of company while I go get the car. I'll double-park and come in to get you. Zip, and you'll be back in the car. Minimum exposure."

She nodded. "Very good. I'm in favor of any plan that doesn't include you trying to chase down some suspicious character."

"I'm sure I could handle that if we decided it was necessary." He wasn't the least bit sure, but he hated looking like a wimp to her. Fortunately, his brain was busy manufacturing an excuse for not challenging the stalker. "You know, it's always possible this person following us is a decoy. Maybe my chasing him would be exactly what they want. If I'm distracted, a second person could grab you."

"Exactly. So you'd better stick close to me."

"Just what I was thinking." He didn't know if she bought his line of reasoning or if she were humoring him, but at least he now had a graceful way out of a potentially risky situation. Using brawn wasn't wise in his case, and he knew it. He'd have to outthink these bad guys, whoever they were.

Red wine, an excellent steak, and sharing dinner conversation with Harry allowed Lainie to push her worries to the back of her mind. She told him a little about her background, giving him a version that didn't make her parents seem quite as cold and uncaring as she feared, deep down, they were. She suspected Harry drew that conclusion, anyway. It was hard not to if you took into account that her parents hadn't been interested in Dexter, simply because Lainie hadn't married Dexter's irresponsible father.

There was certainly nothing cold and uncaring or irresponsible about Harry, Lainie decided. She had no doubt that he'd literally take a bullet for her if the occasion demanded it. That meant she had to watch out for him and make sure he didn't do anything stupid. He had unlimited courage, but she doubted he'd had any recent street-fighting experience.

She, on the other hand, had taken a couple of self-defense classes offered by the casino she'd worked for in Atlantic City. The management had recommended that their female employees get some training, and so she had. Whether she could remember much of what she'd learned was another matter. But she wouldn't be helpless in an emergency.

Telling Harry that, however, didn't seem like a great idea. She'd already implied that he wasn't up to the job of chasing down the bad guys. If she let it be known she could protect herself, his ego might get permanently deflated. And when a guy's ego was deflated, other parts of him could suffer the same fate. She'd didn't want any deflation of any sort going on tonight.

Chances were they wouldn't need to worry about bad guys, anyway. The longer she sat in this cozy restaurant drinking wine, the more she became convinced that she'd imagined someone was following them. Maybe she was getting as paranoid as Leo.

Feeling pleasantly full and extremely mellow, she gazed across the table at Harry. He'd cleaned his plate but had barely touched his wine, even though he'd been the one who'd insisted they order a bottle of red to go with the filet mignon they'd both ordered.

She gestured toward his wine glass. "Don't you like it?"

"Sure." He took another small sip.

"Then you must be holding back on purpose."

"Well, sort of." He pushed his glasses more firmly onto the bridge of his nose. "I don't want to risk slowing my reaction time, just in case."

Now she felt guilty, especially considering that he was paying for the meal and it wasn't cheap. "I should have thought that way, too. We could have skipped the bottle of wine. It's not like I had to have wine with my meal."

He smiled at her. "Yeah, you did. It's your first dinner date in five years, remember? Gotta have wine for that."

She propped her chin on her fist and gazed at him with affection. "You're such a sweetheart."

"Don't give me too much credit. Any guy who had the privilege of taking you home tonight would have to be pretty dumb not to treat you like a princess. I mean, considering the potential rewards involved."

She laughed, remembering the red nightgown hanging on the back of the bathroom door. Then she noticed the way he was looking at her and started getting warm and squishy with lust. "Speaking of rewards, let's leave."

"You're entitled to dessert, you know."

She gave him a lazy smile. "I know. That's why I want to leave."

"Uh-*huh*." He nearly knocked over his water glass in his haste to signal the waiter. "Check, please."

As he signed the charge slip, she admired the elegance of his long fingers and the bold strokes of his signature. No doubt about it, she'd developed a serious case of the hots for Harry Ambrewster.

He tucked his card back in his wallet and glanced at her. "So what's my Visa number?"

She rattled it off without thinking, then stared at him in horror. "Are you afraid I might—"

"Good grief, no. I'm just curious about this photographic memory of yours. You could probably tear up the blackjack tables, at least until they made you quit playing."

"I suppose." Gambling had never interested her. "If I could sit still long enough. And then there's Dexter. I hate leaving him while I'm working, let alone hiring a babysitter so I can gamble."

"Especially babysitters like Mrs. Flippo, who won't even play Chutes and Ladders with him."

"He told you about that, huh?"

"Yeah."

"Poor Mrs. Flippo. She's sweet and honest, but she's not smart enough for Dexter. Then again, I don't know many people who are. That's why he was so excited to have—" She caught herself. "Oh, God, that sounded like I was trying to manipulate you into continuing to watch him. I would never do that. I only—"

"I know you wouldn't." He put his hand over hers. "I've never met anyone more determined to take care of her own responsibilities than you. And just to set the record straight, I've had a great time taking care of Dexter. It hasn't been a chore." He squeezed her hand. "And the cookies were terrific."

"Thanks, Harry." She swallowed a sudden lump in her throat. From the moment she'd given birth to Dexter, she'd felt the burden of caring for him by herself. Sure, she'd hired babysitters, but none of them had acted as if the job were a privilege. Harry and Rona had both given her that feeling, and for now, her burden was lighter.

"I'll go get the car. Give me five minutes before you head for the front door." He released her hand and switched wine glasses with her. "You can sip on this while I'm gone."

She slid the glass aside. "I'm going, too. Waiting here feels silly. I've decided I was seeing things, anyway." And if she hadn't been seeing things, she didn't want Harry heading out to face whoever it was all alone.

"I'd feel better if you stayed in here until I get the car."

"And I'd feel better going with you. We've handled this together so far—why split up now?" She could see him hesitate, so she pushed her advantage. "I feel safer when I'm with you."

"Tell you what. We'll compromise. I'll go get the car, but you can stand right by the front door and watch me. We're not parked far away. I think you'll be able to keep an eye on me the whole time."

Deciding that was reasonable, she nodded. "Okay." As she walked ahead of him to the front of the restaurant, she felt his hand at the small of her back and her skin grew warm there. Soon she'd feel his hands all over her body. She could hardly wait.

Right before he left her, Harry surprised her with a quick kiss. "Stay right here," he said, and walked out onto the sidewalk.

Her mouth tingled as she watched him stride toward the car. How wonderful to feel a man's lips on hers again, especially Harry's lips. He was a darned good kisser. She'd thought an accountant would be predictable when it came to kissing, but Harry was all about improv.

She continued to keep track of his progress. Nearly halfway there. One side street and a couple of stores to pass, and he'd be at the car. Once he was behind the wheel, she'd breathe easier.

Then, as he was crossing a side street less than twenty feet from his black Lexus, he spun suddenly to his left and started running.

Chapter Twenty-one

Lainie flung herself out the door without thinking, slipping her purse strap over her body bandolier-style as she ran. Wherever Harry was going, she was going with him. He needed her help.

Years of dancing in four-inch heels meant she could run perfectly well in them, too. Her purse thumped against her hip, but otherwise she was good to go. She rounded the corner and started down the side street as Harry caught up to a man wearing dark clothing, the same man she'd seen earlier.

Just then the man rounded on Harry and shouted something. But Harry had already launched himself into the guy's midsection with a solid thump. They both went down and started thrashing around in the mud beside the narrow paved road.

Lainie had never been so scared in her life. She wasn't close enough to do anything yet, and any minute she expected a knife to flash or a gun to go off, leaving Harry limp and lifeless. She wasn't about to let that happen if she could help it.

The two men rolled and twisted in the mud, with Harry grunting and trying to land blows, and the other guy cussing a blue streak. Once she was within range, Lainie pulled her purse off and used both hands to swing it at the guy's head. With the weight of her makeup and small bottle of perfume, she might be able to do some damage. The purse connected with a satisfying crack.

"Dammit!" The guy gave a mighty shove that temporarily dislodged Harry. "Dammit, Harry, it's Leo!"

Lainie froze. *Leo?*

"Leo?" On all fours and weaving a little, Harry gulped for air. He'd lost his glasses sometime during the scuffle and had to squint. "What . . . what are you doing here?"

Leo sat up and tried to brush the mud off the sleeves of his silk shirt, but it only smeared. He puffed out a few swear words. "You know, I ask myself the same question. Aw, will you look at that? You put a hole in the elbow of my good shirt. I just bought this shirt. Cost me three big ones."

Lainie stepped cautiously toward him. "Leo, I'm sorry that I hit you over the head with my purse. I didn't know it was you."

He moved his fingers lightly over the back of his head and winced. "At least I'm not bleeding. The head injury I can deal with. It's the shirt that gets me upset."

Harry staggered to his feet. "You're upset? *You're* upset? What the hell are you doing sneaking around here, scaring Lainie and me half to death?"

"Oh, Harry, you're the one who's bleeding." Lainie hurried over to inspect a scrape on his cheek.

"Oh, yeah? Good. I'll just wipe away the blood using the sleeve of this gray silk shirt belonging to one Leo Pirelli." He rubbed the sleeve over his cheek.

"Hey!" Leo staggered to his feet. "It's bad enough that this one is ruined. Don't go getting blood on that one, too, for chrissake."

"Leo, I don't care, okay? Lainie's been worried sick that someone was following us, and—"

"I wasn't *that* worried." Lainie had been more worried that Harry would try to play hero. And sure enough, he had tried exactly that. He was damned lucky the person he'd chased had turned out to be Leo.

"Yes, you were worried," Harry said. "And don't try to pretend you weren't. And all because of Leo."

"I can explain," Leo said. "But let's all go get a drink, first. I know I could use a drink. I ache all over." He braced his hands on his hips and arched his back. "So where's the nearest bar?"

"We just came from it," Lainie said. "The restaurant where we ate dinner has a bar."

"Then let's go." Leo sounded weary as he set off and motioned for them to follow him. "I'm buying." He walked toward the main drag.

"Wait," Harry said. "I have to find my glasses."

Leo paused. "If you hadn't made that flying tackle, you'd still be wearing your glasses, Einstein. Hell, I didn't think you knew how to do that."

"If you hadn't been sneaking around like some hit man, I wouldn't have tried to tackle you, now would I?"

Lainie decided trying to keep the two men from arguing was a waste of effort, so she looked for Harry's glasses. Fortunately, a car went by and the headlights glinted off a pair lying on the ground. Lainie snatched them up. "Here they are. And they're not even broken."

"Which reminds me," Leo said. "Aren't you supposed to be wearing my glasses? As part of your disguise?"

"Uh, yes." Lainie thought of the broken glasses back in their room. She wasn't looking forward to telling Leo about those, after his reaction to his damaged shirt. "I, um, forgot them."

Leo sighed. "Usually Boom-Boom's plans are better than this. But I have to say, so far it's been a total disaster. Come on. A stiff belt will make us all feel a hell of a lot better." He started down the street again.

Lainie glanced over at Harry, who was still standing there. "Are you going?"

"I guess." He put on his glasses and tried to get some of the mud off. Finally he gave up and rubbed his hands on whatever clean spot he could find. "But Leo's going to have to do more than buy us drinks to make up for this."

"Why did you run after him, anyway? I thought we agreed you wouldn't try that? Sure, it turned out to be Leo, but what if the guy had been dangerous?"

"That's exactly why I went after him." Harry still sounded furious.

"But that's not logical, Harry. He could have been armed, whereas you had no weapon at all!" She began to shake as her adrenaline rush wore off. "I was frantic, thinking any minute you could be killed. I find you rolling around in the mud, and now you're bleeding, and it was just dumb, Harry!"

"Which brings up the question of what you were doing there, doesn't it? The plan was you staying inside the restaurant until I brought the car up. What happened to the plan, Lainie? You were supposed to stay put!"

"If you think I would stand there like a good little girl while you went tearing off down the street chasing who knows what, then you need to adjust your thinking. I'm not about to let you get yourself killed while I hang around waiting in the wings. That's not my style."

"But what if there had been two of them, one to lure me away and the other to grab you?"

She hadn't wanted to bring up her training in consideration of his tender male ego, but he was ticking her off. She'd run to his rescue, and he wasn't even slightly grateful. "I know self-defense, okay? I could have taken care of myself."

"What kind of self-defense?" He sounded belligerent, very un-Harry-like.

"I don't know what kind, exactly." They reached the main street and turned right. "A course specifically designed for women, so we have some options if we ever got attacked. I took the course back in Jersey."

"Well, that's good, then." But he still sounded mad. "I'm glad you had that course. But you weren't being attacked. You went out there looking for trouble, and that's a different—"

"I went out there looking for you!" She was sick of being lectured. "How about a little gratitude on your part?"

"I had everything under control."

"Ha! If that's having everything under control, then I'd hate to see the day when you . . ." She lost her train of thought as a car cruised by, going slow. She realized now it was the same car that had passed when she was looking for the glasses. The headlights had helped her find them.

The car could be going around the block looking for a parking space, except for one thing. The man in the car looked like . . . "*Joey,*" she whispered.

"Joey?" Harry stopped in his tracks and glanced quickly in all directions. "You see Joey? Where? Where is he?"

"There!" Lainie pointed to the taillights as they continued on down the road.

"Which car? Leo! Hold up a sec!"

Just then an SUV blocked her view. "Auggh! Damn, now you can't see a thing! And the way the road curves . . . that's it. He's out of sight."

"But you saw him? Leo! Shit, I don't think he heard me. You really saw him?"

She pictured the person in the car. At the time, she'd been sure it was Joey. Now she wondered if she'd imagined it. Her brain was on overload, and maybe she was seeing things. "I thought it was him. Maybe not. Then that Navigator pulled out and blocked him."

Harry continued to stare down the street, his whole body clenched. "What did the car look like?"

"Sort of a gold color, two-door sedan." Lainie was so busy being fascinated by Harry's reaction that she forgot to be scared for a little while. He was practically sniffing the air. Give him a loincloth and a club, and he could pass for a guy on the trail of the woolly mammoth.

"Dammit." Harry's jaw worked. "I'll bet it's him. That describes the rental I saw him driving back at the casino."

"You saw him back in Vegas? You didn't tell me that!"

"I didn't want to scare you."

How incredibly sweet. She began to forgive him for being such an idiot a few minutes ago. "Did he see you?"

"Sure did. I knew it had to be him, and I didn't want him to know I was connected to you, so I made up some story about being a groundskeeper for the hotel. He seemed to buy it."

Leo walked back toward them. "So I look around, thinking you were right behind me, and here you are still way back here. What's up?"

"Lainie thinks she saw Joey. The guy was driving a gold-colored sedan."

Leo's attitude changed from weary to businesslike. "If it's the rental, it's a Ford Escort."

Lainie's tummy started to churn as she pictured the back end of the car. "It was an Escort."

Harry glanced at her. "License plate?"

The moment ran like a video clip in her head, and she rattled off the plate number.

"Good memory," Leo said.

"Photographic," Harry added.

"Let's see if the plate matches what I have." Leo pulled his wallet out of his back pocket and fished out a slip of paper. He held the paper at arm's length and squinted at what was written on it.

"Here." Harry grabbed the paper. "Where are your glasses, anyway?"

"In the car, and it's a good thing, too, or they'd be smashed to smithereens. And those things don't come cheap. So, is it the same car?"

"Sure is," Harry said. "Looks like Joey's in town."

The churning in Lainie's tummy became a heavy

ache. She tried to tell herself Joey was searching for her so they could talk and work something out, that there was nothing threatening about his being here. But the fact remained that she'd run and he'd found a way to follow her. No matter how much she tried to rationalize his behavior, she felt hunted.

Harry moved closer to Lainie, wanting to shield her, even though Joey's car was out of sight and there was no immediate likelihood that she was in danger. "What now?" he asked.

"We make some calls," Leo said. "Get some backup. You two go on into the bar and order me a Scotch. I'll get my cell phone and meet you in five minutes."

"Backup?" Harry was trying to imagine how any of Leo's boys would make it down to Sedona in time to help. "We're not in Vegas, Leo."

"I have contacts in Phoenix."

"Oh. Good." Harry had never been particularly keen on the underworld, but at times like this, mobsters could come in handy. He'd shelve his scruples for a guarantee that Lainie wouldn't get hurt. Shoot, he'd been doing that for years with his mother.

Lainie put her hand on Leo's arm. "Uh, I don't want to interfere in your program, because I don't know exactly what your plans are and don't want to know, really, but can I make one teeny-tiny request?"

"Sure." Leo glanced at her with fondness. "What is it?"

Harry could tell from Leo's expression that he'd taken a fatherly liking to her. Harry had always wondered if Leo wished he'd had kids of his own, but once he'd hooked up with Rona, he'd been stuck with Harry and no prospect of anything more.

Lainie cleared her throat. "The thing is, I don't want Joey rubbed out."

Amusement flashed in Leo's eyes. "That wasn't my intention."

"Good. That's good. Because I know he's a pain in the ass, but he's still Dexter's father."

Leo nodded. "I understand. All I want to do is contain him. Now go order me that drink."

"We will." Lainie took hold of Harry's arm. "Come on. We need to get Leo's drink." She started toward the Cowboy Club.

"I thought he was buying us a drink," Harry grumbled as he followed her. His evening was not going well. He was grateful to Leo for providing protection for Lainie, truly grateful. But there was no question that with Leo's arrival, Harry had been demoted.

And as for the sex he'd been hoping to have with Lainie, that might be up in smoke, too. On top of that, Joey was in town. Harry no longer had the illusion of having Lainie to himself, and that was making him grouchy.

Knowing his limitations, he should be thrilled that Leo had taken over. But during that brief time when he'd mistaken Leo for a stalker and chased after him, he'd felt terrific. Suddenly he'd been the man, the go-to guy who was making the world a safer place for Lainie Terrell.

Now Leo had that role, and logically, that was how it should be. Leo knew what he was doing, and Harry was only acting on gut instinct. Obviously his instincts were faulty, causing him to tackle one of the good guys. Joey had driven by in a gold car Harry should have identified, and he'd been too busy arguing with Lainie to notice. She'd noticed.

Yeah, he needed to step aside and leave this up to the professionals, but he didn't want to: He wanted this to be like in the movies, where he was handed the crisis and he solved it. And then . . . well, in the movies, the guy got the girl. That idea hadn't been part of his original scheme. And it still wasn't . . . was it?

He was thinking about that when they stepped inside the Cowboy Club. Some stares came his way, probably because of the blood and the mud on his clothes. In some ways he felt more at home in the Cowboy Club after that scuffle with Leo. A scuffle proved that he was a man's man, worthy of sitting at the bar and ordering something manly.

As he and Lainie slid onto bar stools, he turned to her. "Do you want anything?"

"Harry, there's something I need to tell you."

"Yeah?" He'd always hated that intro. It usually meant news that he'd rather not get.

"The first time Joey called me in Vegas, he gave me his new cell phone number. I tried to forget it, but you see how things stick in my mind."

Harry wondered how long he'd stick in her mind after this was over. Selfishly, he wanted to be a guy she never forgot. "You have an incredible memory," he said. She was incredible all over, come to think of it, and he thought about that a lot. "What are you planning to do with this cell phone information?" He had some idea but hoped he was wrong.

"I've been considering whether I should call Joey. And although I'd love to just discuss this on the phone,

I know Joey. He'll want to meet me somewhere. He thinks he's very persuasive in person."

"That doesn't mean you have to meet him."

"No, but if I don't, then I might be ruining Dexter's future. I think I have to meet him."

He'd been expecting something like this. Although he didn't like the idea of her being within a hundred miles of the jerk, he couldn't ignore the Dexter angle. No matter which way he cut it, Joey was still Dexter's father. As such, he had legal rights. Plus there was a fortune hanging in the balance, one that might someday go to Dexter, depending on how this played out.

"I've been putting off the idea of calling him," she said.

"I don't blame you."

"But maybe I should."

"Let's see what Leo thinks about it."

"What I think about what?" Leo slid onto a stool next to Harry. "So where's my drink?"

"We haven't ordered it yet," Lainie said. "We were talking, and I guess the bartender's been busy, because he hasn't come down to this end."

"Ah." Leo leveled a Sicilian glare in the bartender's direction, and like magic, the guy came right to them.

Harry had admired that glare for years. He'd practiced it in the mirror and tried it out a few times, but it had never worked for him. Maybe you had to be Sicilian or a member of whatever brotherhood Leo belonged to. When Leo got into his godfather mode, he commanded attention like nobody else Harry knew.

In no time at all, Leo had his Scotch on the rocks and Lainie and Harry each had a glass of mineral water. Harry had thought about ordering Scotch, too, because it seemed to fit the occasion, but he hated the taste. And despite the fact that he might not be needed as Lainie's bodyguard anymore, he wanted to stay sharp, just in case.

Leo took his first swallow and exhaled with pleasure. Then he turned to Lainie. "What were you going to ask my opinion about?"

"I know Joey's cell-phone number. I could cut to the chase on this deal and call him. Knowing him, he'll want me to meet him somewhere so we can talk. Maybe it's time."

Leo didn't act surprised by the information. "Probably. I have the number, too. I was going to suggest something like that, but not quite yet."

"Why not?" Lainie asked. "Wouldn't it be nice to let him know we know he's here?"

"In some ways." Leo sipped his drink. "But I'd like to wait until the Phoenix guys show up. We need to give them a couple of hours, and I like daylight better than dark for this meeting. More people around, and we can see better."

"Yeah, I like the daylight plan better, too," Harry said, although no one had asked his opinion. Clearly Lainie was looking to Leo for guidance, now.

"So you think I should wait and call Joey in the morning," Lainie said.

"I do." Leo gazed at the two of them. "I'll follow you back to the resort, to make sure he doesn't try anything there. However, it's not too likely, which is why I wanted you to stay there and not venture out. And now that I've put Dudley Shearson on the payroll, he—"

"Dudley?" Lainie and Harry said together.

"Yeah." Leo seemed to enjoy their reaction. "After observing him for a while, I decided he'd be a good man to have on our side. The guy isn't selling a whole lot of time-shares, so he was glad to get the pay."

"There's a reason he's not selling time-shares," Harry said. "The place is a dump."

Leo nodded. "I got that impression. Are the locks decent, at least?"

"They seem to be," Lainie said.

"And the place is old, so the doors are solid wood." Harry wanted Leo to know he'd checked that out. The door wouldn't give way like the one in Lainie's apartment.

"Then it should be fine for now," Leo said.

"So Dudley knows we're not Fred and Rona?" Harry asked.

"Not exactly. I didn't spell everything out, and fortunately, Dudley's not looking a gift horse in the mouth. But he's a tough old bird, him and his six-shooter, and—"

"Omigod," Harry said. "Dudley's carrying a *gun*?" He thought about the wild ride in the golf cart and shuddered.

"Ah, he won't need it," Leo said.

Harry gazed at Leo. "Do you carry a gun?"

"Only when I have to."

"Okay." Harry drained the rest of his mineral water and set the glass down with a determined thunk. "You said you'd explain why you were down here following us around. I can understand sending someone, but why come down here yourself?"

"Because your mother didn't trust anyone else to be discreet."

Harry started to laugh. "You call sneaking from store to store, scaring us out of our wits, discreet?"

"I haven't shadowed anybody in a long time, okay? I'm not as quick as I used to be."

"So why not send someone else?" Harry had been about to say "somebody younger and quicker," but thought better of it.

"Like I said, your mother wanted me to do it. And I have a big favor to ask. I'd like you to keep this evening's . . . events . . . from getting back to her. If I've ruined the mood for you two by getting caught spying, she's not gonna be happy."

Harry felt heat climbing up his neck. "Oh." So his mother had sent Leo because Leo would keep his distance and let nature take its course. Which it certainly had.

Leo took another swig of his Scotch. "So what I'm saying is that even though Dudley and I will be keeping watch tonight, I'm hoping you can forget we're even there."

Chapter Twenty-two

"Are you feeling as weird about this as I am?" Lainie asked as she and Harry drove back to the resort. Every time she looked in the side mirror, there were the headlights of their chaperone trailing behind them in his silver Jag.

"Maybe not quite as weird as you. Leo followed me around some when I was a teenager."

"Because you were wild and crazy?"

He glanced over at her. "You don't have to say it like it's impossible. I might have done some wild and crazy things. You never know."

"Yes, I do." She squeezed his arm. "And there's nothing wrong with being steady and reliable. It's very appealing." Wow, was it ever. Then throw in Harry's recent tendency to get physical whenever he thought she was in danger, and presto, you had the Clark Kent/Superman thing going on.

"Maybe for now, when your life is in turmoil, but in the long run, steady and reliable might get boring."

She didn't think so, but she wasn't going to argue with him and make it seem she was angling for a relationship. "All I can say is, I'm not bored so far."

"Me, neither. But you're right about having Leo hanging around. It seems very strange. We're supposed to go back to our hideaway knowing that Dudley and Leo are on duty. And we're supposed to forget they're there."

"Harry, you don't think Leo's had the place bugged, do you?"

He shook his head. "That's why he's here instead of someone else. He'll respect our privacy. His guys would be told to respect it, too, of course, but in their eagerness to do a good job, they might overstep. I'm not worried that anybody can actually hear . . . whatever we're doing." He cleared his throat. "If that's what you meant."

She thought it was so cute that the thought of sex with her could still get him flustered. "I wasn't really worried about that, either," she said. Although she was. What if they were in the midst of being friendly and something happened, like Joey tried to break in and Dudley started shooting up the place with his six-shooter, and she and Harry were caught with their pants down? Literally?

"Okay, I was worried," she said. "We're not exactly free to do whatever we want. At least I don't think so, under these new circumstances."

"I guess you're right." He sighed. "Everything's different."

"Yes, it's different. I just wish . . ."

He reached over and took her hand. "Yeah. Me, too." Then he gave her hand a squeeze and released it so he could pull into the parking spot behind their unit. "So here we are. Just us, Leo, and Dudley."

"Home, sweet home." She turned in her seat and watched the silver Jag glide by. "I wonder where Dudley's keeping himself?"

"I'd rather not think about it." Harry sighed again. "We might as well go in." He opened the car door.

"Might as well." She got out and they walked together up to the entrance without touching at all, not even holding hands.

He put the key in the lock.

"I'll probably skip the red nightgown, tonight." she said. "Considering the circumstances."

"I understand." He pushed the door open and flipped the light switch, which activated the end-table lamps. "Want me to take the couch?"

"I suppose that makes sense." She walked into the room while he closed and locked the door. Then she turned to find him watching her.

She watched him right back. If he could look, so could she. The space between them began to heat up. She swallowed.

He licked his lips and swore softly.

Then it was all over. In an instant they went from motionless to frenzied, clinging to each other, kissing every available inch of bare skin and wrenching off pieces of clothing. In the process they maneuvered their way through the door into the darkened bedroom, and by the time they were naked, they'd reached the mattress and tumbled onto it, panting and moaning.

At least she was almost naked. She hadn't taken the time to unbuckle her red shoes. And Harry was naked until the moment he rolled on a condom. She had no idea when he'd grabbed one, but suddenly there it was, in his hand. In no time he'd put it on and slid right inside. She wrapped her legs around his, holding him precisely where she wanted him, needing the tight connection, needing . . . Harry.

"I could never have stayed on the couch." He kissed her throat, her chin, her mouth.

"And I never wanted you to." She clutched his thighs and arched upward. "Ah, this is so . . . so—"

"Necessary," he finished, his voice thick. "Absolutely . . . necessary." In spite of her tight grip, he managed to move, thrusting in short, intense strokes.

"Uh-huh." She closed her eyes and concentrated on the incredible pleasure of having Harry back inside her. "Necessary."

"You know what really knocks me out?" He pumped faster.

"No." She gasped, hovering on the edge of her climax.

"That you . . . ah, I'm starting to . . ."

"Me . . . me, too. There, Harry. There!" She catapulted over the edge.

One more thrust and a mighty groan later, he joined her. His body shook with the force of it, and he murmured her name as he quivered in her arms.

The connection between them was so electric that she wouldn't be surprised if they glowed in the dark. She held him and rocked him and wished the moment would never end.

"What really knocked you out?" she whispered as they lay locked together, seemingly molded from a single piece of clay.

His chuckle was soft and intimate, his voice lazy with satisfaction. "That you're still wearing your shoes."

• • •

Harry's goose was well and truly cooked, he concluded some time later as Lainie paraded around the time-share unit wearing her shoes and nothing else. She thought it was hilarious that seeing her naked except for those high-heeled red sandals had such an effect on him. Therefore she deliberately kept them on and even included a few dance steps.

"I'm going to make us another pot of coffee," she announced, prancing into the tiny kitchen.

"Coffee's good." Great idea, in fact, because he didn't want to waste time sleeping. Not when Lainie was wearing those red shoes. He followed her into the kitchen so he could watch her make coffee naked.

She emptied the old grounds into the plastic-lined wastebasket, her breasts bobbing around as she worked.

"You know," he said, leaning against the sink. "I've decided naked is the best way to brew coffee."

"Oh, really?" She peered down into the trash can.

"Uh-huh. And I love the view when you lean over like that, and I get the most excellent look of your—"

"Harry, I see a bug."

"Leo's been *listening* to us?" Harry nearly had a heart attack. "Leo! Forget it! I was making a joke! Lainie and I are fully clothed and making some coffee so we can sit and discuss . . . the history of modern dance! That's it! Lainie has some interesting theories. We—"

"Lots of bugs," Lainie said. "The kind with six legs. This trash can is full of ants."

Harry stared at the trash can and slowly sagged

against the counter. "Oh. I thought you meant you'd found a *bug*."

"I did. A bunch of bugs. Now what do we do about this?" She scanned the kitchen counter. "Here's their trail. They're coming through this crack in the wall, and they're overrunning the trash can."

Harry took a look and confirmed her assessment. "Yuck. It must be the burger bag they came after. I need to take this trash can outside."

She glanced at him. "Looking like that?"

"Good point." Reluctantly he started toward the pants he'd left lying on the living room carpet.

"I have some astringent in my purse. I can pour some in the crack, and maybe that will discourage them." She went into the living room and glanced around. "Where did I toss my— Oh, there it is." She picked her purse up off the floor beside the rag rug. "And this thing has been crooked ever since we got here." She straightened it and began to laugh.

"What?" Harry zipped his pants and came over to look. The rug had been covering a huge purple stain on the carpet. "Isn't that lovely? Can you believe they are soliciting business for this place? It should be condemned!"

"I know." Lainie grinned at him. "But I'm starting to like it a whole lot."

He smiled back. "I know what you mean. It's ugly, but it's ours."

"So are you taking the trash can out the front or the back?"

"Good question." Harry hadn't gone back through the sliding glass doors ever since the rattlesnake incident. He didn't relish going out there now, considering that snakes loved the dark, or so he'd been told. But Leo was probably watching the front. Still, Harry hadn't ever met a rattlesnake on that side of the building, and he guessed Leo was better than chancing a snake encounter. "The front."

"Then you might want to put on your shirt, too."

"Right." He located it dangling from the bedroom doorknob, where it must have landed when he tossed it aside.

"Unless you want me to get dressed, and do it."

"Are you kidding? Don't change a thing. I'll be right back." He grabbed his shirt and put it on. "I'm setting this trash can out in front and totally ignoring the fact that Leo's Jag is parked out there. Totally ignoring it."

"Okay."

And he tried to do that, but once he'd opened the door to set the trash can outside, he couldn't help noticing who was in the parking lot. Leo's Jag was there, but no gold Escort. That was a good thing. There was, however, a battered pickup. It had Dudley written all over it.

Closing the door, he came back into the kitchen, where Lainie was busy eradicating ants. "I think Dudley's out there, too."

"I thought you weren't going to pay attention?" She squashed another ant with a napkin.

"I couldn't help it." But he also couldn't help noticing how nicely her assets jiggled every time she went after another ant. The longer he watched, the less he cared about Dudley and Leo. He began taking off his shirt. "You about done, there?"

She glanced over at him. "Just about."

"Good." He tossed his shirt over his shoulder and started unfastening his slacks.

"I thought you wanted coffee?"

"Not anymore." He stepped out of his slacks and caught her hand. "Let's do it on the couch. We've never tried that."

She laughed and allowed herself to be led out of the small kitchen. "Just don't move that blanket they have over the back. No telling what we might find."

"I have a feeling we're going to be way too busy to worry about the condition of the couch. Just pray it doesn't collapse on us." Sex with Lainie, he'd discovered, could block out lots of things, including the knowledge that in a few hours, their time together would be over. Harry planned to focus on sex.

Leo had arranged to meet Dudley in the parking lot directly across from Lainie and Harry's time-share unit. No more than ten minutes after Leo had parked the Jag, Dudley showed up in his ragtag pickup with a camper shell on the back. The guy was prompt. Leo appreciated promptness.

He climbed out of the Jag and winced. That flying tackle from Harry might have bruised a rib, and it had definitely done a number on his hip. Keeping those injuries from Rona would be a real trick, especially considering the bedroom gymnastics they enjoyed.

"Howdy-doody!" Dudley called out as he hopped down from his pickup and strapped on a gun belt like Wyatt Earp at the OK Corral. "Any sign of the bastard?"

"Uh, Dudley, it might be best if we kept our conversation quiet." Leo eyed the six-shooter. Probably had a kick like a mule. "I doubt the resort would appreciate knowing there's surveillance going on."

"Oh, sure, sure." Dudley reached back into the truck and pulled out a duffel bag. "I'm not up to speed on this line of work, so you'll have to fill me in, let me know where I'm going wrong."

Leo wondered what was in the duffel bag. Probably a lasso. "Basically, we have to cover the next three hours until the Phoenix boys arrive. Then we can both get some sleep." Leo couldn't believe how exhausted he was.

"You planning on sleeping in that fancy-dancy car of yours?"

"Guess so. I need to stay close by in case something happens."

"You'd be welcome to share the back of my camper. I got a couple of sleeping bags in there. At least you could stretch out."

Leo imagined what the back of that truck would be like versus the semi-reclining position in his Jag. Sure, his car seats were cushioned leather, but he'd never been good at sleeping in a semi-reclining position. Still, if the sleeping bags were in the same condition as the truck, they'd be marginal at best.

"I snore some," Dudley added.

"Me, too." Leo made his decision. Sleeping was more important than cleanliness. He wasn't all that clean, anyway, after the way Harry had worked him over. "Thanks, Dudley. I'll take you up on that."

"No problemo, partner. So now what?"

Leo handed him a two-way radio. The match to it was on the dash of his Jag. "We'll use the radio to communicate, and each of us needs to stake out an entrance."

Dudley nodded and tucked the radio under his free arm. "Then you'll want me on the golf course side, on account of my boots."

"Your boots?"

"Yep." Dudley lifted his leg to show what he was talking about. "Genuine emu."

"Emu, huh? I've never seen that before." In spite of himself, Leo was impressed with the boots. He'd always had a thing for expensive footwear.

"I don't skimp on my boots. Emu's comfortable, but it can also take a snake bite."

"Oh, shit. I forgot about the snakes." Leo took a quick look around and didn't see anything slithering toward him, thank God.

"You don't need to worry so much here in the parking lot," Dudley said. "They like the golf course side better. More rodents for 'em to eat over there."

"Oh. Then I'll take the parking lot."

"Figured you would." Dudley unzipped the duffel bag and pulled out a thermos with Spider-Man on the side of it. "I brought coffee. Here's yours."

"God, what a wonderful idea." Leo was starting to really love this guy.

"And sandwiches. Hope you like tuna." He handed over a fishy-smelling paper sack.

"Love it." Leo would have been overjoyed with stale bread and peanut butter at this point. Eating on the run, which he'd been doing since morning, had meant eating very little. "This is great, Dudley. Thanks."

"No problemo." Dudley looked pleased with himself. "Seems as how we needed something to sustain us."

"Good thinking, Dud." Then he realized Dudley

might not be partial to a shortening of his name, but there was no taking it back, now.

To his relief, Dudley laughed. "My ex-wife used to call me that. I didn't have the heart to tell her that I was a dud because she'd turned ugly as a fence post after ten years. Anyway, that's all behind me, now, but you calling me Dud put me in mind of it."

"Sorry." Leo really was sorry. The guy was a diamond in the rough. Well, maybe a cubic zirconia in the rough. "I won't call you that anymore."

"It's okay if you do, partner. I have a thick hide. Now I guess we'd better get motatin'."

"Right." Leo gave Dudley a quick description of Joey and the rental car and sent him on his way. Then he settled into his car and opened the Spider-Man thermos. The coffee smelled like heaven and tasted like motor oil. Just the way Leo liked it.

He'd just taken a bite of the tuna-fish sandwich when he heard a car. A glance in the rearview mirror told him the gold sedan had just pulled into the parking area, dammit. Wouldn't you know, Joey would show up to ruin his meal. He got on the radio. "Dudley, our guy's here."

"Roger."

"You don't have to say that. Just talk normally."

"Oh. Okay. Want me over there, partner?"

"You can start moving in this direction, but don't show yourself yet. Keep to the shadows. I want to see what he's going to do."

"I'm on the move. What's he doing?"

Leo peered at the gold sedan. "Nothing. Just sitting there with the motor turned off."

"Thinking, most likely."

"I don't know how much of that he's capable of." Leo took his night-vision binoculars out of the console and trained them on the car. "Looks like he's drinking, not thinking. I hear he's a heap of trouble when he starts hitting the bottle."

"That's okay. I've got me an idea. I'm coming around. Don't worry, I'll be casual."

"Hold it. I'll meet you halfway, at the side of the building."

"Roger. Over and out." Then the radio crackled again. "Forget the 'Roger' part."

Leo sighed. Amateurs. He left his car as quietly as he could, not bothering to close the door tight. The heavy-duty coffee was probably eating away at the lining of his stomach, but at least he was alert. As he walked, he alternated between looking at the gold sedan and scanning the ground, in case Dudley had misjudged the snake situation and one had ventured out to the parking lot.

"Pssst! Over here!"

Leo rolled his eyes and headed over to the shadowed area where Dudley stood beckoning wildly. If Joey had his window open and had any instincts at all, he'd probably hear Dudley acting like some demented secret agent. Leo was counting on Joey's lack of instincts and general stupidity to see them all through this.

"I've got the perfect solution," Dudley said the minute Leo stepped into the shadows at the side of the building. "Got it right here in my duffel."

The duffel bag rattled, and Leo jumped a mile. "Jesus! Is that what I think it is?"

"Just a baby." Dudley put the duffel down and the rattling stopped. "I found a forked stick so I decided to get it now, as long as I was here. Plopped it right in my duffel. Then I got the idea about how to get rid of Joey for the time being, anyway."

Leo had trouble concentrating on what Dudley was saying because he was too busy squinting at every inch of ground. "Are those things everywhere?"

"Nah. It's unusual that two showed up in the same day. Could be the storm we had brought 'em out. Anyway, I was thinking if I took this duffel over to Joey's car, we could—"

"No, Dudley, you're not going to dump that snake in his car. I have strict instructions on this guy. We don't want him getting bit."

"I wouldn't do that. Wouldn't be fair to the snake. No, I'll just go over, let him hear the rattle, and tell him we've had a real epidemic in the past couple of days. Didn't you say he's a city boy?"

"Yeah." And so was Leo. He wasn't used to thinking of snakes as weapons. "But I really—"

"This'll work. You watch. I'll tell him I'm the resort snake expert, which is the God's truth, and that we're evacuating people on account of this extreme snake situation. There's no point in him staying around if he's afraid to leave the car."

Leo had to admit the plan had merit. "Then what'll you do with the snake?"

"Just keep him in my truck for the night, take him out somewhere in the desert tomorrow mornin'."

"You expect to keep that thing in the front of the truck or the back of the truck?"

Dudley grinned. "I keep forgetting you're a city boy, too. I'll keep the snake in the cab. Then we can catch us some Zs in the back. I figure you don't want to leave the parking lot, even if Joey takes off."

"That's right, I don't."

"So what do you say?"

Leo eyed the duffel bag. "Exactly what do you mean by this thing being a baby?"

"Oh, it's less than two feet."

That was about twenty-four inches too many for Leo. "So can it get out?"

"I put the little padlock on the zipper tab. I've never met a snake yet that can pick a padlock."

"Then I guess it's worth a shot."

Dudley nodded. "It's definitely worth a shot. Be right back."

As it turned out, Dudley's plan worked like a charm. Joey left, laying some rubber in the process. On the strength of that exit, Leo decided to call the Phoenix boys and advise them to get a motel room instead of heading on over to Crimson Canyons. They could meet in the morning to discuss strategy.

Finally, when all was quiet, Leo and Dudley crawled in the back of the pickup. Leo spent a few seconds worrying about the snake in the cab up front, a few more seconds wondering what kind of bugs might be living in this musty sleeping bag, and another few seconds listening to Dudley snore. Eventually, however, even the snake, the bugs, and the snoring weren't enough to keep him awake. His last thought as he drifted off was that he was most definitely getting too old for this.

Chapter Twenty-three

Although he'd only slept a couple of hours, Harry woke up before daylight. He didn't want to wake up, but there he was, wide-eyed and fighting a sense of dread. Lainie would probably be seeing Joey today.

With the backup from Leo and his contacts in Phoenix, Harry wasn't worried that Lainie could get hurt. He was afraid she might be manipulated, though. She'd do most anything for Dexter.

As he thought about that, he marveled at her devotion. She was willing to deal with a creep like Joey because it might ultimately benefit Dexter. He really admired that. Plus she was smart and funny, great company.

He'd found the perfect combination—a woman who stimulated him both mentally and physically. Unfortunately, he was afraid she wouldn't want him, a nerdy person who worked with numbers all day. And that made his heart ache, because it looked like he'd fallen in love with her.

She might never return that love, but he could be

running out of time to find out if she would or not. Today she might have to make a deal with Joey that included leaving Vegas. Leaving Harry.

The thought made him so restless he couldn't lie there anymore. He climbed out of bed as carefully as he could and moved through the suite, gathering his clothes. He wouldn't go far, because he still felt responsible for protecting Lainie, but he was really curious to see if Leo was still parked outside and if that was Dudley's truck he'd seen.

Finding his glasses was a trick, but eventually he located them on top of the TV. After grabbing a key, he opened the door very quietly. Instead of birds twittering, he heard some kind of machinery. Maybe the grounds crew was hard at work. Hah. Like this place could afford a grounds crew.

He saw the Jag immediately, and the old truck was still there, too, a few spaces away. No gold sedan, though. Harry walked toward the Jag, expecting to find Leo asleep in it.

The Jag was locked and empty. But he noticed the back window of the camper shell was open, and the sounds he'd thought belonged to gas-powered landscape tools seemed to be coming from there.

Walking behind the truck, he peered in, blinking in surprise. "Leo?"

Leo came awake instantly, struggled to get up, and hit his head on the roof of the camper shell. He swore loudly in Italian.

Harry winced. "Leo, I'm sorry, but I sure never expected to see—"

"Stand back," Leo said. "I'm climbing out of this

contraption, and I don't expect my exit to be pretty."

"Were you in there all night?" Harry still had a tough time imagining Leo sleeping in the back of Dudley's pickup alongside Dudley. Leo was a guy who insisted on the executive floor and turn-down service.

"Most of it." Leo groaned as he heaved his leg over the tailgate. "I wanted to hang around, even though Dudley got rid of Joey."

"What do you mean, 'got rid of'?" Harry didn't want the guy around, but he didn't want murder on his conscience, either.

"Oh, take it easy." Leo climbed the rest of the way out of the pickup and stood brushing lint off his dark shirt and slacks. "We're not going to bump him off."

"Good."

Dudley climbed out of the camper shell and clapped his cowboy hat on his head. "I brought my pistol along to scare this Joey character. Turns out I found something better, right, pardner?" He grinned at Leo.

"Which reminds me," Leo said. "Feel free to take that friend of yours for a ride in the country." He glanced at his Rolex. "We both need to get cleaned up. We're supposed to meet the Phoenix boys at eight."

"What friend?" Harry had a bad feeling that he already knew the answer.

"Just a snake," Dudley said.

"Please tell me you didn't turn that big snake you caught yesterday loose on Joey." The idea made Harry queasy.

Dudley laughed. "Nope. That snake you located is enjoying life way up Schnebly Hill Road. This one's a baby, kind of cute, in a way."

Leo met Harry's gaze. "Don't mind him. What happened is, Dudley took his duffel over with a snake inside and told Joey we were having a snake problem. Joey left. End of story."

Harry's heart pounded as he glanced around. "*Are* we having a snake problem?"

"Nah," Dudley said. "After finding two yesterday, I'd be amazed if I spot any the rest of the week."

"Fortunately, that won't matter to us," Leo said. "We'll be out of here."

"So, uh, where's this baby snake now?" Harry tried to sound casual, but he really needed to know.

"I put the duffel in the cab," Dudley said. "I should probably go check and see how the little cuss is doing." He walked up to the passenger-side door.

Harry's admiration for Leo grew. "You slept all night in the same truck with a rattlesnake?"

"Sure." Leo acted nonchalant, but his chest puffed out. "No big deal."

"I have to tell you, I couldn't have done it. Was the back window in the cab shut tight?"

Leo's eyes widened. "Shit, I forgot about the back window."

"Whoopsie!" Dudley called as he opened the door. "Musta had a hole in my duffel!" He pulled it out, unzipped it, and peered inside. "Sure enough." He waggled his finger through a hole in the bottom.

Leo and Harry both backed away from the truck.

"Goddamn that Dudley," Leo muttered. "I hate snakes. They give me the willies."

"Me, too," Harry said.

"That's probably my fault. I'll bet you picked that up from me." Leo said it apologetically, but there was a certain pride there, too, as if he liked knowing he'd passed something on, even if it was a fear of snakes.

"Yeah, maybe I did get it from you." Harry had never considered that Leo might enjoy thinking of Harry as the son he'd never had.

"Found him!" Dudley shouted. "Curled up in a corner of the truck bed, fast asleep. I'll just leave him there and drive him out to his new home. See you boys later." Dudley hopped in the cab. Starting the engine took a couple of tries, but eventually he drove away.

"And good riddance." Leo gazed after the departing truck and shuddered.

"So that's that, then," Harry said. "What next?"

Leo glanced at him. "You'd better have Lainie make her call."

"Yeah. Okay." Harry's gut twisted.

"How are things between you two?"

"Uh, exactly what do you mean by that?"

Leo gave him the Sicilian glare. "You know what I'm talking about. I can't believe I have to write you a memo. Is there a chance of you two working something out, maybe?"

"I don't think so."

"Why not? You're getting along, right?"

"Um, yeah." Harry glanced away, afraid Leo would see too much in his expression. "But she has to think of Dexter and this fortune the little guy could be in line for. Getting involved with me wouldn't be a good idea."

Leo snorted in disgust. "I've known a lot of rich

people in my life, kid, and you can't predict 'em. Rearranging your life so that they'll leave you their money is a mistake, in my considered opinion."

"Maybe." Harry rubbed the back of his neck. "But it's not up to me. It's up to Lainie. And she wants the best for her kid."

"Like any mother worth her salt. Oh, by the way, her apartment door's been repaired."

"Thanks. I should've known you'd arrange for somebody to do that. Let me help you pay for—"

"Nah, forget it. The great thing would be if we could eliminate this Joey situation and give you two a chance."

"I'd say the percentages are against us on that one, Leo."

"Ah, don't count yourself out too quick. We're a long way from dealing the last hand of this particular game. But we need Lainie to contact this joker. If he wants to meet her, have her pick a nice public spot, say about ten o'clock this morning. Let me know if she reaches him."

Harry nodded. "So you'll be out here?"

"Yeah, until Dudley shows up, showered, shaved, and snakeless."

"Listen, once he's back, you're welcome to use our bathroom to clean up if you want."

"Thanks, but Dudley already said I could use his place, and . . . I don't want to disturb your privacy."

"It doesn't matter."

"Sure it does," Leo said softly. "If you have something good going there, kid, try to keep it going. She's all right."

"Yeah." Harry nodded. "Yeah, she is." Then he turned and walked to the time-share unit, all the while wishing he could turn back the clock.

. . .

When Lainie woke up to find Harry gone, she panicked and went looking for him. He'd become her anchor, her rock, and she wanted to see his face. But he wasn't in the unit. Finally she peeked out the front window.

To her immense relief he was there, looking solid and Harry-like as he talked with Leo in the parking lot. Whew. He hadn't deserted her. No doubt he'd be back any minute, though, and she was a wreck, especially her hair. Sometime during the night she'd pulled off the red wig and finger-combed her long hair. Harry had finger-combed it, too. Now that had been a sensuous experience.

But then they'd taken another magic mattress trip, and her hair was now a tangled mess. This was their first morning-after encounter, and she didn't want to greet him looking like she'd stuck her finger in a light socket. She'd use this chance when he was AWOL to jump in the shower and make herself presentable again.

She was halfway through her shower when she heard footsteps. For one awful second she wondered if she should have locked the bathroom door, just in case Joey had managed to slip past her two guardians. "Harry?"

"Yeah, it's me."

She let out her breath in a whoosh. How she loved hearing his strong, steady voice. "I'm glad it's you. For a minute there, I was afraid that—"

"Sorry. Didn't mean to scare you. I guess I was a little distracted. I should have said something right away, so you'd know it was me."

She slicked her hair back. "I woke up and wondered where you'd gone." Grabbing the edge of the shower curtain, she looked out and found herself staring at Harry's broad back. "Why are you standing like that?"

"So I won't be tempted to climb in there with you. I tend to lose track of time when we . . ." He paused and cleared his throat. "Anyway, I've been talking to Leo. He had your apartment door fixed."

Another wave of indebtedness hit her. "That's . . . terrific. I'll find a way to pay him back."

"I doubt he'll take it. He's never let me repay him for anything. But you do need to call Joey. And soon."

Lainie closed her eyes. The fun was truly over. "Yes, I know." She let the curtain fall back into place and starting soaping her body, the body Harry had loved so thoroughly during the night. "Did Leo spend the night in his car?" she asked.

"Uh, no. If you can believe it, he spent the night in the back of Dudley's pickup. With Dudley." His voice seemed farther away.

"You're kidding." She stopped what she was doing to check again, and he was now standing in the bathroom doorway, still with his back to her.

"Nope, not kidding. It's quite a story. But maybe I'd better save it."

"Because I'm in the shower and that gets you hot?" she said softly.

With a groan, he reached back and fumbled for the doorknob. Then he left, closing the door firmly behind him.

It was one of the nicest compliments she'd ever been given. He still wanted her desperately, even after the sex-filled night they'd spent together. She still wanted him, too, as it turned out, in more ways than one.

Oh, sure, she wouldn't mind having him strip down and join her in the shower, but she understood they didn't have time for that. Almost as much as the sex, though, she would have enjoyed having him on the other side of the shower curtain, filling her in on Leo's adventures. She liked Harry's company as much as his impressive package. She plain liked being with him.

Admitting that meant admitting that she'd found a guy who satisfied her on all levels. She was now officially in love with Harry. Unfortunately, she was in no position to do anything about that because of her past mistakes. And that sucked.

Lainie decided in respect for Harry's urges she'd stay out of his way until she had clothes on again. Apparently he had the same idea, because once she was out of the bathroom and wrapped discreetly in a towel, he announced that he'd take his shower next so she could have the bedroom to herself.

She took her time getting dressed and putting on her makeup because she wanted to look good for Harry. Also, she was trying to ignore the fact that he was in the shower, naked. Now he'd be toweling off. Now he'd be putting on his clothes, darn it. She liked that he wasn't one solid slab of muscle. He was huggable, approachable, comforting. And when aroused, he was all the man she could ever want.

"I'm ready." He leaned in the bedroom doorway looking even more approachable than he'd seemed in her mind's eye.

She craved everything about him, from his glasses to his gentle smile, from his broad shoulders to his capable hands. "I am, too." She shoved her lipstick brush back into the tube of lip gloss.

"You're so beautiful."

She gazed at him and thought of all the wonderful things that made Harry such a terrific guy. She cataloged his kindness, his generosity, his bravery, and his unselfishness. "Not half as beautiful as you."

He blushed. "I'm not beau—"

"Yes you are." She turned to face him. "To me, you are."

"You're talking about the inside of me, then. You think I have a beautiful soul and all that. It's not true, though."

"I'm talking about the inside and the outside. I'm talking about the person who's given me the best twenty-four hours of my life."

He shifted his weight and looked uncomfortable. "Look, you don't have to say that."

"I know I don't." She held his gaze, determined to give him some idea of how she felt even if she couldn't spill everything that was in her heart. "And you probably think the only reason I am saying it is because I finally had sex after five years and anything would feel good. The first time, maybe that was so. Even the second time, maybe, but after that, it wasn't just about getting some. It was . . . special."

"For me, too," he said softly.

She wanted to touch him in the worst way. Just to feel his arms around her right now would be worth a million dollars if she had a million dollars. If she had a million dollars, though, she wouldn't be in this fix in the first place. She'd never thought money was very important until now. She'd been naïve about that.

"You need to call him," Harry murmured.

"Yes."

He reached down and laced his fingers through hers. "Come on. I'll sit right there beside you."

She nodded, wishing she could have him sitting right there beside her forever and knowing it wasn't in the cards. She allowed him to lead her over to the sofa.

He picked up his cell phone and handed it to her. "If he wants to meet with you, Leo thinks ten o'clock would be a good time."

"Okay."

"And he also said to pick a place that's nice and public, so I was thinking that open-air coffee shop where we went yesterday morning."

She hesitated, thinking of that beautiful spot that would now be forever spoiled in her memory. "I hate this."

"Me, too."

"But I have to talk to him and see what we can work out about Dexter. Maybe he'll be willing to do it over the phone." But she didn't think so. Not Joey, who believed he could turn on the charm and always get what he wanted. Taking a deep breath, she punched in Joey's number.

When he didn't answer after three rings, she found herself praying that he was passed out drunk somewhere. But of course that would only delay the inevitable. On the fourth ring, he picked up, and sure enough, he sounded hungover.

Just hearing his voice made her start to shake. She thought of all that Benjamin money and how he might use it to take Dexter away. Then Harry put his arm around her shoulders and instantly she felt calmer.

She cleared her throat. "Joey, it's Lainie."

Silence.

"Joey, are you there?"

"Why are you calling me? I thought you were trying to avoid me like the plague."

She thought the plague was a perfect description of Joey. "I needed time to think everything through."

"Yeah, yeah, I guess. Listen, did you know that place you're staying in has a serious rattlesnake problem?"

"A rattlesnake problem?" Lainie glanced at Harry, who shook his head.

"Yeah. I drove over there to see if I could talk to you, and some old dude in a cowboy hat had this snake in his duffel bag, if you can believe it. I almost shit a brick when that thing rattled. He said they had like a rattlesnake epidemic going on, so I left, man. I didn't want to talk to you that bad."

Lainie's mood lifted. So Dudley had scared Joey with a snake in a bag. She would have loved to see that. "Now that you mention it, we had a six-footer on the patio yesterday. I understand they're quite common around here."

"Well, you can have that place, then! It's a wonder they're not ass-deep in lawsuits, with snakes slithering everywhere. Stupid situation, if you ask me. Listen, we need to talk."

"We're talking now. What do you want to talk about?"

"No, I mean in person." His voice grew silky. "I've missed you, babe. I'd like to see you again."

She didn't believe that for a minute. "Would you like to come to Crimson Canyons?" Although she had no intention of setting up the meeting here, she couldn't resist suggesting it to get his reaction.

"Hell, no! I'm not coming within five miles of that snake pit! You take your chances if you want to, but I'm not getting bit by no rattlesnake. Not this boy. Somewhere else. Maybe some cozy little restaurant. You know, like old times."

"I don't remember any cozy restaurants, Joey." She remembered hotel rooms and room service, but no cozy restaurants. Joey had always wanted to meet her where there was a bed readily available.

"Then there should have been cozy restaurants. We could—"

"How about a coffee shop?"

"A cozy coffee shop?" He sounded hopeful.

"Actually, it's outdoors. But I like it there. I'll meet you at ten this morning, if you want."

"Okay, fine." He abandoned his seductive routine. "Ten o'clock. Just tell me where it is."

She gave him directions and got off thc phone as quickly as possible. Then she shivered. "I feel icky, like I need another shower."

"Come here." Harry gathered her close, nestled his freshly shaven cheek against hers, and stroked her back. "It'll be okay."

"I don't know if it will or not." And yet, here in his arms, she could make herself believe that everything would be okay. For the first time in their short but fiery relationship, Harry's touch was about comfort instead of sex. And comfort was exactly what she needed now, just as pure sex had been exactly what she'd needed last night.

But she also had a job to do. She gave him a squeeze and moved away, out of that charmed circle where life was perfect. "I should probably switch my ring from my left hand to my right. Joey's not the most observant person in the world, but I don't want him asking questions."

"Right." Harry watched as she took off the ring and put it on her other hand. He made no move to do the same.

She wondered if that was on purpose or if he'd forgotten about his ring. In any case, she liked the idea that he still wore it as if they were married. The matching bands meant nothing, of course, but they didn't feel like nothing, and she was glad he kept his exactly where it was.

She was as ready as she'd ever be. "Let's go see Leo," she said.

Through the next couple of hours, while Leo and his backup guys set up their surveillance plan, Harry fought the urge to grab Lainie and make a getaway. All his instincts screamed that he needed to do something to protect this woman he'd managed to fall in love with. He'd kept his ring on his left hand as if that would somehow keep the connection between them.

By nine-thirty, the Phoenix guys had left the resort to take up their positions near the coffee shop. At fifteen minutes before ten, while Dudley and Leo stood a tasteful distance away, Harry handed Lainie the keys to his Lexus. "Be careful," he said.

She gave him a tiny smile. "I promise not to wreck your car."

"I don't give a damn about the car, and you know it."

"I know," she said softly.

"Remember what Leo told you. If he tries to grab you, start yelling. And run."

"Right." She stuck out her foot. "I'll be a blur in these." Leo had outfitted her for this caper, sending Dudley off with a wad of cash to buy running shoes, white shorts, and a bright red T-shirt.

She'd be fine, Harry told himself. But he didn't want her to go.

"I should leave," she said.

He wanted to hold her once more, but not in front of an audience. "Yeah. It's time."

"I'll see you back here when it's over."

"Yep."

"It'll be fine." She stood on the balls of her feet and gave him a quick kiss on the cheek. "Bye."

As he watched her get in the car and drive away, he wondered why there had to be assholes like Joey in the world. Then again, if it hadn't been for Joey, Lainie wouldn't have moved to Vegas. So maybe even assholes had a purpose in life. Joey's purpose was over, though, so he could get the hell out of here any time now. Harry would love to assist him out the door.

"Let's go, kid," Leo said. "We don't want to be late for the party."

With a nod, Harry climbed in the back seat of the Jag. Dudley had probably never ridden in a car like this, so Harry gave him the front seat. Sure enough, Dudley had a ball adjusting the seat, tuning the radio, and rolling the window up and down as they headed off toward town.

Glancing at his watch, Harry tapped Leo on the shoulder. "Let's speed it up."

"I'm over the limit, now," Leo said. "Relax. We're almost there."

Harry sat with his hands clenched as they rounded

the bend leading into town and the coffee shop patio came into view. "She's not there." He quickly scanned the people sitting at the tables. "Neither's Joey. Maybe I should get out and—"

"Take it easy," Leo said. "It's not ten yet."

Harry's gut was a twisted mess. "I know, but she should be there by now." Then he saw her, about two blocks away, hurrying toward the patio. "Damn, she must have had trouble finding a parking spot."

"Which would be our problem, too." Leo cruised slowly down the street, getting farther away from the coffee shop.

"I'm getting out," Harry said.

Leo shook his head. "Don't do that."

"I am doing that." He unfastened his seat belt. "Either stop the car or don't, but I'm getting out. You can circle the block all you want, but I need to be there when she meets Joey."

"There's a parking garage down a ways," Dudley said. "If it's not full, that is. Sometimes—"

"I'm getting out." Harry opened the door.

Swearing under his breath, Leo jammed on the brakes. Tires squealed behind them. As Harry jumped out of the car, he heard the clunk of bumper hitting bumper. Well, he was sorry about the Jag, but being there for Lainie was more important than a fender-bender.

He crossed quickly to the sidewalk and headed back in the direction of the coffee shop. He would keep out of sight, but he wanted to be close enough to do something if he had to. Sure, Leo had guys stationed around the area, and maybe they were professionals who knew exactly what they were doing.

Harry, on the other hand, was only an accountant with no experience in this kind of thing. But he was the only person around who was in love with the woman sitting alone at a table in her new running shoes, white shorts, and a stop-sign–red T-shirt. And he figured that made him the most valuable guy on the job.

Chapter Twenty-four

Lainie had noticed the silver Jag go by as she hurried toward the coffee shop. Catching a glimpse of Harry in the back seat had helped settle her butterflies a little bit. Then she'd heard the squeal of tires and had turned just in time to see Harry jump out of Leo's car and a blue station wagon hit the Jag's bumper with a sickening thud. Poor Leo.

She didn't have time to find out what happened after that, and certainly didn't dare wait for Harry to catch up with her. Instead she walked even faster toward the coffee shop. Once there, she looked around for Joey and didn't see him.

Okay, this was it. Trying to breathe normally instead of like a long-distance runner, she looked for a table. The place was packed, but right then a couple left a table shaded by a large green market umbrella. Lainie made a beeline for it, barely claiming it ahead of a family of four.

She ignored their glares as she sat at the table alone, with no coffee, no excuse for being there. Then she couldn't decide where to sit. She tried all four chairs before settling on the one facing the street.

A cop car went by, no doubt headed for Leo's fender-bender. Lainie could imagine Leo down there fuming, ready to strangle Harry for getting out of the car so fast, which probably caused the accident. But Lainie thought it was wonderful of Harry to be so worried about her that he couldn't wait for Leo to find a parking space.

She'd known the minute she'd driven into town that parking would be a problem. For some reason no one had thought to plan for that, and yet they should have. They were in the height of the tourist season, and crowds were everywhere.

But no Joey. At least not yet. Trying to calm herself, she looked to her left at the spectacular view of red rocks and pine-covered mesas that had so inspired her the first time she'd seen this vista. Today the inspiration was lost on her. But maybe if she concentrated on the panorama long enough, she'd recapture that sense of awe. She could use some awe about now.

She forced herself to focus on the rocks, hoping the natural beauty would soothe her. Didn't work. Soon her attention was skittering all over the place as she looked for Joey. She studied every approaching male figure, but nobody looked even slightly like him.

So he wouldn't be here by ten. That wasn't surprising. He was never on time, and she should have remembered that and told Leo. Too late now, though. But if Joey hadn't arrived yet, maybe she could figure out where Harry had stationed himself.

Once she spotted him she would have laughed if she hadn't been so nervous. He'd picked out a bench in front of a store close by, and he was using an open newspaper to shield the upper part of his body. It wasn't a bad disguise, except that the newspaper was upside down.

The upside-down newspaper indicated exactly how shook up Harry was about all this. Someone as methodical as Harry had to be pretty upset to open a newspaper upside down. She watched him, thinking that eventually he'd notice what he'd done and rotate the newspaper so it was right-side-up. Then, for a few seconds, she'd be able to see his face. That would calm her far more than the view.

When he sat up straighter on the bench, she figured he'd realized he needed to fix the paper before someone decided he was nuts. One chance to look into his eyes was all she needed. Maybe she'd smile at him, to let him know that she'd seen him and appreciated his being right there. If only—

"As if finding a parking place isn't already a bitch, now a couple of bozos run into each other on the main drag. This place is full of idiots."

Lainie's stomach pitched at the sound of Joey's voice. When she could finally bring herself to look up, she wondered how on earth she'd ever found this guy attractive. Five years of late nights and great quantities of booze had left his skin blotchy, and he was starting to get a belly on him, too. His mirrored shades covered his eyes, but she'd bet they were bloodshot.

"Hello, Joey."

"Yeah, hi. Listen, I need coffee bad." He glanced down at the bare table. "You're not having any?"

"No, thanks." She noticed he hadn't offered to buy it for her.

"I'm getting some, then. Hold down the table." He headed for the entrance to the shop.

Had he always ordered her around like that? She admitted to herself that he probably had, and she'd been too insecure to question it. Harry would never dream of speaking to her in that tone of voice. She glanced over toward the bench and noticed the newspaper was right-side-up now.

As she stared at Harry, he slowly lowered the newspaper. With sunlight reflecting off his glasses she couldn't see his eyes, but she didn't need to. From the tense set of his shoulders she could imagine how his eyes would look—filled with the same kind of concern as before, when he'd sent her off in his car.

Obviously, he'd fallen in love with her the same as she'd fallen in love with him. It was as plain to see as an upside-down newspaper. And for a little while, she bathed in the glow of that. Even though their relationship was doomed, she drew strength from knowing that a man like Harry loved her. Then a crowd of people piled out of a bus and the sidewalk between Lainie and Harry filled up with tourists. She couldn't see him anymore.

"There are too damn many kinds of coffee these days." Joey set his cup on the table and plopped into a chair opposite Lainie. "I don't know what the hell this is going to taste like, but at least it's caffeine, so I'm going for it." He took a swig and swore again. "Shit, that stuff's hot. Took off half my taste buds."

Joey, she realized, was mad at the world. He'd been mad at the world when she'd met him, and that had been okay with her, because she'd felt rejected by her parents and only too happy to find a bitching buddy. But being a parent herself, now, she understood her mom and dad a little better. They wanted good things for her, and they didn't think being a showgirl was a good thing.

They'd tried to use disapproval to get her to change her mind, but instead it had driven her away. Then both she and her parents had hardened their positions so that the gulf between them grew wider every year. She didn't know if she could bridge that gap now, but maybe one of these days she'd give it a try. Dexter should know at least one set of grandparents.

Joey's next sip of coffee was more cautious. Then he set the coffee down and looked at her. "Emil's gay."

So he was going straight to the heart of the matter. Good thing he'd abandoned any idea of charming her into getting back together. She did her best to act surprised by his announcement. "Really? Wow. What a shocker that must be for your family."

"My dad disowned him." Joey sat back, his expression smug. "So that leaves the door wide open for yours truly."

"I guess it would, at that." *If you hadn't pickled what little brain you have.*

Joey reached for his coffee and took another careful sip. "The thing is, dear old Dad wants to be sure the business stays in the family. I've seen several doctors, and they all say the same thing. Dexter was a fluke. The chances of me having another kid are next to nil."

"I see."

"I hope you do. Here's how I think this could work so everybody benefits. We get married."

She felt sick to her stomach. "Joey, I don't—"

"Don't worry. I wouldn't expect you to act like a wife except in front of my parents. Hell, I want my freedom to do whatever, too, you know."

She didn't know what she'd expected him to ask of her, but this was horrible. "I couldn't do that. But even if I could, I wouldn't want that kind of life for Dexter. Kids sense things. He'd know immediately we're not a devoted couple."

"Okay, he might, but I'd be away a lot. And think of this, before you get all high-and-mighty on me. Dexter would have anything a kid could want. My mom and dad would dote on him. I'm guessing he's never had that, unless you've suddenly made up with your folks."

Her stomach knotted up. "My relationship with my parents is none of your business."

"I'll bet they'd be a whole lot happier with you if you married the father of their grandson," he said softly. "And you'd have access to the Benjamin money, too, Lainie. You could move your parents into a place right near our house. Then Dexter would have it all."

Oh, God. It would have been easier if he'd tried to pretend he still wanted her. That she could have dealt with. Instead he'd described the charmed life Dexter would lead if she'd simply agree to go along with his plan.

She didn't believe money was the answer to happiness, not by a long shot. But the senior Benjamins could provide private schools, music lessons, trips to Europe, all the things Dexter would relish. She'd struggle to give him a tenth of those opportunities.

Then she also had to consider the shaky legal position she was in, taking Dexter out of New Jersey without getting written permission. For all she knew, if she didn't cooperate with Joey, he'd use that against her to get custody. Because he was basically lazy, he wouldn't want to go that route unless he had to, but if pushed to the wall, he might.

No doubt about it, Joey had tremendous motivation to claim his son. If she thought he could find a way to separate her from Dexter, she'd be wise to grab this first offer no matter how much she hated the idea. At least this way, she'd be with her child.

"I can see you're thinking about it," Joey said. "Don't be dumb about this, Lainie. Think about the kid."

She wished he'd take off those mirrored sunglasses. "Are you thinking about him?"

"Sure I am. I think about him all the time."

"Do you think about him, or what he means to you, now that you have a chance to get control of Benjamin, Inc., someday?"

Joey snorted. "Like, how am I supposed to separate those two?"

"A loving father would have no trouble separating them."

"Oh, for Christ's sake. I'm a loving father, okay?"

She didn't think that deserved a response. She just looked at him, hoping against hope that there was some decency left in him, some kernel of real caring for this little boy he'd helped create.

He cleared his throat. "In fact, I've been meaning to ask you. How's he doing?"

"Fine."

"Have you bought him a computer?"

Now there was a sore point. She lifted her chin. "Not

yet." Another thing that she'd thought about and hadn't been able to afford. Another thing Joey could use in court to convince a judge he'd make a better parent.

"Kids these days need computers. Especially a smart little guy like Dexter." He paused to take a drink of his coffee. "Tell you what. I know this is hard for you, because you've never met my parents. Maybe it would help if you talked to my mom."

Her eyes widened. "You want me to do that?" She'd never anticipated this move.

"Yeah. She's so excited to meet you and her grandson."

"You told your mother about me? What did you say?"

He shifted in his chair. "Well, I had to change things around a little. You know how moms are."

Or fathers. She remembered his stories about Doyle, a guy who made the Puritans look like partying fools. "Does your mother know I'm a showgirl?"

"Not exactly. I said we dated five years ago, and you left without telling me you were pregnant because you didn't believe in forcing a guy into marriage. I told her I've been looking for you ever since."

Lainie stared at him, unable to believe that he could ever pull off such a big, fat lie, even taking into consideration a mother's willingness to believe.

He shrugged. "She bought it."

Lainie pictured a woman so desperate to think well of a son run amok that she'd accept any wild and woolly story if it was what she wanted to hear. "Okay, so she bought it. What does she think I do for a living?"

"She, um, thinks you're a secretary, but it totally doesn't matter, Lainie, because after we're married you won't have to work a day in your life. You'll be on Easy Street. Dexter, too."

"But I love to dance." What he was suggesting felt like throwing herself over a cliff. But this change could be exactly what Dexter needed. She'd never have to hire another babysitter. She could be available twenty-four/seven.

"So dance around the house! You'll have a big house."

She wouldn't expect him to understand her passion for dancing, so she decided to let that part of the discussion go. Nobody wanted her to dance, it seemed. Her parents hadn't approved, and she was afraid Harry didn't want a dancer for a wife, either. Now, in order to set up Dexter for life, she'd have to forget doing what she loved.

"Talk to my mom." Joey pulled a cell phone out of a holster on his belt and punched in a number. "Mom? It's Joey. Yes, I have her right here." Then he handed the phone across the table. "Her name's Celeste, by the way," he added.

Lainie hesitated, as if taking that phone would be the signal for a jailor to swing the prison doors shut with a clang, locking her in forever.

"She's Dexter's grandma," Joey said.

That much was true, at least. Lainie took the phone. "Hello?"

"Lainie, how wonderful to talk to you at last!" Celeste sounded very youthful.

Lainie had wondered if she was a child-woman, because Doyle seemed to rule the roost. "It's, uh, good to talk to you, too, Celeste."

"And I can hardly wait to see little Dexter! I've already

started shopping for toys, and clothes, and . . . everything!"

"That's very generous of you."

"Not at all. I'm his grandma! How soon will you be coming to meet us?"

"I, uh . . ." Lainie couldn't help herself. She looked over at the bench where Harry had been sitting, needing the reassurance of that comforting presence. He wasn't there.

She couldn't scan the area and risk letting Joey know she had protectors lurking around. Harry might have changed locations so he wouldn't appear suspicious. That made sense, but she desperately needed to see him right now, even though he couldn't really help her with this.

No one could help her with this. She had to make the decision by herself. And if this woman had already bought presents for Dexter, how could Lainie refuse to take him back for a visit?

"Soon," she told Joey's mother. "We'll come soon. We'll let you know when we have plane tickets."

"That's wonderful news. Just wonderful. We'll have such fun. We'll go . . . we'll go to the beach! And play in the sand. I can't wait. Bye, now."

Lainie disconnected the phone and handed it back across the table. Suddenly she felt exhausted. Until now, adrenaline had kept her going, but the thought of flying back to New York and pretending to be Joey's wife drained all the life out of her.

"I heard you talking about plane tickets, so does that mean you're gonna play ball?" He watched her as if he expected her to bolt at any minute.

"Joey, what about your father? Does he know anything?"

Joey shrugged. "He'll come around. It's better if we work through my mother. Once she gets a look at Dexter, it'll be a done deal. And my father's partial to boys. He'll be fine."

The whole business made her uneasy, and she decided to leave herself an escape route. "Okay, but in case he's not fine with it, here are my conditions. You can tell your parents we're married if you want, but don't make me go through with a ceremony yet, okay?"

"Why not? It'd be easy in Vegas."

"I know, but let's just go back for a visit, so Dexter can meet his grandparents, and vice-versa. If that all goes well, we'll talk about making the marriage legal." Her stomach twisted at the thought.

"They're not going to welcome you and Dexter unless we're married, you know."

"I know, but if you're lying about everything else, why not lie about this part, too? What difference does it make?" Lainie thought of the ring Harry had bought her, but she wasn't about to offer that as part of the bargain. If Joey wanted her to look like a married lady, he could come up with his own ring.

Joey sipped his coffee, as if deep in thought. "All right. We'll go back to Vegas, get Dexter, and then we'll all fly to New York day after tomorrow."

She panicked at the idea that she'd have to leave with Joey and spend hours in the car with him. She didn't really believe he'd try to hurt her, but the drive back would be disgusting. Plus she wouldn't have a last chance to be with Harry.

"I'll get myself back to Vegas," she said. "You can come and pick up both me and Dexter from the apartment day after tomorrow."

He didn't look happy about that idea. "How do I know you won't try to run again?"

"Because I'll give you my word that I won't. I just talked to your mother, Joey. She's invested in this, and I wouldn't dream of letting her down, now that you've told her she has a grandson." Celeste's excitement was something Lainie couldn't ignore. Her parents hadn't ever acted like that. But maybe Joey was right. Maybe her mom and dad would change their attitude if she was married to Dexter's father.

Joey set down his coffee cup. "Okay, then. I guess I'll have to trust you. Just don't forget what's in it for Dexter."

"Believe me, I won't." She pushed back her chair. "Call my apartment when you have plane tickets."

"About your apartment . . ."

"I know you busted the door. I'm assuming you did some other damage. Obviously, it's not in my best interests or Dexter's to prosecute you for it."

"You've got that right." But he looked relieved, as if he hadn't been sure she'd let that business go.

"Call me when you have information." She stood and headed down the sidewalk toward where the Lexus was parked. She hadn't even started this new chapter of her life, and already she felt like a condemned inmate taking that last walk.

Joey grabbed his coffee and walked back in the direction of his car. He'd had to park way the hell and gone, in the exact opposite direction of where Lainie was parked, apparently. He'd be so glad to get out of this godforsaken place and ditch this dopey rental car. As he walked, he hit redial on his cell phone.

Mandy picked up immediately. "How did I do?"

"You did good. She totally believed you were my mother."

Mandy sighed. "Whew, that's a relief. I did my best to sound older. But for what it's worth, I think it sucks that you have to marry her after the way she's treated you."

"Don't worry. It won't slow me down. The marriage thing is for the parents. What they don't know can't hurt 'em. But I wish she'd go through with the marriage part right now, and she won't. She wants to wait and see how my folks react to her and the kid."

"What a fool. Too bad I can't do it instead of her. I'd stand in front of Elvis and promise to love and cherish any old day you asked me, Joey."

"Thanks." Joey just bet she would. She'd been dazzled by the tennis bracelet he'd promised when he'd asked her to help him with this phone call.

"I mean it."

"I wish I could take you up on it, Mandy." *As if*. "But right now I have to get this project off the ground. My idea was to surprise them with the kid and the new wife. And that should work for the first twenty-four hours, but I know my dad. Once the shock's worn off, he'll assign a flunky to find out if the marriage is real. If it's not, I'm screwed."

"Wow. Your dad must not trust anybody."

"I guess that's why he's got billions." Except Joey didn't trust anybody, either, and he wasn't exactly rolling in it. But he would be, if Lainie didn't crap out on him.

"From what you're saying, Lainie is your whole problem. Without her, you could do whatever you wanted. You really only need the kid, right?"

"Yeah." Joey kept coming back to that same conclusion. "I really only need the kid."

Chapter Twenty-five

Harry followed Lainie at a safe distance as she walked back to the Lexus. He could tell by the droop of her shoulders that something was definitely wrong, but then, he couldn't imagine how anything could be right when she had to deal with a creep like Joey. The guy looked even more obnoxious than he had the first time Harry had seen him.

"Hey, kid." Leo, his ear to a cell phone, beckoned from the doorway of a shop.

Harry hesitated, not wanting to stop. "Leo, I need to talk to Lainie."

"I know. But first you might want to hear what was said during their conversation."

"You know?" Harry had tried to read lips, but between staying in disguise and moving around so Joey wouldn't see him, he hadn't been able to tell what was going on between them.

"One of our guys was right there at the coffee shop

and picked up everything. And don't worry, another one's watching her all the way to the car. And we've checked the car out for explosives."

"Explosives?" Harry had a sudden horrible mental image.

"Standard procedure. Don't freak. Here. I'll have them play the tape again so you can listen." He gave instructions to the person on the other end. "Okay, they're ready. Just say hello and they'll start it."

Harry didn't take the phone. It felt like an invasion of Lainie's privacy. "Maybe I should just let her tell me."

Leo rolled his eyes. "You're so loaded down with scruples it's a wonder you can walk without tipping over. Take my word for it, when you're dealing with women, you need all the information you can get."

Harry didn't think he had so many scruples. After all, he had been trying to read lips to figure out the conversation. Leo's method was just more sophisticated. So he took the phone.

What he heard broke his heart. He was ready to strangle Joey for making Lainie choose between her career and her child. What a diabolical thing to do to someone, and the worst part was that Joey seemed oblivious to the carnage.

When the conversation ended, Harry gave the phone back to Leo.

"Not a pretty picture, is it?" Leo said.

"No." Harry didn't trust himself to say any more. His throat hurt from choking back words of fury. But other than wiping Joey off the face of the earth, he didn't know what options he had. And Lainie wouldn't thank him for eliminating Joey permanently. The amazing thing was his driving urge to do exactly that. He'd never felt so violent toward anyone in his life.

"I'll walk with you back to your car," Leo said. "Dudley hitched a ride with one of the Phoenix boys, and the other two are following Joey all the way back to Vegas."

As Leo fell into step beside him, Harry realized he'd forgotten all about the damaged Jag. "What happened with your car?"

"I'm pretty sure it's been knocked out of alignment." His tone was conversational. "I'm having it towed on a flatbed back to Vegas, so my regular garage can work on it."

"Leo, I'll pay for whatever it costs to fix it. The accident was my fault."

Leo chuckled. "Yeah, it was. And once I got over being pissed at you, I loved it."

"You loved that I leaped out of the car?"

"Absolutely. That's twice now you've acted out of character. It's good to know you've got an impulsive streak under that buttoned-down persona."

Harry chewed on that comment for a while and had to admit there was something to it. Lainie brought out a side of him he hadn't known existed, a side that ignored logic and simply acted according to what his heart told him to do.

But at the moment, his heart wasn't talking to him. It was still numb from the realization that Lainie was considering a loveless marriage to Joey for the sake of Dexter's future.

When he and Leo were about half a block from the Lexus, they could see Lainie sitting in the passenger seat with the windows down. She was leaning back against the headrest with her eyes closed, as if she couldn't bear to look ahead. Harry didn't blame her.

Leo caught Harry's arm and pulled him to a halt. "You know what? I think you two need some time alone. I'll take a stroll back down the street. When you're ready to drive on over to the resort, call my cell."

"I have no idea what to say to her," Harry murmured.

"Just be your usual comforting self. She's got a tough row to hoe right now. And don't give up hope, kid. Nothing's cast in stone yet. She didn't agree to marry that nimrod until after she's met his folks."

"Yeah, but you know how everyone reacts to Dexter. His grandparents are going to love him. Once she goes back there with Dexter, it'll all be over."

"You never know. And I'm still not convinced Joey's put all his cards on the table. I'm going to have my boys keep a watch on him until that flight takes off."

"Good. Because if they weren't going to keep tabs on him, I was."

Leo grinned. "Before you decide to switch professions, let me tell you that you're terrible at surveillance. The Phoenix guys were cracking up watching you today. Lucky for you Joey's not the brightest bulb in the chandelier, or you would've been made."

"And I almost wish he'd recognized me so I could take him on."

"See, that's what I'm talking about. Lately you've been showing a lot of spunk and a lot of heart. I'm glad to see it. I only wish we could make sure Lainie sticks around. She brings out all sorts of interesting things in you."

"Yeah, she does." Harry couldn't pretend that he wasn't involved right up to his eyeballs. "I wish we could get her to stick around, too."

Leo clapped him on the shoulder. "You go talk to her. Let her know she can count on you no matter what. You still have a shot, kid."

"Maybe." But he didn't think so.

"No maybe about it. Okay, I'm taking off. Call me." Leo sauntered away.

Harry walked over to the car, put both hands on the door, and crouched down so his face was even with Lainie's. "How're you doing?" he asked quietly.

She swallowed and didn't open her eyes. "I heard you walk up." Her voice was unsteady. "I can tell your footsteps, now."

"I could find you blindfolded, just by your scent."

"I . . . I could probably do that with you, too." She swallowed again. "Harry, the Benjamins could give Dexter the moon. How can I turn my back on a chance to give him everything I've ever wanted for him?"

Except a decent father. "What about Joey? I thought you were worried about his influence."

"I was. I am. But I doubt he'd be around much. In fact, I'm sure he wouldn't. He doesn't want a wife, just the chance to take over this business."

"But you thought his father wouldn't be so stupid as to give it to him."

When she opened her eyes and turned her head to look at him, her gaze was dull with despair. "I don't, but I've been sitting here thinking about it and I realize Joey doesn't really matter. Doyle and Celeste Benjamin will fall in love with Dexter. Everyone does. Doyle won't retire for another fifteen or twenty years, probably. By the time he does, he could hand the whole shebang over to Dexter and skip Joey completely."

Harry had to admit it was a likely scenario.

"That's assuming I do the right thing and marry Joey. Doyle wouldn't give his empire to someone who didn't have the Benjamin name."

He searched her expression. "Is that the right thing?"

She studied him for a long moment. "Harry, we don't always get what we want in life."

"I know." And he was finding that out the hard way. "Lainie, whatever you decide to do, I'll support you."

As her eyes filled with tears, she swiped at them angrily and looked away. "Thanks. Listen, we should probably get back to the resort. We have a long drive ahead of us."

But his attention had been drawn to the flash of silver when she'd wiped away her tears. "You put the ring back on your left hand." Suddenly he had an awful thought. "You're not planning to use it when you go back to New York, are you?"

"Absolutely not!" She looked down at the ring. "I just . . . felt better with it there. For now."

Marry me. Forget this terrible plan and marry me. He choked back the proposal and pushed himself to his feet. "I need to call Leo. He went off to do some shopping."

Her laugh had a tinge of hysteria. "Oh, I'm so sure. He's giving us some private time, is what he's doing. I figured you'd both need to ride back with me when I saw Leo's car being hauled off on a flatbed. In fact, I expected Dudley to show up, too."

"Dudley's riding with one of the Phoenix guys. But I guess Leo still feels like he has to watch out for us, so he stayed."

Lainie sniffed and wiped her eyes again. "He's a good man."

"The best."

"So are you."

His heart turned over. "You're pretty damned wonderful, yourself, Lainie." Then he grabbed his cell phone and dialed Leo before he blurted out what he had no business saying.

Lainie didn't try to make conversation on the way back to the resort. Then while Leo waited outside, she and Harry packed up their suitcases in record time, not talking, careful not to touch. She tucked the little plastic toy for Dexter in her purse and fluffed the red wig before putting it in a plastic bag so it wouldn't get crushed. They were almost finished when someone rapped on the door.

Harry answered it. "Hey, Dudley."

Pulling her packed suitcase behind her, Lainie went to the door. "Hi, Dudley."

"I just came to say so long," Dudley said. "And to ask you one last time if there isn't some way you can buy a one-bedroom."

Lainie smiled, blessing this funny old guy for lightening the mood a little. "No, Dudley, I'm afraid we can't." But dumpy as the place was, she wished she could buy a time-share here . . . with Harry.

"Thanks for all your help, though," Harry said.

"You're welcome. And I still can't shake the notion that you two are going to buy a one-bedroom unit."

Dudley handed them each a very cheesy business card that looked as if he'd typed it up himself. "So don't lose this."

"I won't," Lainie said as she held out her hand. "And thank you, again, Dudley. For everything."

"My pleasure." Dudley shook her hand and touched the brim of his hat, like a true cowboy.

Then he shook hands with Harry and left, careening away in his golf cart, backfiring all the way.

"I'm going to miss that guy," Harry said.

"I'm going to miss everything about this place." Lainie took one last look around.

"Even the ants?" Harry said, his voice tender.

"Yes." She glanced at him. "Even the ants." Then she drew in a breath and let it out. "Ready?"

He held her gaze for one long, intense moment. "Yeah." He grabbed his suitcase. "Ready."

Lainie gave Leo the front seat and she took the back, telling them she wanted to sleep on the way to Vegas. In fact she couldn't bear to ride all the way home next to the man she wanted so much, the man she couldn't have. So she pretended to sleep and tried to put emotional distance between herself and Harry.

She didn't have much success. Instead she spent most of the trip watching him through half-closed eyes. She studied the back of his neck and the way his hair grew into a neat little point. She noticed that his ears were nicely shaped and close to his head.

When he turned his head to say something to Leo, she admired his profile. He had a good nose and a great chin. She'd been so swept up in lust that she hadn't taken time to register that sort of thing, so she took the time now. She might never have another chance to observe him and record every little gesture, every variation in tone as he and Leo talked.

Their conversation was relaxed and easy, the way it would be between two people who'd known and liked each other for twenty years. The subject was usually Rona. But they also talked about Crimson Canyons, and how somebody with vision could fix it up and turn it into a gold mine.

"I don't dare tell Rona that, though," Leo said. "Or she'll talk me into making it our project. And she wouldn't care a bit about the snakes, either. I'm the one with the snake problem. She'd think they were exotic. And she'd want to get the TITS involved. It would be a nightmare."

"Probably," Harry agreed, "although as an investment, you could do worse than Crimson Canyons. The location is excellent."

"Wanna go in on it with me?"

As Harry hesitated, Lainie held her breath. If Harry said yes, then he'd be coming back here many times. And he'd be without her. Selfishly, she didn't want him to.

"No, I don't think that's my kind of deal," Harry said.

Lainie sighed in relief.

"Too risky?" Leo asked.

"Yeah. Too risky for me."

"Then I don't want to do it, either. And we have to make a pact not to mention it to Rona, or I'll never hear the end of it."

"Can't you just tell her it's a terrible investment? You'd be the one taking the financial hit if it fails."

"I know, but once she gets hold of an idea, she won't

let go. She'd make me do it." Leo sounded exactly like Eeyore.

Lainie couldn't help smiling. Leo, the man who put the fear of God into other men with one piercing glare, was a complete slave to the woman he loved. Then Leo started discussing a houseboat trip Rona wanted to take on Lake Mead, another thing Leo wasn't crazy about doing but probably would.

As the guys debated the pros and cons of houseboats, Lainie found herself getting sleepy, after all. Maybe it was the sense of absolute safety she felt riding in the car with these two men. Maybe it was the soothing quality of Harry's voice. In any case, she drifted off and didn't wake up until Harry pulled into the driveway of Rona's condo.

When she opened her eyes and realized where they were, she scrambled to unfasten her seat belt and climb out of the car so that she could see Dexter again. But as she hurried up the walk to the front door, she paused to glance back at Harry, who was hauling the suitcases out of the trunk. Her special time with that special man was over.

Then she had no more time to think of that, because the door flew open and Dexter came running out to meet her.

"Mommy, I just got a royal flush! I caught it on the river card, Mommy! I'm not just a card shark, I'm a great white! That's what Cherie calls me."

Lainie swept him into her arms, her throat tight from holding back tears of joy.

"Did you have a good time on your trip with Mr. Harry? Did you— Oof, you're squeezing me too tight!"

Lainie loosened her grip and set him back on his feet. Then she cleared her throat. "I was just glad to see you." She reached in her purse and pulled out the little action figure. "Look what I brought you!"

"Oo, cool! Thanks!" He clutched the toy against his chest and took her hand. "Come on inside. I'll bet Miss Rona's friends will deal you in if you ask them. Miss Rona has really nice friends. The only bad thing is I couldn't take Fred for a walk, but Miss Rona said maybe another time I can. Can I, Mommy?" He tugged her inside the house.

"Maybe." But Lainie didn't see how that was possible, now. She should tell Dexter that he was about to take a plane trip, but she couldn't bring herself to talk about it yet. Instead she crouched down to pet Fred, who was dancing around her feet while Dexter giggled.

"He's happy you're home, too," Dexter said.

Lainie had no idea where home was anymore. This place sure felt terrific, though, with the sound of happy voices back in the kitchen and the aroma of food cooking. Then Rona came walking down the hall and held out her arms. Lainie walked right into them and accepted Rona's warm hug.

"Just remember, you'll always be welcome here," Rona said as she released Lainie.

Something in her expression made Lainie suspect Rona knew about the meeting with Joey. "Leo called you from the road?"

Rona nodded, her expression sober. She glanced quickly at Dexter, who seemed engrossed with Fred. "And I understand why you have to do this. But if you need any help, or a shoulder to cry on . . ."

"Thanks, Rona." Lainie kept a tight grip on her emotions. Blubbering now wouldn't help the situation and might scare Dexter. "That means a lot."

"Come on in and have something to eat before Harry takes you back to your apartment."

Lainie looked into Rona's eyes and saw the sadness there. Saying goodbye to Dexter wouldn't be easy for her. No reason to make it abrupt. "Sure," she said. "I'd love to stay a little while."

"Mr. Harry!" Dexter stopped playing with Fred when Harry came through the door with one suitcase. Leo brought up the rear with the other one. "Mr. Leo!"

"Hi, there, kid," Leo said. "I hear you've been cleaning up playing poker with the TI . . . ladies."

"Yep." Dexter beamed. Then he sidled over to Harry and tugged on his pant leg. "I played with some of your toys."

Looking confused, Harry set down the suitcase. "What toys?"

"You know. Your stuff that was in the box. 'Cept you'll have to teach me about Dungeons & Dragons, and the Atari cartridges, but the machine that plays them is broken, but there's a chess set, and a Rubik's Cube, and—"

"Oh, *those* toys." Harry glanced at Rona. "You still have some of that old stuff?"

Rona shrugged. "Just one box full. I thought someday you might . . . well, I got the box out for Dexter."

"Good idea." Harry looked down at Dexter standing there expectantly. "You want to learn Dungeons & Dragons?"

"Yeah! It looks really cool!"

"Well, um . . ." He glanced over at Lainie. "I'd be

glad to explain the game, but I'm not sure what the schedule is, here."

"What schedule?" Dexter looked from his mother to Harry.

Lainie found herself swamped in emotion as she imagined Rona getting out Harry's old toys. Now Harry was here to show Dexter how to play with them. That was the kind of special treat that should be allowed to unfold without time constraints. But time was running out.

She couldn't bear to bring the curtain down just yet, though. "Tell you what, if it's okay, Mr. Harry can show you about Dungeons & Dragons while I'm . . ." She'd be packing for the trip, but she didn't want to say that. "While I'm doing some other things." She met Harry's gaze. "Will that work?"

"Of course."

"Yippee!" Dexter started dancing around while Fred barked happily. "Can Fred come?"

"No, I'm afraid not." Lainie couldn't work miracles. "The apartment complex doesn't allow dogs, remember."

"Oh, yeah." Dexter looked forlorn. "Mommy, can we move? Can we move someplace where they let you have dogs?"

And there it was, the bribe she needed to convince Dexter this trip was a good thing. If they moved back to New York, she could promise him a dog. Somehow, it didn't seem like nearly enough.

Chapter Twenty-six

Harry spent a couple of hours on the floor of Lainie's apartment taking a trip back into his childhood. As it turned out, he still loved playing Dungeons & Dragons, and so did Dexter, partly because of the extra challenge involved. The game was technically geared toward much older kids, but Dexter valiantly studied the principles and accepted his losses as the price of learning "Mr. Harry's game."

Although Dexter's attention span was amazing for somebody less than five, Harry decided to give him a break part way through the session. They fooled with the Rubik's Cube and paged through some of his *Choose Your Own Adventure* books. If Harry could choose his own ending to this adventure, it would involve him hitting a huge jackpot on the Strip so that Lainie could forget about the Benjamins and their money.

She'd used the time to sort and pack for the trip. Dexter didn't know that. He thought she was cleaning up from Joey's rampage. The mess hadn't been as bad as it could have been, though, thanks to Leo.

Harry figured eventually Lainie would gather her courage to come in and tell Dexter what was about to happen. He knew it wouldn't be an easy conversation, and he was prepared to leave if she didn't want him horning in.

About the time Harry was ready to suggest buying dinner, Lainie walked into the living room where Harry and Dexter had their activities spread out on the floor. From her resolute expression, Harry knew she'd chosen her moment to give Dexter the news.

He stood. "I probably should go on down to my own place and . . . check on things." He had nothing to check on—no plants, no goldfish, and probably nothing interesting on his answering machine, but it sounded like a reasonable excuse. It also made him realize his life sucked without the kind of excitement Lainie brought to it.

"Aw, Mr. Harry!" Dexter got to his feet and grabbed Harry's hand. "We're not done yet."

They never would be done, either. Harry could play with this little guy forever. What fun it would have been to watch him grow up.

"Please don't leave," Lainie said. Her gaze pleaded with him to stay and offer moral support.

And just like that, his life sparkled with meaning again. "Well, if you're sure . . ."

"Absolutely sure." She sat on the floor. "Whatcha got there, Dexter?"

"I'll show you!" Dropping to his knees, Dexter proudly displayed his knowledge of Dungeons & Dragons, the

Rubik's Cube, and the wonder of a book that had more than one ending.

"Looks like you've been having a blast," Lainie said as Dexter began to run out of steam.

"*We've* been having a blast, both of us, right, Mr. Harry?"

"Definitely." Harry sat on the floor across from Lainie. He'd used the past few hours to adjust to not being able to touch her. It was quite an adjustment after the touch-fest they'd engaged in at the time-share.

Lainie cleared her throat. "Dexter, you know how you've always wanted to take a plane ride?"

"Yep." Dexter gazed up at her. "But you always said it's out of our price range."

Harry worked not to smile. Dexter was such a little parrot, and it was so cute to listen to him repeat exactly what he'd heard the grown-ups say.

"Well, it is out of our price range," Lainie said. "But Daddy's treating us to a plane ride so you can go see your Grandma and Grandpa Benjamin."

Dexter stared at her, and Harry could almost hear his brain working on that statement. "Daddy's mommy and daddy?" he asked at last.

"That's right."

Dexter blew out a breath. "Are we talking about those people who didn't teach him to behave right? 'Cause if that's who we're talking about, I don't want to go."

Lainie gulped. "Well, just because they weren't very strict with your dad doesn't mean they wouldn't be very nice to you. And it doesn't matter if they're strict or not, because you already know how to behave."

"Does Daddy have to come with us?"

"Yes, he—"

"Nope." Dexter crossed his arms and shook his head. "I'm not going if Daddy goes. He yells."

Harry was caught in the middle. He completely agreed with Dexter, but Lainie needed help. If she didn't take Dexter back to meet his grandparents, she'd never forgive herself.

So Harry plunged in on Lainie's side. "I don't think you have to worry about your dad yelling," he said. "You'll just drive to the airport, which isn't very far, and then get on a plane. People aren't allowed to yell on planes. Then when you get there, your grandma and grandpa will be around."

"Yeah," Dexter said, his expression dark, "but they won't keep him from yelling. If they couldn't make him stop when he was little, they won't be able to make him stop when he's big."

Perfect logic, Harry thought. But he was good with logic, too. "I happen to know that your dad wants to make a very good impression on his parents. That's why he wants to bring you back there, because he knows they'll like you a lot. Yelling wouldn't help his cause, so I'm betting he won't do it." He glanced at Lainie. "Isn't that what you think?"

"Exactly what I think." Gratitude shone in her eyes.

Dexter propped his chin on his fist and thought some more. "I guess that makes sense. Okay, I'll go, then." Then he looked at Harry. "I wish you could come with us."

"Believe me, so do I." This time Harry didn't meet Lainie's gaze. He was afraid the yearning he felt was way too obvious, and a guy had to salvage a little of his pride.

As if on schedule, the phone rang. Lainie got up to go into the kitchen to answer it, and Harry knew instinctively that Joey was on the line.

Lainie confirmed it when she came back into the living room. "Our flight leaves at eight thirty-two in the morning," she said. "Joey will be by to pick us up at six-thirty."

That was it, then. Everything was in place for Lainie and Dexter to start a whole new life, a life where Harry would have no role. But for now, they were still right here, and he wasn't going to miss a single moment.

"Let's go out for burgers," he said.

"Yeah, that would be cool!" Dexter said.

With that kind of encouragement, Harry decided to pile on the activities. "And after that, if there's time, you can both come to my apartment and we'll play Space Invaders on the Internet."

"Space Invaders?" Dexter scrambled to his feet. "Like that Atari cartridge that doesn't work anymore?"

"That's right. We'll pick up a couple of joysticks while we're out." He'd heard that the game was available on the Web, and he'd thought about looking into it, for old times' sake. Now he had the perfect excuse. "If it's okay with your mom, that is." He couldn't believe she'd say no. Distractions should be welcome about now.

"Can we, Mommy? Can we, please?" Dexter's face was alight with anticipation.

"Sounds like fun." Lainie smiled bravely at Harry. "I used to play Space Invaders, too."

• • •

The evening whizzed by, when all Lainie wanted was to stop the clock. Eventually she had to call a halt to their hilarious game of Space Invaders because it was past Dexter's bedtime.

"I'll walk you back to your apartment." Harry grabbed his keys and ushered them out the door.

Dexter spent the entire walk between apartments raving about how much he loved Space Invaders, so Lainie had plenty of time to make a decision. She would tell Harry goodbye now, at the door to their place. If she let him come in, she'd end up kissing him. Maybe she'd end up doing more than that, although probably not, with Dexter in the next room. But even a kiss would destroy her right now.

She got out her key way ahead of time, and when they reached her door, she glanced down at Dexter. "Tell Mr. Harry goodbye. We'll see him . . . after we get back from New York." She knew there was a chance they'd never be back. The Benjamins could easily hire somebody to pack up her belongings and have them shipped.

Harry's quick intake of breath told her he hadn't expected this. But he crouched down in front of Dexter without any protest. "Goodbye, then, Dexter. I've had a great time."

"Me, too." Dexter gave him a hug. "Don't worry. We'll be back soon. Then we can play some more."

"Right." Harry hugged him back. "I'll see you soon."

Lainie busied herself unlocking the door so she wouldn't have to watch them saying goodbye. She swung the door open and flipped the switch by the door that turned on the living room lights. Someday she'd have to repay Leo for the door, too.

"Okay, Dexter," she said, "go on in and start getting ready for your bath."

"Okay." Dragging his feet and mumbling to himself, Dexter went inside. A few feet beyond the doorway he turned and waved. "Bye, Mr. Harry. See you soon!"

"You bet." Harry's voice was suspiciously hoarse.

Lainie steeled herself and turned to him. "I don't know how I'll ever be able to thank—"

"You don't have to thank me, and you know it." His voice trembled. "I hate how this is turning out."

"Me, too." She was sure her eyes reflected the agony in his. "But that's life. I'll . . . see you when I get back."

"If you get back."

She had no answer for that. Pressing her lips together, she went inside. As she closed the door, she had one last glimpse of his face. He looked as if his world had just ended.

Harry played Space Invaders until three in the morning, when his hand-eye coordination was totally shot and he was punch-drunk from staring at the screen. Then he staggered to bed, only to stare into the darkness and worry about Lainie and Dexter going off to New York with Joey. His goal all along had been to protect them, but he didn't know how to protect them now.

At five-thirty his phone rang, and he must have been semi-asleep because he leaped out of bed as if shot from a cannon. He prayed it was Lainie, telling him she'd changed her mind, and if he was willing, they'd run away to some remote country and . . . do what? Farm? God, he was so out of options.

The caller turned out to be his mother. "What time is that loser picking Lainie and Dexter up?"

"Six-thirty." The hour was burned into his brain. "Why?"

"The TITS have officially decided we can't let Dexter leave without a send-off at the airport," she said. "We're taking Trixie's van, and you can go if you want. It'll be a surprise, so we'll come by and pick you up at six-forty. We'll see if we can catch up to them on the way and follow them in, which would be fun. They'd never expect it."

As stupid as it sounded, Harry knew he'd take any excuse to see Lainie one more time. "I suppose you've made a banner."

"Of course we've made a banner. What's a send-off without a banner? And we have balloons and confetti. We're taking Fred. Dexter didn't get to say goodbye to Fred, and Fred's very depressed about that."

"I'm sure he is." Harry was pretty damned depressed, himself. "Okay, I'm in."

"Good! You can drive the van. Trixie's not a morning person, so I'm not sure I trust her behind the wheel so early."

"Then I'll definitely drive the van. Is Leo coming, too?"

"Oh, you know Leo. Hates these kinds of mushy displays. Tried to talk me out of it, so, no, he's not coming. His loss. Gotta run. We have more to do. Bye."

Harry hung up and wondered what sort of undignified

event he'd let himself in for. But he didn't really care. They needed him to drive the van, and he needed to see Lainie . . . one more time.

Lainie didn't sleep much. By the time she hauled herself out of bed, she ached all over and her eyes felt gritty. She hoped that eventually she'd become resigned to this plan. Right now all she wanted was to run away, far away, and take Dexter with her. And Harry, if he'd be willing to go.

She still wasn't sure what to think about Harry. He obviously adored Dexter, and he seemed to have fallen in love with her, but that didn't mean he'd changed his mind about wanting a wife with an ordinary day job.

She was prepared to give up dancing so that Dexter could inherit the Benjamin empire, but if that all fell through, she wasn't prepared to give it up for Harry. If she did that, she'd resent him forever. Resenting the Benjamins and Joey didn't matter, because she already resented them. But resenting Harry would poison what had been a wonderful relationship. So she and Harry were probably doomed, no matter what.

She got herself ready and packed her last few toiletries. She'd packed a separate small suitcase for Dexter, to make this trip seem more special for him. At the last minute she'd remembered to put in a tube of kid-safe sunscreen, in case Celeste followed through on her promise to take Dexter to the beach. A new grandma might not think of such things.

Lainie's final step was to switch her silver ring from her left hand to her right. She did it quickly and tried not to think about it too much, but once she'd moved the ring, she thought about it constantly.

The secret was to keep going, keep doing all the little chores that were necessary. She set out some juice, cereal, and milk for Dexter. Then she went in to wake him up.

He was already awake, his hands propped behind his head as he stared up at the ceiling, where she'd hung mobiles. He had one of the solar system, another of various kinds of fish, and a third that was all butterflies.

"Time to get dressed," she said.

Dexter didn't move. "Mommy, are you sure this is a good idea?"

No. "I talked to your Grandma Celeste yesterday, Dexter. She really wants to meet you. She wants to take you to the beach, so I packed a tube of sunscreen for you. You'll love the beach."

Lainie didn't mention the toys Celeste had bought. She didn't want Dexter to start getting greedy right off the bat. Being rich had some disadvantages, too. Dexter wasn't spoiled now, but she'd have to work hard to make sure he didn't get that way.

"Why didn't she want to meet me before?"

Lainie could tell Dexter had put a lot of thought into this, and he deserved as much of the truth as she dared give him. "Daddy didn't tell them about you until now."

Dexter turned his head toward her. "Why not?"

She wasn't about to get into the moral stance of his grandparents. "He wasn't ready to settle down and be a daddy. If he told them, they would have expected him to do that, so he didn't tell them."

"If he didn't want to be a daddy, then why did he make a baby?"

Lainie decided that was enough truth for one morning. She didn't want to use the word "accident" when it came to someone as awesome as Dexter. "Let's just say he was confused. Come on, now, I need you to get dressed and go in and eat your cereal."

With a resigned sigh, Dexter climbed out of bed and started taking off his SpongeBob pajamas, a gift from the TITS. "Mr. Harry wouldn't be like that."

Her heart beat faster just hearing his name. She'd thought of little else but Harry all night long. "What do you mean?"

"If he made a baby, he'd stay there and be a daddy. He likes kids."

"Yes, I believe he does." Her heart ached for the impossible, Harry as the father of her children, including Dexter, of course. Harry would welcome Dexter as his own—she could already see that. But it didn't matter. She was going to New York with Joey, because that was the hand she'd been dealt.

As Joey drove the gold sedan to Lainie's apartment complex, he thought how glad he'd be to get rid of the damn thing and finally drive his Vette again. But it was good he had this car for now, because he needed a back seat to transport the kid. He glanced at the Game Boy on the seat next to him. That should keep Dexter distracted for a while. The clerk who'd sold it to him had said all kids loved those things.

He pulled up in front of the apartment at six-thirty on the dot. Usually he didn't care much about being on time, but today was different. Today everything had to go like clockwork.

When he got to her front door, he noticed it had been replaced. Well, that was good. Somebody else besides him had paid for a new door. He'd been afraid that expense would come out of his pocket, but apparently not.

He rang the doorbell and worked on his smile. By the time she opened the door, he had it going on. "Hey, Lainie, good to see you."

She didn't smile back. "We're ready."

"Glad to hear it! Hey, Dexter! How's it hangin', buddy?"

Dexter didn't look real happy to see him. "Okay," he said.

"Don't you have a hug for your daddy?"

"Not really."

"Maybe we'd better just go," Lainie said. "We'll have plenty of time to get acquainted on the plane."

"Right, right." Joey hoped the Game Boy would do the trick with Dexter, though. If not, he'd buy him more stuff at the airport. Kids liked getting stuff. He always had.

"Let's get Dexter settled in the back first," he said when they reached the car. "Dexter, look what I got for you!"

Dexter took it, but he didn't act all excited, like the clerk had promised he would. "Thank you."

Little jerk. Joey ground his teeth together. "You're welcome! Come on, let's get you belted in, and then you can play with it on the way to the airport."

"Okay." Still no enthusiasm.

Joey got the ungrateful little brat into the seat with his seat belt on and put his little suitcase next to him. From the corner of his eye he saw the dark sedan pull up behind his rental car. Good. Right on time.

"Lainie, if you wouldn't mind taking a look at these

tickets, I'd appreciate it," he said. "I picked our seats, but we can change them if you want."

She looked at him with the same dull expression as Dexter. "I'm sure they're fine."

He handed her the ticket envelope, anyway. "Just take a look. I want to be sure." Then he leaned into the back seat again. "Got that thing turned on? Pretty cool, huh?" With his body, he blocked Dexter's view of Lainie and kept talking about the game Dexter was playing. He talked loud.

He barely heard the scuffle and moans behind him, so he knew Dexter wouldn't, especially with the bleeps and clanging of the game. The guys he'd hired were pros. They snatched Lainie cleanly and quietly. An engine started and he turned in time to see the black sedan speed away, taking with it the only obstacle to his becoming a very rich man.

"Okay, then!" He closed the back door and hurried around to the front. "Time to get to the airport!"

"Wait! Where's my mommy?"

"Dexter, she decided not to come." He put the car in gear and drove quickly out of the parking lot.

"She wouldn't do that! Stop the car!"

"But she did, Dexter. She decided to stay in Vegas. She didn't want you to be sad, so she just ducked back inside the apartment."

"I don't believe you! Let me out of here!"

Joey glanced in the rearview mirror. The damned brat had unfastened his seat belt. Joey hit the door and window locks. "Sorry, but you're going with me. And you're lucky you are, because once we get there, you can have anything you want. Toys, ice cream, candy—you name it."

Dexter began to scream.

"Stop that, dammit! I can't drive while you're doing that!"

Dexter screamed louder.

"Listen, you brat, if you ever want to see your mother again, you'd better shut the hell up!"

Dexter stopped screaming.

"Now that's more like it. Play with your Game Boy."

Chapter Twenty-seven

Driving a van full of TITS to the airport reminded Harry of taking a bus in a third-world country. Maybe he wasn't carrying goats and chickens, but he'd bet the noise level was about the same, and Fred did his part to provide the animal element.

"Lower the balloons," he called back to Cherie. "You're blocking my mirror."

"I keep trying!" Cherie yelled over the general hubbub. "They float back up!"

"Tie them down!" Harry had trouble when the balloons appeared in the mirror, and even more trouble when Cherie bobbed into view, because now that she had her red wig back, she'd decided to wear it. Harry had way too many memories of that red wig.

Trixie sat next to him with a traveling coffee mug the size of an ice bucket. She was the only one in the group not saying much, because she kept dozing off and jerking herself back awake, which made her long rhinestone earrings jingle. How she could doze was beyond him.

Rona, Suz, Babs, and Cherie had decided to sing show tunes to get in the mood for the gala send-off. They were currently running through "Oklahoma!" and Harry was mightily sick of wind sweeping down the plains. They accused him of being a bad sport for not joining in. After all, he knew all the words.

But all he cared about was getting one last glimpse of Lainie. That pretty much indicated how far gone he was. Freeway traffic was sluggish this morning, and he hoped to hell there wasn't an accident up ahead. He tried to tell himself that Lainie and Dexter weren't part of that potential accident, but of course he worried himself sick about it, anyway.

To reassure himself that Lainie wasn't part of an accident, he searched for the gold sedan in the mass of vehicles. The chances of catching up to the car in this kind of traffic were remote, but he would love to see that car and know that Lainie and Dexter were okay.

Then he thought he spotted it in the far right lane. Damn, it wasn't close enough for him to be sure. He had to ease around a couple of semis to get a better look, and first thing he knew, "Oklahoma!" had come to a halt and the TITS started carrying on about his driving. Even Trixie woke up and began to gripe.

He ignored them all. The closer he got to the car, the more certain he was. He didn't have a photographic memory like Lainie, but he thought the license plate sounded about right.

He was about two car lengths away when he saw the writing in the back window. It was backward, and the letters were dripping like they'd been made with something liquid, like lotion or shampoo. But the word was "HELP."

"Hang on, ladies!" Harry cut someone off so he could veer into the lane next to the gold sedan. "Mom, call Leo! Get him here! I think Joey's kidnapped Dexter."

"Omigod, omigod. Harry, where's here?"

"On the freeway, two miles from the airport exit! Trixie, can you see into that gold car?"

Trixie hunkered down. "I see a blond guy driving, and somebody's in the back seat . . . it's Dexter!" She rolled down her window. "Dexter! We're here!"

Harry lay on the horn and came right up beside the sedan. He'd never forced anyone off the road before, but at least he had a van. He had to be careful, though, because he didn't want Joey to wreck.

By now all the windows on the passenger side were down and the TITS were hanging out, waving and screaming at Dexter.

"Can anybody see Lainie?" Harry's heart beat so loud it almost drowned out the racket.

Trixie leaned halfway out of the window as she looked down at the car. "No! It's just the guy, and he's totally pissed!"

A deadly calm took hold of Harry. The noise faded into the background, leaving him with one clean, white-hot purpose, to get that car off the road and kill the man driving it. He turned the wheel so that Joey was forced to run into him or pull over.

"He's pulling over!" Trixie yelled.

Harry expected him to. Joey was going to pull over. It was a given. He slammed on the brakes, positioning the van across the car's left front fender. Joey wasn't going anywhere.

Harry was out of the van and around by the car, ready

to pull Joey out through the window if necessary. Joey beat him to it, boiling out of the car, swearing a blue streak.

"What the hell do you think you're doing?" he shouted. Then he saw who was coming toward him and his eyes widened. "You!"

"Where is she, you son of a bitch?" Harry had never thought of himself as a strong man, but he had Joey pinned against the car in no time as he wrapped both hands around his worthless throat. *"Where is she?"*

Joey's eyes bugged out. "She's fine, man! Fine!"

"Tell me where she is or I'll kill you right now." It was not a threat but a promise.

"Harry!"

He heard Lainie's voice, but wondered if he was hallucinating.

"Harry, I'm here!"

He turned his head, and there she was, running down the shoulder of the road, followed by two guys who'd just come out of a black sedan. They looked vaguely familiar.

Before running to meet her, Harry shoved Joey away so hard that he fell to the pavement. "What happened?" He clutched Lainie by the shoulders. "Who are these guys? Why weren't you—"

"I'll tell you in a minute." She gasped for breath. "We have to get Dexter. He must be terrified."

"Oh, God. Dexter. He wrote 'HELP' in the back window." Harry ran with her back to the sedan, only to discover that the TITS had everything under control. Cherie, Suz, Babs, and Trixie were sitting squarely on top of Joey, and Suz had a grip on his privates. Rona had Dexter, holding him tight and rocking him back and forth as she murmured reassurances.

Harry stepped back and let Lainie reunite with her son. He still had no idea what had happened, but at least Lainie and Dexter seemed to be okay, and Joey . . . well, Joey was in good hands. Harry still wanted to kill him, but the primal urge had faded and his brain was back in control. Killing Joey would only mean getting sent to jail, and that wouldn't help anyone.

Left with not much to do, he turned back to the two guys he'd vaguely recognized. "Why was Lainie with you instead of with Dexter?"

"Maybe Leo should explain it," one of the men said. "He should be here any minute." He glanced at Joey pinned to the ground by the TITS. "We could take him off your hands, though, if you want."

"Don't you dare," Suz called. "We're having a great time over here."

At that moment a maroon Jag pulled in behind the black sedan and Leo climbed out looking extremely unhappy. He was followed by Eric and Brett. "What the hell is this mess? I thought we agreed that we'd nab him at the airport?"

Rona came storming over. "You *knew* about all of this? You *planned* it?"

"No, we planned something totally different. I was at the airport waiting for the gold sedan, and these guys were following the sedan. We had it under control."

Rona clenched her fists. "You'd better explain better than that, Leo Pirelli."

Leo blew out a breath and rubbed the back of his neck. "My contacts found out that Joey was looking for a couple of guys to do some dirty work, so we sent him these two. That way, Joey would think his plan was working, but Lainie wouldn't be in danger."

"And you scared Lainie and Dexter out of their wits!" Rona's eyes flashed fire.

Leo cleared his throat. "Because I thought Lainie needed to know who she was dealing with. Don't get me wrong, it wasn't a murder plot. He just wanted to keep her from going to New York. Once he had Dexter inside his parents' compound, he'd deny her entry and convince his folks she should never be allowed near her son. Oh, and that phone call to his mother? It was some waitress, not his mother. His folks still don't know Dexter exists."

Lainie approached, holding Dexter. "You're right, I wouldn't have believed Joey would do something like that, but I hate that you scared Dexter so bad. That was not a good thing, Leo."

"That was an inexcusable thing," Rona said. "What were you thinking?"

"I was thinking to expose the creep! Dammit, I did what I thought was best." He walked over and looked into Dexter's eyes. "I'm sorry, Dex. I shouldn't have scared you so bad."

Dexter took a deep breath. "Does this mean I don't have to go to New York with Daddy?"

"It certainly does." Lainie's jaw clenched. "We're through with anybody named Benjamin."

"Then it's okay if I got scared," Dexter said.

Harry saw a little ray of hope. If Lainie was through with anybody named Benjamin, then maybe she'd be ready for somebody named Ambrewster.

"Something else you should know," Leo said. "My

guys talked him out of a hundred grand for snatching you. Cash. It's yours, Lainie. If you buy some long-term CDs in Dexter's name, in sixteen years you'll have plenty to send Dexter to one of those highfalutin colleges."

Lainie blinked. "Wow. Thank you, Leo."

"It's the least he could have done, after what he put you through," Rona said. She was still shooting daggers at Leo.

He pretended not to notice. "So all that's left is making absolutely certain Joey doesn't ever consider coming back here. We need to make sure he's scared straight."

"The pleasure will be all mine." Lainie gave Dexter a hug. "Will you go with Miss Rona for a little while?"

"Can I go see Fred? He's looking out the window of the van, and he really wants to see me."

"Then let's go see Fred." Rona held out her arms.

Once Dexter was inside the van, Lainie turned to Leo. "All right. Let's go put the screws to Joey."

Leo smiled. "That's my girl."

No, that's my woman. But Harry didn't say the words out loud. Just because one obstacle had been removed didn't mean he had clear sailing.

The three of them marched back to where Joey was still being expertly pinned down by the TITS. They all looked up and grinned as Lainie, Harry, and Leo approached.

"Whatcha want us to do with this piece of garbage?" Suz asked.

Joey moaned.

"Be quiet, you." Cherie rapped him on the head with her knuckles. "Or else Suz will start twisting the family jewels."

Lainie crouched down next to Joey. "I have Leo here with me, and I think you already know that Leo is well connected, if you get my meaning. By now you must realize that the guys you hired to snatch me were actually his guys."

"They were?" Joey's voice was a pitiful squeak.

"Yes. And all it takes is a word from Leo, and you'll disappear without a trace."

Joey gulped.

"So unless you want a short and not-very-bright future, you'll leave on that plane and never come back." Then she glanced up at Leo. "Your guys will make sure Joey gets on that plane, right?"

"Oh, he'll be on the plane," Leo said. "And Joey, all it takes is a phone call and your creditors will be alerted that you're probably not going to pay them at the end of the week."

"Oh, dear God." Joey's eyes bulged. "Don't make that call. I'm gonna get the money. Please don't make that call."

"Then you'll be on the plane, right?" Leo said.

"Absolutely. I will definitely be on it, and that's a promise."

Leo nodded. "I believe you. Let him up, ladies."

"Aw, do we have to?" Babs bounced a couple of times on Joey's chest. "This has been such fun."

"Yeah, you have to," Leo said. "We don't want him to miss that flight."

The TITS all reluctantly piled back into the van and Trixie took the wheel to pull it forward. Then Harry stood beside Lainie as Eric and Brett got into the gold sedan with Joey in the passenger seat. When the car eased into traffic, the black sedan with the two Phoenix men followed.

"I doubt we'll see him again," Leo said.

Lainie shuddered. "I hope not."

Leo glanced at the van, which rocked merrily from the movement of the women inside as "Oklahoma!" drifted from the open windows. Then he turned back to Lainie and Harry. "Listen, I think you two and Dexter need some time to regroup. I'll ride back in the van and you three take the Jag."

Harry turned to study the maroon car. "You didn't buy a new one, did you?"

"Ah, it was easier than waiting for the old one to get fixed." Leo dug for his key. "Damn, I must have left it in the ignition, which shows you how shook up I was when I saw this circus. Anyway, just don't race the engine or use the cruise control. It only has forty-six miles on it."

Harry looked at him. "This is me you're talking to. I don't do stuff like that."

Leo smiled. "A week ago I wouldn't have thought so, but lately, I'm not so sure."

"But Leo, your new car?" Lainie sounded doubtful. "We shouldn't be taking a brand-new car."

"In case you two hadn't noticed, I'm in deep shit with Rona. Loaning you my car might earn me some points, and I'm desperate for points."

"Okay, then. Thank you, Leo." Lainie put her hand on his arm. "You're probably right that Dexter and I need to decompress a little, and that van sounds wild. The other thing is, I should stop by the Nirvana, pick up my car, and see if I can have my job back. The sooner the better on that. I'll go get Dexter."

After she walked away, Leo shoved his hands in his pockets and looked at Harry. "So, are you gonna pop the question?"

"With Dexter around?"

"Well, yeah, I suppose that's not the time. Don't wait too long, though. You just played the hero. Take advantage of it."

"I wasn't trying to be a hero. I . . . I don't really know what happened to me. It was like I had no choice but to annihilate the guy."

Leo nodded. "It's called love, kid. And you need to—"

"Here she comes, and no Dexter."

"He wants to stay there with Fred," Lainie said. "I keep forgetting how easily kids bounce back. And he's a real celebrity in that van. Everyone's talking about how smart he was to use his little bottle of sunscreen to write on the back window."

Leo gave Harry a glance filled with meaning. "Then take off, you two."

The first few minutes of the ride in the Jag passed in silence. Lainie thought Harry might be concentrating on driving the new and unfamiliar car. Neither of them wanted to be responsible for damaging another of Leo's vehicles.

But as the silence stretched out, Lainie concluded that Harry was feeling awkward, now that she was a free woman. It was one thing to say he wished for a different outcome when it looked as if they had no future together. He might have said it to make her feel better, knowing they didn't have a snowman's chance in hell. But now they had all the chances they wanted.

Harry could very well be getting cold feet.

She cleared her throat. "I just want to say that I'm not holding you to anything you said in the heat of the moment."

"Lainie, I think we should get married."

She groaned. He thought they *should* get married, which meant that he was willing to step in and fill the gap in her and Dexter's lives. "No, we shouldn't."

"Why not?"

"Because all along you've given me the distinct impression that you want someone with an ordinary job, someone who'll be home at five to cook the dinner and tuck the kids into bed. We both know I'm not that woman."

"That's okay! We could work it out fine, with me babysitting at night and you babysitting in the daytime. The kids would be covered. That's a more logical arrangement than two parents who both work during the day. I see that, now."

She cringed. "This is about logic? You're basing a marriage proposal on logic?"

"No, not totally, but I've had time to think about it, and I see how everything could work out for us. And Dexter seems to like me, so there's—"

"Dexter does like you." *And I love you.* "But if this is about giving Rona the grandmother experience, then we don't have to get married for that. I'd be thrilled to continue taking Dexter over there for visits. I'll even have Dexter start calling her Grandma Rona if she wants him to."

"This isn't about Rona's grandmother experience." Harry's jaw clenched. "It's about us. Getting married is the next logical step. We wouldn't even have much moving to do. We could pick your apartment or mine, whichever you'd rather."

"Actually, I'm leaving that apartment complex." She'd been toying with the idea before, once she saw what having Fred around meant to Dexter. "I'm moving into a place that allows pets."

"Fine! We'll move into a place that allows pets!" He pulled into the parking lot behind the Nirvana. "Lainie, why can't you see that this is the best thing for everybody? You, me, Dexter . . . everybody?"

She stared at him and wondered how such a smart man could be so dumb. "You figure it out." She opened her door. "Thanks for the ride." Then she walked to the back door of the Nirvana.

At the door, she turned around and glanced back. Harry sat behind the wheel of the Jag, looking completely confused and completely adorable. But she wasn't going to marry a man who insisted that it was the "logical" thing to do.

She wanted a lot more from Harry than that. She knew he was capable of more, or at least she thought so, judging from what a hottie he became in bed. Then again, maybe he was one of those men who couldn't get himself to say those three little words.

If so, then she'd have to learn to live without him.

Chapter Twenty-eight

Thank goodness Tim hadn't replaced her, Lainie thought as she stepped back on the Nirvana stage that night. Dancing was exactly what she needed to recover from the emotional roller coaster she'd been riding for the past few days. She'd spent the day taking care of details, but for the moment, all she had to think about was the music, the rhythm, the routine.

Between numbers, thoughts crept in, though. She had to consider herself one lucky woman now that she and Dexter had escaped Joey's clutches and Dexter's education fund was a reality. She'd bought the CDs today after retrieving Dexter and her "Fever" costume from Rona's house.

She'd promised Rona she and Dexter would be back in a couple of days, but she'd avoided any discussion of Harry. He'd been such a hero that she found it hard to believe he'd make such a boring proposal, but he had. She wanted a proposal she could tell her grandchildren about, and "we should get married" didn't cut it.

Unfortunately for her, she still loved the guy, boring proposal and all. She even looked to see if he was in his usual seat at the Nirvana, but he wasn't. Maybe he was rearranging his sock drawer.

Except . . . except he could be wild and passionate, too. She'd seen that side of him at the time-share. And then twice he'd risked his neck in her name. So why couldn't he sweep her into his arms and tell her he couldn't live without her?

Because that's not his first impulse. Deep in her heart, she understood that and loved him anyway, but damned if she'd marry him without something more dramatic than "I think we should get married." That wasn't getting cold feet, as she'd first imagined, it was reducing life to a spreadsheet. And she wouldn't have it.

After the last number ended, Lainie checked her watch and calculated how much she'd owe Mrs. Flippo for tonight. Mrs. Flippo was back on the job, even though Rona had said she'd be glad to babysit. Lainie had gently declined.

Besides the inconvenience of taking Dexter all the way to Rona's, Lainie didn't want to use Rona as a regular babysitter. That would be expecting way too much of a friend. Mrs. Flippo had to go eventually, though. She wasn't smart enough for Dexter. The trick would be finding someone who was.

Like Harry.

Oh, yes, Harry had made perfect sense in what he'd said today. Get married and juggle the babysitting. How terrifically romantic. When during that carefully mapped-out schedule of his would they have wild and crazy sex?

He hadn't mentioned that. She wanted it mentioned. A lot.

She was still thinking about that as she walked out to her car, keys in hand. Recently she'd been spoiled by automatic keys, but now she was back to the old-fashioned kind that you had to push into the lock.

As she started to turn the key and open the door, an arm came around her throat.

"You ruined my life!" Joey hissed into her ear. "Damned bitch, you ruined my life!"

The stench of his breath told her he'd been drinking, but that didn't seem to have affected his strength. She used her elbows, as she'd been taught in her self-defense course, and connected satisfyingly with his ribs. She was more mad than scared, and quite ready to take this guy on. How dare he show up again, let alone attack her?

She kicked backward and missed his groin, but not by much. One more try and she'd disable him. Relishing the prospect, she planted her left foot firmly and started to swing her right foot back and up so it would land squarely on his crotch.

Then she heard a cry of rage and suddenly she was free. Gasping, she turned around to see Harry throwing punches like a madman. Joey went down, and Harry followed him to the pavement, his fists moving like pistons. He was going to kill Joey.

She rushed over and tried to tug him away. "Stop it, Harry! That's enough! Let me call the police!"

He didn't seem to hear her, so she started shouting for anyone who would. "Help! Someone help!"

"Excuse me, miss."

"Step aside, please."

As she watched in amazement, the two men who had been with Leo earlier this morning moved in and effortlessly pulled Harry away from his victim while Harry bellowed in protest.

"Hey, kid, that's enough, now." Leo stepped out of the shadows and over to Harry. "You don't want to get arrested for manslaughter. Rona would have a fit."

His chest heaving, his shirt splattered with Joey's blood, Harry stared at Leo. "He . . . he tried . . . to kill her."

"I know. I found out he never made the Chicago–New York leg of his flight. Probably spent the layover in the bar, nursing his grievances, then caught a flight back to Vegas. Good thing we all had the same idea, to hang around after the show and be sure Lainie got home okay."

Harry's gaze flicked to Lainie. "I . . . wasn't here for that."

"No? You were taking an evening stroll and happened upon this scene?"

"No." Harry looked directly at Lainie. "I came to tell her I love her and I can't live without her."

"You did?" Her heart leaped. "You do?"

Harry nodded. "I didn't expect to find this Neanderthal trying to choke her to death."

"So, boss?" The guy with a shaved head had dragged Joey to his feet. His nose was spouting blood like a broken fire hydrant. "What are we gonna do with him?"

Leo stroked his chin. "That's a good question, Brett. Joey, I thought you understood that you weren't to set foot in Vegas ever again."

Joey began to blubber. "Please let me go! I promise

this time! I'll never come back here. Please don't feed me to the fishes!"

"We wouldn't do that," said the blond guy. "It's too far to Lake Mead from here. I think dropping him off the balcony at the Rio sounds like a good idea."

"Noooo. I hate heights!"

"Then maybe the Rio it'll be. Good idea, Eric," Leo said.

Lainie started getting nervous. "Couldn't we just have him arrested?"

"That's no fun," Eric said.

When a patrol car cruised into the lot, lights flashing, Lainie sighed with relief. "Oh, good. The police are here."

"The police!" Joey broke away from his captors and ran toward the cruiser. "Arrest me, arrest me! I'm afraid of heights! They're going to kill me!"

Lainie thought Leo and his boys would fade into the night once the cops arrived, but to her surprise, Leo sauntered over to the cruiser.

"Hi, Bob," he said. "You might want to slap the cuffs on this one. He assaulted this young lady, and I'm sure she'd be willing to prosecute."

"I would," Lainie called out.

What followed was an incredible amount of paperwork which they filled out under the lights of the parking lot. All the while Lainie kept glancing over at Harry. Had he really said that he loved her, or was she just imagining it?

Finally the cruiser left with Joey in the back seat.

"So that's that," Leo said. "You'll get your day in court, and Joey Benjamin will undoubtedly get off with his family's money behind him. They won't want a jailbird in addition to a gay guy. But I don't think he'll try this a second time."

Harry was looking at Leo with great interest. "You acted like you were good friends with those cops."

"I am, as it happens."

"But . . . isn't that kind of unusual, in your line of work? To be friends with the cops?"

Leo glanced from Harry to Lainie. "If I tell you something, you have to swear you'll never repeat it to Rona."

"We won't," Lainie said.

"Definitely not," Harry added.

"The thing is, I'm not connected to the Mob. I own a personal protection business, hired bodyguards, if you will, and I have a great relationship with the cops around here."

Lainie still didn't get it. "Why wouldn't you want Rona to know you have a legitimate business?"

"Because she thinks me being a Mafia type is mysterious and sexy. And with Rona, I need all the help I can get."

Harry started to grin. "You're kidding."

Leo shrugged.

"I'll be damned." Harry glanced at Lainie. "There's your answer. Leo's not the Godfather, after all."

"I wouldn't mind being *a* godfather," Leo said. "If you get my drift."

Harry walked over to Lainie. "That's up to this lady. What do you say, Lainie? Care to make Leo a godfather?"

She gazed up at him. "Would you say it one more time?"

"Care to make—"

"No, the other thing. The reason you came here tonight."

"You mean that I love you and I can't live without you? That thing?"

"Uh-huh."

He held out his hands, which were bloody, and looked down at his bloody shirt. "I should be holding you at a time like this, and I'm a mess."

"I don't carc."

He wiped his hands on his pants, anyway. Then he gathered her close. "I love you and I can't live without you. Please marry me, or I'll die. Not literally, but in every other way. I'll shrivel up and become nothing but a human calculator, with no heart, no soul, no—"

"Sex life?" She smiled.

"I think this is where we fade out of the picture," Leo said. "But before I leave, let me put in a plug for you to name your first kid after me."

Harry gazed down into Lainie's face. "How do you feel about a girl named Leo?"

"Sounds fine to me."

"Great," Leo said. "Then we'll be off."

As the maroon Jag pulled away, Harry tightened his hold on Lainie. "Your turn."

She didn't have to ask what he meant. "I love you and I can't live without you. If you won't marry me, I'll die. Not literally, but in every other way. I'll become a dried-up showgirl with no heart, no soul, no—"

"You couldn't be dried up if you tried. Me, I could dry up, but you will always be one juicy woman."

"All right, then, I'll float away on my tears of grief."

"Can't have that. Are we on, then? Wedding, reception, honeymoon, the works?"

"We're on."

"Good, because it's really the logical thing to do, you know."

"Harry Ambrewster, if you use that word one more—"

"Just kidding! Still have your ring?"

She held up her right hand to show him. "I decided to keep it on the right hand for now, but if you want me to switch it over, I will."

He took her hand and kissed her fingertips. "Mine's on the right, too. I think we should wait and put them on our left hands when we're standing in front of the minister."

She was so happy that nobody would ever be able to wipe the grin off her face. "Sounds good."

"Come on, I'm taking you home."

"What about my car?"

"We'll get it tomorrow. I want to take you home in my car, which is the equivalent of riding off with you on my trusty steed. And I'm staying the night."

"Oh, really?"

"Yep." He circled her waist with one arm and led her over to his Lexus. "And the night after that, and the night after that, and so on."

"Okay."

"That's all you have to say?"

"Nope." She wrapped her arm around his waist. "I'd say Mrs. Flippo is so fired."

"Anything else?"

"Yeah." She gave him a squeeze. "I want the one-bedroom."

Epilogue

The TITS occupied the front row of folding chairs, and as mother of the groom, Rona sat in the middle. Suz and Trixie flanked her to the right and left, with Babs and Cherie each one seat over. They'd drawn numbers to figure out the order so that nobody felt slighted.

Rona gripped her friends' hands and blinked back tears as Harry, dressed in a dark gray tux, walked across an emerald lawn and took his place next to the minister in front of a makeshift altar. She'd never seen her son look so handsome or so happy.

Next to him stood Leo, also gorgeous in his tux, and Dudley, far less gorgeous and already tugging at his collar. An arched trellis behind them framed red rock formations rising above a green velvet fairway. A breathtaking setting for a wedding, if Rona did say so, and well worth three months of concentrated effort on everybody's part.

The rest of the wedding guests sat in neat rows arranged on the newly landscaped patio behind the renovated Crimson Canyons clubhouse. Inside the clubhouse, caterers prepared the tables and chairs for the reception. A recording of flutes and drums, Lainie and Harry's choice for the pre-ceremony music, wafted from state-of-the-art equipment concealed behind a folding screen.

"Doesn't he look yummy?" Suz whispered.

"You mean Harry or Leo?" Rona would have been hard-pressed to say who looked the yummiest of those two. One inspired her mother's pride and the other one flipped all her switches, even if he had given up his underworld connections to go into this time-share business with Harry. Leo wasn't getting any younger, and he probably needed to try something legitimate for a change.

"I mean *Dudley,*" Suz said. "What a man. Hubba, hubba."

Rona managed not to laugh. She never would have guessed that Suz would meet Dudley and fall madly in love, and vice-versa. Suz stood at least five inches taller than her new conquest, but neither of them seemed to give a damn. And thanks to Suz's tutoring, Dudley had become quite the salesman.

The Crimson Canyons project had turned out to be a shot in the arm for all the TITS, as a matter of fact. Everyone had bought in and were now part of the sales team. Business was booming. Babs had even sold a time-share—Rona paused and corrected herself. Babs had sold *resort ownership* to Lainie's sour-faced parents.

Rona, Leo, and the TITS split their time between Sedona and Vegas, and Suz had announced that once she talked Dudley into marrying her, she'd move here permanently. Lainie and Harry could only come once in a while, though, because Lainie needed to stay close to work. That girl would be a headliner before long, or

Rona didn't know her stuff. And Rona definitely knew her stuff.

As for Dexter, he was about the happiest kid Rona had ever seen. Harry and Lainie had bought a house in Henderson near Rona's condo, and the yard was perfect for a dog. Everywhere Dexter went, there was Mitzi, a little bundle of champagne-colored Shih Tzu energy who also had a crush on Fred. When Dexter came to visit Rona, Mitzi always came along to profess her doggie love.

"This music makes me want to get into the lotus position and meditate," Trixie said. "Why did they choose it, again?"

"It's all about their memories of this place," Rona said. "I wish I could have talked them out of the fast-food burgers for the reception, but they wouldn't budge on that, either." And she didn't really care. Harry was getting married to Lainie, and by dinnertime she'd be legally a grandma, and that was all that mattered.

The flutes and drums trailed off and the first chords of the wedding march began. Heart swelling and eyes moist, Rona stood up in unison with her friends. She flashed Leo a triumphant smile before turning to face the procession coming down the carpeted aisle.

Dexter appeared in the darling little tux she'd picked out for him. He had Mitzi on one leash and Fred on the other. Mitzi had Harry's silver ring tied to her collar, and Fred had Lainie's matching ring on his. Rona had voiced some misgivings about this plan, but the two dogs seemed to be behaving themselves.

Dexter started forward, just as they'd practiced, with the dogs trotting on either side of him. Then flashbulbs started going off. Mitzi reacted first, barking and pulling the leash right out of Dexter's hand. Fred ran after Mitzi, and Dexter chased both of them through the rows of chairs, in front of the altar, and toward the folding screen hiding the sound equipment.

Chaos erupted as the guests—plus Harry, Leo, Dudley, and even the minister—tried to help. Both dogs raced past the folding screen, knocking it over onto the sound equipment. The resulting crash sounded very expensive and brought an abrupt halt to the wedding march.

Suz whistled through her teeth. "TITS, take charge!"

The five women moved with the agility and awareness that came with years of dance experience. In moments Rona had Dexter, Babs grabbed Mitzi, and Cherie got a good hold on Fred. Trixie shooed the guests into their seats and Suz hurried back to reassure the shell-shocked bride that all was not lost.

Rona set Dexter down in the middle of the aisle, adjusted his little bow tie, and gave him a kiss. "Go on and walk up there," she said. "Miss Babs and Miss Cherie will be right behind you with the dogs. They can hold them until time for the rings."

"But we don't have music," Dexter said, his eyes wide.

Rona glanced at Babs and Cherie. "We'll sing it. Right, girls?"

"Sure thing," Cherie said. Then she turned to the guests. "You all know this. Join in."

"Right," Trixie said. "I'll direct." She raised her hands and began to sing and conduct at the same time. *"Dum-dum-de-dum, dum-dum-de-dum."*

Fortunately they had quite a few show people among the guests, and soon they had a respectable wedding march going on. As the crowd sang, Lainie's two attendants, dancers she'd been close to back in Atlantic City, started down the aisle. Behind them, with a grin wider than the sky, came Lainie, walking toward her groom on the arm of her father.

Rona's eyes misted again as she thought of how much reconciling with her parents had meant to Lainie. Although Rona wasn't sure she'd ever forgive them for the way they'd treated Lainie and Dexter in the beginning, they seemed to be warming up a little more with each trip to the Southwest. Someday Rona might even decide to like them.

As the bride approached the altar, Trixie brought the singing to a stop with a dramatic downbeat. Then she walked over to stand with Rona and Suz. Babs and Cherie stayed with the wedding party and held the wiggling dogs.

The ceremony was short and sweet. Because the sound system was broken, Suz volunteered to get up and sing the theme song from *Annie.* The rings were detached from each dog's collar. The reverence with which Lainie and Harry bestowed those rings made the tears stream down Rona's face. Then, before she could believe it was over, the minister instructed Harry to kiss his bride.

Cheers erupted, and as Harry and Lainie started back down the aisle, the guests sang the recessional without being prompted. All except Rona, who had such a big lump of happiness in her throat she couldn't sing a note. As she stood there watching her son and new daughter-in-law hurry down the aisle, laughing as they went, she felt a tug on her sleeve.

She glanced down at Dexter and smiled.

He smiled back and held out his hand. "Come on, Grandma Rona. Time to party!"

She held his hand as they walked together toward the clubhouse. Indeed it was.

Look for Vicki Lewis Thompson's
Next Fabulous Romance—

NERD GONE WILD!

Coming in February 2005 from St. Martin's Press